# WHAT WAITS IN THE WOODS

Books by Terri Parlato

ALL THE DARK PLACES

WHAT WAITS IN THE WOODS

Published by Kensington Publishing Corp.

# WHAT WAITS IN THE WOODS

TERRI PARLATO

www.kensingtonbooks.com

KENSINGTON BOOKS are published by

Kensington Publishing Corp.
119 West 40th Street
New York, NY 10018



Library of Congress Control Number: 2023944246

ISBN: 978-1-4967-3859-2

First Kensington Hardcover Edition: January 2024

ISBN: 978-1-4967-3861-5 (ebook)

10 9 8 7 6 5 4 3 2 1

Printed in the United States of America

For all my muses here and gone

# ACKNOWLEDGMENTS

I am so grateful for all the amazing people at Kensington Publishing. Thank you doesn't begin to cover all that you've done for me. To my wonderful editor, John Scognamiglio, thank you for all your encouragement and your keen sense of what makes a story infinitely better.

To my incomparable agent, Marlene Stringer, you've made a fifty-year-plus dream comc true for me. There are not enough thank yous to convey my appreciation.

To Sandra Erni, Tacey Derenzy, and R. H. Buffington, thank you so much for reading my works in progress, for keeping me on track, and for letting me know when I've gone off the rails. To my good friend and excellent proofreader, Karen Street, thank you for everything.

To my husband, Fred, and our children, Brittany, Becca, and Nick, you are my world and without your support, none of this is possible.

And to my readers, I appreciate you so much. Because of you, I get to do what I love.

**Sweet Dancer**

The girl goes dancing there
On the leaf-sown, new-mown, smooth
Grass plot of the garden;
Escaped from bitter youth,
Escaped out of her crowd,
Or out of her black cloud.
Ah, dancer, ah, sweet dancer!

If strange men come from the house
To lead her away, do not say
That she is happy being crazy;
Lead them gently astray;
Let her finish her dance,
Let her finish her dance.
Ah, dancer, ah, sweet dancer!

—William Butler Yeats

# CHAPTER 1
# Esmé

SOMETIMES, THE ONLY THING YOU CAN DO IS LEAVE. THAT WAS MY mindset when I was eighteen. There was no thought of staying put and duking it out, fighting to make things better. I didn't have the slightest inkling of how to do that.

But eleven years later, teetering on the edge of thirty, the world looks a lot different. So I'm going home. The thruway is gray and damp, and my ancient car thumps along at fifty-five; any faster and it makes a noise that drowns out the radio. I'm not in any hurry to get to Graybridge anyway. I'm sort of liking the road between Syracuse and my Boston suburban hometown. I'm alone with my thoughts, boyfriend—ex, actually—in the rearview mirror, my family, or what's left of it, at the other end of my journey. Here, on the road, I'm in a dreamland of my own.

It's early. The weak October sun is just rising, and the dying leaves look gray, their brilliant colors hidden in the morning mist. Kevin is still asleep, most likely. He'll get up in another hour and find my note on the kitchen table; such a cliché, but I couldn't face him, see that look in his eyes, the folds in his forehead when something unpleasant and out of his control happens. I need all my strength for my brother and dad and whatever else I have waiting for me at home. I have nothing to spend on Kevin. It's been over for months, although he's refused to even consider that our relationship has ended. Six years of fighting and making up is all I had in me. I'm ready for the fighting to be over. That's why I'm going home. For one last stand maybe, to settle things there. And, besides, I have nowhere else to go.

My coffee has grown cold, sitting in the cup holder, forgotten. I sip, and the taste is bitter in my mouth, and I wonder again why I bothered to sit in the long line at the drive-thru to purchase it. Habit, I guess. Black coffee, and lots of it, has been my mainstay for years. Zero calories and a good jolt of energy. What more can a dancer ask for? I glance at the paper grocery bag sitting in the passenger seat like an old friend, or a relative who fills me with pain and disappointment. But I can't part with the contents. In some ways, they are my world. Pointe shoes, scuffed and worn, fit only for the dumpster, but their pale pink satin peeks through the grime, belies the hours of work, and I can't let go.

I'm going home a failure, never an easy prospect. The end of my dance career, which, at one time, had seemed so promising, has left me adrift, my painful hip sending shock waves when I move my foot from the gas to the brake pedal. *Ha,* it taunts. *Thought you could stretch me and plié me to death? I'll show you!*

I wipe a tear from my cheek. I don't know what home has to offer me. A father who's desperately ill, a brother whose phone calls have only gotten colder as the years have gone by. A mother in her grave since I was sixteen, and a man who threatened to kill me the night of my mother's accident. My phantom. Is he still lurking, waiting for my return? Or is he a figment of my imagination, like everyone said?

I sigh and turn up the radio and let the strains of Tchaikovsky lead me into a mindless numbness as a cold rain begins to fall from the dark sky.

# CHAPTER 2
# Rita

THE BODY IS LYING IN THE WEEDS AT THE EDGE OF THE WOODS, THE woman's red sweater a beacon in the gray day. From the kitchen window, the scene outside looks like a far-off movie. Crime-scene investigators and cops circle the corpse, like wrestlers trying to find a way to wrap their arms around what's happened here. The ME walks through the crowd, which parts respectfully to let her through.

I look up from my notebook at the young man, dark brown hair feathering his forehead, sweat dotting his stubbled upper lip.

"So, Mr. Foster. You knew the victim?"

"Yes," he mumbles.

"How did you know Kara Cunningham?"

He heaves a great sigh. "We went to school together. High school."

"You've seen her since?"

He scrubs his hand over his eyes. "Yes. Uh, some. It's a small town."

He's already told me that he works as a nurse, hospital night shift. When he got home at around seven-thirty this morning, his father told him that he'd heard a scream from outside.

"When was the last time you saw her?"

"Last Saturday, I guess."

"You know or you guess?"

"I know."

"Okay. We'll get back to that. I need to speak with your father. He's still here?"

Byron Foster blinks his eyes. "He lives here. I moved back in a year ago to take care of him. He doesn't leave the house."

"What's wrong with him?" I ask, which comes out a little insensitive, but that's me. I don't always get the PC phrasing right. Force of habit.

"He's an alcoholic."

I nod. Lots of people are alcoholics. My mind drifts unwittingly to my brother Danny, and I have to pull it back. *Stay on task, Rita. Think of Danny later.*

Byron continues. "He's in the last stage of cirrhosis."

"Sorry. Okay."

"He's dying, Detective," he adds matter-of-factly.

"He told you he heard a scream coming from the backyard?"

"Yes. So I went out to look around. I really didn't think I'd find anything. My father is so out of it, it's hard to believe anything he says." Mr. Foster's gaze shifts to the window, where a stretcher is being pushed through the tall grass. It gets stuck, bogged down in the mud, and two guys drop to their haunches to try to free it. "I think his mind is caught in the past. He hears things, sees things that aren't there."

"You can't get him any help?" I bite my tongue the minute this leaves my mouth. I've tried for years to help my brother, but he insists he doesn't have a problem and, if I push, tells me it's none of my goddamn business, which has me backing off. Being on the outs with Danny isn't something I'm willing to live with. He and I are the youngest and the closest siblings in a big family.

Mr. Foster's eyes find mine, and they're filled with not grief exactly, anger maybe. "You can't help people who don't want help."

I nod again. Swallow. "Okay. I still need to talk to him."

We rise from the table, and I follow him down the hall and up a dark and squeaky staircase. As we near the top, a slight sour smell, vomit and alcohol, wafts over me. My partner, Chase, picked a great week to take vacation.

Inside the dim room, a tall man, thin as a skeleton, sits shriveled into a ratty recliner. His breaths come in ragged gasps. Young Mr. Foster flips on the overhead light, and the room is thrown into garish brightness. The old man blinks his eyes like a young pup. He's wearing a flannel shirt in a cheerful red and blue plaid, unbuttoned at the neck, where white hair peeps over the top of a gray undershirt. His wrinkled hands shake, and the smell of alcohol leaches from his pores.

I glance around for a place to sit. The son moves a yellow plastic and chrome kitchen chair from the corner and places it in front of his father.

"Mr. Foster, I'm Detective Rita Myers, Graybridge Police Department," I say, settling in the chair. The old man nods, but I'm not sure if he understands what I've said. I pull out my notebook and turn to a fresh page.

"I'd like to ask you a few questions." He looks over at his son, who has seated himself on the edge of the double bed. "You told your son you heard a scream last night." He nods absently. "What time did you hear the scream?" His dark eyes cloud over like I've just asked him to explain nuclear fission. His left hand twitches and digs at a spot on his arm. "Mr. Foster?"

He shakes his head and glances out the window. "I don't know," he says finally in a trembling voice.

"Where were you when you heard it?"

"In the living room, watching TV." He stretches his mouth wide, and the wrinkles in his cheeks gather. "I heard a scream." He points to the window. "I heard someone scream out back somewhere."

"You don't know what time it was?"

He shakes his head.

"Can you guess?"

He shakes his head again.

"What were you watching?"

"The news was on."

"The six o'clock news or the ten o'clock news?" I sketch his troubled, rheumy eyes in my notebook, give him time to search through the cobwebs of his brain. Drawing helps me think, slows me down. It's something I've done since I was a kid, and it has followed me into my long career in law enforcement. My notebooks are filled with pictures of suspects and victims and crime scenes. And sometimes the visuals help lead me to answers.

"I don't know," he says at last. His voice is stronger than before.

"What time did you go upstairs to bed?" I just get a vacant stare. "You have anything to drink before you went to bed, Mr. Foster?" I hear the son huff out a breath.

The old man nods.

Young Mr. Foster says, "When I got home from work, I went upstairs to check on him, and he was agitated. He told me about the scream, so I went outside to look."

"Did he say anything to you this morning about when he heard the scream?"

"No." He shakes his head. "I really don't think he knows. His concept of time is pretty skewed."

I turn back to the old man. "Did you go outside, look around?"

"No. I stayed right here."

"Is there anything you can tell me about last night besides the scream? Did you hear any other noises? Did anyone knock on the door? Did you hear any cars stop by the house?"

He cringes in his chair as if my questions were punches. I sigh. This is getting me nowhere. "Okay, Mr. Foster. If you think of anything, please give me a call, or have your son call me," I say, standing, stashing my notebook under my arm.

We head downstairs and back into the kitchen. The body is still on the ground, the crime-scene investigators still hard at work. When I arrived on scene, I'd had a quick conversation with the first responders before heading inside. But I need to get out there and talk with the ME when I'm through here.

"Mr. Foster, you said you saw Kara on Saturday night, correct?"

"Yes."

"Where was that?"

"At Hartshorn's Brewpub. She was having drinks with a friend."

"So, you weren't with her?"

"No. I was there with a buddy from work. Kara was at another table."

"Did you speak with her?"

"No. I don't think she saw me. We weren't sitting near each other. I just noticed her on my way out."

"You didn't stop to say hello?"

"No."

"Who was she with?"

"Christy Bowers."

"Who's that?"

"She's a friend of Kara's."

"Okay. I'll need to talk with you again." I hand Mr. Foster my card. "I'll be in touch, but don't hesitate to call me if your father remembers anything."

# CHAPTER 3
# Esmé

IT'S JUST AFTER TEN WHEN I EXIT THE HIGHWAY. I HAVEN'T BEEN BACK to Graybridge in two and a half years. I'm a coward. I know that. I was here last to see my brother's new baby and stayed just long enough to be able to tell myself that I hadn't abandoned my family. But that's exactly what I did. I knew then that my father was in awful shape, but I told myself that Byron was the best person to take care of him. He's a nurse, and besides, they were closer. I wasn't close to anyone, not after my mother died. Her death signaled the end of the family as we knew it. Some families draw closer together after a death. But some don't. Some go the other way. My mother, tall, elegant, beautiful, was the leader, the maypole that we all danced around. When she died, we retreated into ourselves, and all thoughts of family dissipated like a dream.

I turn down Hogsworth Road. The house where I grew up is in the country, at the edge of woods and fields, the outskirts of Graybridge. I follow the curvy road, pass our few neighbors, drawing closer to our house. Past the Grady barn: I see it in the distance.

Cop cars line the road, and my heart hammers. *What happened?* My thoughts race, and I dig for my phone, which I'd silenced. I glance at the screen. Five missed calls, all from Byron.

I swing my car into the crowded driveway and run for the front door.

The familiar smells hit me as I step over the threshold. Voices buzz in the kitchen, and I nearly run headlong into a slim older woman with a leather bag over her shoulder. She stops short.

"You are?" she asks.

"Esmé Foster," I manage. "What happened?"

Byron appears behind her. "Ez, what are you doing here?"

"Is Dad okay?"

"He's fine. Well, you know. I left you a ton of messages."

"What happened?"

"Let's sit back down in the kitchen," the woman says. She introduces herself, and we get settled. My heart is pounding as I take in the scene out the window, a clutch of cops circling something on the ground.

Detective Myers pulls out a notebook and looks at me expectantly. "So, Esmé Foster, who are you?"

"His sister." I glance at Byron. He's still in his scrubs, his eyes fuzzy with fatigue.

"Do you live here?" Her eyes are a serious, piercing blue, her dark hair pulled up in a messy bun.

"No. I live in Syracuse. I was coming home." My gaze meets Byron's. "What happened?"

"We got a call this morning of a body found," the detective says, her eyes on her notebook.

"I don't understand." All I see is a group of cops and an empty stretcher at the edge of the woods.

Byron takes a deep breath, his gaze on his hands, which are folded and tapping nervously against the table.

"We don't know what happened," Detective Myers says. "That's what we're trying to figure out. When did you leave Syracuse?"

"This morning. Early."

"Why were you coming back?" She glances sidelong at Byron. "Sounds like your brother wasn't expecting you."

"No. I didn't tell anyone."

"When was the last time you were in Graybridge?"

"A little over two years ago," I whisper.

"Coming for a visit?"

This twists my stomach. "No," I say softly. "I was coming home to stay."

She raises her eyebrows, scribbles in her notebook. "Helluva homecoming."

Byron clears his throat. "Really, Ez?" He smirks. "When did you decide this?"

I don't want to fight with him. Not now. Not when I'm so off-kilter. Not when there's a *body* in our backyard. "Dad's okay then?"

"As okay as he can be with barely any liver function." My brother's eyes are like two dark stones. "Good thing you're here. You'll get to see him before he dies. I wasn't sure that was going to happen."

Detective Myers raises her gaze from her notes, like a teacher facing an unruly class. "Okay, then." She digs a business card out of her satchel and places it in front of me. "I'll need to talk to you all again." She and I rise from the table.

"Wait," I say. "You have no idea why there's a body in our yard?"

"Not at the moment."

"Who is it? Do they know?"

Byron stands so suddenly his chair scrapes halfway across the floor. "It's Kara," he says, his eyes meeting mine. "Kara Cunningham."

I drop back down in my chair.

"Do you know her?" Detective Myers asks.

I nod, my chin trembling. I glance out the window and see a flash of light brown hair splayed on the ground between two cops. "She's my best friend."

# CHAPTER 4
# Rita

A SHARP CHILL PENETRATES MY LEATHER JACKET AS I TREAD ACROSS the yard through the tall grass to where the victim lies, near the woods. I greet the techs and cops as I make my way to Kara Cunningham's body. Byron Foster ID'd her before I arrived, and the driver's license in her purse confirmed it.

She's lying on her side, a mane of long hair draped over her face. She's fully clothed in black pants and a red sweater and looks like she could be sleeping. That is, until you walk around behind her and see the dark blood clotted against her skull.

Cops are walking the woods, eyes on the forest floor.

"They find anything?" I ask the ME. Susan Gaines and I are of an age, veterans among the mostly younger cops and techs. She readjusts the sunglasses atop her head, which function more to keep her hair out of her eyes than anything else. There's no sun out today.

"Just the purse, so far."

I shiver in the cold and pull up the zipper of my jacket. "No coat?"

"Nope. At least, we haven't found one."

I drop down on my haunches, close to the young woman's head. "Blunt-force trauma?"

"Looks like it, but you know I can't say until the postmortem."

"Anything that might be a weapon?" I stand and brush the wrinkles from my pants. There are numerous branches and rocks lying around that could've done in Kara Cunningham.

Susan shrugs. "The guys have bagged up a few possibilities."

I walk slowly around the body but don't see anything significant. She was a small woman, and I can't help but think she resembles a bird, tiny and small-boned and forgotten out here near the woods. I inhale deeply of the chill autumn air and close my eyes, trying to get a feel for this young woman's last moments. What was she doing out here? Who was here with her, and why would they leave her here to die alone? What emotion drove them to end her life? I sigh. My gut isn't giving me any help.

"No sign of another person?" I ask Susan.

She shakes her head. "Not that I noticed, but somebody was out here with her."

"I guess she couldn't have just fallen?"

The ME smirks. "No."

"Time of death?"

She gives me that look like, *Really, Rita?*

"Just a wild guess, Susan. Mr. Foster heard a scream last night but has no idea what time it was."

"I'll let you know." She turns and starts barking out instructions. I trudge back to my van and set off down the road. The nearest neighbor is less than a quarter mile away. It's a good place to start.

The farmhouse looks like it's been here at least a hundred years. The clapboards were painted white once. Now they're a dull, peeling gray. The porch steps sag and sway slightly as I make my way up to the front door. But there's a shiny new truck in the driveway, so hopefully someone's home. I rap on the wooden door, and a man opens it right away, as if he'd watched me pull into the driveway.

He's tall, thirty-something, with long, wavy brown hair and crooked teeth. The smell of weed envelopes him like a cloud.

"Can I help you?" he asks.

"I hope so. Detective Rita Myers, Graybridge Police Department." I show him my identification.

He nods like he's considering whether to believe me or not.

"I'd like to ask you a few questions."

He swings the door wide, and I follow him through the hall and into a fairly bare front room. There's a couch with a stained brown throw cover over it and a big flat-screen against a wall that was painted pink sometime in the distant past. There's an end table that he pulls around and sits on, leaving me the couch. I sink into its springless depths and pull out my notebook.

"This about all the cop cars over at the Fosters?"

"Yes. What's your name?" I ask, pencil poised.

"Ray. Raymond Ridley Junior."

"You live here alone, Mr. Ridley?"

"With my sister." An image slowly forms in my mind. A little girl with a tangle of white-blond hair. And the name Ridley. I joined the Graybridge PD nearly twenty years ago, after years as a cop in Boston. A few months before I got here, there'd been a drowning in a pond on the Ridley property. There were two little girls in a rowboat. The girls had gotten into an argument, and the older girl had knocked her little sister out of the boat. It was an ugly, tragic story that made the Boston papers. I remember the picture of the girl, the one who died. She was a little thing, almost angelic-looking, and the community was taking it hard, still taking it badly when I moved out here. I remember hearing that the older girl was charged in the case but ultimately went to a psychiatric facility. Since she was convicted as a juvenile and so long ago, she's probably been released by now. Is she the sister who lives with Ray Ridley?

"What's your sister's name?" I ask.

"Cynthia." He smirks. "I'm sure you know who she is."

I nod. "Is she home? I'd like to talk with her."

"No. She's at a doctor's appointment."

"Was she home last night?"

"Yeah." He stretches his arms over his head, and his T-shirt rises, revealing a slack, white, hairy stomach.

"Will she be back soon?" A worn armchair is squeezed into a corner near the window. A huge orange cat sits in it like a sphinx and eyes me suspiciously. Yarn is heaped in a basket on the floor. Two long knitting needles are thrust into a bright yellow skein.

"Not for a couple hours."

I'll need to talk to her another time. "Okay, Ray, you hear anything last evening?"

"No. What happened?" He tips his head in the Fosters' direction.

"Were you home yesterday?"

"Most of the day."

"Where did you go?"

"Ran out to the grocery store."

"Time?"

He shrugs. "Afternoon, I guess."

"Can you be more specific?"

"Somewhere around five, I think."

"What timc did you get home?"

"About six maybe. I'm not sure."

"When you left or returned home, you see anything strange, out of place? A car parked around here you didn't recognize?"

"No." He jumps up from the end table and walks to the window that looks out on the road. The Fosters' place is visible in the distance.

"What the hell happened?" He chews his bottom lip.

"What time did you go to bed?"

He digs at his nose. "Uh, I can't remember. Late. I watched some TV and fell asleep on the couch."

"What time did you wake up?"

He snorts. "A while ago. Don't remember."

"So, you slept straight through? Didn't hear anything?"

"Nope. What happened? Byron's old man okay?"

"Yes. Mr. Foster is alive and well." Although *well* is a stretch.

"What happened then?" Ray bounces on his heels and walks over to the chair in the corner, lifts a knitting needle from its nest, then pushes it back into place. The cat has disappeared, annoyed by my presence maybe.

"We've got a body by the woods behind the Fosters' house."

Ray's eyes glance up and catch mine. "No shit?" He swallows and licks his lips, his eyelids twitch. "Who is it?"

"We can't say yet."

He nears the window again. "In Byron's backyard?"

"Yes. You been out in those woods lately?"

He shrugs. "Yeah. I go for nature walks now and then."

I suppress a smirk. He doesn't exactly look the nature-walking type. But who knows? He reminds me of a couple of old hippies who lived in my Boston neighborhood when I was a kid. They'd sit in the park across the street, legs folded, listening to an old radio, communing with nature. Ma warned us to steer clear of them, which only fueled my curiosity. I would sneak into the park with my trusty notebook and spy on them from the bushes, always the nosy Nancy, as my big sisters used to call me.

I clear my throat. "When was the last time you were out there?"

He draws a deep breath, looks at the ceiling. "Yesterday."

"What time yesterday?"

"Afternoon."

"See anything unusual?"

"Nope."

"You know the Fosters?"

"Yeah. I grew up in this house. They grew up over there. I went to school with Esmé. Well, she was two years behind me."

"What about Byron?"

"He was two years behind Esmé, so I didn't know him that good. When I graduated, he was still in middle school." He turns toward the window, interested in the commotion.

"You see much of him these days?"

Mr. Ridley turns back toward me, his hands in the pockets of his dirty jeans. "Not much. He works nights. We were never really friends, you know?"

"What do you do for a living?"

"I used to do construction." He sucks on his teeth. "But mostly now I take care of my sister."

Huh. "Why does she need you to take care of her?"

He shrugs. "She's got a lot of issues. She was in a group home for a while, but she kept running away, coming back here, so my mother told me I could stay in the house and take care of her. She'd pay me to do it."

"Where's your mother?"

"In Florida, in a senior apartment place. You can't live there if you're not fifty-five, so my mom couldn't take Cynthia with her." He snorts. "Not that she wanted to anyway."

"So, what exactly is wrong with Cynthia?" I need to know what to expect when I question her.

Ray lets go a deep breath. "When she was little, about two years old . . . I was just a baby, so I don't remember it. Anyway, my dad told me that while he was at work, Mom fell asleep on the couch, and Cynthia fell down the cellar stairs. She hit her head and had brain damage. She was in the hospital in Boston for a long time. She has trouble thinking straight and remembering things. She can't live on her own."

Okay. Not exactly a diagnosis, but I guess it's the best Ray can do. The injury might make Cynthia an unreliable witness. But we'll see. Maybe she saw or heard something last night, maybe not. Or maybe . . . I'll need to take a look at her records.

"Who's with Cynthia now, at the doctor?"

"A lady, a home health aide. She comes once a week to take her."

"Okay, Ray. Here's my card if you think of anything, notice anything that might help. And give me a call when your sister's home. I'll need to speak with her."

He takes the card and shoves it in his back pocket. "You can't tell me whose body they found?"

"Nope." I walk toward the front door, Ray on my heels.

"Did Byron do it?"

I stand still, look back over my shoulder. "What makes you think he did it?"

Ray reaches his arm past me, grabs the doorknob. "Just wondering. Body was found by his woods, right?"

"It was."

"Well, then." He shrugs. "I wouldn't put it past him."

# CHAPTER 5
# Esmé

"SO, YOU'RE REALLY MOVING BACK?" BYRON ASKS.

"Yes," I whisper, my mind awhirl, trying to comprehend that my friend is dead in our backyard. I clutch my brother's arm. "What happened to Kara?"

"I have no idea. When was the last time you talked to her?"

I walk toward the window. "Not in a long time, years."

Byron snorts. "And she's your best friend?"

"She was. You know that."

"Back in high school. Before you ditched us all for your career."

I wheel on him. "Is that how you saw it? Me taking off to dance?"

"That's what you did, didn't you?"

It's more complicated than that, and I don't want to talk about it now. Tears gather in my eyes, and my stomach knots up. Kara and I had been friends since kindergarten. Growing up, we did everything together. And because her single mom worked, I convinced my mom to pick Kara up after school and take her home with us so that she didn't have to go to day care. We played every day in the house when rain pattered on the roof or outside in those same woods when the weather was warm. We stayed friends right through high school, and it was Kara I confided in when I decided to leave Graybridge and start a new life as a dancer in another state. She was heartbroken. We were more like sisters at that point. I told her we'd keep in touch. But I didn't. I'd cut her off, like I did all my friends after I left. I just wanted to get away from Graybridge and all the painful memories here. I was young and selfish, and now it's too late to make things right. How could I have let Kara down that way?

Guilt floods over me as Kara's body is lifted from the ground and placed on the stretcher by uniformed strangers. Byron joins me at the window, and we watch, helpless and confused. The stretcher gets stuck a time or two in the muck and tall grass. Finally, the men wheel her around the house and out of sight. There are still cops out by thc woods, eyes on the ground, searching.

"What was she doing out there, Byron? I don't understand. What could've happened to her?" I cover my eyes with my hands. "Her mother must be devastated. Oh, my God." I sink down in a chair, emotions rippling through me thinking of Mrs. Cunningham. Kara was her only child, all she had. More memories of my friend flit through my mind, her high-pitched giggle that never changed as she grew older. Her pixie face that grew into real beauty as we became teenagers. A sob bursts through my lips.

"I have no idea." Byron scrubs his hands over his face. "It's surreal. I found her at the end of the path like she was coming out of the woods. When Dad told me he heard a scream, I walked out there and saw her lying in the grass. I checked her right away, called her name. But it was no use. She was dead. Had been for a while. There was nothing I could do except call 911."

My brother looks exhausted, not just his usual coming-off-his-shift tired. He shakes his head and clears his throat. "Someone killed her, Ez."

"How do you know?"

"The back of her head was covered with blood."

"Maybe she fell."

"No. I've seen my share of falls when I worked in the ER. Someone crushed her skull."

I shiver, cover my mouth with my hands, and look back at the woods.

"I better make Dad's breakfast," Byron says. "He should've eaten hours ago."

"Is he still upstairs?"

"Yeah." Byron turns and heads to the kitchen counter.

The hall leading to Dad's bedroom is dark. I have to pass my old room to get to his, so I stop, turn the knob, and go into my room first. I'm drawn to the window that looks out on the backyard. The forest stretches for acres behind our house; paths lead through it from various points and converge at the pond. It was our magical playground when we were kids, filled with wonder and then danger too. Thrilling and scary at the same time. Then, as teenagers, it became our rebellious haunt, a place to get away where we could drink stolen beer and pretend we were grown-up and so much smarter than the adults in our lives.

Thoughts of Kara and our friends fill my mind. Our little group that made up my world before I moved away. When we were five years old, Kara and I started ballet lessons together. My mom signed me up, and I, of course, asked for Kara to sign up too. At the Graybridge Dance Academy, we met and befriended two other little girls in the class, Laney Morelli and Christy French. Soon, my mother was the designated driver for the four of us. The other moms were busy with work or multiple children, and they were only too happy to have my mom take charge. That's where we bonded, in dance class, as little, bun-headed, pink-clad girls. Friendships that would only deepen as the years went by. I wonder where Laney and Christy are now. Do they know yet about Kara? Are they still as close as we all used to be? The thought of facing them sends shivers down my spine. Do they hate me now for cutting them out of my life? Tears spring anew, and I quickly wipe them away. I need to see my dad. I'll have to think about Kara later.

My father's room is even more depressing than it was when I was home last. The bed has been pushed into the corner, with its old quilt dangling to the floor. The rest of the room is nearly bare. But my mother's picture still sits on the bedside table, the sole decoration in the spartan room. She smiles her radiant smile, blond hair lying in curls over her shoulders. The photo was taken at one of the backyard parties she liked to throw in the summer in the sunshine, the last summer before she died.

I sniff back tears as I near my father. He's looking out the window and doesn't hear me as I cross the floor.

"Dad?"

He doesn't move, his eyes transfixed on the backyard, where cops search the woods like busy ants.

"Dad?" He slowly turns his head. His sunken eyes meet mine.

"Esmé?" His voice is scratchy.

"Hi. I thought I'd come home and see you." I reach down and grab his hand. It's thin and feels like old paper.

He nods like he's trying to process what I just said. He places his other hand over mine, and tears gather in his eyes. I feel a stab of guilt for staying away so long. He looks worse than I ever imagined. I inhale a ragged breath as he drops my hand and points to the window.

"Something bad happened, Esmé," he says, his voice close to normal.

"I know, Dad. But it's okay. The cops are going to figure it out."

Tears spill over his cheeks. "She's not coming back . . ."

I know he's not talking about Kara. This is another reason home is so hard. My father's grief is still raw, even all these years later. Byron pushes the door open. He's carrying a tray, sets it on the bed, and tucks an old striped dish towel over Dad's shirt. He places a half-full cup of black coffee in Dad's trembling hand.

"Drink, Dad. You'll feel better." I stand back and watch as Byron efficiently helps our father eat a piece of toast, drink a cup of coffee, a routine that I'm not a part of, a life I've left behind.

Dad shakes his head. "I'm done, By. No more."

My father seems as helpless as a child. I follow Byron out of the room. "He looks terrible," I whisper.

"He's dying, Ez. I told you that. I've been telling you that for the last six months."

Byron and I talk on the phone about once a week, and he did tell me that Dad was going downhill. But I didn't want to believe it.

"He's only fifty-eight. He looks eighty-eight."

"With as much as he drinks, I'm surprised he looks as good as he does."

Back in the kitchen, my eyes are drawn to the window again. The cops are still there, still searching. Byron places the dishes in the sink.

"Why do you buy it for him? He can't go get it himself, can he?"

My brother turns to face me, his eyes flashing, and I step back. "I don't buy it for him. He hasn't driven since last spring, when he ended up in the ditch in front of Ray's place. Irene buys it."

"She's still coming over?" Irene and her husband were friends of Mom and Dad. They seemed to always be around, sitting at the kitchen table, playing cards with my parents, bringing over casseroles for dinners shared on the picnic table in our backyard. Then Mom died and Irene's husband left, leaving my father and Irene to carry on.

"Same as always. She's here most days when I'm at work. But you'd know that if you were here."

I drop down in a kitchen chair. "Well, I'm here now. I'll help."

Byron leans against the counter. "Why? Why bother now? You and Kevin finished finally?"

I'm too tired, too upset about Kara to rise to the bait. "Yes."

He nods and runs water over Dad's dishes.

"You need to get to bed?" I ask.

Byron turns to face me. "Normally, I'd take a shower and try to get some sleep, but . . ." He points out the window. "I can't sleep now." He rubs his hand over his mouth.

"What was Kara doing out there, Byron?" I haven't been out there in years and can't think of any reason Kara would've been back there now.

Byron shrugs. "I have no idea. I need to get in the shower. Then I'll be back down," he says and leaves the kitchen. I sit at the table and watch the cops work.

# CHAPTER 6
# Rita

As I drive back to the station, Ray Ridley's statement tumbles through my mind. Why would he suspect Byron Foster? When I pressed him on it, he offered nothing but that he thought young Mr. Foster was a dick. That might be, but that doesn't make him a killer.

And old Mr. Foster has me shaken. Is this what's in store for my brother? Wasting away, mind gone? But they're nothing alike. Danny's an English professor at a local college. He's the smartest one of all nine of us, the only one who made it all the way through college and then some. He works, shops, socializes, lives a normal life, sort of. Most people don't even suspect he has a drinking problem. But I know. I see the glass that's always in his hand when he's at home. I know there's a stockpile of booze in the kitchen cupboard. I know his mind floats too often to Ricky and Jimmy, our brothers who should be here but died long ago.

A lady in the car behind me lays on her horn as the light turns green. *Yeah, yeah, I'm going.*

I called ahead and had Detective Broderick do a background search on all parties involved so far. Lauren, young and eager, reminding me too much of myself sometimes, is waiting for me in my office when I get there.

"Didn't find much, Rita," she says as I hang my jacket on the back of my chair.

"Let's hear it." I settle behind my desk.

"Byron Foster, twenty-seven years old. Works at Graybridge General hospital. He and his wife divorced a year ago. They share custody of a two-year-old daughter." She glances up at me. "No criminal record. Thomas Foster. Fifty-eight. Was cited for drunk driving twice in the last ten years. His wife was killed in a car accident thirteen years ago. He was driving."

"Was he intoxicated that time?"

"No. Just an accident on an icy road. He wasn't charged."

"Okay. Anything else on him?"

"Nothing." She clears her throat, flips her long and often troublesome braid back over her shoulder.

"What about the daughter, Esmé?"

"A couple of traffic tickets. That's it. I did find a bunch of articles about her going way back."

"What kind of articles?"

"She was a ballerina of some note. She danced locally as a kid. Got parts in the annual professional production of *The Nutcracker*. Then she went to Syracuse and got a job with a ballet company out there."

"Huh." I can see that. She definitely had that dancer look. Skinny, light brown hair pulled up in a tight bun. "Anything else? Any run-ins with the law?"

"Just the speeding tickets."

"What about Raymond Ridley, the neighbor?" He certainly seemed nervous.

Lauren juggles her laptop, takes a deep breath. "He's got quite a rap sheet. Mostly misdemeanors. Minor drug charges. One B and E when he was seventeen."

"He do any time?"

"Doesn't look like it."

I'm fumbling with my bootlaces. Must've tied them too tight this morning, and they're pinching the tops of my feet.

"I found articles about his sister," Lauren says quietly.

"Yeah. I remembered the incident when I started questioning

him. It happened right before I moved out here, but I remember the coverage. His older sister lives with him."

Lauren's gaze meets mine. "I saw that she'd been released from a psychiatric facility about a year and a half ago. Did you talk to her?"

I shake my head, wiggle my toes. "She wasn't home."

"I read some of the articles. I was just a kid when it happened, but I remember overhearing my mother and her friends talking about it. I remember them saying that the Ridleys were odd, and that Mrs. Ridley was an unfit mother. I wasn't sure exactly what they meant by that. I just remember that people were really upset." Lauren tips her laptop in my direction. She's got one of the old articles from the *Graybridge Gazette* pulled up. There's a black-and-white photo at the top. Two little girls in ballet costumes. I lean in to read the caption: *Wendy Ridley and Esmé Foster ready for the Graybridge Dance Academy annual recital one month before Wendy was killed.* Huh.

"People were still talking about it when I started here." I sniff and bend down to retie my boots. Graybridge, like many small towns, has a strong sense of community. When a kid dies, it hits everyone. Kind of like my old neighborhood in Boston. When my brother Jimmy died of leukemia when he was eleven, everyone rallied around my parents. They stopped by the house with casseroles and money. Back in those days, you gave money to grieving families. "Just in case," they'd say. Maybe a leftover tradition from long-ago days in Ireland when money was scarce and death a whisper from everyone's doorstep. I sigh, thinking of Jimmy. Clear my throat.

"Dig up our files on Wendy Ridley's death. And see if you can track down Cynthia's files from when she was incarcerated."

"You think she might've been involved in Kara's murder?" Lauren asks.

"Let's cover our bases. I hope they wouldn't have let her out if she's still a danger to society." I snort. "But we all know how that goes."

Lauren clicks the keys of her computer. "Will do."

"What about our victim? What about Kara?"

Lauren looks up over her laptop screen. "A couple of traffic tickets is all I found so far."

"You guys get anywhere with her phone, social media?"

"I finished the paperwork for her phone records. Working on the social media now."

"Chief back yet?"

She shakes her head.

Bob Murphy and I go back years. And while we're nearly the same age, he's counting the days to retirement. Bob's looking forward to leaving all this excitement behind and dividing his time between Graybridge and his little place in Florida. He muses about spending his summer days at Fenway and playing cards with his buddies, who include my ex-husband, Ed, and fishing in the Gulf. I'm happy for Bob. He's earned his retirement more than most people. When Kara was identified, Bob took it hard. He knows her mother. They were neighbors for a number of years before Bob bought his condo. He remembered Kara, an only child, growing up with her single mom. He said he helped Cathy out once in a while with minor repairs and the like. She took care of his dog when he was gone. When the ID came in, Bob sighed, put on his coat, and trudged out of the station. He said he'd break the news to Cathy himself.

That's the worst part of this job, bar none. Over the years, I've done my share of shattering parents' worlds. Those days are the worst, and in those moments, I'm always glad I never had kids.

"Thanks, Lauren. Let me know what else you come up with."

"Will do, Rita." She leaves, holding her laptop and somehow clicking keys as she walks.

Bob is back in his office, door closed. No one dares disturb him, and everyone looks to me as his old friend and contemporary. Well, I've got to know what he learned from Kara's mom, so I take a deep breath, knock, and walk in without waiting for an invitation. Bob's sitting behind his big, messy desk, his head in his hands. He's gone nearly all gray, and his face droops like an old bulldog's. He glances up as I sit in the chair opposite him.

"You okay?" I ask.

"I'm too old for this, Rita." Everything about Bob sags. "What the hell's wrong with the world?"

I don't know what to say. I've asked myself that same question over the years, and so far, I haven't come up with an answer.

He huffs out a tired breath. "She was just a kid, Reet. Younger than my own daughter."

"It's tragic," I agree.

"I remember when she was little, riding a scooter in her driveway." He points a meaty finger at me. "I yelled at her one day because she was getting too goddamn close to the street."

"I'll do everything I can to find the bastard who did this to her."

He nods and fishes his old notebook out of his coat pocket and drops it on the desk. The leather cover is scarred and battered. It's the same one, paper replaced as needed, that he carried years ago as a detective.

"Let me give you what I've got."

I open my own notebook and wait.

"Kara was twenty-nine years old, living with her mother because she couldn't afford rent on her own. She worked as a junior insurance agent." Bob spells out the name of the company. "Her mom says she was fine. No trouble. Acting completely normal in the days leading up. Mom was a little worried that she hadn't come home last night but figured she stayed with a friend, which she did occasionally. The last time Cathy spoke to her was yesterday about lunchtime. She called her mom every day at the same time."

"Anything unusual in the conversation yesterday?"

Bob shakes his head. "No."

"When was the last time her mom actually saw her?"

"Yesterday morning, when they were both getting ready for work." Bob blows out a breath.

"How's Mrs. Cunningham taking it?"

"Not good. Kara was all she had. Her sister's with her. I called her on the way over, and she got there before I did. Thank God. But Cathy's barely hanging on. The sister called her doctor, and he called in something for her." Bob takes a deep breath, runs his massive hands through his gray hair. "Jesus. Let's get everyone together and meet in the conference room in fifteen minutes."

"All right."

"This is your investigation, Rita."

"What about Doug?" He's the other lead detective in our small department and has been champing at the bit for a big case.

Bob shakes his head. "Not this time. It's yours. Besides, you've already done the initial work. Doug and Lauren will help out, but you're the lead."

The room is chilly. Bob has gone quiet, his mind somewhere else. I only hope he's thinking of his place in Florida and not all the misery he's witnessed over the years. He pushes his notebook over to me. "The names of Kara's friends," he says.

I start to copy them into my notebook.

"No, Rita. Just take it. Take the whole goddamned thing." He shuffles to his feet and walks out.

# CHAPTER 7
# Esmé

When Byron comes down from his shower, he heads past me and finishes cleaning up the dishes. I should've done it, but I can't seem to move from my chair at the kitchen table.

Someone's coming through the front door, but Byron doesn't move from the sink, as if he's expecting company.

"Byron! What happened? Why are the cops here?" Irene Musgrave looks the same, only older. Her dark brown hair hangs just past her ears, and the straight-across bangs give her both a severe and a childlike look at the same time. She's bigger than I remember, wide through the shoulders, with a belly that protrudes between the wings of her royal blue jacket.

He turns to face her. "Dad heard a scream last night, and I found Kara Cunningham dead out back this morning," he deadpans.

She blinks behind her glasses, and her mouth hangs open. "Oh my God. What happened to her?"

"We don't know yet."

Irene rushes to the window. "What was she doing out there?"

"We don't know."

"Was Tom here alone?" She glances at me. "When did *you* get here?"

"This morning."

She drops a grocery bag on the table and throws a tangle of keys next to it. "How could this have happened?" her voice breathy. She narrows her eyes at my brother. "How did Kara end up dead in your backyard, Byron?"

"I was at work, Irene. I have no clue."

"Jesus, I can't believe it. What happened to her?"

"Someone killed her," Byron says, wiping off the countertop.

"Who? Who could've been back there?"

Byron shakes his head, folds a kitchen towel, and lays it next to the dish drainer.

"Is your father still up in his room?" she asks.

"Yes," Byron says.

Irene turns on her heel, and I hear her heavy footfalls as she stomps upstairs.

"She's over here every day?" I say.

"Yes. And I don't want to hear it. Dad wants her here. I know she brings him beer, but she also sits with him and fixes his meals while I'm sleeping, so I don't need to worry that I'll wake up and find him dead in his own vomit."

I shake my head. "Why? Doesn't she have her own life?"

He shrugs. "She still lives in the same house. She's got her ninety-two-year-old mother with her, so she goes home to her at night, but otherwise, she's over here most of the time."

I hear a game show, beeps and whistles and canned laughter on TV in the living room. Irene must have gotten Dad settled in his chair. She bustles into the kitchen.

"Did he eat good?"

"A little."

She nods, places two six-packs of beer in the fridge, tearing one can off its plastic ring and popping the top. She rifles through the cupboard, completely at home, and pulls out a bag of potato chips. She sets the beer and the chips on the table. "Did the cops question him?"

"They tried. He couldn't tell them anything," Byron says.

She glances out the window at the activity outside. "God, this is nuts. Kara's mom must be a mess. Who would do something like this? Do they have any clues?"

"Not that they've told me."

"Thank God your dad's okay with a murderer in the backyard. *Jesus,* Byron." Irene walks right up to the window and watches silently.

Dad calls from the other room, a high plaintive drone. Irene gathers the beer and the chips and walks out.

# CHAPTER 8
# Rita

We're packed into the conference room. Detective Doug Schmitt smirks at me from where he's standing against the back wall, perfect suit and tie, stylish as usual. I guess Bob's already told him that I'm the lead on this investigation and that he and Lauren will answer to me. Too bad. I've got years more experience than he does, so he'll have to suck it up.

I stand in front of the whiteboard, which will soon be covered with photos and notes. Lauren is assembling the crime-scene pictures now. I place my notebook beside Bob's on the table in front of me. I feel strange with his notebook in my possession. It seems wrong, like something has cataclysmically shifted in the universe.

I take a deep breath and update the team on what we have so far.

"Mrs. Cunningham said Kara didn't come home last night after work, and she assumed Kara had stayed with friends. But mom was a little worried because Kara would usually call her, and Kara wasn't answering her phone." I skim through Bob's notebook. "She said the following people were Kara's closest friends." I list the names on the board: Jack Crosby, Christy French Bowers, and Laney Morelli Addison. "She also said we should question Byron Foster, which I have done at least initially and will follow up on since the vic was found in his backyard. Lauren, you get contact information for the friends. Doug"—I clear my throat—"you head out to Kara's office and interview her coworkers. And we still don't know where her vehicle is." I consult Bob's notes. "A white Toyota Camry." I finish handing out assignments, and everyone is pretty eager to get going. Most cops don't like sitting still.

I stop in my office to quickly catch up on some paperwork and wait for Lauren to get me info on the friends. I check my phone and see I have a message from Jack Crosby. He wants to talk to me. Hmm, good timing.

He sits across the table from me at a little coffee shop around the corner from Graybridge High School. It's warm inside, and the scent of coffee and pastries fills the air.

"I've only got thirty minutes," Jack Crosby says with that rushed, exhausted look of every teacher I've ever interviewed.

"That's fine. I'll take what I can get."

His dark auburn hair is fairly long, hip, and his blue eyes are red-rimmed. He wipes his nose on a brown napkin. We spoke briefly on the phone, and he already knew about Kara. That happens in a small town, especially in these days of social media. Surprising a person of interest is pretty much dead.

He shakes his head and sniffs. "I can't believe it. I saw it on Twitter this morning. The kids are all talking about it."

"They're a little young to know anything about Kara Cunningham."

"Doesn't matter. Someone was killed in Graybridge. Someone young and pretty, even if she was my age. They all want to know if I knew her."

"What did you tell them?"

"Yes. Of course. We went to school together." He clears his throat.

"Were you friends?"

"We were close friends back in the day. After graduation, I went to college in New York. I was living in Albany until last month. Then I moved back to Graybridge."

"Have you seen Kara since you've been back?"

"Yeah, a couple times."

"When was the last time?"

He runs his hands through his hair. "Two weeks ago, I guess. Our friend had a party."

"Which friend?"

"Christy Bowers."

I glance down at my notebook. She's one of the friends Kara's mom listed. "Haven't heard from her after that?"

His gaze shifts to the door. He draws a deep breath. "Actually, Detective, I was supposed to meet Kara last night. That's why I called you."

I lean in, pencil poised. "Where? What time?"

He stabs the table with his finger. "Here. We were going to meet for coffee at seven, but she never showed."

"You call her?"

"I tried. Went to voice mail. I hung around until eight. Kara was always late." His eyes water, and he wipes them with a napkin he's crumpled into a ball in his fist. "Then I went home."

"Why were you two meeting?"

He draws a deep breath. "She wanted to get together for drinks, but I told her I was tired, but I could do a quick coffee. It was a school night."

"You guys still close friends?"

"We were close in high school. She was part of my inner circle. Kids form groups. She was part of mine. Then we graduated, and I went to New York. I've been slowly getting in touch with my old friends since I moved back."

"Who else was in your inner circle?"

He clutches his stubbled chin. "Austin Swanson, Laney Addison, Christy Bowers." He smiles. "And Esmé Foster. Sometimes Justin Reeves," he adds. "But he moved in eleventh grade. Austin moved too, after I left for college. Someplace down south."

"You been socializing much with the old gang since you've been back?"

His gaze rests on the table, and he shakes his head. "Some. But I've been really busy." He sits up straight, sips his coffee. He's handsome in a professorial way. Teaches AP History, he told me.

The door opens, and a draft of frigid air whips past us. Mr. Crosby glances at two teenage girls, who giggle as they come through the door. They seem to notice him and avert their eyes, hurry by. "They're not supposed to leave campus," he says, raises his eyebrows. "But some of the seniors manage to sneak out at lunch."

I tap my pencil on my notebook. "When did you last talk to Kara?"

He clears his throat. "Monday night when she called to see if I wanted to meet."

"Any particular reason she wanted to see you?"

"No. I don't think so. Just to hang out. Catch up."

"Huh."

His full lips are clamped shut. I add laugh lines to my sketch, but there isn't anything funny about Jack Crosby. He's nervous, eyes darting around, knee bouncing under the table.

He blows out a breath and runs his hand through his hair again. "I can't believe she's dead. That someone killed her."

"Where did you go after you left here last night?"

His mouth drops open. "Home. It was a school night."

"You live alone?"

"Yes. In Grand Valley Apartments."

That's one of the new complexes that have been sprouting like mushrooms around Graybridge. "Can anyone vouch for you?"

He shakes his head. "No." He glances at his watch. "I've got to get back to class." He stands and grabs his coffee.

"What about Esmé Foster? Have you kept in touch with her?"

He shakes his head. "No. I haven't seen Esmé since the summer after graduation." There's a softness in his eyes, like regret.

"You been over to the Fosters' house lately?"

"Not since high school. Why?" He glances out the window, in a hurry to get away, seems like.

"That's where we found Kara. Out by the woods." I watch his eyes, and they flicker with surprise? Concern?

"What was she doing there?"

"We don't know." I pick up my pencil. "We'll be in touch."

He nods and hurries out the door. I finish my notes. Add to my sketch. I ask the manager if they have surveillance video. They don't, but he tells me that he was working last night, and he saw Mr. Crosby, and he was alone. No sign of a woman who fit Kara's description. I drop my notebook in my satchel and head out.

# CHAPTER 9
# Esmé

I WALK PAST THE LIVING ROOM, WHERE DAD AND IRENE SIT SIDE BY SIDE in matching recliners, the only pieces of furniture in the house that look like they've been purchased in the last thirteen years. I put my jacket on and head out onto the front porch.

I wonder what Kevin's thinking. He must've read my note by now and realizes our relationship is over. The note left no room for doubt. But I can't help my mind wandering back over our years together.

Kevin is a chef, and he's wanted to open his own place for the last two years. It was supposed to be our big dream, even though my dream had sputtered and died with a career-ending hip injury. Kevin figured I could join my star to his. Let my dream go and follow him in his, just like that. But it wasn't that easy. I'm still grappling with the end of my ballet career, and he just didn't get it. To be honest, I stayed with him too long. After I knew it wasn't going to work, I stayed because of his family. And that isn't fair to either of us. I love Kevin's family. They welcomed me like some long-lost daughter. Their beautiful home in North Syracuse was always full of light and laughter. I reveled in the atmosphere that surrounded them. His tall, thoughtful dad, his bubbly sister, and especially his mom. She's kind and loving and was so interested in my career. They attended my performances, and when the pain started, clucked over me and researched the best doctors. Despite their help, no one could fix what years of strenuous dancing had done to my body.

I stand and walk around the side of the house. Across the weedy backyard, the cops have set up a folding table with papers on it held down with rocks. They are canvassing the woods. Through the trees, I see them, heads down, scouring the forest floor. There's a narrow path that leads to the pond that separates our land from the Ridleys'. When we were growing up, Byron and I explored those woods. Ray and his sisters played out there too. Ray sometimes had a gang of boys who ran with him. They taunted my brother and me. We were younger and made good targets. It always ended with a screaming match across the pond. You stay on your side, and we'll stay on ours. But despite Ray, I loved those woods.

Then when I was nine, everything changed. It was only a week after school had let out for the summer. Eleven-year-old Ray came down the path and stood crying in our backyard. My dad, Byron, and I ran outside. Ray was nearly incoherent, tears rolling down his face. Through stuttering bursts, he told us that his sister had drowned in the pond.

My mother had left to take Christy and Laney home. They'd been over to play. We'd been in the backyard when we'd heard the sirens, and Mom decided it was a good idea to get everyone home. She returned as Ray was telling us what happened. She grabbed him in her arms and cried along with him. Wendy was dead. She was my age, and we were in the same ballet class. But we weren't friends exactly.

The Ridleys kept their distance from other people. Mrs. Ridley sat in her car, the radio turned way up, while Wendy was in class. We'd pass her without a word in the parking lot, cigarette smoke twirling from her cracked window, as Mom herded the four of us into our car. Wendy would always tag after us, and it makes me feel guilty, even now, that we never included her in our little group. I don't know why. Maybe it was the adults' attitudes toward the Ridleys that rubbed off on us. They were a strange family, people apart from the rest of the respectable Graybridge citizens. But I remember Wendy, her angelic face, her white-blond hair, and her shy smile. I remember clearly the last time I saw her. We were leaving ballet class, and she waved to me and said, "Bye, Esmé. See you next week." But there was no next week. She was dead, and I never had a chance to return the friendship she so clearly desired.

The night she died, my parents, my mother particularly agitated, sat me and Byron on the couch and warned us to stay out of the woods. *Don't go near the pond.* We heard our parents whispering about Cynthia. It was Cynthia's fault. She'd killed her little sister, and we were afraid. She'd always been strange, even for a Ridley. When we played in the woods, Cynthia would hide behind trees, watching. But she'd been taken away, so Byron and I didn't understand why we couldn't go back there. By that fall, our parents seemed to have forgotten about their edict, and we crept back, slowly, worried that Wendy's ghost now haunted our woods but drawn there just the same.

Then as teenagers, my friends and I would sneak down the path after dark with beer filched from our parents' refrigerators. We'd sit on old mesh lawn chairs and build a fire, drink, and blast music from a boombox. By then, Ray had grown up too, and we, at least us girls, were more interesting to him. He'd join in our parties sometimes, a creepy presence, but not entirely unwelcome. He grew to be a good-looking teenager, and the whiff of bad boy that clung to him was a little exciting.

Why would Kara have been in the woods last night? From where she lay, it almost looks like that's where she'd been, like she'd gone into the woods, and someone had followed her out. I sigh and stick my cold hands in the pockets of my jacket and head back inside.

# CHAPTER 10
# Rita

BACK AT THE STATION, I CATCH UP ON SOME OF MY OTHER CASES, wanting to get some paperwork and phone calls out of the way so I can concentrate on the Cunningham homicide. Nothing from the crime-scene techs yet. I glance out my window. The sun is headed for the horizon, and daylight is slipping away. I need to talk to the rest of Kara's friends. I pick up my phone.

Mrs. Addison says she's available this evening, so I'll stop by her place on my way home.

I pack up my satchel and head out. She lives in a nice new subdivision with flowerpots on the front porches and swing sets in the backyards. I pull my old van to a stop, turn the key, and wait for the engine to sputter and quit.

She opens the door, eyes red, a clump of tissues pressed against her nose. She's dressed in black yoga pants and a T-shirt. Her dark hair is pulled up in a long ponytail, and her complexion is as smooth and clear as that of a model on the cover of a magazine.

We settle in her cozy family room, where a small playpen sits in the corner, a plastic bin of toys snugged next to it.

"I can't believe someone killed Kara." She chokes out a sob. "You found her this morning?"

"Yes." I give her a minute to pull herself together.

"Where did it happen? Did someone break into her house?"

"No. We found her out by some woods. Hogsworth Road."

I see a flicker of recognition in her eyes. "Why would she be out there?"

"That's what we're trying to figure out. Mrs. Cunningham listed you as one of Kara's close friends."

She nods. "That's right."

"When was the last time you spoke to her?"

She lets go a long, teary breath and tips her head back to look at the ceiling. "A few days ago. Sunday, I think."

"What was going on in Kara's life?"

"Nothing big. Same stuff." Tears build in Mrs. Addison's brown eyes. "Why would someone kill her?"

"What did you two talk about on Sunday?"

She licks her lips, lets go a trembling breath. "Uh, I don't remember. Ordinary stuff. She was thinking about looking for a new job. She felt like she was in a rut at the insurance office."

"Any problems there?"

"Nothing major. Just that the woman who holds the senior position isn't going anywhere, and Kara felt like she was stuck where she was in the company."

"Anything personal she was concerned about?"

Mrs. Addison blinks, and her gaze shifts to the window. A look that has me on alert. She reaches for a tissue from a box on the end table, clears her throat. "Actually, she seemed really upbeat. A friend of ours moved back to town recently, and she was really excited about that."

"Who would this friend be?" I glance up from my notebook to meet her eyes.

"Jack Crosby. An old high school friend."

I nod. "Were they an item back in the day?"

"No. Just friends. We had a tight little group, but Kara always had a thing for Jack." Mrs. Addison blows out a breath, sinks back against the couch cushions.

"Tell me about your high school friends." I sketch her face and thin shoulders, which are hunched with tension.

"Well, Kara, Christy Bowers, Esmé Foster, and I were all in the same ballet class. We started at the Graybridge Dance Academy when we were just five years old!" This makes her smile before she remembers that her friend is dead and pulls back into her grief. "Anyway, we've known each other since then. We also went to school together. By middle school, Jack Crosby and Austin Swanson and another guy kind of rounded out our group."

"So you've all known each other for years?"

"Yes." She sighs.

"What happened after graduation?"

"Jack and I went off to college. Kara and Christy stayed local. I came back after I got my degree. Got married a couple of years later."

"What about Mr. Swanson?"

"Austin? He moved to North Carolina, I think. He has family down there."

"What about Ms. Foster?"

"Esmé." Mrs. Addison takes a big breath. "We all kept dancing right through middle school. We were at that point in ballet where you have to decide, do I keep going? Try to go on pointe and work my butt off? I decided to quit. Soccer tryouts for high school were coming up, and that appealed to me more than dance. I wasn't going anywhere with it anyway. Wasn't good enough and didn't care."

"What about the others?"

"Kara and Christy wanted to keep going, but they weren't really that good either. But Esmé was amazing. She got all the lead parts in our little recitals. She was just way better than the rest of us. Miss Felicity told her mother that Esmé should apply to the ballet school downtown, and, of course, Mrs. Foster was thrilled."

"What about the other girls?"

"Well, they figured if Esmé was going to try out for the big school, then so were they, but neither of them was accepted."

"How did that affect the group?"

"They were kind of mad at first, but we all came around, supported Esmé. Although we didn't get to see her as much. She left right after school every day to go downtown to dance."

"Ms. Foster has just moved back. She told me this morning."

Mrs. Addison's mouth pops open. "Really? You saw Esmé? I didn't know she was coming back." Her gaze drops to her hands, which are knotted in her lap. "You found Kara out on Esmé's road?"

"Yes. In her backyard, in fact." I watch her reaction.

Mrs. Addison clamps her hand over her mouth. "That's crazy. Did Esmé see her?"

"No. She got home after Kara was found. When was the last time you spoke to Esmé?"

"Uh, well, forever. I don't remember." A tiny cooing noise quickly morphs into a wail, and Mrs. Addison jumps up and lifts an infant from the playpen. She shushes him sweetly and bounces him on her hip. "You don't mind if I feed him here?"

"No. Of course not." It's her house. The baby's hungry. She settles back on the couch, whips the baby into position and pulls up her T-shirt. I keep my eyes on my notebook while she strategically settles a small blanket over her shoulder. And I think how times have changed. My mother and her friends would've fainted at the sight of a woman breastfeeding. All nine McMahon children were bottle-fed. My ma considered herself a modern woman, and a modern woman in the fifties and sixties wouldn't have dreamed of breastfeeding. That was for country women stuck in the past and hippies.

"When did you last talk to Esmé?"

"I really don't remember. I haven't seen her since that summer after graduation."

"Huh. Thought you were all such good friends."

"We were." She sighs. "Esmé's had it rough. When her mother died sophomore year, she understandably went to pieces. We were devastated too. We all loved Mrs. Foster. She was the one who drove us to ballet class when we were little. Kara's mom had to work. My mom had three other kids to worry about, and Christy's mom was some big executive. But Mrs. Foster loved it. She wanted to do ballet when she was young, but her parents couldn't afford the lessons, she said, so she enjoyed taking us to class, being involved. When she died, we were all kind of a mess for a while. We started drinking on the weekends. Getting a little rebellious. But Esmé kept dancing. It was her mother's dream as well as hers, so I guess that gave her some comfort. But she really went downhill to the point where all she was doing was drinking and dancing. She was failing her classes and got in trouble at the ballet school. They warned her that if she didn't shape up, they'd kick her out. So she rallied, did better, and managed to graduate too. Then she told us she was going on auditions out of state. She got a job in Syracuse, and that was the last we saw of her."

"You never tried to contact her?"

"I texted her for a while, but she just didn't seem interested in staying in touch. I've heard she's been back occasionally to see her dad, but I haven't seen her. She just seems to have wanted to cut everybody off." Mrs. Addison's gaze meets mine. "We all worried some about Esmé's mental state, if I'm being honest."

"Why's that?"

She shrugs. "Just all she'd been through, and she just started to pull away from us after a while. We didn't understand."

"Uh-huh." I add to my notes. The "we" she keeps referring to is interesting. I was never one to belong to a clique, even when I was a teenager. "What can you tell me about Kara's love life?"

Mrs. Addison snorts. "Kara was always after guys who weren't interested in her. She'd date someone for a month or two, then they'd break up."

"She wasn't presently seeing anyone?"

A shadow passes Mrs. Addison's face. "Well, she was seeing Byron Foster, Esmé's brother."

I look up, lean forward. "Really?" I take a deep breath, tamp down my interest, but my heart is thumping. "How'd that go?"

"They broke up right after Jack came back last month."

"Who initiated the breakup?"

"I think Kara did. That's what she said anyway."

"What do you know about Byron?"

"Not a lot. He's had a rough couple of years. His wife cheated on him, so they got a divorce, and Kara said he was really down about that. His wife, Sonia, is a bit of a"—she whispers, as if the baby knows what she's saying—"bitch. Then he moved in with his dad, who's dying, I hear. He's an alcoholic. He never got over his wife's death."

I contain an inward chuckle. I think Mrs. Addison would fill me in on every family secret in Graybridge, if I asked. But the fact that Byron Foster didn't mention that he and the victim were involved is huge, and I scrawl quickly in my notebook, questions popping, Mrs. Addison forgotten for the moment.

She sniffs and draws a deep breath. "You don't have any clue what happened to Kara?"

"Not at this point."

"I can't believe she's gone." She glances away. "Did you talk to Byron?"

"I did. Anyone else you think I should talk to?"

"Christy. They hung out more than I did." She glances at the baby. "I just don't have time. Maybe she told Christy something that might help."

"Uh-huh." I finish my notes, glance up. "Where were you last night, Mrs. Addison?"

Her mouth pops open, and she blinks her eyes. "Me? I was here. Home. With my husband and the kids."

"Okay." I rise. "I appreciate your help." I hand her my card. "I'll let myself out."

By the time I get back in my van, it's dusk. I check my phone and see that my brother Danny texted, reminding me I was supposed to stop by his house after work. I sigh. It's been a busy day, a big new case, and I'd rather just get home. I've got a lot to sort out, but seeing Mr. Foster today has me feeling guilty about my brother, so I throw on my blinker and head for the highway.

Danny lives about twenty minutes west of Graybridge in one of those tiny historic towns Massachusetts is so full of. He teaches English at a small private college full of dim-witted rich kids who couldn't get into the Ivy Leagues. I told him I'd stop by since he wanted to give me something he unearthed from one of the boxes from Ma's attic. And besides, it's October.

His house is a white, clapboard, century-old two-story. The architecture has a name I can never remember. He's been restoring it for like twenty years. Anyway, I ring the bell, shiver on the porch. Feels like it might rain. The air is chilly and damp, smells like rotting leaves.

A woman opens the door. She's blond, her dark eyes adorned as though she uses a professional makeup artist, slim pants, and a cream-colored silk blouse. Pearls too. *Really, Danny? A clone of your last three girlfriends.*

"You must be Rita." She extends a thin hand and clasps mine.

"Yeah. And you must be Vivian."

She smiles. Lips thin and clamped. "Vivi*enne*."

I follow her through the foyer and into the living room, where embers glow in the fireplace.

"Dan's in the study. He had a call and asked me to let you know he wouldn't be long. Would you care for a drink?"

"Some water would be nice." She heads into the kitchen, and I'm left standing in front of the mantel. I notice the McMahon family portrait isn't in its regular place. I glance around the tidy, antiques-filled room. Don't see it anywhere. Maybe Danny and Maureen are on the outs again. He and our eldest sister don't always see eye to eye, and he's put the portrait away during their spats before. My brother is always the grown-up, poised, levelheaded, except when it comes to Maureen, who thinks she's the head of the family now that our parents are gone. They fight like two little kids. Maureen calls him Dr. Fancy-pants, and he refers to her as Mrs. Danvers, a character from a book he teaches.

The last family portrait (not that there were too many of those) was taken the year before Ricky left for Vietnam. After that, we began to come apart, and nobody was going to suggest Ma and Dad load the other eight of us into the station wagon and head down to the Sears portrait studio. We all have a copy of the picture. Don't know where mine is. In a box in a closet someplace. I don't need it hanging on the wall to recall every detail.

Dad in his one suit and a skinny tie, stomach straining against his dress shirt, his thin hair combed straight back and gelled into place. The look on his face could be indigestion or resignation. I can never decide which. Ma, hair tightly curled, wearing her best go-to-Mass-on-a-holiday dress, sits next to him. Our eldest brother stands in the back next to Ricky, a couple of spots on his chin clumsily touched up by the photo tech. My two eldest sisters, Maureen and Joanie, are on the back row too. Linda and Debbie sit on either side of our parents. The youngest, Debbie, is five years my senior. And the three musketeers, as we referred to ourselves, sit cross-legged in front of our seated parents, me between Jimmy and Danny. I wore a green dress that I hated and had my bangs brushed back and clipped with a barrette (which I also hated). I remember that, on the way over, Ma kept turning around to check that I wasn't getting all wrinkled. When we were nearly at the plaza, she gave me a once-over, reached for a Kleenex in her big purse, dabbed her tongue with it, and cleaned my cheek. Gross, I know, but nothing that I hadn't seen everyone else's mother do in a pinch.

Vivi*enne* returns with a tumbler filled with ice water. I get a good look at her in the lamplight. She's late forties, I'd guess, to Danny's sixty-two, but he's a handsome man, youthful and fit. Ma always said he was the best-looking of the litter, and she wasn't wrong. My other living brother, Bill, is seventy-three and has let himself comfortably slide into old age, gray and glasses and content. He retired years ago from the power company. Has a good pension and builds birdhouses in his garage.

Viv and I sit in wing-back chairs on either side of an end table culled from an estate sale. I notice she's holding a short glass of amber liquid, which makes me think of Mr. Foster again and his shaking hands and beer breath. So, she keeps Danny company in the drinking department, must be. His last girlfriend, a nice woman named Sandra, tried to curb Danny's drinking, and she didn't last long. I sip my water and set the glass on a crystal coaster.

"Dan tells me you're a detective in Medfield?" she says.

"Graybridge. And you work at the college with Danny?"

"Yes. We met last semester at a seminar. I teach art history."

Huh. Wonder if Danny told her that I draw. Not that I'd call myself an artist. Probably not. "That's nice. Interesting."

"Yes. I think so." She smiles, but her eyes dart toward Danny's study door. I'm not much for small talk, so I sometimes make people nervous. Vivienne's perched on the edge of her chair, sipping her drink in tiny convulsive sips, faint wrinkles around her mouth.

I glance at my watch, not that I have anything to rush home to, but my mind is churning with the Cunningham case. Danny and I are the closest in the family, and we regularly see one another, but when I'm at the beginning of a new, tough case, I get laser-focused and tend to draw into myself until I get it sorted out.

Viv clears her throat, checks a small gold watch on her wrist. "Dan tells me that you . . . work on some really difficult cases."

"Yeah. Yes. I'm the lead detective. It's a pretty small department, but the most difficult cases usually land on my desk. I've got a lot of experience. I was with the Boston PD for years before I moved out to Graybridge." I sit up. I was starting to slouch, my mind wandering to Byron Foster and his demeanor while I questioned him. I think of Ray Ridley's accusation and Laney Addison's revelation. I glance at Viv and rack my brain trying to think of something interesting to ask her.

She sips her drink again, clutches her glass like a lifeline. A blond tress has worked its way free and lands across her forehead. She swipes it back, takes a deep breath, and bolts up from her chair as Danny's door opens.

"Sorry," he says, hurrying into the room. Viv sets her glass on the end table.

"No problem. Your sister and I had a chance to get acquainted." They smile at one another like people do when they're first dating—best behavior and good manners. "But I do need to run along, Dan. I've an early class tomorrow."

"Yes. Right." He walks her to the door.

She peeps over her shoulder. "Nice to have met you, Rita."

"Same here," I call. Danny pecks her cheek and shuts the door behind her.

"Hope you weren't waiting too long," he says, walking back to the center of the room, glass of whiskey in his hand.

"No. Gave me a chance to talk to Vivienne."

"She's great." He smiles, sips his drink. "We haven't been going out long. Still in the getting-to-know-you stage."

"She hasn't met Charlotte yet?" Charlotte is Danny's daughter from his first marriage. Of all my many nieces and nephews, Charlotte is the one I'm closest to. She's thirty years old, works as an admin for the Dean of Fine Arts at Danny's college, where she's working on her master's degree.

My brother shakes his head. His hair is still mostly dark, but the little bit of gray works for him, and he's got just enough facial hair to give him a suave, professorial look. "Not yet. Charlotte's been busy anyway. Soon probably."

"So, what's up?"

He drains his glass, sets it on the mantel. "I was going through another one of the boxes from Ma's." Maureen's been living in our old house in Boston since Ma died a few years ago, and all the stuff that's accumulated for decades is in the attic. Turns out, Ma was something of a hoarder, and she seems to be the person who ended up with everybody's junk as her family and Dad's passed away. "I wanted to give you something." He heads back into the study and returns with a large, flat-bottomed ceramic chicken.

"What's that?"

He plops it on my lap. "You don't remember it?"

"Should I?"

"It's a roaster pan. It used to sit on a shelf in Grandma's storage room when we were kids. Don't you remember? We took it down one day to play with it, and Gran had a hissy fit when she saw it was full of plastic Army men. She said it was old, and we weren't to touch it."

A memory vaguely comes back to me. "And I need this why?" Not like I'm ever going to roast anything.

Danny sips the drink he's refilled. "Maybe you can take a cooking class?" He arches an eyebrow.

"Right. So, where's the family portrait? You fighting with Maureen again?"

"No." Danny's gaze shifts to the dying embers in the fireplace. "I guess October is hitting me harder this year for some reason. I decided to put it away for a while."

"Oh." I sink back into my chair. I can't believe our big brother has been gone so long. Over fifty years. Ricky was KIA this month, while back home the leaves were dying and Jimmy, Danny, and I were fighting over who was going to be which character for Halloween.

"Anyway, let's plan something, Rita. I don't get to see you often enough."

"I'm pretty busy at the moment. I'm working a homicide," I say automatically, not stopping to think about Danny's pain.

"You work too much," he says and sips his drink.

"Yeah. I know." My refuge, just as whiskey is his. "But okay, yeah. Let's plan something."

"Have you talked to Joe lately?"

I set the roaster on the coffee table and slip my jacket off. The room is getting warm. "Yeah, actually." Joe Thorne is my friend from the FBI. Well, we're a little more than friends, and he wanted to get together over the summer, and we did manage to meet for drinks downtown a couple of times. "We've both been really busy, though." I stand and slip my jacket back on. "I better get home." My gaze lands on Danny's nearly empty glass, but I bite my tongue.

"Why don't you call him, Rita? We could get together. The four of us."

"Yeah. We'll see."

Danny's gaze meets mine. "It doesn't do you any good to be alone, Rita."

*And it doesn't do you any good to get drunk every night.*

"Okay. I'll call him. All right?" I can't hide the touch of annoyance in my voice. I zip up my jacket and turn to leave.

"Don't forget your chicken," Danny says.

# CHAPTER 11
# Esmé

Irene fixed Dad's dinner and left a while ago. He's watching TV and finishing the last of the beer she left in the fridge. It's a strange relationship, but aren't they all? Byron walks into the kitchen in a fresh set of scrubs and rifles through the cupboard.

"Did you get any sleep?" I ask.

"An hour or two," he says, pouring milk over a big bowl of cereal.

"You think you should go to work?"

He replaces the milk and shuts the fridge door. "I can't just call out. We're short-handed." He sits at the table, hunched over his bowl. He looks terrible.

"Well, under the circumstances . . ." I glance out the window. The autumn-draped trees are just visible in the back-porch light, bright yellow tape tied to their trunks. The woods seem somehow closer and more menacing than they did in the daytime.

Even though her body's gone, it almost feels like I can see Kara lying there. And I can't help but look for a man lurking in the trees, menacing, his eyes fixed on the house. That's what finally drove me to leave home and not come back. Mom died when I was sixteen. I had been in the car with her and Dad when we crashed into a tree on an icy winter night. Before the cops and ambulance got there, a man poked his head in at the car door, his face concealed in the dark. A man who seemed to know us. But he wasn't there to help. He growled, "I'm going to kill you! I'm going to kill you!" I tumbled out of the back seat and into the snow. He circled the car and grabbed me by the neck. I can still feel his icy fingers. And then I heard the sirens, and the man melted away, back into the night, and disappeared.

When I lived in Syracuse, I could forget about him. Like a ghost, he seemed tied to this place. But now that I'm back, I instinctively look for him again, especially now that it's dark and there's been a murder in my own backyard.

Byron shovels a spoonful of colorful cereal into his mouth. "If it's not too much trouble, maybe you can make sure Dad gets upstairs and into bed, so I don't find him down here asleep in his chair when I get home."

I swallow, ignore Byron's tone. "Does he do that?"

"Sometimes."

"Will I be able to support him? I don't want him to fall or anything."

"He can walk. Hopefully, he hasn't had too much today. So, what are your plans? You really going to stay here?"

"Yes. I think so." I glance at my phone, but there's no one to call me now that Kevin and I are through. All our friends back in Syracuse were really his, and I've isolated myself from everyone here. My own fault. "Maybe I'll look for a job," I say.

"Yeah?"

"I'm broke, By. I need to do something."

He smirks. "Maybe you could go to college."

"My grades were so bad, that's not an option, and you know it." I get up from the table and walk to the window, drawn there as if by an invisible force.

"Sorry," he says. "I don't mean to be such a fucking dick, but it's been a helluva year, and I could've used your help." He rises from the table and rinses his bowl in the sink. "And now Kara. This is crazy."

"I'm sorry too. I can't believe someone killed her." I shudder. "What if the murderer is still out there in the woods?"

"The cops have been all over the place. I don't think he'd be hanging around. Still. Lock all the doors when I leave, and Dad's gun is right where it's always been."

I turn to face him. "God, Byron. Not where he can get it?"

"No. Where we hid it after Mom died. I fire it at the range occasionally, so it works. You hear anything strange, call 911 and get the Glock."

Byron left for work, and Dad's in bed, his raspy snores echoing down the hall. Byron was right; Dad walked up the stairs okay and even got into his pajamas and brushed his teeth. I really didn't have to do too much to help him.

I had left my suitcase and bag of ballet shoes in the garage earlier, so I walked out there and grabbed the suitcase and carried it upstairs. It's the same one I fled Graybridge with over ten years ago. I flick on my bedroom light and take stock of my present situation. My bed, with its lavender comforter, sits against the far wall. Posters of bands I liked in high school are still thumbtacked to the walls. Mom had put up wallpaper, wide pink and white stripes with little ballerinas scattered over it. My dresser still has makeup lying across the top that hasn't been used in years. It needs to be thrown out. My boombox sits in the corner, where Nickelback and Rascal Flatts and *The Nutcracker* CDs mingle in a messy pile. My closet is full of old costumes from when I was little and danced at the local school, where Miss Felicity taught tap and jazz along with ballet. The sequins and polyester shimmer under the harsh overhead light.

I close the curtains at the window that overlooks the backyard and drop down on the bed, tired and teary. What am I going to do now? Like I told Byron, I'm broke, with no plan for the future. I think of my mom and how she'd know what to do. She'd help me fix my life. I glance at my phone. It's just after midnight.

I doze off and on. I can't seem to stay asleep. Thoughts of Mom and Kara tangling up together. Kara murdered in my backyard and my mom dead in our crushed car thirteen years ago. And the man who showed up at the accident. Is he still around? Perhaps looking for young women to kill? I can't get the thought out of my head, and the knowledge that Kara and I resembled one another, at least from behind. Same straight, light brown hair, same short, petite build. When we were in high school, people were always mistaking one of us for the other. What if her murderer was the man who threatened me? What if he's been lurking around Graybridge, waiting for his chance? Kara was struck from behind. Maybe he thought she was me.

I get up from the bed, wrap my arms around my middle, and pace. *Get a hold of yourself, Esmé.* It's been thirteen years. That man might not even have been real. No one thinks he was real but me. When I asked my dad afterward, he told me that there was no man. I imagined it. I had a concussion, that's why I was confused. And why would anyone want to kill me? It didn't make sense. But my family's and friends' calming words didn't banish the man from my dreams, which still haunt me occasionally. I pinch my sides, trying to distract my mind with the pain.

I go to the window and pull the curtain aside—nothing but trees in the moonlight. I cross the hall, the floor cold on my feet, and go into Byron's dark room and look out on the road. Nothing. Still, when I head back to my room, I stop at the closet and reach under the blankets stored there and grab the gun.

# CHAPTER 12
# Rita

THURSDAY MORNING, I YAWN AND SIP MY COFFEE. IT'S EARLY YET, BUT the station is quickly filling up, people starting their day. I leave Byron Foster a message to call me. We need to get him in here for more questioning. I tap my fingers against my blotter. He's got some explaining to do.

Lauren raps on my door frame.

"Hey. You got anything?"

She flips her braid back over her shoulder, but little brown curls frame her face, refusing to be restrained. "Not a whole lot, Rita. I called the hospital, and they verified that Byron Foster worked the seven-to-seven shift Tuesday night." She glances at her computer. "They told me he works on the med-surg floor. I spoke to the charge nurse, and she did say that Byron had a break about three-thirty."

"Huh. How long was the break?"

"She said usually about thirty minutes, but she couldn't remember exactly when he left and returned."

"That's not much time. See how far it is from the hospital to his house."

"Already did." Of course she did. "Fifteen-minute drive during rush hour. But probably quicker than that at three-thirty in the morning."

"Still be tough to murder somebody in that small window." And why would Kara have skipped out on her date with Jack Crosby and then met Byron Foster at three-thirty in the middle of the night? Doesn't seem logical. "Anything on Kara's phone records?"

"Not yet."

"Okay. Good deal. Let me know if you find anything."

"Will do."

Doug sticks his head in at my door. As always, he's neat and stylish, nary a wrinkle in his snow-white dress shirt, nor a fold in his expensive suit pants.

"I thought you'd want to know what I found out at Kara's office yesterday."

"Have a seat," I say.

Doug consults his notebook. "I talked to her boss, Clark Littleton; he's seventy-something, I'd guess. He had retirement brochures all over his desk. He didn't seem to have any grip on what actually goes on in his own place of business. He referred to Kara as Carla three times. I don't think he knows his ass from his elbow."

Doug shoots me a look from under his neat, heavy eyebrows.

"What else?"

"Well, Mr. Littleton wasn't even in the office Tuesday. Said he had a ton of vacation days that he was taking here and there before he retires in December. He was no help at all." Doug flips a page. "Marie Romano, middle-aged, has worked at the agency for twenty-four years. She didn't have a lot to say about Kara except that she thought Kara was on her phone too much. But she didn't know anything about Kara's personal life. Said Kara practically ran out of the office at quitting time every day." Doug leans back.

"What about Tuesday?"

"Marie said that Kara left at five-thirty, as usual. Kara told her she'd see her tomorrow, and that was it."

"Hmm." Well, we know that Kara was going to meet Jack. "You didn't get a sense that Marie knew more than she was telling?"

"No. She said she didn't see anything out of the ordinary Tuesday."

"They have security cameras?"

"One outside on the parking lot. We haven't received the video yet. I'll give them another call."

"Let me know."

"Will do. "He stands and tucks his notebook in his jacket pocket. "We hear anything back from the lab?"

"Not yet. Hopefully, we'll have something soon."

He nods, buttons his suit coat. "Okay, talk to you later, Rita."

Kara's autopsy is scheduled for this afternoon, so I called Christy Bowers and arranged to talk with her this morning.

Mrs. Bowers is an executive at a medical supply company, but she's working from home today. When she heard about Kara yesterday morning, she left the office with no set plan to return, so her admin said.

A tall, slim blonde answers the door of a big two-story colonial in the swanky, old-money Graybridge Hills neighborhood.

"Come in, Detective." She swings the door wide, turns, and patters down the hardwood hall. We get settled in the family room. Huge windows look over a meticulous fading garden with woods beyond. Mrs. Bowers tucks her long legs under her, red-painted toenails peeking out from her black slacks.

She sniffs and wipes her bloodshot eyes. "I just can't believe it," she says, as I get my notebook out of my satchel. "Who would do such a thing?"

"We're trying to figure that out," I say. "You've known Kara since you were a kid?"

"Yes."

"And you were still close?"

"Yes. Close friends."

"When did you talk to her last?"

Tears trickle from the corners of her eyes. "I'm not sure. I talk to her quite a lot. You know? She and I call each other all the time."

"Did you talk to her the day she was killed?"

"No. I don't think so. I spoke to her Monday, though. I remember that."

"Why? What was memorable about Monday's conversation?"

She shrugs, takes a deep breath. "Nothing, really. I just remember I was sitting in the kitchen eating takeout I'd picked up on the way home from work. My son was at a friend's house, and I hate to eat alone, so I called Kara, and we talked while I had my dinner."

"You don't remember what you talked about?"

She wipes her nose with a clump of tissues. "Just stuff. How work was going. Oh." She drops the wad of tissues on the end table. "I met Kara at Hartshorn's Brewpub for dinner last Saturday night." Her lips tremble. "That was the last time I actually saw her." She glances around at the big, open floor plan, which seems to echo in its emptiness. "Anyway, Kara and I had dinner and a couple of drinks. She's looking for a new job and wanted my help."

"She was unhappy at work?"

"Yes. She needed a new challenge. And the guy she works for is a real creep. She needed to get out of there. Anyway, she was unhappy at work, and I wanted to help. That's what we were talking about again Monday, as well as the usual, gossipy stuff, you know."

I sketch her face, how her bangs slip over her intense green eyes, and give her a minute.

She coughs into her elbow. "Do you have any leads, Detective? Kara was the sweetest person in the world. No one who knows her would've hurt her. Was she . . . ?"

"Raped?"

Mrs. Bowers nods. "I heard she was found out behind the Foster house in the woods."

"We don't know yet. The autopsy is pending." But Kara was fully dressed. If she had been raped, she'd had time to put her clothes back on, which could've happened, before the murder.

Mrs. Bowers closes her eyes, and tears continue to seep from the corners.

"What do you know about Kara's love life?"

Her eyes flutter open, and she glances out the window, where a cold rain starts to fall. "Kara wasn't seeing anyone at the moment."

"Who had she been seeing?"

Her gaze meets mine. "Byron Foster." She snorts. "Pretty strange that someone killed her in his backyard, isn't it?" she mumbles through damp tissues.

I nod. "When did they break up?"

"About a month ago."

"How did she feel about the breakup?"

"She was glad it was over. Byron is a jerk."

No one seems to have a good opinion of Mr. Foster. "How so?"

"Well, he just is. He wouldn't call her for days, then want to hook up out of the blue. He never treated her very well."

"So did she end it?"

"Yes. She finally told him not to call her anymore, that she was done with him."

"How did he take it?"

Mrs. Bowers lowers her eyes. "He wasn't happy about it. That's what Kara said."

Hard to understand a man killing a woman over a breakup. Still, I've seen women murdered for less. Jilted boyfriends make good suspects. "Anyone else that Kara might've been interested in?"

"Not right now, no."

Huh. Not what Mrs. Addison said. "What about Jack Crosby?"

Mrs. Bowers's face reddens slightly. "Jack? Yeah. Well, he just moved back to town. He teaches at the high school. Kara always liked him." She swishes her hand as if this is no big deal. "But I don't think they were seeing one another. She would've told me." Mrs. Bowers clears her throat. "My friend told me that Byron's sister was back."

"Esmé? Yes. She was at the house yesterday."

"What's she doing here?"

"She said she was moving back."

Mrs. Bowers nods. "Huh."

"You haven't kept in touch?"

She clamps her lips and shakes her head. "No."

"Where were you, Mrs. Bowers, on Tuesday night?"

Her gaze meets mine, eyes widen. "Here, home."

"Alone?"

"Yes. Well, except for my son." Her eyes shift to the mantel, where a framed photo sits of a boy about seven or eight years old posing in a soccer uniform. I give her my card and tell her to call anytime if she thinks of anything.

# CHAPTER 13
# Esmé

With Byron in bed after his shift, and Irene and Dad in their recliners in the living room, I grab my car keys and head into town. I don't feel like hanging around with them, so I'm off. I haven't been back to Graybridge proper since I left eleven years ago. When I visited Dad, I got off the highway before town and had no reason to drive through. I'm nervous about what I'll find. Obviously, things will be different. But if I'm staying, I might as well get reacquainted with my hometown.

I park in a slanted spot on the square. Cold rain dots my windshield, and I pull the collar of my jacket up around my ears. My hair is up in a bun, as usual. An old habit, but it keeps it out of the way. I walk slowly past the shops. Some have been here forever; some are new. The Graybridge Dance Academy is closed. Its second-story windows are dark and dusty. Miss Felicity has probably retired. She was old even when I started dancing there. I take a deep breath, emotions rolling through my chest. I can almost hear the piano music tinkling on the breeze, smell the resin.

I keep walking. I pass Graybridge Books on the corner and turn down the other side of the square. Tony's Superette is still here. That makes me smile. My friends and I used to stop there for candy when we were young. When we were thirteen, Austin slipped a six-pack of beer under his hoodie. Luckily, Tony didn't call the cops, but Austin almost wished he had, rather than call his dad, which is what Tony did.

I come to a stop halfway down the block in front of a place called André's Café. The Dash-In Deli used to be here. André's is new, or at least new to me. There are wrought-iron tables out front for the warm weather, and the big plate-glass window is slightly steamed. There's a small HELP WANTED sign in the corner.

A bell chimes when I open the door. Vivaldi plays softly over the sound system. There are small round tables clustered in front of the plate-glass windows. On the wall behind the register is a board with the café's fare written out in colorful chalk. A man about my age emerges from the back. He's slim and neatly dressed, a white apron over his black jeans and white button-down shirt. His dark hair is thick and neatly combed back.

"Good morning," he says. "What can I get you?"

"Um, well. I haven't decided." I try to smile. *Be personable, Esmé.*

"Take your time," he says and busies himself bagging up cookies.

I take a deep breath. "I noticed you have a help-wanted sign in your window."

He turns toward me and folds his arms. "Yes. The girl who works the morning shift decided not to show last week. When I called her, she said she didn't feel like coming to work anymore, like, no big deal. She had better things to do."

"No notice?"

He blows out a breath. "I guess that was her notice. Ghosting me."

"That's rude," I say.

His eyes widen. "I know, right? We're running a business here." I can't help but smile. "And we're swamped." He glances out the front window as if expecting a crowd to come storming through the door any minute.

"I'm looking for a job, actually. I have experience."

"Let me get you an application." He touches my sleeve and heads into the back. I like the looks of the café. The walls are a creamy pale yellow, and a mural is painted on the big side wall. Interesting cartoon people drinking coffee, their pets at their sides, like something out of the *New Yorker,* but in color and three feet tall.

Rich desserts fill the cold case, and I notice that the menu includes soups and sandwiches, plus a few heartier entrées. André's Café has all the coziness and charm that the restaurant where Kevin works lacks. It's all chrome and neutrals, really upscale, but cold.

"I'm Collin Flynn, by the way." He hands me a paper application on a clipboard and scurries off as two elderly women have come in and are standing impatiently at the counter.

I take a seat by the window and fill out the application. I've only done this one other time, when Kevin got me a job serving at his restaurant after my ballet company let me go. I was nervous then. I'd never done anything but dance. It was the only world I knew, and the thought of interacting with the public so closely was frightening. On the stage, you were protected, the audience at a safe distance. But I didn't know what else to do. Kevin said he would take care of everything. His restaurant usually wouldn't have hired someone who'd never worked a day in her life, that was how his boss put it. Dancing professionally didn't count in his book. His servers were well-trained, heavily experienced in the culinary world. I didn't know a merlot from a cabernet, a London broil from a rib eye. But Kevin got me the job, and I was terrible. After two weeks, his boss wanted to fire me, but Kevin lobbied for more time, and he trained me himself. We'd go home at night, and he'd go through proper place setting, appetizers 101, bar orders, until I was a passable server. And then I was absorbed thoroughly into his world. For the last two years, I worked like a dog, trying to forget my dancing life.

When I finish the application, I look up and see that the tables around me have begun to fill, but Collin is standing behind the counter, free of customers for the moment.

I hand him the clipboard.

"Esmé?" He cocks an eyebrow.

"Yes. My mother loved all things French."

"It's lovely." His gaze shoots down the page. "A ballerina?"

"I was."

His eyes linger on my face a moment. "That must have been amazing." I force a smile. "But I see that you've been a server the last two years."

"Yes."

"What brings you to Graybridge?"

"Actually, this is home. I decided that it was time to come back." I feel myself start to tear up, and I don't want him to think I'm a nutcase, so I blink and glance away, hoping he doesn't notice.

"Well, let me go over this, and I'll be in touch."

# CHAPTER 14
# Rita

Detective Broderick is driving an unmarked car to the crime scene, while I look over my notes in the passenger's seat. The afternoon is gray and chilly, but at least the rain has stopped.

This is the first time that Lauren has been out in the field with me since making detective, and I'm glad for her help. I got busy after talking with Ms. Bowers and had to send Lauren to the autopsy in my place, so she fills me in on the ride over.

"Cause of death was blunt force trauma," she says.

I nod. "Figured."

"The perp struck her twice in the back of the head. One of those blows resulted in a skull fracture, which was eventually fatal."

Lauren turns onto Hogsworth Road, and trees and fields spread out on both sides. The autumn leaves have rapidly picked up color and are peaking, and despite the lack of sunshine, the countryside is a picture.

"Eventually?"

"Yeah. She said that Kara was alive, unconscious probably, but alive for maybe a couple of hours after she was attacked."

I take a deep breath. Not what I wanted to hear. To think that girl was lying by the woods and someone, had they known she was out there, might've helped. If only Mr. Foster hadn't been too drunk to go outside when he heard the scream. Timing can be cruel.

"Okay, what else?"

"She had scratches on her arms and looked like she might've fought back."

"Anything under her fingernails?"

"Fake. They're at the lab. She also had a good bit of debris from the woods in her hair and on her clothes."

"Anything that might belong to her attacker? Fibers? Hair?"

"They collected stuff, but we'll have to wait for the lab. Tox report too."

"Sexual assault?"

"No obvious signs of that."

"Time of death?"

"Dr. Gaines said between eight p.m. and midnight, she thinks."

I turn to look at Lauren. "But she said that Kara was possibly alive for two hours after she was assaulted?"

"Yes."

I blow out a breath. "Which means she could've been attacked as early as six o'clock, not long after she left work. How long does it take to drive from her office to the Foster place?"

Lauren bites her lip, her short chin wrinkling. "I looked it up. It's in my notes." She pulls into the Foster driveway. "But not long."

"Okay. Let me know." I close my notebook and stow it in my satchel. The fact that Kara was killed early in the evening changes things. There's a window that would've allowed Byron Foster to have killed her *before* he left for work. I check my phone to see if he's called me back. Nothing yet.

A stout older woman with dark hair and large-framed glasses opens the door. We introduce ourselves, and she says her name is Irene Musgrave, a family friend, and leads us into the living room. The remains of what looks like lunch cover two TV trays, those old plastic ones that snap onto the metal legs. Ma used to have some just like them. Mr. Foster gives us a quizzical look, and I notice the beer can sitting next to his half-finished sandwich.

"Is your son here, Mr. Foster?"

"He's asleep."

"Would you be sure to tell him to call me when he gets up?"

He nods, but I'm not exactly convinced that he'll remember. "We're going to be in your backyard, Mr. Foster. Just wanted you to know. Also, I wanted to see if you remembered any more about Tuesday night."

He shakes his head, and Ms. Musgrave, who's hovering over his chair, folds her arms across her ample bosom.

"I've asked him, Detective," she says. "He doesn't remember a thing. He's not well."

"Yes. I'm sorry about that. But, Mr. Foster, you told us you heard a scream. Was it one scream? A few screams?"

His gaze meets mine, and his brain seems to clear. "One. One scream. Very faint. Like from a long way away. Then it was quiet."

"Where were you when you heard it?"

"I was in my chair here. I'd fallen asleep in front of the TV."

"But you don't have any idea what time it was?"

"No."

"Was it dark out?"

"I don't know. My son pulled the drapes before he left for work."

"Was he still here when you heard the scream?"

"I don't believe so. He went to work. And I dozed off."

"Did you get up to check it out?"

"No." He glances up at Ms. Musgrave, who leans her hands on the back of his recliner.

"He doesn't do well in the evenings," she says. "He's ill."

And drunk too, I think to myself, but anyway. "Okay, well, we'll be out back. Let us know if you remember anything."

I start to turn to leave, then stop. "Ms. Musgrave, what do you know about this? Were you here on Tuesday?"

She sticks her hair back behind her ear. "I was here until about five-thirty. I fixed Tom his dinner, and then I left for home."

"You see anything unusual?"

"No."

"Any cars on the street?"

"Not that I remember."

"Was Byron still here when you left?"

She hesitates. "Yeah. He was in the kitchen, I think, when I went home."

"Okay, let me know if you think of anything that might help."

Lauren and I head outside and trudge around the house. The yard is mucky from the rain, and the wet makes for a raw day. The crime-scene team has finished up, and Hugo Martinez, their lead, waits for us by the woods.

"Hey, Rita, Lauren." He nods. "I'd walk with you, but I've got another call. The rest of the team has already left."

"That's fine."

"We're finished up here." He turns, gestures to the woods, his dark hair flopping in the wind. "I'll send you my initial report when I get back to the office, but here's a hand-drawn copy of the diagram we made so you know what you're looking at."

"Thanks, Hugo." He takes off like a kid released to recess, and Lauren and I put our heads together over the diagram.

Lauren looks up. "We're standing about where the body was found." The weeds are flattened from the trampling of the team and the ruts from the stretcher. She glances back at the map, which shows the pond in the middle of the woods, with several paths running from it. One of the paths ends where we're standing.

I point to the side of the pond. "They've marked it here, where they think she was first attacked."

Lauren blows out a breath. "She was trying to get to the house, don't you think?"

"Possibly. Wonder what she and the perp were doing at the pond. How did he get her out there? Let's have a look."

Just as we get ready to start down the path, Esmé Foster runs up to us from across the yard.

"Detective! Have you found anything?"

"Not yet. What do you know about these woods?"

She catches her breath. "Uh, our property runs back a ways. Past the pond a little bit."

"Why would anyone be out there, you think? It's private property, right?"

"Yes. But several properties run together back there."

"You want to show us?" Maybe she knows something helpful.

"Okay." She nods, her cheeks red from the cold.

I lead the three of us down a muddy, but well-worn path. I don't see anything of note except colorful trees interspersed with fragrant pines.

We walk about five or six minutes before the trees start to thin out and the pond comes into view. Here things are interesting. There's a large fallen log that's covered with half-burned thick candles on either end, with space between, where people can sit maybe. There's a pile of charred branches near the pond's shore, apparently the remains of a bonfire. The pond is dark and still, with a slight ripple across the surface when the wind blows.

On the far side of the pond sits Ray Ridley in a rusted lawn chair. His head is tipped back as he enjoys a smoke. We move around the shore, and he straightens up and opens his eyes. The smell of marijuana pervades the air as he puffs, his lips smiling around the joint.

"Detective. Nice to see you."

"That's only legal on your own property, Mr. Ridley."

He nods, clamps the joint firmly in his lips, and gets halfway to his feet. Clasping the lawn chair to his ass, he shuffles a couple of feet away from us, sits back down and continues with his smoke. "That should do it. Ridley property starts at that pine tree."

"Great. Okay. What are you doing out here?"

His gaze shifts to Lauren and then to Ms. Foster. He pinches out the joint and drops it in the pocket of his flannel shirt underneath his open thermal vest.

"Sugar Plum! I'll be damned. It's been years!"

She retreats halfway behind Lauren, who's tall and wearing an open, oversized jacket.

"Ray," I continue, "what are you doing here?"

"My property, as I said. I usually come out here in the morning for a smoke, take in nature. I saw your people, and they gave me the all clear."

"When were you out here last?"

"I don't remember. Not yesterday, because the cops wouldn't let me. Tuesday, I guess. I told you that the other day."

"Remind me. What time?"

He shrugs. "Afternoon."

I skim through my notes. "Before or after you went to the store at five?"

"Before."

"You come out here Tuesday night? Maybe after you got back from your grocery-store run?"

He shakes his head, his long curly hair fluttering in the breeze. "Don't come out here in the dark, Detective. You never know what's lurking in the woods."

"Like what!" Lauren says, her voice exploding.

He shrugs. "I was home that night like usual. Tucked up safely with my Xbox and a six-pack of Corona."

"What's with the candles?" I ask, pointing at the fallen log.

"I entertain occasionally."

"When was the last time you *entertained?*"

He squints one eye, thinking. "Not since August probably, when it was warm."

"All right. We've got work to do." We walk around the edge of the pond and over to the log with the candles. Lauren peers over my shoulder and points at the map.

"This is where they think she was attacked, here by the log." I glance around but don't see anything interesting. I take a deep breath, close my eyes, and try to picture Kara here, feel her presence, her fear. A cold breeze chills my cheeks, and I open my eyes.

I turn toward the pond. Its dark depths cast a sinister feel over this clearing in the woods. Maybe because of the little girl's death years ago. Maybe that's what I'm feeling.

There's a note on the map that a large rock that might be the murder weapon was found here. It's presently at the lab. And a fake fingernail that matched the other nine on Kara's hands was found here as well.

"But how did they get out here?" That's another mystery. The logistics of the whole thing. Unless the perp forced Kara into her vehicle and made her drive out here. Then he took off in her car. That's possible.

Ms. Foster pipes up and points to the map. "There are four paths to the pond," she says, voice shaking slightly in the cold.

"Where do they lead?"

"One back to our house. One to the Ridleys. One to Mr. York's place, and one to a parking area down the street from Mr. York. It's not a real parking lot. Just a place people have made with their cars over the years.

"What about this Mr. York? Where's his house?"

She points to a path on the far side of the pond.

"Okay, Esmé. Thanks. You can head back now, and we'll let you know if we need to talk to you again."

She nods and takes a surreptitious glance at Ray, who's still relaxing in his lawn chair.

"You want me to walk you back?" Lauren asks.

"No. I'm fine," she says and heads toward the path to her house. We turn toward the trail that leads to the York place and hear Ridley call.

"Hey, Sugar Plum! Where you going?"

Lauren and I head down the path. Off to the side of the trail, there's a shack, gray boards and a rickety roof, in a little clearing not far from the pond. I glance at the map, where Martinez's group has dutifully drawn it.

"Let's take a look," I say.

There is no door, and we step gingerly across the threshold. The floor is dirt, and there's a musty, animal smell inside.

"Wonder what this was," I say.

"It was all farmland out here," Lauren replies. "I researched it. The Ridley house was built in the nineteen-twenties and belonged to a family who farmed this area. There was a barn on the property at one time, and I bet this was one of the old outbuildings. You know, for supplies or hay or something. Not sure. I was raised in the suburbs."

"Probably." I was raised in the city, so I'll take Lauren's word for it. There's a wooden shelf against the far wall. I take a look and find the skeleton of what might've been a mouse, small, with delicate white bones. There's also a tiny rubber ball and a stick with a feather tied to it. The feather is bedraggled and gray with grime. Lauren comes up next to me.

"Cat toys?"

"I guess. Well, there's nothing else in here." The breeze whistles through gaps in the walls and a big opening that resembles a window. Lauren and I look out, and the pond is dead ahead. I glance back at the map, and there are no notations beside the shack; apparently, nothing of interest was found here, so we head out to the trail.

After five or six minutes of walking, the trees come to an end, and we're standing in someone's backyard. There's a huge Victorian house, three stories high, sitting by a small road.

"Must be Mr. York's place," Lauren says.

"Nice color," I say, not sure it works for me, though.

The house is gray—no, more a mauve, I guess, with white painted trim. It looks slightly run-down, as if it's just starting to slide into decline, and I can't help but picture it as a house in a ghost story, huge and silent, out on a lonely road. A weeping willow stands at its side, with tendrils so long they sweep the ground. There's an English garden with box shrubs and fading rose bushes angled around several gray garden sculptures of women who look menacing in the cold.

I turn the map sideways. "What road is that?"

Lauren shrugs. "Didn't know it existed."

"Let's go see if Mr. York is home."

We trudge across the grass to the front yard. The big wraparound porch squeaks as we approach the door. There's no bell, just a huge, burnished brass knocker, which I lift and let fall. Immediately, a chorus of dogs—small yappers, by the sound of them—rush to see who's there. We wait several minutes, but no one answers. I turn and look back over the front yard. There's a gravel driveway next to the house, but no car.

"Must be out," I say.

The sun is peeking out finally, just in time to start setting, and Lauren shades her eyes and looks up the road. "You want to try and find the place Ms. Foster was talking about, the parking spot?"

"Yeah. Let's go."

The little road has no shoulder, let alone a sidewalk, so we basically have to walk on the pavement. I'm still turned around. Don't know where we are. I've lived in Graybridge for years, but I've never been down this road. Mr. York's place seems to be all alone out here. No other houses or buildings, just thick woods on either side, dark and silent. We round a curve and still nothing but road and trees.

"Maybe it's the other way," I say, stopping and looking back.

"Don't think so, Rita. Looks like the road dead-ends just past the house, and according to the map, it would be this way."

"Right. Let's keep walking."

I'm starting to sweat, so I unzip my jacket. All the walking and the sun are combining to make this something of a workout. We start to hear traffic—faint, but there's civilization somewhere up ahead. "Is that Singleton Road up there?" I squint and point. But Lauren grabs my arm.

"Look, Rita." Off to the side of the road is a matted-down, muddy place big enough to act as a makeshift parking area for three or four vehicles. Next to it, the trees split, revealing a path. There's one car there now. My heart hammers. I whip out my phone and call Martinez.

"Get your guys back here ASAP. We've got a white Toyota Camry near the scene."

# CHAPTER 15
# Esmé

It's dark already, the sun setting more quickly each day as we head deeper into fall. I wonder if Detective Myers and her partner found anything in the woods. I certainly felt uneasy out there, and it didn't help seeing Ray, sitting in his lawn chair like he did when we were teenagers. I guess he hasn't moved on.

Byron got up, showered, ate, and left for work a while ago. Now it's just me and Dad and Irene. I managed to avoid them most of the day, and I wonder how this is going to work. It's Dad's house, and if he wants Irene here, that's his prerogative. It just makes me feel like an outsider, but where else can I go? I've got no money to even think about living on my own, so I'll just have to make the best of it for now.

I'm sitting in the kitchen with a cup of coffee, while Dad and Irene watch TV in the other room. The doorbell rings, and I hear Irene answer it. I hear a man's voice. A cop maybe?

Then he walks into the kitchen, and I jump to my feet.

"Jack!"

"Hi, Esmé. I hope you don't mind me dropping by. I heard you were home."

He's wearing a tweed jacket and jeans, and he's filled out some from the skinny teenager I remember. Except for the beginnings of laugh lines around his mouth, he looks just like he did in high school.

"What are you doing here?" I ask, but I can't keep the happiness out of my voice. We were good friends, and regret makes me teary.

Jack and his friend Austin joined our little group in middle school. We all sat at the same lunch table; up until then, we girls had been a tight little exclusive female group. But we immediately welcomed the two boys. We were twelve, after all, and Jack was especially cute. All four of us were a little smitten. Then, as we got older, the friendships deepened and altered. Austin dated a few girls, who made short appearances in our circle, but Jack never had a serious girlfriend back then, and we all had crushes on him, although they never came to anything. He seemed to straddle this nebulous world of friend/brother/crush that we couldn't seem to penetrate. It was as if, had one of us claimed him as our own, it would have tilted the dynamics of the group in a way that might have broken us apart. So Jack remained our good friend, equally shared by all.

"I would've called first," Jack says, "but I don't have your number anymore."

"It's great to see you." I catch him in a hug that feels good and welcome. "Are you living in Graybridge then?"

"I moved back just before Labor Day. You weren't here, right?"

I shake my head. "No. I've been living in Syracuse. I came home yesterday." My gaze sweeps past him. "Probably for good."

His eyes turn somber. "Well, it's great to see you again. Sorry I haven't kept in touch."

"No worries. I didn't do a very good job of that either."

I glance around the sparse kitchen, hear Irene chuckle, along with canned laughter from the other room. She's usually gone by now. Must be something special on TV.

We fall silent. "I heard about Kara," he says quietly.

I nod, tears catching in my throat. Seeing Jack here again, standing in my kitchen, floods me with memories of my friends, of Kara. "It's surreal. I got home yesterday morning, and there were cop cars in the driveway. I thought something had happened to my dad. In a million years, I couldn't have imagined that a friend of mine would've been killed in my backyard." I shiver, wipe my face with my sleeve.

"It's unbelievable," he says, clears his throat.

Irene's gravelly voice echoes down the hallway. I sniff back tears. "You want to head out someplace?"

We sit in a dark corner booth at Hartshorn's, a brewpub that we'd been too young for when we were in high school. Before we left the house, I'd run upstairs and brushed my hair, which was wavy from the bun I'd worn all day, and traded my hoodie for a dark green sweater.

We both order a Trillium, and I feel strange and grown-up sitting with Jack and ordering beer. High school seems like yesterday and a hundred years ago at the same time.

"So, Jack, had you been in touch with Kara?"

"I'd seen her a couple of times. I was stunned when I heard. She was the sweetest of us all. Who would've hurt her?"

I shake my head. "I can't make sense of it. But she was also the most naïve about people. She trusted everybody. Maybe she met somebody . . ." I feel that nagging guilt well up in my chest again. Kara and I had been so close. I'd always looked out for her since she didn't have anyone except her mother. She trusted everyone, and after my mother's accident, I trusted no one. In the years I'd lived here, Kara spent a lot of time at my house. Mrs. Cunningham worked long hours to support the two of them, and she had little time to spend with her. And then I'd gone to Syracuse and left Kara on her own.

"Maybe. I feel awful for her mom," Jack says.

"Me too." My mood starts to slip. "I hope they catch the bastard." I sip my beer, and it goes down smoothly. I blink my eyes, sniff, and wait for the alcohol to relax my tense muscles.

Jack nods and falls silent.

"Have you seen anyone from, you know, our old group besides Kara?" I ask.

"Yeah. Christy had a party a couple of weeks ago. Laney and her husband were there. Kara too. Austin moved away, though. I haven't heard from him since the summer after graduation."

"Is it like old times now that you're back?"

Jack shrugs. "I've kind of been busy at work and haven't had a chance to see everybody all that much." He smiles and pulls on my sleeve. "I'm teaching at our school. I've got Mr. Lang's old room."

"Really?" This makes me laugh. Mr. Lang was the worst teacher we had. Pompous and condescending and perpetually getting things wrong. "Remember when you corrected him when he mispronounced . . . what was it?"

Jack sips his beer. "Hue. We were studying the Vietnam War."

"And he called you a jackass? Right?"

"He did."

I shake my head. "You were such a nerd."

"Still am," he says, smiling.

"Kind of ironic, huh? You were so anxious to get out of Graybridge."

A server, a woman younger than we are with a short blond pixie haircut and a colorful sleeve, comes up to the table. "Can I get you guys any food?" She throws menus on the table.

"What do you think, Esmé?" Jack's eyes meet mine. "You have dinner yet?"

I'd had a bowl of cereal with Byron before he left for work. "No, not really."

Jack orders a cheeseburger and onion rings. I order a basket of cheese fries. The server snatches up the menus and goes on her way.

"It's really good to see you," Jack says.

"Same here. I guess I should call Laney and Christy, but I'm afraid they'll hate me for disappearing on them."

"I don't think so. Why don't I call them and see if they want to meet somewhere with the two of us, if that'll make it easier?" His gaze falls to the table where he's reduced a napkin to a small pile of white shreds. "We should all go see Kara's mom."

I nod. "Yes. Let's get together and make a plan."

He smiles and squeezes my hand. "What was your life like in Syracuse, Esmé? Why did you come back?"

I draw a deep breath. Where to start? "I'm not dancing anymore." I peep up and catch his gaze.

"Was it your choice?"

"No." My throat constricts. "I developed a problem with my hip. It's common for dancers and can be career ending, which it was in my case. My company didn't renew my contract."

"I'm sorry."

"Me too." I sniff back tears. The beer is doing its job. I'm starting to relax but am feeling sad at the same time. "Anyway, a dancer's career is pretty short-lived in the grand scheme of things."

"What else have you been doing?"

"Waitressing. If you can believe that."

He nods, probably not knowing the right thing to say. "Is there anyone special in your life?" He sounds like an awkward old man, and that makes me smile.

"There was. Another reason I came home. I broke up with the guy I was with the last six years. There wasn't any reason to stay in Syracuse."

Our food comes, and we order another beer. We both seem glad for the distraction, and I dive into the fries, which are perfectly greasy and salty.

"What brought you home, Jack?" I ask after a big sip of my IPA.

"My family, for one. And the woman I was seeing in Albany left me for another dude a few months back."

"Sorry."

"It's okay. We weren't headed for the altar or anything."

"What's up with your family? Everybody all right?"

"Yeah. They're good. My brother's got two kids whom I'd rarely seen. Parents are getting older." He shrugs. "I felt like I was missing out. Time to come home."

"Yeah. Things change, don't they?"

"They do." He smiles and sips his beer. "I'll be right back. Got to hit the restroom."

I relax back against the booth, check my phone, and I'm surprised I've got a text. It's from Collin Flynn offering me the job at the café. I can come in tomorrow for training if I'm interested. I text him back. *Yes!* Maybe home won't be so bad.

Then laughter explodes from the bar. A husky blonde and her date are in deep conversation with the bartender, their words punctuated with guffaws. My gaze drifts to the end of the bar, where a man sits alone, hunched over a draft. A gray newsboy's cap sits atop his head, and he's huddled in a navy peacoat, a scarf bunched around his neck. Something about him sends chills down my back. Nothing I can put a name to, but like a bad dream. My phantom man. *Not real, Esmé.*

"What's wrong?" Jack asks, sliding back into his seat.

"Nothing." I tear my gaze from the man as he lifts his glass in one hand and fingers a crumpled napkin in the other.

Jack and I talk for another half hour, then rise to go home. As I pull on my jacket, I shoot a glance toward the man in the cap. He's standing, back to us, and tosses a couple of dollars on the bar. I hurry in front of Jack as we leave the pub.

I glance over my shoulder as I get in the passenger seat of Jack's car. I can't see where the man has gone. Maybe he walked home. Maybe he lives close by. But maybe he's watching us from his car somewhere in the shadows of the parking lot.

I take a deep breath and realize that Jack will probably take the same route back to my house that he took on the drive here. It's the closest way. It makes sense unless you're me. I never drive down Miller Road if I can help it. I'll drive out of my way so as not to go by that lonely stretch where my mother's life ended. But Jack—or probably anyone else, for that matter—wouldn't give it a thought. On the way here, Jack and I had been chatting away with the excitement of seeing one another again, so I'd been distracted as we passed the spot. But now, the beer has got my mind loose and off guard.

The headlights illuminate the road, while leaving the surrounding countryside completely in the dark. We round a bend, and the oak tree, big and ominous, sits up ahead, just off the shoulder. The lights shine on it a moment as we round the curve. There are still gashes, like battle scars, across the wide weathered trunk. I feel my muscles tense, and despite my best efforts, that awful night fills my mind.

Someone was following us. His headlights shone through the back window. My father cursed and sped up. Then everything went black, like the snapping off of a light, until I realized that we'd stopped. Icy air seeped into the car through the wreckage. My mom was still, so quiet, crumpled against the dashboard, her blond curls visible in the moonlight. Dad shouted her name. *Jen . . . Jen . . .*

*Jen.* I hurt, and sticky blood dripped down my forehead. Then a man appeared beside the car. He tried my mom's door, but it was crushed, so he opened the back door, leaned in. His hat was low, concealing his eyes, his face blurred in the dark. *I'm going to kill you. I'm going to kill you,* he growled. With my heart skittering in my chest, I managed to crawl out of the back seat on the other side and fall into the cold, wet snow. Then thick fingers found the back of my neck, the collar of my jacket. I gulped for breath, tears on my cheeks. The man had been following us, and now he was going to kill me. Then I heard sirens bleating in the distance, and the man faded away. My memory of the accident ends there. The next thing I remember is waking up in the hospital, screaming for my mom.

I take a deep breath. Jack changes the radio station. I glance over my shoulder, looking for the man from the bar.

"So," Jack says, "I told the kid if his mom said he didn't have to read the book I assigned because she thought it was boring when she was in high school, I would email her and—" He gives me a sideways glance. "You okay, Esmé?"

"Huh? Yeah. Fine. Sorry. So, what happened?"

Jack continues with his story, but I can't keep my mind from the accident. I'd worked up the courage to ask my dad about it. But he said I was wrong. There was no man. Just the three of us, and he told me he never wanted to talk about it again, and the dad I had known disappeared into a fog of alcohol and denial.

# CHAPTER 16
# Rita

When I get to my building, Mrs. Antonelli and her son Leo are standing in the foyer. Since she moved in a few months ago, the place has become Grand Central Station. I miss the days when a skinny grad student named Gregory lived across the hall. In the four years he was there, I never saw anyone come from or go to his place. I worried a little bit that he might be building bombs in there and planning Armageddon, but not too much. I just enjoyed the peace and quiet.

"Hello, Rita," Mrs. Antonelli shouts. She's elderly and hard of hearing, so I guess she assumes everyone else is too. I glance down at her. She's even shorter than I am.

"Hi, Carmela, Leo." Leo is about my age, dark-haired and polite.

He tips his head. "Working late?"

"Always. Well, have a good night," I say, squeezing past.

Before I can get my door open, Mrs. A calls, "Rita? You want to come over for dinner tomorrow night? I'm making lasagna."

"That sounds great. Can I let you know? I'm pretty busy at work. I've got a new case, and my hours are kind of irregular."

She huffs a little. "You still need to eat." She's already asked me why I'm not married, and what possessed me to want to be a detective. "Well, that's okay. I've got Leo and his kids coming, so you just drop by when you get home."

"Thanks. I appreciate the offer." I get inside and shut and lock my door. All I want to do is get out of my boots and work clothes and have a glass of wine.

My phone rings as I'm slipping into my sweatpants. Maybe Lauren's got something, but it's not her.

"Hey, Collin." The son I never had who lives in the apartment above mine.

"What's all the commotion in the foyer?"

I chuckle. "Nothing. Mrs. Antonelli and Leo."

"You just getting home?"

"Walked through the door a few minutes ago."

"Have you had your dinner yet?"

"Haven't even thought about it."

"I brought home some beef Burgundy from the café." Collin and his partner, André, run a catering business and café on Graybridge Square. "I can run some down if you want."

"Sure. Great." He hangs up, and I know that he just wants some company, and that's fine by me. I don't mind Collin. I didn't see André's Lexus parked in its spot, so I get a good meal that I don't have to cook, and Collin's pretty good company besides.

The next morning, we get confirmation on Kara's vehicle. Martinez and his team had the car towed to the impound lot and are processing the vehicle now. Hopefully, there will be DNA or something that will help. But the perp must've had his own vehicle. He got out of there somehow. Still, he might've left a fingerprint or something on Kara's door. And her coat hasn't been found, which is odd.

The other scenario is that Byron Foster killed her. He met her in the woods, had her park in the far lot to avoid having her car in his driveway. The fact that he neglected to tell me that he and the victim had been involved is certainly a red flag.

He finally got back to me and is scheduled to come in later for questioning. He can't be here until this afternoon, so I grab Lauren, and we head out to see if either Mr. York or Cynthia Ridley is home.

There's a late-model black Mercedes parked by the Victorian, so York's probably there. When we knock on the door, the dogs start up again, but this time, the door swings open and a man, sixtyish, stands on the threshold.

"May I help you?" He's average height, slim, with dark hair mixed evenly with gray.

We identify ourselves, and he steps aside while three small dogs—one a pug, the other two some fluffy, probably French breed—continue to yip.

"Let's sit in the parlor," he says.

The interior of the house is dim. Several lamps glow even this early in the day. A dark mahogany staircase winds down into the foyer. The walls are painted a deep cherry red, and oil paintings hang in nearly every inch of the space. The biggest one, over a table, looks really old. Lauren stops to admire it.

"The nine muses," she says. *Is there anything this girl doesn't know?*

He smiles. "Yes. My favorite."

We sit in his fancy living room on two stiff, padded chairs while Mr. York arranges himself on a velvet couch. The dogs hop up and huddle around him.

"How can I help you, Detectives? I assume you're here about all the commotion out in the woods Wednesday." He crosses his legs.

"Yes. Where were you Tuesday night, Mr. York?"

He squeezes his chin. "Out. It's a shame about the girl. I heard she was one of the group who used to be friends with Esmé Foster."

"What do you know about her?"

"Well, they used to hang out in the woods by the pond when they were teenagers, but I didn't know they were still coming around. Esmé moved away years ago, so I was quite surprised when I heard."

I sketch his wrinkled hand in my notebook as he taps a tasseled pillow at his side. Lauren has her own notebook out. I like that she documents her work the old-fashioned way. Chase, my regular partner, uses his phone, like a lot of other young cops.

"Tell me, Mr. York, how long have you lived in this house?"

"Thirty years or more. I'm from New York originally."

"What do you do for a living?"

"I'm a costume designer for film and stage productions."

"Huh. How's that work out here in the middle of nowhere? Shouldn't you be in Hollywood or New York?"

"Well," he brushes a wrinkle from his slacks and strokes the back of one of the fluffy dogs, "I made my reputation back in New York. Once I moved up here, I traveled pretty frequently in the early days. Still travel some. Now I can do a lot of my work over the internet. The beauty of technology." He smiles.

Still a pretty isolated place to conduct any kind of business. "How well do you know the Fosters?"

"Well enough, I suppose. I knew Jennifer." He sighs. "She was a lovely woman. A tragedy that she died so young."

"Mrs. Foster?"

"Yes. Killed in a car accident. She and I were friends. I'd make blueberry scones when I knew she was coming for a visit. She was a great conversationalist."

"What about the kids?"

"Byron and Esmé? I don't know Byron very well. I know that he's moved in with his father, who's quite ill. I knew Esmé and her friends a little bit. I'd run into them by the pond sometimes while walking my dogs back in the day."

"Do you walk these dogs in the woods?" I point at the pug with my pencil.

"Yes."

"When was the last time you were in the woods, Mr. York?"

"I'm out there every day. Usually early, sometimes in the evenings too, before dark." He gently moves one of the fluffy dogs off his lap. "I was walking Wednesday morning when a police officer stopped me. That's how I heard about the girl."

"Were you out there Tuesday night?"

His gaze flicks past me to the window. "No. I was in town Tuesday evening. The dogs didn't get their evening walk that day."

"Where in town?"

"The bookstore."

"Graybridge Books?"

"Yes. Was that when the girl was killed?"

"What time were you there?"

He squeezes his chin. "Let me see. I'm not sure what time, to be honest."

"Guess. Was it dark when you left home?"

"Not quite."

"What time did you get back?"

"It was seven maybe."

"What were you doing before you left home for the bookstore?"

"Working. I've got several projects going right now."

I nod, add to my sketch. "What do you know about Raymond Ridley?"

A shadow flickers over his face. "Not much, really. He's a bit of an unseemly fellow. Then that bad business years ago when the girl was killed. They're not a very respectable lot, Detective. There were rumors then that the mother might be arrested for neglect. She let her kids run wild in those woods. The older girl was quite strange. I wasn't surprised when I heard that she'd pushed her sister out of the boat. I was relieved when they sent her off to that institution."

"Did you know that Ms. Ridley is back living with her brother?"

"Yes, actually. I've seen her skulking in the woods when I've been out with the dogs. It's a little unnerving."

"Have you spoken to her?"

He shakes his head. "No."

"What about Ray? Why is he 'unseemly'?"

Mr. York shrugs. "I really don't know him. Just what I've heard."

"And what have you heard?"

"Just that he doesn't work. That he does drugs, although I can't testify to that."

I finish up my notes, add a few details to my sketch, wait for Mr. York to add anything. The room falls silent until geese, honking as they fly past the house, send the dogs yapping to the window. Mr. York follows the dogs, and Lauren and I stand.

"Can you see that parking area up the road from here?" I ask.

"No." He turns from the window. "It's around the bend."

"On your way to town or coming home Tuesday night, did you see anyone there? Any cars?"

"I didn't notice."

Huh. Kara's car might've been parked there by then. "Did you see anything? Hear anything unusual?"

He shakes his head. "Sorry. No."

Lauren wanders into the foyer and across the hall. "You have a beautiful home, Mr. York," she says.

"Thank you, my dear."

Creepy, if you ask me. Dim inside, corners dark. I follow them into the next room. There's a huge dining room table covered with bolts of fabric, a sewing machine at one end.

"Tools of the trade?" I ask.

"Yes. My workroom."

"The muses in the foyer inspire you?" Lauren asks.

They've drawn together in front of another large painting of a half-naked woman reclining on a couch of some sort.

"Yes, they do." He points at the painting. "And their mother, Mnemosyne, the goddess of memory. For without memory, no art is possible."

I'm standing behind the two of them like a simpleton, wondering what kind of wacko this guy is. Danny and Viv would be right at home here, drinks in hand, discussing paintings of ancient Greeks, laughing together at some witty remark one of them made. I turn toward the huge table, which holds stacks of fabric. It looks like organized chaos. Definitely looks like Mr. York is still a busy man. He and Lauren continue to chat about the painting. He seems harmless enough, but you never know.

We drive back down the street and swing around to Hogsworth Road, hoping to catch Cynthia Ridley at home. The clouds have thickened, and the day has turned grim. I glance up at the sky as I get out of the car. Hope it doesn't rain.

Ray greets us at the door, his mouth turned down, none too pleased to see us, I guess, but that's too bad.

"Your sister home?" I ask.

"Yeah." He turns, and we follow him into the living room. She's sitting in the armchair in the corner, her head bent over her knitting, needles flashing rhythmically. Her long hair is a strange white-gray. She's probably only in her mid-thirties. But some people turn gray early. She's wearing a floral-print dress with a faded, navy-blue sweatshirt over it.

"Cyn?" Ray calls, and she slowly tips up her head to look at him. Her small features are pinched, her face strangely childlike beneath the graying hair. She continues to knit, the yellow yarn trailing over her lap. "There are people here to talk to you." She cranes her skinny neck, and her deep-set, dark eyes run over me first, then Lauren.

I move closer to where she sits and introduce myself. She blinks but says nothing.

"Ms. Ridley? Cynthia? We need to ask you about Tuesday night." Silence. "Were you home?" Ray already told us she was, but I want to hear it from her. She merely nods. "Did you leave the house at all on Tuesday?" She shakes her head. "Did you hear about what happened in the woods?"

Her face changes like a child who's working up to a good cry, but her eyes remain dry. "Uh-huh," she says at last.

"Do you know anything about it?"

"No. I wasn't there." Her voice is strangely deep, gravelly, like a smoker's.

"Okay. So you were in the house all day?"

"Yes. I was in the house all day." Knitting needles click compulsively.

"Did you know Kara Cunningham?"

She glances at her brother.

Ray says, "She knew her years ago when they were kids. Not too well, though. Cynthia keeps to herself." There's anger in Ray's eyes. "She doesn't know anything, Detective. I told you she was here in the house the night Kara was killed." He angles his head, wanting to talk in the foyer, I guess. Lauren and I follow him.

"She doesn't know anything about Kara, okay?" he whispers.

"Fine, Ray. Just doing our job. Don't mean to upset her. Where was she when you went to town to the grocery store?"

"In the house. You don't have to watch her every minute."

"How do you know she wasn't in the woods then?"

"She doesn't go outside when I'm gone. She knows better."

"All right," I say. "We'll be in touch."

He opens the door, and Lauren and I step out into a freezing rain.

# CHAPTER 17
# Esmé

André's Café is warm and snug. I got in earlier than Collin said I needed to, but I was antsy to get started. It was quiet, just the two of us, as I helped him unload and arrange the fresh pastries in the cold case. He was pleased that I knew my way around the industrial coffee pot and espresso machine. And he had time to show me how to run the register before people started filing in for breakfast.

We were busy, customers nonstop all morning.

Before I know it, it's ten-thirty.

"Why don't you grab something to eat and catch your breath?" Collin says, wiping the counter. "We'll pick back up in an hour when the lunch crowd starts."

"Are you sure? I'm fine." I like to keep busy.

"Yes. I insist."

I pour myself a cup of black coffee and select a cinnamon roll from the case. I'd been too nervous to eat breakfast before I came in, and my stomach is letting me know about it now. I sit at the little table in the break room and drink my coffee, nibble my roll, which is heavenly. I feel momentarily content. I can do this; it's maybe not a career path, but this will work for right now. After about ten minutes, I get back up and head behind the counter, where the menu has flipped to lunch and Collin is busy prepping sandwich ingredients. I pick up next to him, and we work easily in tandem.

The lunch crowd is heavier and livelier than the breakfast people had been. I can see why Collin needed help. Another woman appears beside me in a white apron and introduces herself as Margo as she falls into line. Collin said she'd be coming in at eleven, and we work without much time to talk. By two-thirty, the crowd dwindles, and I bus tables around the three still occupied. It was busy, but the clientele was much more appreciative and less demanding than at Kevin's restaurant.

Collin disappears into the office to take care of paperwork, leaving me and Margo to run the counter and dining room. She's friendly and asks me about Syracuse and why I came back to Graybridge. I give her the easy, noncommittal answers. She's from Maine and takes classes at the local community college, hoping to be an accountant someday, which I never would've guessed based on her pink hair and colorful tats, but you never know about people. I pictured her an art major, something creative.

I sip a cup of coffee and finish unloading the dishwasher. The bell tinkles, and a tall man enters. My stomach knots.

"Sugar Plum!"

"Hi, Ray."

Margo gives him a sideways glance.

He's wearing a ratty pair of jeans and a thermal vest over a flannel shirt. His uniform, I guess. His long hair hangs over his shoulders.

"You working here now?" he asks.

I point to my apron, with its embroidered *André's* across the bib.

"Cool."

"What can I get you, Ray?"

He purses his lips like he's thinking. "I'll have a large peppermint mocha and a slice of pumpkin bread."

"Okay." I try to hide my smile. I can't picture Ray with anything but a Bud Light and a bag of pretzels. Times have certainly changed when Ray Ridley orders a coffee topped with whipped cream and sprinkles.

He leans on the counter. "Hey, Margs. Got any new ink?" He wiggles his eyebrows.

"Nothing you'll ever see, Ray," she says and walks away.

He lowers his voice. "They figure out what happened to Kara?"

I place his pumpkin bread in a to-go sleeve and set it on the counter. "I haven't heard anything."

"Well, I have my suspicions."

"Tell them to the police."

"I just might."

I hand him his coffee.

"Things have changed around here," he says. "Not the same little town it was when you left." He touches my hand a moment too long when I hand him his change, and I pull away. "Or maybe that's not true. Maybe we just all hid it better back in the day. See you around, Sugar Plum."

# CHAPTER 18
# Rita

Byron Foster is waiting for me and Lauren in an interview room. I let him cool his heels for a little while before we join him. I'm about to get up when there's a rap on my door. It's the new young officer, whose name I still can't remember. He hands me a couple of envelopes. "Here's your mail, Detective Myers." His eyes are downcast as if he's handing me a dead snake.

"Thank you," I say and try to smile, but he's not looking at me. He wipes a tissue across his nose, coughs, and mumbles, "You're welcome" before scooting out the door.

I drop the envelopes on my desk, then feel around for the small bottle of hand sanitizer in the top drawer. The last thing I need is a cold. I find it and slather on the sticky concoction that smells like pine trees and is guaranteed to knock out all germs.

Hope it works. When I was growing up, we didn't have all these products designed to wipe out microscopic pathogens; we just had to rely on our immune system to do the job. And we did our share of playing in the mud, handling insects and unvaccinated pets, you name it. Then there were no car seats, and we hardly ever used seat belts. There weren't enough for all of us in the station wagon anyway. And bike helmets? We would've laughed at the idea. It's a wonder any of us survived a 1960s childhood.

I can't help but let out a sigh. We didn't all survive. I think of my brother Jimmy. Even a McMahon immune system couldn't beat leukemia. But modern medicine might've saved him. I guess not everything was better in the old days. I grab my notebook and head down the hall.

Byron Foster is wearing blue scrubs and is holding a paper cup of coffee that someone brought him. His eyes are red, and he looks like a man who hasn't slept in days.

"Mr. Foster, thanks for coming in." Lauren and I take seats across the small table from him.

"I have to be at work soon, so I don't have a lot of time."

"Won't take long." I go through the formalities, state your name, etc.

"I didn't have anything to do with what happened to Kara," he blurts out.

"We just have a few questions for you. First, how come you didn't tell us that you and Kara were romantically involved?"

He bites his lips. He was ready for this. "I didn't think it was pertinent."

"Huh. Well, we think it's pertinent, Byron."

He shakes his head. "We broke up over a month ago. It was no big deal."

"Who broke it off?"

"We both did. It wasn't going anywhere."

"How did Kara take it?"

He shrugs. "It wasn't a big deal. It hadn't gotten serious."

"Okay." I flip through my notes. "You told us that you saw her at Hartshorn's last Saturday. What did you talk about?"

"I didn't talk to her. I told you that. I saw her at another table with her friend."

"Who were you with?"

"A guy from work. Pete Savage."

I write this name in my notebook. "He works with you at Graybridge General?"

"Yes."

"He a good friend?"

"Yeah. I guess."

"Got a phone number for this friend?" My gaze meets his. There's concern, surprise in his eyes.

"You're going to call him?"

"Maybe. We've got to get a clear picture of what was going on here."

His fist hits the table with more force than he probably intended. "Nothing is going on. I was traumatized when I found her out there like that, and I'm as confused as anybody by what she was doing there."

"When was the last time you talked to her?"

"I have no idea. A long time." He glances around the room as if looking for an escape route.

"What time did you leave for work Tuesday night?"

"I'm not sure. I usually leave by six forty-five. My shift starts at seven."

"That the time you left Tuesday night?"

"I guess." He shakes his head, gaze on the table.

"Think." I raise my voice a notch. "What time did you leave the house that night?"

"Six forty-five."

Lauren puts down her notebook and picks up her phone.

I nod and sketch his eyes, letting him stew a minute. "Charge nurse's name?"

He drops his hands on the table with a thump. "I don't remember."

The room quiets, and only the frantic, irritating clicking of Lauren typing on her phone fills the room. She's doing this on purpose, making him think she's made an interesting observation about him.

"Janice Wilson," he says at last.

I glance at Lauren, who nods and keeps clicking.

"So, Byron, you didn't meet Kara in the woods that night?" His mouth drops open, and a dot of saliva trembles on his lower lip. I add his tense jaw to my sketch. Lauren pauses her clicking and glances over.

"No," he says. "I told you I haven't seen Kara since Saturday night."

My gaze meets his. I wait a beat. "You didn't arrange to speak to her in the woods? Maybe you'd heard about the new man she was going to meet, and you wanted to talk to her about that."

"No." He shakes his head. "Why would I?"

I lean back in my chair, peruse my notebook. "Your wife left you last year, right?" He looks at me like I just punched him in the gut. "Left you for another man?"

"What?"

"Come on, Byron. That must not have felt too good, huh? Your wife leaves you for another guy. Then Kara tells you it's over. You heard she was interested in somebody else. That must've been a huge blow. You've had a rough year."

His gaze falls to the table. "Yeah. It was tough when my wife and I split up. We have a little girl."

"Maybe when you and Kara met in the woods, things got a little testy. She told you to leave her alone. There was someone else now, and she didn't need you anymore." I watch his face carefully. He's flushed, agitated.

"No." He shakes his head. "I never spoke to her."

"Maybe Kara was being a little obnoxious. Maybe a little cruel. Maybe things got physical. She pushed you first. You pushed her back, and she fell. Totally unintentional. You leave her there because you've got to get to work. You had no idea that when she fell, she hit her head."

He gulps like a goldfish. "No. No. That didn't happen. I had no idea she was out there. I left for work that day same as usual."

I wait, my eyes on his.

He blinks and swallows. "I want you to catch the bastard who did this, but it wasn't me. I swear. I'll take a lie detector, anything." His panic is rising, and he looks around as if cops have come into the room to drag him off to jail.

"All right, Byron. We can set that up," I say, make a note, and stand. "We'll call you about the polygraph. You're free to go, for now."

It's getting late, but I want to go over what we've got with Doug and Lauren before the weekend. We meet in the conference room,

Doug on his phone as he walks through the door. The whiteboard behind me has filled up with notes and maps, but as yet, nothing really helpful.

"Okay," I say, opening my notebook. Doug sets his phone on the table, and Lauren closes her laptop.

"The biggest problem, as I see it right now, is we've got no motive, so . . . let's consider the usual suspects: lust, hate, money."

"Back to detective school 101, Rita?" Doug says.

"You got a better idea?"

"You forgot serial killer." Which is a category all its own.

"You really think that's what we've got going here?" I smirk, tap my notebook with my pencil.

"Probably not. Just saying."

"Right. Anyway." I push my chair back so I can look over at the whiteboard. "Lust. Based on the autopsy, we have no evidence whatsoever that it was a sex crime. No indication that she was raped. No other telltale signs somebody was getting his jollies. So let's move on to hate. Who have we talked to that might hate Kara enough to kill her?"

"The ex?" Doug says.

"We just had him in here. Maybe."

Lauren opens her laptop. It's like she can't resist. Like it's her right arm. "Maybe he just snapped, Rita. Like you were saying. Maybe she taunted Byron about the new man in her life, and after his wife cheated on him, he flew into a rage. Didn't mean to kill her."

"Maybe. Let's do a deeper dive on Mr. Foster. See if he has an explosive temper. See if we can find anybody else he's gotten physical with. And he's agreed to take a polygraph," I say to Doug. "Maybe that will be helpful." My eyes sweep over the people we've questioned. Kara's friends. "No one else we've talked to so far has said anything except nice things about Kara. So, what about money?" I throw that out there just for the sake of completeness.

"She had nothing," Lauren says. "She couldn't even afford to live on her own, her mom said. And she had twenty-two dollars in her wallet, and all her credit cards were accounted for, so it wasn't a robbery."

"Right." I rock back in my chair. "What about Cynthia Ridley, Lauren? You find anything yet?"

"I went through our records from when her sister was killed. There was a statement from Ray, although he was only eleven at the time, but he said that he saw Cynthia and Wendy arguing. Wendy threw Cynthia's cat out of the rowboat. Cynthia picked up an oar and hit her sister, knocking her into the water. Ray ran off to tell their mom, and Cynthia paddled to shore and ran after him. Mrs. Ridley had been out and had just pulled into the driveway when Ray and Cynthia ran out of the woods. By the time they got back down to the pond, Wendy was nowhere in sight. EMS was summoned. A dive team eventually found Wendy. She was pronounced dead at the scene. Cynthia was taken into custody."

I blow out a breath. "What about when she was incarcerated? Any violent episodes?"

"I haven't been able to track down those records yet. But I'll get on it ASAP."

"Good deal."

The door opens, and Officer Connors walks in with an evidence bag. "Here it is, Rita."

"Thanks, Anna." She leaves and shuts the door.

"What you got there?" Doug asks, eyes on his phone.

"Kara's purse. It's the only personal item we've recovered from the scene. The techs went through it and itemized the contents, but I wanted to look for myself." I pull latex gloves from my pocket and weed through the inexpensive red handbag. Wallet. Lipstick. A pack of tissues. And a bottle of pills. It was listed on the report, but this is the first I've actually seen it. I hold up the vial.

"Looks full, Rita," Lauren says. "What is it?"

I skim through a file folder and pull out the lab report, which just came in this afternoon. I'd printed it out on my way to the conference room but hadn't had a chance to look it over. My eyes scan the page. "Hmm. Oxycodone," I say. My eyes meet Lauren's.

"The vial is unlabeled," she says, the implication dawns on us.

My heartbeat kicks up. "Kara was taking pain killers that may not have been prescribed for her," I say. "If they weren't prescribed by her doctor, then she would've had to be seeing a dealer. That certainly puts her in the company of unsavory characters." This is the first indication that Kara might have had a dark side we hadn't known about before, something that might indicate a problem in her life that might give someone a reason to harm her.

"That gives us a new angle, Rita," Doug says, standing. "I've got to hit the road, guys. My wife made dinner reservations, and I haven't been home before seven-thirty all week."

"Don't let us stand in your way, Doug. Keep the wife happy." I'm not being sarcastic. You've got to keep a balance in your life, or you'll crash and burn in this business.

"Have a good weekend," Doug says as he leaves.

"You go home too," I say to Lauren. "Do something fun." She looks at me like, aren't we having fun? "I'm leaving too."

I hear laughter as I open the heavy front door to my building. Mrs. Antonelli's door is ajar, and that's where all the noise is coming from. *Shit.* But they'll never hear me if I tiptoe and don't jangle my keys.

Just when I think I'm in the clear, Collin opens Mrs. A's door.

"There you are. I told everybody you'd be home pretty soon."

*Damn him.* He monitors me like an old mother hen. "What are you doing down here?"

"Mrs. A invited me. Come on, we're just getting ready for tiramisu. She saved you some lasagna." He lowers his voice. "It was divine. The dessert is André's, my contribution."

"Who else is in there?" I whisper.

"Well, not André." Collin huffs out a breath. "He's meeting a potential catering client for drinks downtown." I see disappointment in his eyes. *Damn, André, sometimes.* "Mrs. A, Leo, and his kids, Alana and Carlo. Have you met them? Really nice. Come on, Rita. You need to eat."

"Well, I suppose. I've got a few minutes."

He puts a hand on his hip. "Don't tell me. You have big plans to sit in front of the TV with a glass of wine, right? Well, we've got wine in there." He tips his head just as another crescendo of laughter explodes from the apartment.

I draw a deep breath. My messy bun is just about to fall out, and the makeup I put on this morning has probably faded away by now. Not that I'm overly vain or anything. But I have some standards. "Let me drop my satchel at my place and run a comb through my hair."

Collin smiles, and that's enough for me.

# CHAPTER 19
# Esmé

Jack and I are headed over to have drinks with Laney and Christy, and I'm nervous. Will it be like old times? Thinking back to high school, we were a unit, the four of us girls. A small tight circle at the center of the larger circle that included the guys. Christy was the bold leader, Laney the cheerleader who had everyone's back. I was the serious dancer with the rosy future, and Kara was everyone's fragile little sister, whom we all protected, until we didn't.

Jack pulls up in front of a huge house in the Graybridge Hills neighborhood. It's definitely Christy. In fact, her parents lived a couple of streets over when she was growing up. They were pretty well off. Her mother was an executive who worked downtown in a high-rise office building, and her dad was an attorney. It looks like Christy has followed in her mom's footsteps. I've heard that Christy married her much older boss, a man she'd interned for during senior year of college.

My heart's thumping wildly as I follow Jack up to the massive front door. When Jack called her, Christy insisted that we get together at her place. I took care to dress my best, slim black pants and a blue silk blouse. I left my hair down and put on a bit of makeup. Christy and Laney always looked gorgeous. Kara too, maybe Kara most of all. I hope my clothes and makeup hide my thinness and overwrought nerves.

Christy grabs Jack in a hug. She turns to me, and I'm stopped in my tracks. She's stunning. Tall and toned, glowing skin, blond hair and makeup perfect; she's even prettier than she was as a teenager.

"Esmé!" She kisses my cheek and pulls me into a hug.

I relax. Maybe my old friends don't hate me after all. We follow Christy into a huge family room, where Laney lounges on a white sofa. She jumps up and hugs Jack and me in turn. She looks great too. Sporty, like in high school. Long dark hair in a sleek ponytail and large dark eyes under perfectly sculpted brows.

Jack and I sit together on a love seat facing Christy and Laney. Hors d'oeuvres adorn the coffee table between us. Laney is drinking a tall glass of seltzer water with bits of fruit in it, while Christy brings Jack and me white wine in tall, stemmed glasses.

Christy takes a swipe at her eyes as she sits. "I can't believe we're back together."

The room goes quiet, as though someone threw a switch. We're all thinking of Kara. You can feel it in the air. I can almost see her sitting between Christy and Laney, her long hair sweeping over her shoulders, her pretty blue eyes full of life.

Christy clears her throat. "What have you been up to, Esmé? Catch us up." Talk of Kara postponed. I feel my face flush. I feel like the only one whose life has been a failure. And I remember, in high school, the little bit of tension between us as my dancing career took off, as articles about me appeared in the local paper. When my friends came downtown to see my performances, my future looked full of rainbows and roses.

"Everything's great. Well," I stutter, "I'm not dancing anymore." I take a big sip of my wine, hoping to steady my nerves. "I developed an injury."

Laney's brow wrinkles. "Was it serious?"

I nod and sip. "It ended my career."

Christy and Laney offer murmurs of condolence.

"That sucks, Ez," Christy says. "So, what are you doing now?"

I'm a waitress at a café, I think to myself. "Uh, my boyfriend and

I were getting ready to open a restaurant in Syracuse, but I decided to come home. My dad's not well."

They again offer condolences, which just makes me feel worthless.

"Well, we're glad you're back," Jack says and wraps his arm around my shoulders in a quick hug.

Laney stands. "I'm going to get a refill. Anyone need anything?" She pads off to the kitchen, totally at home in Christy's house. And I feel like I've been left behind. My friends, who had meant so much to me ten years ago, have gone on with their lives without me. And I feel a strange desperation, a childish desire to be one of the group again. In a way, I feel like an outsider, like Wendy was when we were kids.

The room falls quiet, and Christy dabs at her eyes. She picks up a framed photograph from the end table. "My son," she smiles.

Jack nods. "He's a nice-looking boy."

She bites her lip. "He is." Christy looks at me. "I divorced his dad four years ago."

"I'm sorry," I say.

"Don't be." She shrugs. "I've got a great private investigator. He got pictures of Paul with his admin. Such a cliché. But I got a hefty settlement." She smiles. "The PI was worth every penny."

Laney returns, her glass full. "I guess we need to talk about Kara," she says, taking her place on the sofa.

I inhale a big breath. I feel so guilty for having lost touch. "I wish I'd been around," I say half to myself.

"Well, no one could've predicted this. Who would've thought any of us would be *murdered?*" Laney says.

I shiver and wonder again if the murderer had been looking for me, but I don't dare bring up my phantom. My friends will think I've lost it. "Who could've done something like that?" I ask. "She was behind my house, by the woods, near the path that leads to the pond." I feel like I'm trying to sort out a puzzle. "Why would she be out there?"

A funny look passes over Christy's face. She leans toward me, voice low. "Did you know she was seeing Byron?"

"What?" I utter, disbelieving. I shake my head. That can't be right. "He didn't say anything about it to me."

Christy rests a hand on my knee. "It doesn't mean anything, Esmé. She broke it off last month. I don't think it was serious, but does your brother know why she was back there?"

Sweat sprouts on the back of my neck. *Why didn't he tell me?* "No. He doesn't know. Do any of you go out to the pond anymore?"

They shake their heads. "No," Laney says. "We haven't been back there since you left. What about Ray? He's still around. I saw him last week at the grocery store. He came over to me in the produce section and said hello. Still creepy as ever."

"Maybe," I say. "He was sitting by the pond yesterday when I was out there with the cops. I think they questioned him. Maybe he hurt Kara, and she was trying to get help from Byron." I take a deep breath and sip my wine.

Laney nods. "Or maybe it was some stranger."

Jack blows out a breath. "Anyway, I thought we should go see Kara's mom."

"I called her last night," Christy says and glances at Laney.

"I talked to her too. She's not doing well," Laney adds.

Jack looks at me. "Maybe we should stop by?"

It's the last thing I want to do. Mrs. Cunningham has to be devastated, and my guilt at not having been in touch makes seeing her feel like a betrayal.

"Yes." I nod. "We should," I say, leaving the arrangements to Jack.

We pass the next hour reminiscing about Kara and high school, wiping away tears, and vowing to stick together. By the time Jack drops me off at home, I'm exhausted, hollowed out of emotion.

# CHAPTER 20
# Esmé

In the morning, I wait to see Byron. He's off today and went to bed after his shift before I was awake. I don't know how long he'll sleep. But I have to leave for the café at one. Collin asked me to work the afternoon/evening shift today, so I'm rattling around the house, staying in the kitchen mostly, to avoid Irene and Dad in the living room.

I put the kettle on and grab a teabag from the cupboard. Why didn't Byron tell me that he was seeing Kara? No wonder Detective Myers called him to come into the station for an interview.

Tea in hand, I wander to the window and look out at the woods. The house is chilly, and I shiver in my pajamas.

"Aren't you going to work?" Irene asks.

I turn to face her. She's standing at the kitchen door, an empty beer can in her hand.

"Yes. Later. Why?"

She walks over to the garbage can under the sink, drops the can inside, and shuts the door. She straightens, leans against the counter, and folds her arms across her ample bosom.

"So, you plan on staying then?"

"Yes. I told you that."

She arches her thick eyebrows, and her glasses gleam, hiding her eyes. "Well, just so you know, your dad can't support you. His disability check doesn't go very far."

Not that it's any of her business. "I'm working, Irene. Believe me, I don't expect anything from him."

"That's good because he doesn't have a pot to piss in. If it weren't for your brother's help, he'd be hard pressed to make ends meet. And God knows Byron's stretched thin, with that bitch, Sonia, bleeding him dry."

"I'm not here to take advantage of anybody, Irene." I walk past her and set my mug in the sink.

"Just thought you should know," she says.

Up in my room, I put my hair up, slip into my best jeans and a white blouse. On my way back down the hall, I run into Byron coming out of the bathroom.

"Hey," he says and goes to pass me when I grab his shoulder.

"Why didn't you tell me that you were seeing Kara?"

He heaves a big breath. "It's been over for more than a month. It wasn't a big deal. It wasn't serious."

"Still. Don't you think you might've mentioned that?"

"Why do you care? You weren't here." His gaze meets mine. "You can't believe I had anything to do with what happened to her."

"No. Of course not. But what about Detective Myers?"

"I've got this, okay? I didn't do anything, so there's nothing to worry about." He turns away from me. "Get off my back, Ez. I've got enough people giving me shit without you adding to it." He walks heavily down the hall, stops, and turns back toward me. "Oh, I'm picking up Ashlyn today. You know, my daughter, who you haven't seen since she was born. Maybe you might want to spend some time with her before she heads off to college."

Guilt settles in my chest. That's something else I've missed out on by not having been around for the last two and a half years. When Ashlyn was born, I came home. That was my last visit. Byron and Sonia were so happy, and their baby was a precious, seven-pound bundle. I was enchanted and a little envious. I stayed for three days, but then scurried back to Kevin and his family in Syracuse. On my phone, I've got dozens of pictures of my niece that

Byron's sent, but he's right. I've been neglectful of the only family I've got.

My mind clicks back and forth. I've got to go to work. It's only my second day. "Why don't you bring her by the café? They make really cute animal cookies."

Byron snorts. "Maybe," he says and slams his bedroom door.

My mind turns over all that's wrong with my life and my relationships with the people in it as I drive the curvy road. Graybridge Square is ten minutes away, but I seem to arrive in seconds, my mind still troubled, and I dread going inside the café, facing the public. But I need something to concentrate on other than my problems, so maybe work is the answer. I get out of my car and lock the doors. It's only then that I remember I've left my bag of pointe shoes sitting in the garage and make a mental note to carry them up to my room. I should just throw them out, but I can't. Holding onto them gives me some kind of twisted solace. Like tangible proof that I had a dream, and it was real, at least for a while.

# CHAPTER 21
# Rita

THE SUN PEEKED OUT THIS MORNING, AND YOU MIGHT THINK INDIAN summer is a possibility. Still, I needed my jacket, which I promptly peel off once inside the station. The smell of bad coffee greets me as I make my way through the squad room and back to my office.

I grab my notes and head for the conference room, where the weekend team has gathered for a briefing on the Cunningham case. We got a few reports back from the lab, and I took a minute to do a quick read-through. Lauren stands at the back of the room, and the chief shuffles in and sits heavily in a chair near the door. I stand in front of the whiteboard, which has filled up with crime-scene photos and lists in red and blue marker.

"Good morning. This is where we are," I say and sip my coffee. "The initial lab reports have come back, and we've identified the probable murder weapon." A murmur runs through the ranks. I hold up a large photo. "This rock was found near the pond." I point to the diagram taped to the board. "This is where we believe Kara was attacked. The lab identified blood on the rock as belonging to Kara. We believe her assailant struck her from behind twice. We think Kara then staggered down the path toward the Foster house before collapsing. Dr. Gaines has stated that Kara died approximately two hours after she was struck. That would mean the attack probably happened between six and ten p.m." I draw a breath. "Which means Byron Foster had opportunity. No one sees him until a little after seven when he arrives for work at Graybridge General. Also, he was involved romantically with our vic until recently, so there was history between them. However, that's all we've got really to tie Mr. Foster to the crime." I pause, look over my notes. The room is still, and the ticking of the old clock hanging on the wall over the whiteboard is an irritating reminder of how stagnant this case is.

"Anything else, Rita?" the chief asks, hopeful.

I clear my throat. "We've identified her vehicle." I point to the map. "It was parked here. But nothing of note was found inside it. We don't have anything that puts anybody specifically in those woods that night, including Byron Foster. Now"—I turn to the board and add two names to the suspect list—"Raymond Ridley lives near the Fosters and frequently hangs out in those woods. He doesn't have an alibi. He's got a rap sheet of minor offenses, but nothing violent, and so far, we don't have a motive. Alan York is an elderly man"—I cringe when this leaves my mouth since he's probably only a few years older than I am—"who lives on the opposite side of the woods from the Fosters." I point to the diagram. "He also said that he walks in those woods—every day, in fact—and has no solid alibi, but also no discernible motive either. And Tom Foster, who heard a scream that night. He was at home, but he's ill and says he didn't leave the house. So, these men were in the area when Kara was killed. Oh, and Cynthia Ridley was at home that night as well." I add her name to the list as people murmur behind me. They all know who she is.

I take a deep breath, shoot a glance at the chief. "So far, that's all we've got."

Bob grunts. "What about her coat, Rita?"

I shake my head. "We haven't located it." I glance up at the team. "Kara's mom said that when she left for work that morning, she was wearing a black, three-quarter-length wool coat. She didn't leave it at work, and it wasn't in her car. We also found that a vial of pills in Kara's purse are oxycodone, but there's no pharmacy label, so I'm going to ask her mother about that. It may be something or not." I blow out a breath. We've got a whole lot of nothing so far. I give out what assignments I can. We're at a serious standstill, and I hope that the lab will come up with some DNA, fingerprints even, that'll give us what we need.

Back in my office, I close the door and turn on my little radio on the windowsill. My classic rock station is on commercial; it's an ad for an obnoxious used-car dealership where everyone screams, as if that will make you want to buy a car. Maybe I should just get a streaming service, like Chase keeps telling me. I sigh. He'll be back from vacation Monday, and maybe he'll see something we're missing.

I sit and read through my notes, power up my laptop. My mind wanders back to last night at Mrs. Antonelli's. I had a decent time in spite of myself, and Collin was happy. He likes company, and he was glad that I was out socializing too. Mrs. A's son, Leo, is nice enough and good-looking enough. He was Johnny-on-the-spot when my wineglass was empty. (Thanks for this morning's headache and breaking my two-drink limit on a work night rule.) Collin's been trying to find me a date for the last two years. Still, I don't know. My track record isn't very good, especially with nice men like Leo, a banker. I can see that working out, *not.* Nine-to-five, a suit and tie. *How can we help your business be more profitable?* While I work crazy hours. Spend my time with murderers and rapists, DNA, and blood. And then my mind filters back to Joe. My friend at the FBI. *Shit.* And Danny's words burn in my brain. What's wrong with being alone? You get to do what you want when you want. No one to ask you why you're home so late.

I dive back into my notes. Ten minutes or so tick by, and I notice Lauren in my doorway. "What?"

"I think we've got something, Rita."

"Let's see." I close my notebook as she gets settled across from me.

"The surveillance footage from the insurance office. They finally sent it over." She opens her laptop and cues up the tape. Lauren is literally on the edge of her seat.

The side of the white clapboard building appears in the corner as the footage pans out to the little parking lot. As the tape rolls, we watch Kara, wearing her black coat, walk across the lot to her

Camry. Just as she clicks her key fob, she suddenly turns toward the street.

Lauren stops the tape and points to the screen. "There! Someone calls her name."

"And you know this? Maybe she heard a dog bark."

"Maybe." Lauren starts the tape again, undaunted. We watch as Kara walks out of the shot toward the road. Time ticks on the screen. Five thirty-two. Five thirty-three. Then at five thirty-seven, Kara's back. She gets in her car and drives away.

Lauren stops the tape and leans back in her chair. "The perp called to Kara and arranged to meet her in the woods."

"How do you know that?" I ask, always the devil's advocate.

"There's nothing telling on her phone, Rita. We got the reports just this morning, right after the meeting. I took a quick look. There aren't any phone calls or texts after she spoke to her mother at lunchtime. And there aren't any calls earlier that I couldn't account for. Well, except for one number on Sunday. Still working to track that down. That might've been when she arranged the meeting. We don't know. But I'm thinking the perp might've just showed up at her work."

"What's across the street from the office?"

"A fairly dead plaza. On the end nearest the insurance office, there are two empty storefronts and probably no cameras."

"Let's check on that." I tent my fingers. "You think the perp knew that? Parked over there and called to Kara to get her out of the camera's range?"

"I think so, yes," Lauren says. "It's a theory anyway."

I take a deep breath. "Could be. What does that tell us?"

"The perp didn't want any phone or camera evidence. And he knew that the woods would be a safe place to get her alone."

"What else?"

Lauren taps her fingers on my desk. "The meeting was planned by someone she knew and trusted. And it probably wasn't Cynthia or Tom Foster, since I doubt either one of them drives, but I'll check on that."

"Agree," I say. "With all of it. Now, who would have a motive? Who would want Kara dead?"

"Maybe they didn't. Maybe the perp didn't plan to kill her, Rita. Who hits someone with a rock, then takes off without making sure they finished the job? Kara could very well have gotten help in time."

"Good points all, Lauren. But why was she meeting someone in the woods? Meeting her drug dealer maybe? But why would he hit her with a rock? She's got her pills. Must've already paid for them. Not like she's going to turn him in." I take a deep breath. "Let's see what her mom has to say."

# CHAPTER 22
# Esmé

WE'VE BEEN BUSY AT THE CAFÉ, AND EVERY TIME THE BELL ON THE front door tinkled, I looked up, hoping Byron had forgiven me. Finally, just as the crowd has thinned, he comes through the door with Ashlyn. She's wearing a pink jacket with a purple, glittery unicorn on the pocket. She toddles in, holding his hand. I can't believe how much she's grown.

"Hi!" I come around the counter and drop to my haunches. "Wow, what a big girl you are."

Byron leans over and tugs off her hood, letting loose a headful of dark curls. "This is Aunt Esmé, Ashlyn."

The little girl smiles shyly and points at the brightly frosted cookies on the counter.

"Can she have one?" I ask.

"Sure. And an apple juice, please. I'll take a latte and a cherry Danish." Byron pulls off Ashlyn's coat and slings it over his arm. He glances around the nearly empty café. "Nice place. I've been in here a few times. How's it going?" His dark eyes meet mine.

"Good, so far. Everyone's really nice." I shrug. "It's not hard work."

"That's good. It's something anyway."

I hear a trace of condescension in his voice, and my heart contracts. How did things get this bad between me and my brother? I think back to when we were kids, playing together in the woods. He was younger, but we were close then. We liked to hide out in the shack by the pond, play pirates and explorers. We were happy. Then Wendy died, and the pond lost its magic for a while. I was having regular playdates with Kara, Christy, and Laney by then, and we tried to ignore Byron when we were together, but he never resented me for it, the loyal little brother. But then it changed when I got older and started at the ballet school downtown. I seldom saw him after that. We didn't even eat dinner together as a family at that point. Mom would leave something in the fridge for Dad to heat up for him and Byron, while Mom and I ate later, after getting home from my lesson. By then, Byron and Dad were settled in the dark living room watching TV. Looking back, it seems like my mom was carving out a separate life for her and me, putting distance between us and Dad and Byron. That couldn't have been easy for my brother. I sigh. Hindsight.

Byron and Ashlyn take a seat by the plate-glass window. People start to trickle in again, and Collin comes out of the office to help me. We get busy, and all I can do is take furtive glances at my brother and his daughter. When they finish their food, Byron pulls a packet of wipes out of his pocket and cleans Ashlyn's chubby fingers. He waves as they head out the door.

After the rush dwindles, Collin and I clean up. "Saturday nights aren't too busy," he says. "Now, tomorrow, we have a book club that arrives in the late afternoon, after they finish their meeting at the bookstore. But tonight should be light."

I looked at the schedule when I came in and saw that I work tomorrow but not Monday. That's fine with me. I'd be glad to work every day rather than rattle around at home. "Sounds good," I say.

I enjoy the classical music that Collin plays over the sound system, so much better than modern pop hits, at least to me. It helps take my mind off things, and I find myself behind the counter slipping into what has been my nearly lifelong routine. Stand in first position as I wipe down the counter near the register, slide my foot into second position, close my eyes, feel the music, ignore the pain.

A gust of cool air glides past me as a group of middle-aged women walk in. I wait for their orders as they discuss the day's specials and argue about what they had last time. After they make their selections, I hand them a metal stand with an order number attached, and they saunter off to a table in the corner.

As dark comes on, Collin is right, there are few customers. He slips back into the office to do paperwork, and I'm left to myself except for a young man in a black jacket and a mop of dark hair, sipping his coffee Americano and working on a laptop. A wave of loneliness sweeps over me, and my mind wanders back to Kevin. He's probably super busy right now. Saturday nights at his restaurant are crazy. People jostling for tables, regretting not making a reservation and watching the waitlist like hungry hawks. I take a blueberry muffin from the case and break it into small pieces, eat it surreptitiously behind the register. Collin said to help myself to anything I want, but I don't think eating in front of the customers, or the customer, is very professional.

I watch out the window as a few people walk past. There's a bar down the block, and a group of young women giggle and shout as they move past. I notice that a table in the corner needs wiping. Somehow it had escaped my notice earlier. I carry my supplies over, brushing past the young man. He looks up and smiles.

"Could I have a refill when you get a minute?"

"Sure." I drop my supplies on the dirty table, grab his mug, and head back to the counter. After I take care of him, I return to my cleaning. I'm hunched over a table near the window, wiping cookie crumbs, scrubbing a coffee ring, when I see a man outside, muffled up in a thick dark coat. He slows near the café, bends toward the window, and his eyes meet mine. I squeak like a mouse and jump back, dropping my cleaning cloth on the floor. The man straightens and quickly walks away.

The young man looks up. "Are you all right?"

I bite my lip and nod. "Yes. Fine. Just startled." I shudder and retrieve my cleaning cloth.

# CHAPTER 23
# Rita

ALL'S QUIET WHEN I ENTER THE FOYER OF MY BUILDING. MAYBE Mrs. Antonelli's son or grandkids picked her up for a night out. Hope so. My attempts to contact Kara's mom all went unanswered. Maybe she's away for the weekend and not listening to her voice mail. Who knows? But tracking down where Kara got the pills is our top priority at this juncture.

My apartment is chilly, and I push up the thermostat and turn on the living room lamp. The front bay window looks out onto the street, and it's all quiet there too. Not much traffic. Most people are home relaxing or are already out on the town.

I glance at my old stereo and consider putting on an album from my vinyl collection, but decide I'll relax in the quiet for a change. I lean back into the couch and prop my feet on the coffee table, which I always enjoy. When I was a kid, Ma would pitch a fit if anyone dared put their feet on her furniture. We didn't have much, but Ma watched that we didn't destroy what she did have. I yawn and close my eyes, consider taking a hot bath.

My phone chimes on the cushion next to me. Danny.

"Hey."

"How's it going?" he asks.

"Fine. What's up?"

"How's your new case?"

I grunt. "Okay." He wants to ask me something that he knows I won't be too keen about. I know my brother.

"I was wondering . . ." Here it comes. "Are you busy Thursday night?"

"Let me check my social calendar." I'm just yanking his chain, and he knows it.

"Please, Reet."

"What?"

"I'm having dinner with Vivienne, and I've asked Charlotte to join us. She hasn't met Vivienne yet, and it would be great if you could be there too," he says in one breath.

"Jesus, Danny. You can't manage this alone by now? Charlotte's thirty years old. She can handle a new woman in your life. She's had enough practice."

He takes a deep breath.

I'm the last person to help out with an awkward social situation, but Charlotte and I are close, and I suppose there's no one else Danny can really ask. And I would like to see my niece. It's been a while. Since I never had kids, my nieces and nephews have filled that void. Collin too. And Charlotte and I always have a good time when we're together. We've got the same dry sense of humor, and she doesn't see much of her mom, who lives in Toronto, so I fill a void for her too, I guess.

"Please. You could bring Joe."

I sit up, huff out a breath. "He's probably busy. I can't call him at the last minute."

"It's not until Thursday."

"Still. He's probably busy."

"Okay. Another time then. What do you say, sis? Do a guy a favor. Besides, you haven't seen Charlotte in a while, right?"

"Yeah. Okay. Where? What time?"

I finish the leftover Chinese I'd picked up on the way home yesterday and settle in with a glass of cabernet and an old movie. What's wrong with that on a Saturday night? I wouldn't be good company for anyone with the Cunningham case on my mind. I grab my satchel and fish out my notebook, pause.

Wonder what Joe's doing? Probably the same thing I am, sitting home, mulling over a case. But what if he's not? What if he's out on the town having a good time with his buddies? What if he's got a date? Well, that has nothing to do with me. Not like we're in some kind of relationship. We're friends.

I set my notebook on the coffee table and pick up my phone, tap on my contacts. Scroll down to Joe's number. Maybe he is free Thursday night.

I sigh. He's probably busy. And it would be super awkward to have Joe meet me at some snooty restaurant with my brother and his new perfect girlfriend. And I wouldn't be able to relax and pay attention to my niece, who'd feel like a fifth wheel anyway. Besides, Joe and I are more spontaneous, beer and pizza people.

I close my contacts and stick my phone under a couch pillow. I sip my wine and start clicking through the channels looking for another decent action movie. But, hell, nothing good on, as usual.

# CHAPTER 24
# Esmé

SUNDAY AFTERNOON, IT'S JUST ME AND MARGO AT THE CAFÉ. THE book club Collin warned me about is filtering in, mostly women with what looks like a couple of husbands in tow. They are talking excitedly, not wanting to let the meeting go, I guess, after their time at the bookstore. They've brought an appetite and stand in a chatty group before the counter. Once they're settled, orders delivered, we start to clean up.

The bell on the front door tinkles, and I look up to see Jack. He smiles as he makes his way to the counter.

"Hey. I was in town and hoped I'd catch you here."

I shrug. "You found me."

He leans on the counter. "I was wondering. What time are you finished?"

"Six." We close early on Sunday.

"Do you have plans for dinner?"

"No. Not really." Just go home and scrounge something up and hope that Irene has already left.

"I was going to make some spaghetti, and, well, it's not too easy to cook for one. You want to come by my place and help me out?"

"Sure. I guess I could do that." What else do I have to do?

He straightens up. "Great. I'll text you my address." Just as Jack pulls out his phone, Ray appears over his shoulder.

"What's happening, Sugar Plum?"

"Hi, Ray."

He tips his head in Jack's direction. "You got a date?"

I feel my face flush and see Jack's eyes go wide. "Not exactly, Ray. What can I get you?"

"Haven't decided."

"Take your time." I move down the counter, and Jack follows.

"That Ray Ridley?" he whispers.

"Yeah."

Jack shakes his head. "You okay?"

"I'm fine. He's harmless."

"You sure?"

"Yeah." He's been my neighbor since I was a kid. I can handle Ray. I hope so anyway. But Laney's words come back to me. Maybe Ray killed Kara. Is that possible?

"Okay. I'll see you when you get off?"

I nod. Ray clears his throat. Jack gives him a sideways glance as he walks to the door.

"Who was that?" Ray asks.

"Jack Crosby."

Ray turns and cranes his neck as Jack strides down the sidewalk. "No shit? It's old home week. What's he doing back in town?"

"He moved back last month. What can I get you, Ray?"

His eyebrows draw together. "Just a regular coffee." He taps the glass counter with dirt-stained fingernails, looks down like he's contemplating things. "You heard anything about Kara lately? The cops find anything?"

"No," I say and turn to pour his coffee into a to-go cup.

I start to walk away after handing Ray his order.

"Wait up, Esmé."

"What?"

"Why don't you stop by the house some time. We can catch up."

"Yeah. Maybe," I say, just hoping he'll leave.

"You've been gone a long time. We've got a lot to talk about. Things that might interest you."

I take a deep breath. "Like what?"

He grins. "Stop by, and I'll tell you."

What could Ray know that I could possibly be interested in? Luckily, he doesn't wait for a reply, just nods and leaves.

The Grand Valley Apartments are new since I lived in Graybridge. It's strange to think of Jack, or any of my friends, living on their own. I'm still seeing everyone through high school eyes. And I never could picture Jack in an apartment. His family lived in a nice ranch home in a nice neighborhood. His father had a book-filled, paneled den, and there was a rec room complete with a large projection TV and a Ping-Pong table in the basement. I guess I just pictured Jack still living there, assumed his parents would move to Florida maybe and Jack would take over the family home. A silly thought. It's just hard to picture that people from your past have moved on, have had other lives. You think of them as they were, stuck in your memory.

I smell spaghetti sauce as I near his door on the second floor. I brought a bag of chocolate chip cookies from the café. I seem to remember that they were Jack's favorite.

He's wearing an apron over his jeans and a Mumford and Sons T-shirt, and that makes me smile. "Nice," I say pointing at his attire.

"Oh, this?" His face reddens as he pulls the apron off and tosses it on a nearby chair. "I'm such a klutz. Remember? I'll drip sauce all over myself if I'm not careful. Come in." He shuts the door behind me and takes my jacket. "You want a glass of wine?"

"Sure. Great."

Accepting his dinner offer seemed like the most natural thing in the world, but now that I'm here, I feel strange. He seems strange. Grown-up Esmé and Jack. How do we do this?

I follow him into the kitchen, where a pot of water bubbles furiously on the front burner of the stove. After he hands me my drink, he dumps rigatoni into the pot. "Hope you're hungry," he says. "I always seem to make a buttload of food when I cook."

"Good for leftovers," I say, then walk to the window, sip my wine, and look out over the trees next to his building.

"How's school going?" I ask.

"Busy. I never realized what a hard job teaching is. When we were in school, it all seemed pretty cushy. Sit at a desk, hand out worksheets. Off all summer."

"But the good teachers never sat at their desks and passed out worksheets."

"You're right."

"And I bet, Jack, that you're a good teacher."

He stirs the pasta, places the wooden spoon on the counter. "I try to be."

I walk around the living room and notice stacks of papers piled neatly on a desk in the corner. There are a couple of candles burning on the coffee table, and their woodsy scent mingles with the simmering sauce in the kitchen. I turn to face Jack, who's tossing a salad at the table.

"I like your place."

He shrugs. "It works for now."

It looks like a sanctuary to me after living with Kevin the past few years in a place half the size of this one. Kevin wanted to save every penny we could for the restaurant he planned to open, so we had to economize. The bathroom was so small we couldn't be in there at the same time, and the living room window overlooked an alley full of garbage bins. And now, when I'm living at my dad's, in my childhood bedroom, with Irene ruling the place, Jack's apartment looks like heaven.

"I'm hoping to get my own place eventually," I say.

"How's your dad doing? I meant to ask you."

"Not good." I sigh. "I don't really know if he knows what's going on, how bad off he is."

"I'm sorry," Jack says. He drains the pasta, steam rising. "You ready to eat?"

The sauce is actually pretty good, and that surprises me. Like Jack said, he's a klutz in the kitchen. Senior year we took a culinary class together. It was an intro course, an easy A. But, somehow, Mr. Nerd only managed a C, about which he complained bitterly. But Mrs. Holtz told him he got what he deserved. A soufflé that looked more like a pancake was the last straw. She told him he was hopeless in the kitchen and advised him to stick to his history books.

After dinner, we sit in the living room, me on a blue sofa and Jack in the armchair next to it. The wine and pasta have made me drowsy.

Jack leans forward, his gaze on the floor. "I feel so bad about Kara," he says. "I was supposed to meet her that night." His gaze meets mine.

"What?" I sit up. "The night she was killed?"

"Yes. We were supposed to meet at the little coffee shop near school."

"Why didn't you say anything before?"

He shakes his head. "I don't know. I feel guilty. I didn't want to talk about it to Christy and Laney."

I don't know why Jack feels guilty. If anything, I feel guilty. Not just for leaving Graybridge and cutting off my friends for ten years, but because of the man. My phantom. Was he looking for me? Did he mistake Kara for me? I shake my head. *Stop it, Esmé,* I tell myself. "Did you tell the cops?"

"Yes."

"What happened? Did you see Kara?"

"She didn't show. I waited a while, but I gave up and went home."

"Why were you guys meeting?"

"She'd called me and arranged it. She said she just wanted to catch up." He runs his hand through his hair. "Why didn't I call the police when she didn't show? I keep asking myself. Maybe they would've been able to save her."

"Why would you even think that she was in danger? Kara was always late. It's not your fault, Jack."

"I tried to call her, but every time it went to voice mail."

"There's nothing you could've done." I lean over and place my hand on his arm. He looks up and catches my gaze.

"What if she needed help, Ez? What if someone was bothering her, and I could've done something about it?"

"It's not your fault. No one could've predicted this. I feel bad too for not being here with you guys. We were all so close, then I just took off." But my mind goes back to those days. I didn't know what to do with myself. My mother always hoped I'd dance for a company close to home where she could come to my performances. Where we could still stay close. But after she died, staying local was the last thing I wanted to do. Losing my mother made me feel as if I had no anchor. She was so tied up in my life here that I couldn't see how I could go on without her.

And then there was the phantom man. Kara, Christy, and Laney had gathered at my house after Mom's funeral. Up in my bedroom, away from the friends and relatives who swarmed the first floor, I described what happened. They were sympathetic and, at first, believed me when I told them about the man. Then I began to see him everywhere, and I became a jittery mess. At some point, Christy spoke to my father, concerned about me, I guess, and my friends tried to convince me the man wasn't real. He was a nightmare tangled up in that dark, icy night when I lost my mother. I was angry at first, with my friends, with my father. But, eventually, as no real man appeared from the shadows, I started to believe them. It was easier to live that way than to be on the lookout for danger every minute.

Still, I needed to get away from Graybridge. I just couldn't stay. Things with my friends felt different after the accident, altered in some way, like they thought I was going to fall apart and somehow ruin the dynamics of the group. So I started auditioning out of state, got my dream job, and met Kevin, and his family seemed like the answer to everything. In another town, another state, I could let go of the phantom man and live in relative peace.

"Well, I'm glad you're back now," Jack says, that familiar smile on his face.

"I'm dreading the funeral," I say.

"Me too." Jack sighs.

One of the candles sputters, its flame dying and then flickering back. I change the subject. The thought of seeing my friend laid to rest is more than I can handle right now.

"Do you regret your breakup? You know, the girl in Albany you were telling me about?"

He leans back in his chair, scrapes his hair off his forehead. "No.

We were good together for a while, but she wasn't the one. I wasn't the one for her either. Actually, I just saw that she and the guy she left me for are engaged. What about you?"

I shake my head. "Kevin and I were together six years. You'd think we would have had it figured out before then. You know? Either we were right for each other or we weren't." I sip my wine, finish the glass, and set it on the coffee table.

"So, what didn't work?"

I sigh and let my gaze fall on the candle's flame. "He's a good person. We were happy in the beginning. It was me."

"What do you mean?"

"He didn't really know me." The room has darkened as the last rays of sunlight have flickered out. "I was lonely." I pull my legs up under me. "Kevin knew exactly what he wanted out of life. He's a terrific chef. Loves entertaining, cooking for people. He was so excited about opening his own place. And he just thought I should be too."

"You weren't?"

"No. I mean, I wasn't opposed to the idea, but it just seemed like when my career ended, he was just like, okay, let's get on to the next thing. Open a restaurant with me." I pick my glass back up and tilt it, hoping for a last drop.

Jack jumps up. "I'll get you a refill." He's back in a second with a new bottle of chardonnay and pours us each a glassful. "So then what?"

I shrug. "Like I said, he didn't know me. Not really. I was devastated, Jack, when my ballet career ended. It was all I ever wanted. All I ever dreamed about." My mind drifts back, as it so often does. The music, the scenery, that magical and artificial world when I'm onstage, where no one can hurt me, where everything is perfect. I remember when the pain started, six months before my company let me go. I tried to dance through it, but it didn't escape the careful eye of the director or the ballet mistress. They could see that I was struggling. I'll never forget when they took me aside and sent me to the doctor, and then his somber news. Snapping hip syndrome. And nothing helped. The director sat me down and delivered the news that it was time for me to retire, at age twenty-seven. After years of strenuous dancing, my body had finally had enough.

"Kevin didn't support you? It must have been a terrible thing for you to accept. I remember how dedicated you were."

"He tried. He just didn't get how much ballet meant to me. He was sorry and all, but he didn't understand how deeply I felt." Tears gather in my eyes, and I sniff them away. That's the loneliest thing in the world, when someone close to you doesn't understand how you feel.

Jack walks me to my car. The air is bitter, raw and damp, and I wrap my scarf around my neck.

"You sure you're okay to drive?" he asks.

"Positive." We spent the last two hours drinking coffee and laughing about the old days.

Jack gives me a hug. "I'm glad you're back, Esmé."

"Me too."

"I'll see you tomorrow afternoon at Kara's . . . ?"

"Yeah." Jack can't bring himself to say Kara and funeral in the same sentence. I can't either. Better to pretend we're just getting together, like the old days. He opens my car door and waits until I've started the engine and locked up before giving me a wave under the streetlight and heading back to his place. I slip the gearshift into drive and sputter through the lot to the apartment road that leads to the main street. As I turn right, I notice a car immediately behind me, its high beams flashing through my little car.

*Back off, idiot.* I mumble and hit the gas. He flips his headlights back to normal, and I wonder with a hammering heart if I cut him off. I don't think so. I didn't see anyone coming when I entered the roadway. I turn up the volume on my radio, and an old, mournful Pearl Jam ballad fills the car. There aren't a lot of vehicles on the road, and I try to think back over the pleasant evening I've had with Jack. But when I slow down for a red light, the car is still behind me and close to my bumper. *Don't be paranoid, Esmé,* I tell myself. I decide to turn in at the grocery store a few blocks from home. I pull into a spot near the store entrance and peer into the rearview mirror. I don't see him. I wait a couple of minutes, then pull back out on the street. There's one more traffic light before I reach my road. And, of course, it's red when I approach. I stop, my fingers tapping on the steering wheel, and I venture a glance in the mirror. My pulse kicks up. He's back. I'm sure of it. I peel out when the light turns green and head toward home. Byron should be there. He's not working today. I fumble for my phone, ready to call 911 if this guy follows me onto Hogsworth Road. But as I slow to make the turn for home, he barrels past me and disappears into the night.

# CHAPTER 25
# Rita

ON MONDAY MORNING, MY MIND IS POPPING WITH LISTS OF THINGS to do as I make my way to my office. I glance across the squad room. Chase is back. He's sitting at his desk, buried in emails.

"Hey, Rita," he says without looking up. "Trying to get caught up." He swivels in his chair to face me. "Looks like you've got a tough one with this Cunningham case."

"We do. Glad you're back. I'll send you my files." He's tanned, looks rested. His and the Mrs.'s anniversary cruise came at a good time for him personally. His last six months as a detective were rough, and he was showing signs of fatigue.

"Thanks," he mumbles, and his gaze is back on his computer screen.

In my office, I power up my laptop, skim through my notes. I'd been checking my messages all weekend, hoping Kara's mom would call me back, but so far nothing. I need to talk to her about the pills, and I want to look through Kara's room. Doug has already been through once, collected her computer, but so far, nothing has panned out. Time to go back over a few things.

I keep checking the time, and finally, Mrs. Cunningham calls and says she's home and we can drop by this morning, but she'll be busy this afternoon. Bob said that Kara's funeral was later today.

Lauren offers to drive, while Chase remains behind catching up. I wanted to take my own van, but I'm getting more and more resistance from everybody. Even Bob. *What if you've got to chase down a suspect, Rita? Old Blue could give up the ghost anytime.* I only drive my own vehicle on routine calls. *But you never know.* Okay, fine.

I sit in the passenger's seat, going through my notebook, while Lauren drives us out to Kara's subdivision.

"Any thoughts on the oxy in Kara's purse?" I ask Lauren.

"Hopefully, her mom knows."

"We'll see." I glance back at my notes. "You know, when I talked to Ray, I noticed he had a nice big flat-screen and a new truck."

"Yeah?"

"Told me he's not working, living on money his mom sends to take care of his sister."

We pull up in front of a small two-story, and Lauren looks over at me. "What are you thinking, Rita?"

"Well, let's see what Mrs. Cunningham knows, and then maybe a trip back out to see Ray wouldn't be a bad idea."

The house is a little run-down. Needs a coat of paint. A shutter hangs loose next to the picture window.

Mrs. Cunningham meets us at the door, eyes swollen and red. She knows we're here to search Kara's room.

"Anything, Detective? Anything new?" she asks, her voice thin and scratchy.

"One thing we wanted to ask you." There's a flicker of interest in her tired eyes. "Was Kara taking any pain medication that you know about?"

She draws a deep breath. "Last spring, I guess it was. She hurt her back. A guy rear-ended her. The doctor gave her some pain pills."

"Was she still taking them?"

"No. She told me she finished them months ago. Her back was better."

Huh. "Was Kara acting in any way unusual lately?"

Mrs. Cunningham shakes her head. "No. Not that I noticed."

"But the back pain was gone?"

"Yes."

Mrs. Cunningham doesn't ask me why I want to know. Her daughter's dead, so what does it matter? "Can we see her room?"

She turns and leads us into a tiny foyer. The lumpy cardigan she's wearing seems to hang on her thin back like a shroud.

"Upstairs. The first door on the right," she says, and heads off into the dark interior of the house.

We climb the worn carpeted steps and enter the small bedroom. It looks like it belongs to a teenager rather than a woman approaching thirty. Boy-band posters hang on the walls. Makeup covers the top of the scarred oak dresser. There's a dried nail-polish stain on the nightstand next to a box of tissues and a half-empty bottle of perfume. I stand still a moment, trying to get into Kara's head, get a feel for who she was. A young woman in a dead-end job. No luck on the romance front, but hopeful now that Jack Crosby was back in town. If she was abusing opioids, no one, so far, seems to have noticed.

Lauren is methodically canvassing the room, taking notes, peeking into drawers, assessing the contents of the closet.

"No journal or diary," Lauren says.

"No. Doug didn't find anything like that either."

"She probably used her computer," Lauren says. "Maybe we'll still find something on it."

"Let's hope." I turn and open the drawer in the nightstand. It's full of junk, envelopes, lipsticks, paper clips, and nail files. But then I see a photo shoved into the corner. It's a five by seven. Interesting. I flip it over.

"Holy shit."

"What?" Lauren says.

"Look."

The interview room is cold, small, utilitarian. Chase and I take our places across the metal table from Mr. York. He's dressed in a dark suit, a small bunch of silk violets in his lapel. The harsh overhead fluorescent light bounces off his gelled, salt-and-pepper hair.

I introduce Chase, and Mr. York forces a polite smile. I open my notebook and place it on the table. I have him state his name and the date for the recording; our meeting is being viewed in the other room by Lauren and a few others.

"Really, Detective, what's this all about? You were so cryptic on the phone."

"We have a few more questions about the Kara Cunningham murder."

"I believe I've told you all I know." He brushes a piece of lint from his sleeve.

"Humor me." I tap my pencil against the table. Chase is flipping through a folder, reviewing notes and letting Mr. York wonder what we've got.

"Now, the night Kara was killed, you were at home?"

"I told you before I was. Then I went into town."

"Where did you go again?"

He sits up a little straighter and eyes my notebook. "The bookstore. Surely, you wrote that down last time we spoke."

"Okay. What time did you leave?"

"I'm not sure. About dinnertime, I guess."

"How long were you at the bookstore?"

He sighs. "I really don't remember. Not too long. They had a book on hold for me. I paid for it and went on my way."

"What time did you get home?"

"Seven-ish," he says. "And I didn't walk the dogs that evening."

I look up from the sketch I've started. "Why not? Don't you walk them every night?"

"Not always. Sometimes I just take them out front when I'm pressed for time."

"Okay. You told us before that you know the Fosters, Esmé and Byron."

"Yes."

"But you didn't know Esmé's friends, Christy French Bowers, Laney Morelli Addison, Kara?"

"Not really, no."

"Never spoken to them?"

"Well, I didn't say *that.* They used to spend a lot of time out by the pond when they were younger, and I walk in those woods almost daily. I have for thirty years. So, of course, I've spoken to them."

"That's it then, huh?"

"That's it, Detective."

"Never had them up to your place?"

He shifts in his chair, straightens his shoulders. "Well, Mrs. Foster came by occasionally, years ago. She'd bring Esmé sometimes. She liked to play with the costumes."

"That so?"

"Little girls like dressing up. She was a child."

"What about when she got a little older, a teenager?"

He shrugs. "I don't remember. She might have been by a time or two. We've been neighbors of a sort for years. It's only natural."

"What about Kara? She ever in your house?"

He licks his lips, coughs. "May I have a glass of water?"

"Sure." I glance at Chase, who rises and leaves the room without a word.

"It's quite stuffy in here, Detective. I don't know how you stand it."

"Really? Feels fine to me." I wait, add to my drawing of his eyes and their tense graying eyebrows.

"You're quite the artist there," he says and half-chuckles.

I lean back, tip up my notebook so he can't see it. Chase returns with a bottle of water, and we watch silently while Mr. York twists the cap and drinks self-consciously. I wait long enough to let him calm down, think he's thrown us off track.

"Is that all, Detective?" he asks hopefully. "I really need to get home. I have work to do." He makes a show of looking at his watch. "I have a conference call shortly."

"We're nearly finished." I set my pencil on the table and pull the photo from Chase's folder. I lay it in front of him and watch his face turn a shade of purple.

"We found this in Kara's bedroom. Nice picture." Kara poses in an outfit that makes her look like a nineteen-twenties flapper, a serious look on her pretty face, unlit cigarette in a long holder in her hand.

"I don't know anything about it."

I huff out a breath. "Really?" I flip it over. "'To my favorite muse'? Signed, AY?"

His mouth hangs open.

“And if you look closely”—I flip the picture back over—“look, there’s that painting in your dining room. That goddess of memory or whatever.”

He leans back in his chair and tries to form words, but nothing comes out.

“You still claim, Mr. York, that Kara Cunningham was never in your house? That you barely knew her?”

# CHAPTER 26
# Esmé

I DO MY USUAL FORTY-FIVE MINUTES OF STRETCHING AND BALLET PRACtice, my wooden desk chair acting as a makeshift barre. My hip hurts the whole time, but I won't give up my routine, not entirely. It's too ingrained in who I am. I wipe the sweat from my forehead and do a few pirouettes across my bedroom floor. I sigh, turn off the music. I need my pointe shoes. I've been trying to practice in them at least once a week, just to prove to myself that I still can. I need to bring them up from the garage.

I decide to clean out my room, which will accomplish two things: I make an effort to move forward, leave the past behind, and I avoid Irene at the same time. After a couple of hours, I've got two big garbage bags full of junk. I carry the first one down the stairs and out to the garage. I remember my pointe shoes and look around for the bag, but I don't see it, so I walk back into the house.

Irene's in the kitchen, her back to me, rooting through the refrigerator.

"Irene?" She whirls around.

"You scared the shit out of me. What?"

"Did you see a paper bag in the garage? It was full of ballet shoes."

"Uh. Yeah. When I took the trash out to the curb Wednesday night. I put it next to the bin."

"Next to the trash?" My heartbeat kicks up. The thought of Irene touching my pointe shoes hurts in a childish way, like she'd taken a treasured toy and broken it on purpose.

"They looked like trash to me. You aren't using them anymore, right?"

Tears gather in my eyes, and I glance out the window at the woods, swallow. That was days ago, so the shoes are long gone, covered in garbage in a landfill somewhere.

"What's the big deal, Esmé? If they were so goddamn important, you should've put them away instead of leaving them where your dad could've tripped over them."

I sniff up my tears and walk up to my room. I lie on my bed a while, but the house is small, and I can't seem to shut out the sound of the TV and Irene's voice. My phone rings. It's Christy, inviting me to lunch downtown. I need to get out of the house, so lunch with my friend works.

# CHAPTER 27
# Rita

"MR. YORK?"

He removes a handkerchief from his coat pocket and wipes his nose. "All right, Detective. Yes, Kara has been in my house. She worked as a model for me for years." He raises a hand as if taking an oath. "Only after she turned eighteen. Anyway, in my line of work, you need a flesh-and-blood model. Mannequins only take you so far. You need to see how a particular fabric drapes on a real body, how it hangs and moves as an actress walks across the stage. How a neckline functions as an actress sits and leans forward in a scene."

"Uh-huh. You think you might've mentioned that?"

"I didn't think it was important."

Funny, what people decide is unimportant in an investigation, I think sarcastically. "So, when was the last time Kara was at your place?"

He takes a deep breath. "August."

"But you've worked with her for years?"

"Yes. Kara is a perfect model. Her proportions mirror those of several leading ladies. It was a business arrangement that worked out quite well. She was always short of cash, so modeling for me helped her out."

"There was nothing more to the relationship? Strictly business?"

He swallows, and beads of perspiration gather on his forehead. “Absolutely. Kara was like one of my nieces.”

“Uh-huh.” I add to my sketch, capturing the slackness of his mouth. Chase blows out a deep breath.

“Really, Detective. There was nothing untoward . . .”

“Okay. If you say so. She was just like one of your nieces?”

“Absolutely.”

“Why then your total nonchalance about her death? If one of my nieces died, I’d sure as hell show some emotion. You’ve talked about Kara like she was a dead bird someone found in your garden.”

He shakes his head. “I feel terrible, but some of us were brought up to control our emotions.”

“I see.” I close my notebook. “I’d like to have a look at your place, Mr. York.”

“Search it?” He suddenly looks alarmed.

“No. I’d just like to see where you and Kara worked. Would that be okay?” We don’t have enough to get a warrant, but I’d like to look around the interior of his place if he’s agreeable. You never know what you’ll find. “What do you say, Mr. York?”

He sighs. “I suppose it would be okay.”

# CHAPTER 28
# Esmé

I HAVEN'T BEEN TO DOWNTOWN BOSTON IN YEARS, AND THE TRAFFIC IS terrible, worse than I remember. But eventually I find my way, slip into a parking spot, and stride up the sidewalk. The restaurant is upscale, hip, lots of exposed brick and walls of windows. Christy waves from a table in the middle of the dining room as I come through the door.

"Hey," she says as I sit across from her. "You look . . . tired."

"I am. I haven't slept well since I got back."

Christy nods, her eyes on her phone. She scrolls quickly, then sticks it in her purse. "Any news about Kara?" Her gaze meets mine for a second before shifting away.

"No. The cops haven't found anything yet. At least, they haven't told us anything." A young man wearing round-lensed glasses pours water from a frosted pitcher.

"Let's have a drink," Christy says and tips her face to the server. "I'll have an espresso martini."

I'm not sure I want alcohol. I haven't eaten much today, but I give in. "A glass of pinot noir, please." The young man hurries away.

Christy blows out a breath. "I need something to get me through later." Kara's funeral is only a couple of hours away.

"Are you in the office today?" I ask.

"Just this morning. I needed to get out of the house. I need to stay busy. But I'm heading home after we finish, to get ready."

"I work tomorrow and the rest of the week. I'm glad for that. Irene is driving me crazy."

Christy sniffs. "That old hag is still around?"

"Every day. She acts like she owns the place."

"How's your dad? Any better?" She grasps my arm.

I didn't go into the details when we met at her house. "Not good." I sigh. "Byron says he doesn't have much time left."

"I'm so sorry, Esmé. I didn't realize it was that bad. I always liked your dad. He was a good guy."

The server places our drinks in front of us, and I sip my wine. He takes our orders. A Greek salad for Christy, a club sandwich for me. Sitting here with my friend, my mind wanders back.

"Do you remember when my mom died?" I ask her.

"Of course. We were all devastated. Your mom"—Christy points her fork at me—"she was amazing. We all wanted to be her. Elegant, beautiful. And she took such an interest in you. You were her whole world and, well"—she sips her drink—"we were a little jealous of that. But she was so sweet to all of us that we couldn't be too envious."

"I keep thinking about her since I've been back. I keep thinking about the accident."

"Why?"

"I don't know. I really don't. Except I keep coming back to the man I saw after the crash."

Christy's brow furrows. She was the one who nicknamed the man "Esmé's phantom." After my dad had a talk with my friends, and after weeks of me moping and fearful, they tried to pull me out of my funk. Christy thought the way to do that was to make light of the man. Telling me he didn't exist. He was a phantom. It hurt at the time; her sometimes teasing manner had a bite to it, like she was ready for us all to move on from the accident and was losing patience with my moods. But Kara. She took up for me. She told Christy to leave me alone, and Christy tamped down her annoyance, and the group got back on an even keel, sort of.

She grasps my arm again. "I think Kara's death has you twisted up. I know it's got me on edge."

"You're probably right, but someone harassed me on the road the other night. Riding my bumper and following me."

"It was probably just some asshole you pissed off by driving the speed limit." She waves her hand and sips her drink.

"I guess."

"Even if the phantom did exist, you really think he's still around?"

"What if he was real? He said he was going to kill me, Christy. After the accident. What if, now that I'm back, he's decided to do it?" I know I sound crazy, and I regret the words as soon as they leave my mouth. But my mind won't stop, my thoughts running in a loop. Maybe he mistook Kara for me in the woods that night. But I don't dare utter that idea. Christy's eyes are wide, concerned.

She purses her lips as if she's talking to a child. "If you're really upset about this, ask that detective to pull the report on your mom's accident. Maybe that will put your mind at ease. If there was a man, they would have noted it, questioned him. Don't forget, you had a concussion. You blacked out. Who knows what that did to your memory of what happened? My cousin was in an accident last year, and she doesn't remember a thing. One minute, she's at her desk at work, the next she's in the hospital mumbling about a family of polar bears crossing the road when she was hit. She got T-boned two blocks from Fenway."

"You're right. It's ridiculous." I take a deep breath, will my mind to calm down. Our food comes, and I pick at the chips that come with my sandwich.

"So, any thoughts of going back to Syracuse?" Christy asks, her drink nearly gone.

I shake my head. "No." I don't know what I'm going to do.

"You were pretty serious about that guy, right?"

"I was. We were together six years."

"That's a big investment just to walk away."

"Kevin's a good person," I say.

Christy taps the table with her manicured fingernails. "There's a lot to be said for that. Paul was cheating on me almost from the get-go."

"I'm sorry, Christy. I didn't have that to contend with. Kevin was totally committed." I sigh, thinking about his family. The dinners we'd shared at their house. The warmth and laughter.

"Well, don't sell that short." She takes a bite of her salad.

It's tempting, the thought of going back, slipping into my former life, after what I've found here. But I can't abandon my dad, not now.

"Yeah. I know." But how do I explain how I feel to someone like Christy? She's a successful businesswoman. She has goals, professional dreams. She's right where she wants to be career-wise. As if on cue, her phone chirps.

"I need to take this, but I'll be quick," she says, jumping up and heading for the lobby.

I watch Christy in the distance, pacing in her tailored suit, animated, talking on her phone as if she rules the world. I can't seem to see myself in the same light, heading in a new direction, a new career endeavor. My head is still filled with music and movement, costumes and stage lights, getting lost in the dreamlike stories that make up ballet. How powerful and free I felt on stage. I didn't realize how hard it would be to see it all end. Maybe because my mom didn't live long enough to see me dance professionally. It was something she'd pinned her dreams to as well. I understood, even then, that my mother was a woman whose life had disappointed her. She seemed a fish out of water in Graybridge. At our little backyard barbeques, at my brother's baseball games, she looked like some Hollywood glamour girl, a fanciful bird among the wrens. And I knew, deep in my heart, that my dad wasn't her prince charming. She tried not to let it show, but I could see it in her smile and her eyes, which had a way of looking beyond what was right in front of her.

Christy returns, throws her phone in her purse. "One of my biggest clients," she says. "I swear, they're like toddlers sometimes, ready to throw a tantrum over nothing."

"Not a problem, I hope?"

She smiles, energy radiating. "Nope. I took care of it."

We finish our meals, chat about nothing. But Kara's service is on our minds. "I guess I'll see you later?"

Christy nods. "Although I'd rather stab myself in the eye. I hate funerals. At least it's graveside, short and sweet, Laney said. She talked with Mrs. Cunningham. Offered to help, you know Laney."

"There's a get-together at the house afterward."

"Yes." Christy sighs. "We'll need to make an appearance. I just can't bear to see Mrs. Cunningham like that. I called her the other day, and she just sobbed."

"No one likes a funeral, Christy. That's not the point."

"I know. I'll suck it up. We need to be there for each other."

The server drops off the check, and Christy throws her platinum credit card on top before I can open my mouth.

She smiles. "My treat."

# CHAPTER 29
# Rita

After finishing up with Mr. York, Chase and I head out to the Ridley place. Too much is happening at once, but that's the nature of police work, famine to feast or the other way around. As we pull into the driveway, I see a young man come out of the side door, jump down the steps, and head off toward the path and into the woods.

We get out, and I shade my eyes, trying to get a good look at the guy, but he's long gone, swallowed up by the trees. Chase and I continue to the front porch. Ray opens the door and reluctantly invites us in.

"What brings you by, Detectives?" We walk through the dim foyer.

Chase and I settle on the saggy couch, and Chase's knees pop up like a grasshopper's. Ray paces in front of the picture window, his sister nowhere in sight. I notice the knitting basket is gone as well.

"Just a few questions," I say.

He stops and faces me. "Shoot."

"You told me last time I was out here you couldn't work because you had to take care of your sister."

"Yeah."

"Tough to make ends meet?"

He scratches the back of his neck. "We get by."

Cynthia appears in the doorway, doesn't seem to notice us. "Can I come out now, Ray?" Ray licks his lips, his gaze shifting between me and his sister. "Yeah, Cyn. It's fine."

I look to him for an explanation as Cynthia skirts by us quickly and settles into her chair. She picks up a magazine, a *National Geographic*, that had been lying open on the floor and starts paging through it.

"What's going on?" I tip my head in the sister's direction.

"Nothing. She was just in her room for a while. No big deal," Ray says, running his hand through his long hair.

"She needs your permission to come out?"

He tips his head toward the foyer. Whatever it is, guess we can't discuss it in front of her.

Chase looks up from his phone. "Mind if I use your bathroom?"

"Down the hall on the right," Ray replies, but his eyes are on me. Chase gets up and excuses himself.

Ray stands where his sister can't see him and motions me into the hallway.

"A buddy of mine stopped by," he whispers. "Cynthia can get nervous around some people, so I told her to go to her room while he was here."

"She seems fine with me."

He shrugs. "You never know how she's going to react."

"Who was this buddy?"

"Just a guy I know."

"We saw him leave out the side door as we pulled in."

"So?"

"Why'd he come through the woods?"

"What difference does it make? What are you doing here anyway?"

"Just getting a little background."

"You still don't know who killed Kara? Did you talk to Byron lately? I saw him in town yesterday, and he looked like shit, like a guy with a guilty conscience."

"We appreciate your insight. How well do you know Esmé Foster?"

He shrugs. "A little. We went to high school together."

"You seen her lately?" I juggle my notebook.

He glances down the hall. "Now and then I run into her."

"But you don't hang out anymore?"

"No."

"Nice truck you've got out front."

"Yeah. My grandma left me some money."

"Nice flat-screen too."

He pivots and strides toward the bathroom, but stops short and turns to me, a belligerent look on his face. "Like I said, she left me some money."

Chase reappears and nearly walks into Ray.

"I was starting to worry you fell in," Ray says, a fake smile on his face.

"Sorry," Chase says, patting his stomach. "Mexican for lunch."

*Boys,* I think to myself, but the explanation seems to satisfy Ray. No doubt, Chase used the excuse to do a little unofficial snooping.

I stash my notebook in my satchel. "Well, I think we're finished here for now."

Ray nods and can't walk us to the door fast enough. As his luck would have it, a white Mercedes pulls up alongside the front yard as we step out onto the porch. A woman wearing a pencil skirt and silk blouse emerges from the vehicle. Her gaze shifts right, then left.

"Another one of your buddies?" I say.

"I don't know who the hell that is," he mumbles. The woman looks up, gives Chase and me the once-over, jumps back into her car, and speeds off.

# CHAPTER 30
# Esmé

KARA'S MOM AND HER AUNT LOOK JUST ALIKE, TWO MIDDLE-AGED women bowed down by grief, in their black dresses, one supporting the other. Scenes of my mother's funeral run through my mind, the quiet tears, the soft voices. It occurs to me that this is the first funeral I've attended since then. How can that be? Thirteen years between them, but it's true. A good thing, I suppose.

Back at Kara's house, a loud woman, who introduced herself as Mrs. Cunningham's neighbor, has taken charge of the deli trays, the mound of rolls, the homemade desserts that cover the dining room table. She nudges people along, handing out paper plates and plastic flatware, while offering a kind if generic word to each of the mourners who've gathered at the house after the short service.

There aren't a lot of people here, and that makes me sad. The police chief is among them, a large older man in a worn overcoat, sagging shoulders. Laney said he used to live next door and was friends with Kara's mom. He must feel a heavy burden since finding Kara's killer ultimately rests on him, and so far, it doesn't sound like the cops have a clue.

The house is dim and shabby. Someone brought one of the flower arrangements back from the cemetery to act as a centerpiece? A souvenir? I shudder. The bright pink blooms, Kara's favorite color, make an odd focal point in the dull room. I sit on the sofa with Jack between Christy and me. My gaze wanders to the staircase in the foyer, and I wonder if Kara's room is still the same as it was when we were all giggling teenagers.

"Can I get you guys another drink?" Jack asks, jumping to his feet.

"I'm okay, thanks." I still have half my Pepsi left.

Christy raises her clear plastic cup. "Can you look around and see if there's anything stronger," she whispers.

Jack raises his eyebrows. All we saw when we came in was an assortment of liter soda bottles on the end of the table. "I'll look," Jack says.

Christy fans herself with her hand, although I'm cold straight through.

"How much longer do you think we should stay?" she asks quietly.

I shrug. I have no idea. Laney is across the room with her husband and both kids. She's got the baby on her hip and is still managing to be helpful, guiding newcomers to the food, taking coats.

"Laney seems to have done well," I say. "She was always good at everything."

"She's had her own issues, Esmé."

"Like what?"

"Just like all of us. She's had problems too," Christy says, blows out a breath. "I need to get going."

I keep seeing us thirteen years earlier and absently touch my forehead. I'd hit the front seat when our car collided with the tree. I'd had a concussion and a huge lump there. I barely remember my mom's service or the get-together afterward.

"I don't think we need to stay much longer, Christy," I say finally.

Jack hands her a new cup.

"Root beer. It was the best I could do."

"Thanks," Christy downs the soda like she's doing a shot. "I'm going to go say goodbye to Mrs. Cunningham." She glances at Jack, then me. "You guys want to head out too?"

We follow her lead, give Laney a hug on the way out.

# CHAPTER 31
# Rita

MORNING RAIN PATTERS ON THE ROOF OF THE BIG OLD VICTORIAN as I knock on the front door. Mr. York stands before me like a welcoming host. His earlier reticence seems to have disappeared. His gray suit is immaculate, a red silk handkerchief in his pocket. Doesn't this guy go casual even in his own home? He smiles and nods, but there's wariness in his eyes. Doesn't mean necessarily that he has anything to hide.

"What would you like to see, Detective?"

"The whole tour. This is a pretty cool place," I say, trying to sound sincere.

"All right. Follow me." We walk through the parlor, then head down a hall into the kitchen. Don't think I'll find much there, but you never know. The room looks distinctly old-fashioned, with a farmhouse sink that looks original and dated cupboards.

"Where are your dogs?" I ask, suddenly feeling their absence.

"At the groomers. I have to pick them up at noon."

"I'll be out of your way by then." I glance out the window over the sink. It looks on a faded garden, the gray woods beyond. "So, when was the last day you saw Kara?"

"Sometime in August. I can't recall the exact date, but I can look through my records."

"Were you going to call her for another project?" I walk through an open door that leads to a large pantry.

He draws a deep breath. "No. Kara had become unreliable."

"How so?" I step back into the kitchen.

"She was late more times than not, sometimes not turning up at all."

"Did she give you a reason?"

"Not any that made sense."

But that behavior makes sense if she was abusing opioids. So does her need for the extra money she was making by working for Mr. York. "Where did you and she work?" We head back down the hall and into the dining room, where the sewing machine and bolts of cloth cover the table. On a desk snugged in the corner, sketch-books are piled next to an open laptop.

"Some in here. But also upstairs."

"Let's take a look." The staircase is expansive, shiny with dark polished wood, but the steps creak as if to show the age hidden beneath their beauty. Several bedrooms open off the Persian-carpeted hallway. They are all neat and filled with antiques. "Where up here did you work with Kara?" I raise an eyebrow.

"Not here, Detective. The third floor."

"The attic?"

"It was when I bought the place."

I don't know exactly what that means, but I follow Mr. York to the end of the hall, to a set of narrow curving steps. "Mind your footing," he says over his shoulder as we start up.

We're standing in a small, dark hall before a door. Mr. York takes out a set of keys and lets us through. I blink my eyes, and Mr. York throws a switch illuminating a cavernous room that appears to cover most of the top of the house. And it's painted black: walls, ceiling, floor.

"Huh. You worked with Kara up here?"

He smiles. "Welcome to stage York." He walks out to the middle of the room, his shiny loafers making a tapping sound like he might break into a Fred Astaire routine.

I turn around, look up at the ceiling. "Are those stage lights?"

"Just like the ones they use in the best theaters."

I've never seen anything like this in all the searches I've done, and I've seen some doozies over the years. Elaborate meth labs. Gambling dens. Even a house decked out like a nineteen-twenties brothel, but this takes the cake.

There's a window in the middle of a wall. "What's that for?"

"I'll show you." Mr. York advances to a door that I didn't even know was there. It's painted black like everything else. He takes out his keys again, and we enter a small room.

"Why do you have everything locked up?"

"I invested a great sum of money to have everything exactly right, and if thieves should break in, I don't want them up here."

"Doesn't look like much to take."

He turns to me, smiles. "You haven't seen the costume room yet."

"What about all the artwork you've got downstairs? Aren't you worried about that?"

"It's insured. Now then. This is the taping room."

I notice a desk piled with equipment and a microphone.

"What exactly do you do in here?"

"Well, once my model is in her attire, I can set the lighting from in here and she walks, sits, twirls, whatever. I give her instructions." He taps the mic. "Whatever the project calls for. And I tape her. I then send the tape on to my clients, and they can say either yea or nay." He shrugs. "Adjust the length of her gown. Change the color, fabric."

"Quite an elaborate setup," I say.

He folds his arms. "It's my passion. All I ever wanted to do, Detective. Surely, you understand what that's like?" But his eyes are mocking, as if a cop couldn't be passionate about anything. A lot he knows. But he must have a buttload of money to go this far for his passion.

"You have tapes of Kara?"

"Of course. Still shots too." He angles his chin toward a row of filing cabinets. "Over thirty years of work. All meticulously documented."

"Huh. What about this costume room?" I ask.

"Follow me."

We head back into the stage area, cross the floor. "The prop room is through that door. Do you want to see?"

"I'll take a look," I say and wait while he unlocks the door. He snaps on a light. The room is crammed full of furniture, lamps, screens, you name it. It looks like loot from a fancy garage sale. "Nice. Is the costume room the only other room up here?"

"Yes. The last stop on our tour of stage York." He's almost giddy in his enthusiasm.

We leave the prop room. Mr. York dutifully locks up behind me, and we head to the final door.

Upon first entering, I see a large round mirror surrounded by those light bulbs you see in a movie. There's a little velvet-covered chair before it and bottles and tubes of makeup lying on the vanity.

"This is where my models get ready," Mr. York says.

"Kara sat here? Did her makeup once she was wearing her outfit?"

"Yes. And other ladies and gentlemen over the years."

"People from around here?"

He purses his lips as if thinking back in time. "A few. But not recently. Mostly just Kara. In the old days, I had models and actors from New York come up. But not too many people have time for that anymore." He sighs. "I usually have to pack my trunks and go to them."

"Were you getting tired of Kara? Annoyed with her erratic behavior?"

He shakes his head. "Not annoyed exactly. Disappointed."

"How so?"

He draws a deep breath. "Unfortunately, Kara didn't have the commitment, the passion this line of work demands." He clamps his lips in a taut straight line. "And that came through in the photos and videos, especially in recent months."

"So you needed to get rid of her."

He opens his mouth to speak, closes it again. "I didn't lay one hand on that girl, Detective." He steps away from the vanity. "Let me show you the crowning glory."

He opens an interior door and turns on the lights. A chandelier glitters overhead. Along the walls are rods stuffed with gowns, dresses, shimmering fabrics, dripping lace.

"Wow," I can't help but mutter. "All your creations?"

"Every one." He smiles, flushed with pride. "And accessories too."

On a shelf above the dresses is a huge assortment of hats, gloves, fans, and other stuff I can't identify.

"And, of course, shoes," he says and points to a set of shelves on an adjacent wall.

There are pumps, boots, and flats, some ordinary, some decorated with sequins and big buckles. "Well, I have to admit, Mr. York, I've never seen anything like this before."

"Of course not," he says smugly and crosses his arms. "I'm one of a kind." He chuckles. "But what you're seeing is my life's work. From New York in the early days until now. And I'm still working because of all this, the time and care I put into my art. I'm constantly in demand."

"I can see why. But why here? In the middle of nowhere."

"I told you before. The solitude works. When I left New York, I looked at multiple properties. I didn't want to be too far from the city, yet I needed a house big enough to accommodate all this. And I wanted to be alone," he adds, his gaze sweeping over the costumes.

"Uh-huh." Still, something seems off about this guy. Chase is back at the station looking into his background in more depth than we have at this point. Maybe he'll find something.

"Well, that's it, Detective. I think you've seen all there is to see."

"Would you send us the last video you took of Kara?" Don't know if that will help anything, but you never know.

"Certainly. I'll send you the most recent still shots as well."

"That would be great." We head for the door, and I nearly stumble over a paper grocery bag sitting on the floor near the shoe shelves. Mr. York picks it up and moves it out of my way.

"Sorry. I need to put these away. Ballet shoes."

# CHAPTER 32
# Esmé

After the lunch crowd dies down and I've cleaned up, I head home from the café. I'm a little tired. I didn't sleep well last night. Thoughts of Kara tumbled through my head. I worked the early shift, but now I've got the rest of the day to myself.

Irene's car isn't in the driveway when I get home, and my spirits lift, but her absence makes me wonder. I drop my keys in my purse and set it on the kitchen table. I hear Dad's TV, loud, blaring in the living room. He's sitting, per usual, in his chair, what remains of his lunch on his tray.

"Hi, Dad." He turns his head, dewy eyes straining behind his glasses.

"Esmé? You home already?"

"Yes. I worked the early shift." I sit on the edge of the other recliner. "Where's Irene?"

"She's with her mother at a doctor's appointment. She'll be back later. Byron's asleep."

I haven't had a lot of time alone with my dad since I've been back. "How are you feeling?"

"Okay." He coughs, his hand barely reaching his mouth to cover it. "Just tired."

On his TV tray, his sandwich sits. One half has a few bites taken out of it. The bright orange cheese is starting to dry at the edges.

"You want me to get you some chips or cookies? Byron's got sugar cookies he bought for Ashlyn in the kitchen." I should've brought him something from the café, but I wasn't thinking. Tomorrow. Anything to tempt him to eat.

He shakes his head and reaches a trembling hand to grasp the beer can that sits next to his half-finished meal. "Would you get me another, please?"

I sigh and stand. "All right."

When I return, pop top dutifully lifted, he reaches and takes the can and brings it quickly to his lips. I sit back down in Irene's chair. After a long pull on his beer, my dad sets the can down. He reaches out a thin hand and pats my arm.

"Are you all right, Esmé? I worry about you."

"Why?" My gaze finds his, the dark eyes so like Byron's. "Yes, Dad. I'm fine. Please, don't worry about me."

"I'm glad you're home."

"Me too."

His chest starts to heave under his flannel shirt. "I'm so sorry."

"For what?"

"Everything. Your mother."

"What about Mom?" I hear a car outside.

Dad draws a quavering breath, snuffles.

"It wasn't your fault," I say. Is he still this broken up about Mom's death? Maybe it's me being home, a constant reminder of that awful night. But I need to ask him, maybe for the last time about the man. "Dad?" His eyes slowly shift in my direction. "*Was* there a man? After the accident?"

My father shakes his head, digs in his pocket for a wad of tissues.

"Esmé!" Irene stands across the room, her girth filling the doorway. "What's wrong? What did you say?"

I jump to my feet. "Nothing. And it's none of your business."

"I'm all right, Irene," my dad says. "It's okay."

I march past her and head into the kitchen. I hear her mumble something, and the volume of the TV goes up. I'm pacing the kitchen, my arms crossed over my chest. Irene approaches, drops her big purse on the table.

"What did you say to him?"

"Nothing. Like I said, and it's none of your fucking business."

"Why is he so upset?"

"He started talking about my mother. I didn't bring her up, he did. He still mourns for her, Irene."

She smirks. "Right. Your precious mother." Her voice is filled with derision.

"My mother was a wonderful woman. She was your friend!" I want to say, *Why are you trying to take her place?* But I bite my lips.

"Just don't bring her up to your father, okay?"

"Like I said, he brought her up. Maybe if people had been a little more understanding, he wouldn't have gotten into this state to begin with." My mind goes back to my teenage years, right after Mom's death. I'd turned to my friends, stayed away from the house. I'm just as much at fault as anybody, maybe more so. Did I blame Dad for the accident? I never thought so, but did he feel that? Think that? Have I created this mess? I cross my arms over my chest.

Irene snorts. "Tom has no reason to mourn Jennifer. It was an accident. And she didn't deserve him in the first place."

"What do you mean by that?"

"Just what I said. Tom is a kind, decent man, and your mother . . ." she shakes her head.

"My mother was a good woman, a good person."

Irene's eyes meet mine, her mouth thins, and she nearly laughs. "Your mother was a *slut!*"

I gulp, step back. "How dare you . . ." I can hardly catch my breath. "How dare you say something so hateful?" But Irene's gone. Back in the living room with my dad, a fresh can of beer in her hand. I want to chase her and snatch the hair right off her head. How dare she? But I know I can't. Dad's a mess, and that won't help.

I walk to the foyer, slip my arms into my jacket, and head outside. The air is cool on my blazing cheeks. I wipe tears from my face as I head around the house toward the path. I don't know what to do. I want to throw Irene into the street and tell her to never come back, but I can't. It's my father's house, and while he's not well, he's not incompetent either, not yet.

The trees are bright yellow and deep crimson, a beautiful palette that contrasts with my dark mood. My feet move almost as if on their own, the walk to the pond part of my muscle memory. I stop. What if Ray's out there? I proceed slowly, peering through the trees. The breeze flutters the branches as I near the pond. The coast is clear, no Ray, just his old lawn chair sitting on the shore like a rotting throne.

I walk to the log where I'd sat a thousand times, sometimes alone, sometimes with friends, as a child enjoying the outdoors and as a teenager looking to escape. But who am I now? Not that blissfully happy child. Not that shattered teenager whose mom had died and left her. I take a deep breath of damp air, the smell of fall decay in the air, and wipe my cheeks.

I hear dogs yipping in the distance. I stand, bent on flight. My hip clicks, and pain radiates down my leg. I want to be alone.

"Esmé? Is that you, my dear?"

A familiar voice calls over my shoulder. Mr. York. He looks older, grayer, but still the neatly attired gentleman.

"Yes. Hi, Mr. York. How are you?"

Three little dogs circle him as he comes to a halt.

"I'm well, thank you. I heard you were back. I was hoping you'd come pay me a visit."

"I was going to. I've just been so busy and . . ."

He bows his head. "Ah, yes. Kara. I was so sorry to hear what happened." He reaches down and pulls a stick from the mouth of a white fluffy dog. "I was attempting to walk the girls last Wednesday when the police stopped me and told me what happened."

"It's been so hard. I'd lost touch with her. With almost everybody. I still can't believe it."

Mr. York walks closer until he's right in front of me. "I'm so sorry, my dear. Is there anything I can do?"

I shake my head. "No. Really." I wipe my cheeks. Smile. "You're still living in your big house then?"

"Oh yes."

When I was young, my mom and I would visit Mr. York regularly. My mom enjoyed his company and all his stories of New York and Hollywood. I remember his beautiful house with the high ceilings and, of course, the costumes.

"Are you sure you're all right?" he asks again.

I draw a deep breath. "Yes. It's just that my dad isn't well, and Irene Musgrave has taken over my house and him."

He makes a face. "That dreadful woman? She's still around?"

I laugh. "Unfortunately."

Mr. York swipes at his nose with a handkerchief. "Would you like to come back to the house? I've just made tea and left it to steep while we had our walk."

I clear my throat. I don't want to go home. "Yes. I'd like that."

Mr. York's big house is just as I remember it. We sit in his parlor, a tea service on the table between us.

"I remember when my mom and I would come to visit."

"Your mother," he sets his cup on an end table. "What a lovely woman."

"She was, wasn't she?" I can see her sitting here on the sofa, laughing as Mr. York detailed getting stuck in an elevator in New York with a ventriloquist, who, for the three hours they were stranded, insisted on talking only through his dummy. She'd loved his stories, as if they'd lifted her out of the drudgery of her own life and unfulfilled dreams.

"Such a shame that you lost her so young."

I nod, sip my tea, sniff back the tears that threaten.

"She modeled for me, did you know that?" Mr. York's dark eyes find mine.

"No. Really?"

"She did. A time or two. She was so lovely—tall, though. Too tall for ballet, she once told me. She'd wanted to dance." He points at me like a schoolmaster. "That's why she was so keen on your career."

"I just wish she'd seen me dance professionally."

"She was so proud of you. I know she enjoyed your performances at school. And *The Nutcracker*. That counts, doesn't it?"

When I was young, several years running, I got parts in the professional performance downtown. Every year, they auditioned children for the holiday classic. My mother had been thrilled.

"Yes. I guess it does."

"You were magnificent. Are you home for a visit?"

"No." I sigh. "Here to stay. I'm not dancing anymore."

"I'm so sorry to hear that." He leans back, sips his tea. "But I'm glad you're back."

With one hand, he moves the pug off his lap and prevents one of the fluffy dogs from trying to take its place. "What are your plans?"

I shrug. "Right now, I'm working at André's Café. But long-term, I don't know yet."

"Maybe we could help each other." He sets his cup back on the table. "I'm looking for a new model. Someone who will wear the costumes while I photograph them for clients."

"You're still working then?"

"Busier than ever. And"—he jumps up—"let me show you the designs I'm working on." He walks into the dining room. I remember that was where he worked on the costumes. He returns with a sketchbook, flips it open, and sits next to me. "It's a film set in New York City. Early nineteen sixties." The drawings show a woman in a full skirt, gloves on her hands, and a small hat perched on her head. Another woman is depicted in a filmy nightgown.

"They're lovely," I say, thinking how wonderful it would be to pursue your career for so many years.

"Thank you. I'd pay you, of course. Would you be interested, Esmé?"

My eyes sweep over the sketchbook as Mr. York turns the pages, revealing one beautiful costume after another. "I'd love to do it."

# CHAPTER 33
# Rita

BACK AT THE STATION, I SETTLE BEHIND MY DESK AND GO THROUGH my messages. Chase wanders in and sits.

"I've spent all morning reading about the illustrious Mr. York."

"And?"

"He's a well-respected costume designer. Works regularly. A little eccentric, but a perfectionist. He's been in the business since he was twenty-two. Got all kinds of awards."

"Eccentric? Even in that line of business?" I didn't think there were too many movie and stage types who weren't, but what do I know? "What about his personal life?"

"One brief marriage when he was in his twenties. In the interviews I dug up, when asked about that, he said he was too involved in his career to have time for a wife."

"Anything criminal in his background?"

Chase shakes his head. "Nothing that I could find."

I stretch back in my chair. "You should see his place. Big Victorian, full of antiques. Reminds me of a horror show my brothers and I used to watch when we were kids. There was this big old house we called the monster mansion." I sit up. "Anyway, York's got fabric all over the dining room next to his sewing machine. Upstairs on the third floor is where he does the videos and takes pictures. You should see it."

"Yeah?"

"He's got a whole stage set up in the attic. Lights, dressing room full of costumes, and a taping room."

Chase leans back, blows out a breath. "Really?"

"The works."

"Well, I guess that goes along with his reputation for detail."

"I guess. I thought it was kind of creepy. The stage area is painted all black. No exterior windows. Or if there were, they've been painted over."

"See anything related to Kara?"

"Nope. He's got photos and video he's going to send over. He still claims he hasn't seen her since August when they finished his last project. He did say she'd become unreliable."

"Maybe the oxy then."

"Could be."

"You really think Ridley might be dealing?"

"His place was pretty busy when we were there. I've got Lauren and Doug looking into his activities." Chase's brief, and unofficial, search of Ray's house hadn't revealed anything, but he hadn't gotten much beyond the bathroom. "Anything from the lab?"

"Nope. Not this morning." Chase glances at his phone. "Or afternoon. You want me to call them?"

"Yeah. Can't hurt."

I take a deep breath. Something needs to pop.

Evening sets in chilly. The day's warm teasing of Indian summer has evaporated with the sunset. After I tidy my desk and pack my satchel, the chief and I head across the street to Mac's Bar and Grill.

The place is nearly empty on a Tuesday evening. By now, most of Graybridge's hardworking residents are nestled in at home, enjoying a bit of family time. Mac waves as we walk in. He's involved in a lively conversation about football with a man at the bar who's hunched over his draft. Mac is a great big guy who played a couple of seasons in the NFL a hundred years ago. But now he spends his time dispensing drinks and watching over his busy kitchen, putting up with spent cops who walk across the street to blow off steam at the end of their shifts.

Bob and I take a seat in a corner booth. A middle-aged waitress, who must be new (I don't recognize her), quickly walks over. She takes our orders and heads into the kitchen.

"How's Kara's mom?" I ask, not sure I want to hear the answer.

"Not good, Rita. I went to the service yesterday." Bob grabs his beer as soon as it hits the table and takes a big sip.

"You didn't tell her about the pills in Kara's purse?"

"No. Like we agreed, we'll wait until the tox report comes in. Maybe the pills were old, from last year, when her mom said she hurt her back."

"Maybe." But the vial was unmarked. A red flag. But I let it go. Bob's been down enough about this case without me adding to it. And Mrs. Cunningham can be spared until we get something concrete to tell her that her daughter was abusing narcotics.

"How's your grandson?" I ask. Bob can use some cheering up.

He smiles under his gray, bushy mustache. "He made varsity this year. Running back."

"Good deal. You'll have to give me his schedule so I can catch a few games." I sip my wine, a nice merlot. I have to give Mac credit, for a little restaurant/bar, he stocks decent wine.

Bob nods. Then his face falls. "If I retire, Rita, and head down to Florida, I'll miss Clayton and my daughter."

"You don't have to decide right now. No one's pushing you out." And that's the truth. Bob Murphy is a well-respected and much-beloved Graybridge institution. Not to mention that the position of deputy chief has been vacant for a while, making Bob even less expendable.

Our food arrives. Cheeseburger and fries for both of us. Not a great choice, as I've been eating junk all day. Oh well, I'll do better tomorrow.

# CHAPTER 34
# Esmé

MR. YORK OPENS HIS BIG FRONT DOOR. DUSK IS FALLING. I HESItate on the threshold.

"Would you like me to drive you home, Esmé?"

"No. It's okay. It's not that late." I head down the porch steps and around the house. Time got away from me as Mr. York and I talked. It was soothing to hear good things about my mother, to sit and sip tea without worrying about running into Irene or sniping with my brother.

Now I'm headed through the woods, paths I've walked a thousand times, but things are different. I'm alone in the chilly evening air, and a murderer walked these same woods barely a week ago. I start to run, the ends of tree branches slapping against my jacket. I reach the pond and skirt the shore, making my way toward the path to my house. The water laps the bank, and I steal a look at its dark depths and shiver.

There's a rustling to my right, and my heart starts to hammer. A figure steps out in front of me, and I skid to a stop, let out a scream before I recognize her. I rest a hand on my hip and catch my breath.

"Cynthia?" She stands before me in a long dark coat, but her white hair gives her away. I haven't seen her in years, but her thin figure and pinched, childlike face are relatively unchanged.

"Esmé?" Her dark eyes are unblinking in the shadows.

"Um," I stutter, "when did you get back?" My mind turns to the last time I saw her. She was thirteen, and I was nine. She was hiding in the shack, watching me and my friends playing by the pond. Then, a week later, she killed her sister. Killed Wendy by hitting her with an oar and knocking her out of the boat; she drowned in the pond. I had no idea that she was out of prison or the hospital or wherever they had taken her. I rack my brain to try to remember what my mother had said about her, where she had gone. All I knew then was that it was strange Cynthia wasn't here anymore. She was someplace where she couldn't hurt the rest of us. But now she's standing right in front of me. Grown-up. It hadn't occurred to me that one day she might be back.

"What are you doing out here?" I ask.

"Nothing. You should be careful, Esmé. Someone killed Kara."

"Yes. I know." I can't stop shaking and clutch my arms across my chest. "Neither of us should be out here. Are you living back home?" I ask.

"Yes. My mother went to Florida, and my father doesn't live here anymore."

In my most vivid memory of Mr. Ridley, he's standing on the shore, across the pond. Thick dark hair cut in a mullet, flannel shirt and cowboy boots, his eyes hidden beneath mirrored sunglasses. Ramblin' Ray. That was his DJ name. We were all a little in awe of the fact that Ray's dad was on the radio. But we rarely saw him. Then, after Wendy died and Cynthia was taken away, he packed his bags and left. Only skinny, chain-smoking Mrs. Ridley and a young Ray were left at the house.

I wonder if Detective Myers knows that Cynthia is home. I wonder if she's been questioned. Could she have killed Kara? The thought has me trembling. I glance over Cynthia's shoulder to where the trees part, where the path starts to my house. The sounds of frogs thrum from the edges of the pond in a sinister chorus. "I better get going, Cynthia," I say, stepping around her.

"Bye, Esmé," she says, as I run for home.

# CHAPTER 35
# Esmé

I WOKE UP THIS MORNING FUZZY-HEADED WITH TATTERED DREAMS STILL stuck in my brain. The woods, dark and humming with menacing noises, and Cynthia haunting the pond's edge like a forlorn ghost.

I arrived at the café feeling like someone recovering from the flu. Collin wasn't in today. It's just been me and Margo. The lunch crowd kept us hopping as usual, and before I know it, it's nearly four o'clock.

I finish up my shift feeling lost and unsettled. When I clock out and come out of the break room, slipping my arms into my coat, Jack is sitting at a table sipping a coffee.

"Hey, Esmé." He waves his arm overhead like a kid in a classroom. "You finished for the day?"

"Yes. I was getting ready to head home."

"You have time to keep me company while I finish this amazing coffee?" I notice a pile of papers covered in messy teenage writing sitting next to his mug.

I chuckle. "Sure." I plop down across from him.

"How are things?" he asks, his auburn hair windblown, making him look like the teenager he was back in the day.

"Okay. Nothing new, I guess."

"Nothing about the investigation?" he asks quietly.

"No. I don't think they've come up with anything. But I hope they will soon, for Mrs. Cunningham's sake." She certainly looked bad at the funeral.

Cold air gushes past us as the door opens. Christy, wearing an eggplant-hued coat and white scarf, walks in. Her eyes scan the menu board over the counter a second before settling on Jack and me.

"Hey, you two."

"You knock off early?" Jack says jovially.

"Yes. It's been a day."

"Join us for coffee?"

"I just might have to do that. Don't run off." She shakes her finger at us.

Freezing rain starts to ping the plate-glass window. Clouds have been darkening all afternoon. Christy sits with her steaming coffee, removes her gloves, and stashes them in her purse.

"It's like winter today," she says.

"Typical Massachusetts weather," Jack says. "Wait five minutes."

"Ugh, I hate when summer ends. This time of year, all I want to do is book a Caribbean vacation."

It occurs to me that Christy can do that any time she likes, while I can't afford a car trip to the Cape. I'm not envious exactly, just feeling the depths of my failure to have a post-dance plan, again. What was I thinking? I wasn't, I guess.

"Anyway," Christy says. "That'll have to wait until business dies down a bit. What's new?" Her blue-green eyes turn on Jack.

"Just toiling away at old Graybridge High," he replies, patting the stack of papers. "You?"

"Busy every minute." She turns toward me. "Just get off your shift?"

"Yes. Headed home in a minute." I glance out the front window to where the grassy lawn of Graybridge Square lies empty of people on this dark, blustery day. "Did you guys know that Cynthia Ridley was back?"

Christy's eyes widen over the rim of her mug. *"What?"*

"Cynthia. I ran into her in the woods yesterday."

Christy sets her cup down. "You're kidding, right? I didn't hear anything about it. I thought she was gone for good."

Jack takes a deep breath. "It stands to reason. She was convicted as a juvenile. She wouldn't have had to serve a life sentence or anything."

Christy shudders. "Well, that's creepy as hell. So, I guess she's back living with Ray then if you saw her in the woods."

"Yes. That's what she said."

Jack rubs his chin. "Maybe Cynthia."

I turn to him. "That's what I was wondering. I meant to call Detective Myers before I came in today to see if she's talked to her. I asked Byron this morning, but he had no idea that Cynthia was back either."

"I'd call her, Esmé," Christy says, her eyes on her coffee. "Who knows? Maybe Cynthia is back to her old ways."

Silence fills the café, except for the light strains of Prokofiev in the background.

Christy taps a manicured fingernail against the table, her eyebrows drawn together. "Anyway," she clears her throat, "I had a thought. I invited a few friends from work to my place on Friday for drinks. Why don't you guys come? I'll call Laney too."

"A party?" I say. It seems a little too soon after Kara.

"I know the timing isn't great, but I've had this on the calendar since, well, before. I always host a quarterly business get-together."

"If it's work-related, why do you want us there?" I ask.

"To break up the monotony. We really talk very little business. It's mostly social." She glances at Jack. "And I think we all could use a lift. I know I need it." She sighs. "It would really be great if you guys could come."

I have nothing else to do, that's for sure. Anything to get out of the house.

Jack asks, "What do you say, Esmé? I can pick you up; that way you won't have to drive." I'd told him about my harrowing ride home from his place after our spaghetti dinner.

"Sure. That sounds fun, Christy."

"Great." She jumps up, swings her purse over her shoulder. "See you two on Friday."

# CHAPTER 36
# Rita

It's been another frustrating day. It seems all I got done was paperwork and a few calls on my other cases. My radio on my windowsill is playing an old Neil Young ballad, one you rarely hear anymore. I listen as my tired brain drifts.

"Rita?" Lauren jars me back to earth. I jump up, kill the radio.

"Yeah. What?"

Lauren closes my door and sits in the chair across from my desk. I plant myself back in my seat. "What's up?"

"Geno Lewis was just arrested."

"Again? Okay." He's one of our regulars. But something's up. Lauren's brown eyes are actually twinkling.

"He was caught trying to sell a stash of oxy in the parking lot of the Elm Tree Tavern." Probably the shabbiest and least reputable establishment in Graybridge. "The owner called in about a suspicious person lurking outside. Uniforms made the arrest." She leans back, folds her hands together. "He's looking at real time this go-round."

"And?"

"He says he bought the pills from Ray Ridley."

The chief calls us into the conference room to discuss the Lewis arrest. It looks like my suspicions were correct. Ray's dealing, and that might explain why Kara was in the woods that night with a full bottle of pills in her purse. But why would Ray kill her?

Bob seems reinvigorated by this development, and there's a little fire in his eyes. He points a finger at Doug. "I want you on Ridley. Let Rita concentrate on finding Kara's killer. I want you doing whatever it takes to shut Ridley down and build a case against him for dealing."

Doug sits up straight, nods. "What if it turns out Ridley is Kara's killer?"

Bob wipes his massive hand over his mouth. "You two work together where it makes sense. But I want this guy. I don't want this shit in our town."

I hate to remind Bob that it's everywhere, our modern-day plague. A monster so insidious that every jurisdiction is chasing it and ending up in the same place, like the red queen. But you have to go after the dealers. Too many people are dying, even if it is like playing Whac-a-Mole.

Doug sticks his notebook in his pocket. "I'll have a couple of the guys tail him and see if we can catch him in the act."

Bob nods. "Get right on it. Like today. Before he gets wind that Lewis has been arrested."

My apartment is cold and dark, and I feel the same way. I'm frustrated over the Cunningham case, but maybe something will turn up now that we've got a bead on Ray Ridley. I flip on the lights, unlace my boots, and stick my feet into my slippers. I pour myself a glass of wine and collapse on the couch. I don't even have the energy to hunt for the remote to turn on the TV.

There's a knock on my door. *Please not Mrs. Antonelli,* I whisper under my breath.

"Rita?" It's Collin, thank God. "I've got food."

I pull myself to standing and let him in. He hands me a Tupperware.

"You're an angel," I say.

He folds his arms. "You're really late tonight."

"Tough case," I say, prying up the lid of the container. "Eggplant parm?" I'm nearly crying with happiness.

"Your favorite. André and I have a big catering job this weekend, and we've been trying out recipes all day. One of them called for eggplant, so I whipped this up on the side."

"You're too good to me." I walk into my little kitchen. "I'll throw this in the microwave. Can I get you a glass of wine?" I call over my shoulder.

"Love one."

When I return to the living room and hand Collin his drink, he's made himself comfortable in my armchair, his feet on the ottoman.

"So, what's this big job?" I ask.

"A private party at Wilbur Banks's house. Beacon Hill."

"Ooh, fancy, the senator's father? That should be some shindig."

He rolls his eyes. "Yes, and we've got so much work to do before the event. You should see the menu they came up with. And, of course, we've got one vegan, two gluten-frees, and a shrimp allergy, plus sixteen other people."

I can't help but laugh. "Didn't realize catering's gotten so complicated. Back in my day, you got what you got. If you had a problem, it was *your* problem."

"Not anymore." Collin sighs. "But it'll be fine. It'll be lovely. I'm looking forward to seeing the house. I hear it's gorgeous. And, hopefully, we'll get some nice referrals out of it. He's invited some Boston bigwigs."

Collin sips his wine, and I notice a dusting of flour in his dark hair. That makes me smile. He's always so fastidious. He must've had a rough day.

"Oh, I meant to tell you." He sets his wine on the coffee table. "I hired Esmé Foster at the café last week. She told me that murdered girl was found in her backyard."

"That's right."

"Poor thing. She's really sweet. Have you found the killer yet?"

"Not yet." I blow out a frustrated breath.

"But that's why you've been so late this week."

"Yup." The microwave chimes. I take a big sip of my wine and head into the kitchen. "Be right back."

The parm smells amazing, and I grab a fork to eat it right out of the container. My fast-food lunch was hours ago, long since metabolized, the energy long gone.

Collin looks up as I make my way to the couch. "She isn't in any danger, is she?"

"Miss Foster?"

"Yes."

"We don't have any reason to think so." But we don't have any reason as to why her friend was killed either, which just makes my insides jittery, thinking about the lack of motive. I take a bite and let the cheese and sauce melt on my tongue. I close my eyes. "I'm in heaven," I mutter.

"You need to take care of yourself, Rita. You're not twenty-something anymore."

"You can say that again." I said goodbye to twenty forty years ago. That thought has me nearly choking on my eggplant. I sit up, run my hand through my dark hair, which I've kept long and colored.

Collin leans toward me, lowers his voice. "I was talking to Mrs. Antonelli a while ago. She thinks you're late forties, early fifties."

I chuckle. "Really?"

"That's what she said." He raises his hand. "Honest to God."

"Huh." Well, I do make an effort. I glance over at my exercise bike in the corner, wonder if I've got the energy to get on it later. Probably should, after all the junk I've eaten this week.

"Has Miss Foster talked much about her friend's murder?"

Collin finishes his wine. "Not really. She's sad about it, of course. They hadn't kept in touch, but she still feels awful."

"Let me know, would you, if she says anything that strikes you as important or interesting?"

He smiles. "I could be like an informant."

Collin has a way of making me laugh. "Yeah. Something like that."

# CHAPTER 37
# Esmé

THURSDAY MORNING, I STAND ON A LITTLE STOOL WHILE MR. YORK, pincushion attached to his wrist, pinches fabric and makes adjustments to a blue poplin skirt. My hair is up in a bun, to be out of the way, and he tugs a small hat over it. He stands back, crosses his arms, then reaches over and flattens the Peter Pan collar.

"Lovely, like a young Audrey Hepburn."

I smile inwardly, standing still, erect posture. "Is that what you're going for?" I ask.

"Absolutely. Perfect. Now, go ahead and get dressed, and I'll take in the waist."

I feel something like a spark in my stomach as I walk to the bathroom adjacent to the dining room. This feels good, right. To be back in costume, playing make-believe. Being creative. I slip the skirt down and step out of it.

"Hand it to me, Esmé," Mr. York says.

I open the door a crack and hold out the skirt. He whisks it away, and I finish dressing, getting back into my jeans and top, my café attire.

I hear the whirring of the sewing machine as I walk back into the dining room. Mr. York's head is bent over the bobbing needle with the intensity of a rocket scientist. He finishes the seam, stops the machine, and looks up.

"Leaving already, my dear?"

"Yes. I need to get to work."

"No time for a cup of tea?"

"I'm afraid not. But tomorrow maybe."

"Splendid. I think we need one more fitting for this outfit, so maybe we'll get upstairs to take pictures and film tomorrow afterward."

He told me about his stage on the third floor, and I'm anxious to see it. I wonder if it's always been there. I don't remember seeing it when I was a kid. Maybe we just never went up there. I pick up my purse from a chair in the corner. "Do you have pictures of my mother from when she modeled for you?" I ask, the idea suddenly dawning on me. Mr. York pushes away from the table and crosses his legs.

"I do indeed. I keep copies of all my work." He puts a hand to his forehead. "Let me think, though, when those would've been taken. It was for costumes I was doing for a film set in Roman times, I believe, if memory serves."

The thought of my mother in Roman dress paints a beautiful picture in my mind. Why didn't I know about this? I wonder what else I don't know about her. A dreadful thought passes through my brain.

"Mr. York?"

"Yes?"

"Were men interested in my mother?" I know that sounds weird, but I don't know how else to put it.

He clasps his chin. "Well, Jennifer did have admirers, if that's what you mean. When you're as lovely as she was, it stands to reason. Why?"

"Nothing. Just something somebody said."

He stands and walks me to the front door. "Your mother was beautiful inside and out. There are some people in this town who were jealous. Remember that."

# CHAPTER 38
# Rita

After a quick lunch on the square, I settle back at my desk. Danny's big dinner date is tonight. I sigh. Well, I've got a lot of work to do before then. Doug raps on my door frame. I noticed a spring in his step this morning when I came in. He's finally got a case that has him feeling like the big deal he thinks he is. Doesn't matter as long as he gets Ridley.

"What's up?" I ask, looking up from my computer.

"Nothing yet, but I've got Connors and Reyes in an unmarked vehicle following Ridley."

Connors is one of the best. An experienced cop and single mother of four. Reyes is a rookie but one with promise. "They got anything yet?"

"Not yet. But we will."

"Good deal. Keep me updated."

Doug starts to leave, turns back around. "Keep me in the loop, Rita, about Kara."

"Sure thing. Hey, we're in this together."

He nods and goes on his way. Doug Schmitt and I are like the proverbial oil and water. He has his ways, dresses for success like some TV detective, and I've got mine, practical, don't mind getting my hands or my boots dirty. He's by the book, and I'm sometimes more . . . creative. But, hell, there's nothing wrong with that. There's room for both of us.

Danny wanted to meet at Concetta's downtown, his favorite restaurant when he wants to impress somebody. I left right from the station after a quick trip to the ladies' room to brush my hair and touch up my makeup. I don't have time to run home and change my clothes, so I'm wearing what he calls my detective uniform, white button-up collared shirt and dark pants. It'll have to do.

I fight Boston traffic, glad as always that I don't work down here anymore, and find a spot in the small parking lot next to the restaurant. Danny's Mercedes has just pulled in, and he parks next to me. My van looks like an eyesore next to his vehicle. He and Charlotte jump out.

My niece is petite and blond, like her mother and like every girlfriend Danny has had since his divorce nearly twenty years ago. Danny is wearing a dark suit and a violet tie, looks like the dapper professor, as usual. Charlotte is more casual, which is her style, black turtleneck and dressy jeans.

"Hi, Aunt Rita," she calls as they circle my van.

"Nice to see you, honey. It's been a while."

She looks suddenly contrite. Charlotte has a big-time serious side. "I've been really busy, but let's plan something."

"Yes." I clasp her arm. "When you're free, we'll do something fun." I turn to Danny. "So, where is Vivian?"

"Vivi*enne*. She's coming. She had a meeting downtown." We all instinctively turn toward the street just as a silver Jag pulls in. "Here she is now." We watch as Vivienne looks for a spot. She waves as she drives past us to the back of the lot. Danny walks quickly after her.

"Thanks for being here," Charlotte says when we're alone.

"You met her yet?"

She rolls her eyes. "Yeah. I stopped by Dad's house Sunday to pick up some files I'd left over there. He didn't know I was coming, and she was there. It was super awkward. They'd had a few drinks. I only stayed about ten minutes."

"Sorry, kid."

She pushes her long, straight hair behind her ears. "I'm used to it." She blows out a breath. "I thought she was pretentious. Really full of herself."

My feelings exactly, but I don't say so. "Maybe if we get to know her a little."

Charlotte gives me a look like, yeah, right. "I really liked Sandra." Danny's last girlfriend. "But, of course, she was too nice to last."

"This one may not last either."

"We'll see."

Danny motions to us to follow them into the restaurant.

Our table is tucked away in a little alcove, and we get settled with drinks. Charlotte ordered a sparkling water, and I ordered a glass of red wine, but it's whiskey for Danny and Viv. She's all dressed up in a silk blouse and skirt, classic black pumps on her feet.

"I'm so glad you could join us, Rita," she says, smiling.

"Yeah. Nice to see you again, Vivienne."

"And Charlotte. I've been looking forward to spending more time with you."

Danny is smiling like the Cheshire cat. He grasps Charlotte's hand. "I don't get to see her nearly enough either."

I've been perusing the menu; it's all in Italian, of course, but I've picked up enough to figure it out, mostly. Danny and Viv talk about academia, totally lost in each other until Danny remembers himself.

"How's that big case going, Rita?" I fill him in as much as I can. Vivienne can't help but drop her jaw and open her eyes wide as I detail murder and mayhem. Danny clears his throat. "Better you than me. Anyway, Char. What are you going to order?"

The waiter, in white shirt and bow tie, comes over and recites the day's special, something about fish, which Danny and Viv both order. Charlotte decides on cannelloni del mar, and I stick with the eggplant parm, but I know it won't be as good as Collin's.

Charlotte rises. "I've got to run to the restroom." She walks toward the lobby, and Danny and Viv resume their work conversation.

I fumble with my satchel, take out my phone. "I got a text from the station. I'll be right back." They barely notice as I head into the lobby and turn into the ladies' room.

Charlotte is washing her hands. She glances at the door and whispers, "See?"

"Yeah. I know. When we get back to the table, ask me if I've started my Christmas shopping yet."

Charlotte furrows her brow. "It's October. You never start your shopping until two days before Christmas."

"Yeah. I know. Just ask."

She shrugs. "Okay." We exchange a smile in the mirror.

Our salads are waiting when I return a couple minutes after Charlotte.

"So, Aunt Rita, started your Christmas shopping yet?"

Danny's instantly on alert. He knows me too well. "Not yet, but I'll call you, and maybe we can spend some time together at the mall."

"That would be nice."

"Speaking of Christmas, Danny." I point my fork at him. "Remember when we were kids and you asked Santa for a ukulele?"

"No. How's your salad, Charlotte?"

"Fine."

"Vivienne," I say, "you should've seen Danny on Christmas morning. He was so excited about that damn ukulele. He gave us all his best Tiny Tim impression."

"Who?"

"Tiny Tim. 'Tiptoe through the Tulips'?"

Vivienne looks at Danny. "From Dickens? *A Christmas Carol*?"

"No," I say, between bites of romaine. "Not that Tiny Tim. You don't remember the singer from the sixties?"

She smiles. "Afraid that was before my time."

"Right. Well," I pull out my phone, "Danny did a spot-on impression. Let me pull up YouTube."

"I don't think that's necessary, Rita," Danny says. That little vein in his temple is throbbing like it does when he's pissed.

Viv turns to him. "There's a video of you singing on YouTube?" She's dead serious.

"No," I say. "Now, that would be a hoot. Here it is." I turn my screen so she can see it. "This is the real Tiny Tim."

Danny sips his drink and blows out a breath. I can feel his eyes boring into me as Tiny Tim's warbling falsetto emanates from my phone.

When a man at the next table turns around, Danny whispers, "Come on, Rita, I don't think this is the place for that."

"Oh, all right." I put my phone away and glance at Charlotte. She's trying not to laugh.

Over dessert, Danny catches my gaze. Here it comes. Payback. "So, Rita, I guess Joe turned you down for dinner. Maybe next time. I know Vivienne would be delighted to meet him."

I feel the heat rise to my face. "He was busy."

"Who's Joe?" Viv asks.

"Rita's sometime boyfriend. Or have you sent him packing, like all the others?"

He's a fine one to talk. "Joe and I still see each other when we can."

Danny looks at Viv. "He works for the FBI. Rita says they've been seeing one another off and on for several years. I don't know why she keeps him such a secret. I've only met him once. And that was for a quick drink at some Graybridge tavern." Danny sighs like I'm the biggest loser he's ever met.

"We'll plan something," I say and jut out my chin like I used to when we were kids and Jimmy and Danny would challenge me to do something that I knew I shouldn't.

I behave myself for the rest of the meal, even when Vivienne says she'd love to meet the rest of the McMahons. I really want to give her a rundown on the rest of the clan, but Danny gives me the stink eye, and I keep my mouth shut.

Out in the parking lot, under a streetlight, we can see our breath as we say our goodbyes. Danny walks Vivienne to her car, and I brace myself for his return.

Charlotte giggles. "You think he's pissed?"

"Won't be the first time."

Danny's wearing his best I'm a big-deal, cultured professor face as he puts his arm around Charlotte's waist. "Thanks so much, honey. It means a lot to me that you get to know Vivienne. She's a really nice person, and she's so impressed with you."

"She's very nice, Dad."

Danny shifts his gaze to me. "Thanks, Rita. I know you're busy." His mouth starts to twitch, and we both burst out laughing. "You got me this time. Just wait."

"Oh, it's a sweet story. You were a perfect Tiny Tim."

"Well, I think Joe needs to hear about the boys' locker room story."

I fold my arms. "I don't think he'd be interested in that."

"Okay. I won't mention it. Maybe. I'm serious about getting together, though. Really, Rita. Bring Joe around sometime."

"Yeah. Maybe when this case is wrapped up."

Danny reaches in his pocket and hands Charlotte his keys. She smirks at me, and I nod. It was a fun evening; too bad Danny's had too many to drive home.

# CHAPTER 39
# Esmé

Friday morning, I'm at Mr. York's house. After a half hour of fussing and adjusting a seam, measuring the hem, Mr. York declares himself satisfied with the skirt and blouse costume.

"All right. Time for the camera. Follow me, Esmé."

"What about shoes?" I ask as we ascend the shining staircase.

"Upstairs in the costume room."

I follow Mr. York to the end of the second-story hall to a small set of stairs. At the top, he unlocks a door and flips on the lights, and we're standing on what looks like an actual stage.

"This is incredible," I say.

There's a screen in the middle of the room with a delicate, carved wooden chair in front of it. He has me stand, walk, sit briefly, but not long enough to wrinkle the skirt.

"Wait just a moment." He glances at my feet. "Size seven?"

"Yes."

"Be right back." A moment later, I'm wearing navy pumps, and Mr. York has a camera, snapping pictures and directing me like a photographer. *Turn, head this way, tilt your chin. Good.* I feel like a princess, a feeling that I haven't had in a very long time. As if I'm someone else. Someone whose father isn't dying, whose mother is alive and well. Whose friend isn't dead.

Mr. York lets the camera hang from a strap around his neck. "Wonderful." He takes a deep breath. "I'm going to go into the booth now, adjust the lighting, and I'll take some video."

"What do you want me to do?"

"I'll tell you. Just like you were used to with directors and choreographers. Just listen to my instructions."

After about thirty minutes, I'm actually getting tired. But it's sort of like dancing. The closest I've come to it in ages anyway. My hip snaps, and pain flares just enough to tell me not to get too excited.

Mr. York finally emerges. "Just beautiful, Esmé."

"Thank you. So"—I glance around the dark room; he's shut the stage lights down, and only a single bulb suspended overhead casts an eerie light—"my mother was up here?"

"Indeed she was. While you were at school, probably. We worked together, like I said, on that one project. She really enjoyed herself. A pity she was never able to pursue a career."

"Do you have pictures?"

He raises his index finger, a wait-a-second gesture. "Be right back."

Downstairs, Mr. York insists I stay for tea, and I make myself comfortable in the parlor. The dogs patter behind him as he comes in bearing a tray. "Now then, we'll relax after all our hard work." He pours us each a cup and hands me a blueberry scone on a napkin.

"Made them myself," he says.

I sip my tea, take a bite of pastry. "Do you have the pictures, Mr. York?"

"Oh, yes. Right here." He sets his cup on the coffee table and hands me a manila folder.

I gingerly open it and slide the glossy eight-by-tens out. I catch my breath.

"She was beautiful, wasn't she?" Mr. York says.

I nod. Tears fill my eyes. "I've never seen her like this."

He smiles. "Make-believe, my dear. Art. It can transform everyday life into something divine."

My mother's blond hair is pulled up and fastened with a jeweled headband, and earrings dangle nearly to her shoulders. One shoulder is bare, the other covered in a filmy white material and clasped with a large brooch. "She could have been a real model," I say. "Or an actress."

"Yes. She could have."

We finish our tea, and my mind is awhirl. Maybe just like my mother's was when she posed for Mr. York so long ago.

He sets his empty cup on the tray. "Now then. Let me show you my latest designs." He gets up and returns with a sketchbook. He smiles. "A friend of mine has been after me to collaborate with him for years. I've put him off, but now, Esmé, that you're home, I've been giving it some thought. Well, more than some thought."

"Why?"

He opens the sketchbook. There's a dancer, her face just barely drawn, ghostly. She's wearing a black lace bodice and a full red tutu.

"Ballet costumes?"

"Yes. Since we met the other day, I've been inspired. So I called my friend, and he was delighted. He filled me in on his next project, and I agreed to work up some designs."

My gaze meets Mr. York's. "What's the ballet?"

"*Carmen.* The ballet version, not the opera. Have you ever danced it?"

"No. But I saw a production once. It was amazing. The music is infectious." That's the only word I can think of to describe it.

"Yes. Full of passion and energy." He gazes at his sketch, runs a finger over it. "Kara wouldn't have done it justice," he says quietly.

"What?"

He swallows. "Kara had been modeling for me. I'm sure I mentioned that."

I shudder. "No. You didn't say anything."

"She modeled for me for years. She needed the money, and she was competent, if not stellar."

"You knew Kara? Knew her well?"

"I suppose so."

This is strange news to me, but Kara was certainly model-like. I can see her doing this.

"I was devastated to hear of her death, and so close by," Mr. York continues quickly. "I was in town the night she was killed. Have they made any progress in her case, do you know?"

"Not that they've told me." I feel a sense of sadness that I'm stepping into Kara's shoes. She had always wanted to be somebody whom others would admire. Her father's leaving when she was little seemed to affect her in a way that left her hungering for attention, feeling unworthy. She always seemed to be saying, "Look at me!" First, when she danced when we were little, then as a teenager, she was always trying out for plays at school. But after that, after graduation, I heard she got her degree locally and was working at an insurance agency. That must not have been very fulfilling for someone like her. Modeling for Mr. York must've been exciting.

Mr. York pats my knee. "Hopefully, they'll find the culprit soon." He closes his sketchbook and stands. The dogs circle and yap. "I think it's time for their walk."

# CHAPTER 40
# Esmé

Christy's house is lit up like a Christmas tree, shimmering in the darkness, and expensive cars are double-parked in the driveway. I'm not sure I'm ready for this. Jack seems buoyant, though, but he's always been sociable. He's never had the insecurities that have dogged me my whole life. Perhaps sensing my mood, he holds my elbow and steers me to the porch.

Christy greets us at the door. She's stunning as usual, a headful of tousled curls, sleek red lipstick.

"Hi, guys. I'm glad you finally got here!" She kisses us each on the cheek like we've run into each other on the Champs-Élysées instead of at her home in Graybridge, Massachusetts. She takes our coats and hands them off to a woman in a uniform who looks like she was hired for the event.

In the glittering living room, people lounge in small groups, drinking, chatting breathlessly, and I wonder if I'm underdressed. My eyes search for a familiar face. I see Laney coming out of the kitchen. Our eyes meet, and she makes her way over to us.

"Hey. Did you two come together?" Laney asks.

Christy appears at Jack's side. "Isn't he a gentleman? Didn't want Esmé to have to drive by herself."

"Yeah. Nice," Laney says. "Then you can drink all you want, enjoy yourself." Laney's face seems wistful as she sips her seltzer. "Nursing," she says and raises her glass.

I smile. The room feels too warm, and I get the impression that everyone, Laney excepted, has had a few drinks before we got here. Christy loops her arm through Jack's.

"Speaking of drinks, let's get you guys something."

Laney taps my shoulder. "I need to find Dylan. See you in a bit." She walks off to find her husband.

The kitchen is humming with guests holding small plates of finger foods. Wine bottles sit on the counter. And before I know it, Jack and I each have a drink in hand, and Christy is introducing us to her work friends.

Jack makes easy conversation, and I do my best to smile and nod, not really paying much attention to what's being said until Christy collars a man, handsome, fortyish.

"This is Esmé, the ballerina. Well, she used to be a ballerina," Christy says.

"That's not something you hear every day," the man says with a trace of an accent. Russian? I didn't get his name. Did Christy actually introduce us? He reminds me of someone. An actor in one of those espionage movies? But before I can say anything, Christy whisks us over to a group of three young women.

"This is my killer staff," she says, words slurring slightly. "These are the people who make my working life function."

The women, thin, stylishly dressed, makeup and hair perfect, smile. "We have an incredible boss," the brunette gushes and looks at the other two. "We wouldn't be where we are today without our illustrious leader."

Christy beams and swallows a sip of her cocktail. "We make a great team," she says and steers Jack and me on to the next group.

The evening goes by in a blur. Finally, just before midnight, Jack and I are standing back in the kitchen. "You ready, Esmé?"

"Yes. If you are. I just need to run to the restroom."

"I'll get our coats."

I wander down the hall, pass expensive artwork on the walls. Stop with a door on my right and left. Which one is the powder room? I can't remember what Christy said earlier. I choose the one on the right. The room is dark, and I shut the door behind me, feel for the light switch, and flick it on. I guess I chose wrong. I'm standing in what must be Christy's home office. There's a big, shiny desk dominating the room, with bookcases lining the wall behind it. On the opposite wall hang Christy's diplomas, each one attesting to Christy's many accomplishments. On shelves beneath them are other awards, plaques and trophies and knickknacks. I can't help but take a closer look. Christy was always an overachiever, collecting prizes as if to mark her position among us as number one. I pick up a cheerleader award from high school, and it makes me smile to think that she's held onto it for so long. But a tiny, tarnished trophy that sits on the bottom shelf is even older. It reads Student of the Year, Mrs. Tinker's Third Grade Class. I glance back up at the diplomas and sigh. What's my plan now that my dance career is behind me?

I remember that Jack is waiting for me, so I turn off the light and head across the hall.

When I return to the living room, Christy is talking to Jack.

"You guys really need to leave already?" she asks me when I join them.

"It was really lovely, Christy. Thank you for inviting me, but I probably should be on my way."

"Well, okay." She hugs me and whispers in my ear. "I'll call you." She smells of hairspray, sweat, and expensive perfume.

Out in the fresh air, I feel better, revived. I really don't want to go back to my house yet. Byron is at work. Dad is in bed.

Jack pulls into my driveway.

"You want to go for a walk?" I ask.

"Sure. Where?"

"Out to the pond?" With Jack, I won't be frightened. When we were teenagers, the boys always made the dark woods feel safe.

"Yeah. Okay." We get out of the car, and Jack turns on his phone's flashlight as we make our way around the house. I hurry past the spot where the trail starts, where Kara's body lay just over a week ago.

The temperature drops as we enter the woods. The scent of pine and rotting organic things fills the air. The skinny fingers of a nearly bare maple extend across the path. Something small rustles through the dead leaves off in the distance, and I huddle close to Jack.

"You sure about this?" he asks.

"Yeah. I don't feel like going inside yet, and besides, this was our place back in the day. We were out here every weekend."

"That we were." He holds his phone out to light the path in front of us, and we continue. An owl hoots off in the distance, and we laugh.

"I don't remember hearing all this wildlife back then, though, do you?"

"We were too caught up in ourselves. And we were so loud, I don't think the little creatures dared make a noise. The beer and music helped too."

We come out into the clearing and make our way over to the log and sit. Clouds cover the moon, so it's black as pitch. You can't even see the pond, but I hear it lapping against the shore with the breeze.

"You don't have any matches, do you?" I ask.

"No. Unfortunately. A fire would be nice. Are you cold?"

"A little." I walk my hand over the seamy bark of the log and bump into cold melted wax. "I wonder if Ray sits out here and reminisces. These candles must be relatively new."

"Yeah. Maybe."

"Remember that summer after graduation?"

"We had a good time, didn't we?"

"Yeah, but I was so anxious after I'd signed the contract with my company. The closer it got to leaving time, the more nervous I was."

"You were leaving home for the first time. I was a little nervous too. I was off to college in the fall. Three hours from home. We were kids."

"Did you like living away?"

"Yeah. I did. I had the perfect college experience. Learned a lot and had a good time without getting into too much trouble." He laughs.

"I wonder what my life would've been like if I'd gone to college instead of right to work." I draw a deep breath of the cold damp air. "I mean, I was really happy dancing. I just wonder if I was too young. Lots of dancers go to college first."

He doesn't say it, but I know what he's thinking. My grades were so bad. My head was nowhere in the right place to sit and study. College probably would've been a disaster for me.

"Well, you've got your whole life in front of you now."

The breeze tosses the tree branches and flutters the dying leaves. The pond shimmers as a stray beam of moonlight hits it and sets it alight before clouds snuff it out again. I think about the muck and the slimy toads that live in the reeds near the water's edge, and I remember when Ray held my head under water when I was eleven and how he laughed when he finally let me go. I sputtered and heaved as I came out of the water, dripping and muddy, scared shitless that Wendy's ghost would reach out of the dark water and grab me by my hair. That was the last time I'd actually been in the pond. I can't swim, and while Laney, Christy, Kara, and the boys, in the heat of summer, would jump in and swim the short distance to the other side, I'd stay put on shore.

"I just wish I knew what to do with my life, Jack. Since I've been home, I've felt so lost." I clear my throat.

He drapes an arm around my shoulders. "Hey, you've got plenty of time to figure it out. Give yourself a break. You've got a lot on your plate right now. Your dad's ill. And then . . ."

"Kara." I turn my face to look at Jack. "What was she doing out here? And who would've hurt her?" I sniff and look out across the pond. It's as if I can hear her childlike laugh on the breeze. Picture her in a bright yellow bikini, skin brown from the summer sun. The four of us girls lying on a blanket at water's edge, working on our tans.

"It's senseless. It really is," Jack says.

And I think about the last time we sat out here. We talked about our futures at summer's end. I was going to dance until I was forty, work toward being a soloist. Jack was considering how to turn his love of history into a career. Christy was going to be a big business executive, and Kara laughed, tossed her pretty head, and said she was going to marry a rich man. I sigh, and Jack squeezes my shoulders.

"Remember when Austin dumped that beer can full of water on Kara and Christy when they were sunbathing?" I say.

Jack chuckles. "Christy was so mad!"

I can still see her jumping up like a shot and going after Austin. She had an explosive temper, and poor Austin caught the worst of it that day. But Laney intervened, and soon we were back on an even keel, Christy mollified as Kara handed her a clean beach towel to dry off with. Christy was never one to appreciate a practical joke.

There's a noise in the distance, like someone stepped on a twig and snapped it underfoot. Too big to be a squirrel. Jack turns his head, and we listen. There's someone in the woods. Maybe it's Cynthia again.

Jack stands, whispers. "Wait here." He stashes his phone in his back pocket and quietly walks in the direction of the noise, toward the shack. Why did I want to come out here? I try to slow my breathing, which insists on coming out in loud gasps. I stand quietly, trying to see through the darkness.

Then I hear thrashing, a shout, and I take off toward the shack. Footsteps pound in the distance, rustling through the trees. I stop. My heart feels like it is hammering out of my chest. Where's Jack? But I don't dare call his name. Who knows who might answer?

I take off again and run blindly into the woods, desperate to get away, hide somewhere. I get turned around; branches slap against my face, but I keep running. I trip over a root and fall headfirst onto the forest floor. Dirt fills my mouth, and the scent of decay and wet clogs my nose. I push myself to sitting and rub my forehead where I'd hit something hard. Stones arranged in a line. It takes a few seconds, but my mind clears. I know where I am. Cynthia's pet cemetery.

When we were kids, she always had cats, and when they died, she'd bury them out here. Cynthia and Wendy. They seemed to belong to these woods. Maybe it was because their dad was always off working and their mom was seldom around. They were left to behave like wild children for the most part. Maybe Cynthia's out here in the woods with us now. But why the scream and the thrashing? Would she actually attack Jack? Would they have let her out if she was dangerous? I shiver and scramble to my feet.

I try to make my way back. I need to find Jack, but I'm totally disoriented in the dark. I hear a noise, turn, and step backward, my foot squishing into mud and sliding into frigid water. The pond. I've stepped backward into it. I try to free my foot as dark water closes over my ankle, but the other foot gets trapped as well, sinking into the muck. I choke out a sob as images of Wendy descending to the bottom fill my mind. I drop to my knees and churn my feet, water splashing, my fingers digging frantically into the icy mud, trying desperately to gain traction. I no longer care if there's a killer out here. I'm more frightened of being sucked into the deep water and into oblivion.

Then I feel a hand on my shoulder, and I freeze.

"Esmé?" he whispers.

I collapse on the mucky bank. "Jack?" Tears stream down my cheeks.

He grabs my hands, hauls me to my feet, and pulls me into his arms. "It's okay."

My heart starts to ratchet down. "What happened?" I mumble.

"There was a guy in the shack. But he's gone now. Are you all right?"

"Yes. I'm okay. It wasn't Cynthia, was it?"

"No. It was a man."

I try to catch my breath. "Who was it then? What was he doing here? Are you sure he's gone?"

"Yes. He ran up the path. The one that goes to the parking area." Jack swipes at his jaw. "I followed him for a little while, but then I was worried about you and came back."

"You're bleeding."

"He punched me. Just as I walked into the shack. I didn't even see it coming, and he decked me. And before I could come to my senses, he ran away." Jack lets go a deep breath. "I was afraid he was going after you, so I got up and followed him, but luckily he turned up the path in the other direction." Jack wipes his face on his sleeve.

"We need to get you to the hospital."

"I'm fine. I've had worse scrapes. It's just he took me by surprise in the dark. I didn't get in a swing."

"We need to report this to the police." I'm shivering, the cold night air settling into my bones.

"Yeah. Okay."

We head back down the path toward my house. Jack pulls me close to his side.

"What if that was the guy who killed Kara?" I say, my voice shaking. *What if it was my phantom?*

Jack doesn't respond, just hugs me tighter.

# CHAPTER 41
# Rita

Saturday morning. I'm supposed to be off this weekend, but too much is happening to sit at home. I'm still a little sleepy as I look over the report filed last night by Jack Crosby. Whenever I'm having trouble with a case, it shows in my sleep or lack thereof. Which just pisses me off because I need to be alert and energetic most of all when I'm struggling. I sip my coffee and lean back in my chair.

Lauren appears in my doorway. "Crazy, huh? That a man was out in those woods and that he would attack somebody." Lauren was in even earlier than I was, of course. She knew all about the incident before I'd even powered up my computer.

"Yeah." I drum my fingers on my desk. "And Mr. Crosby definitely identified his attacker as a man."

"Yes."

"So, it couldn't have been Cynthia."

"You think it might've been Ray?" Lauren asks.

"Maybe. But why? Why would he attack Mr. Crosby?"

Lauren shrugs. "Good question."

"Maybe it was one of Ray's customers, now that we know he's dealing."

"Maybe."

"And could the attacker also have killed Kara? What would connect them?"

"Doesn't seem like anything," Lauren says. "But what are the chances there would be two attacks in those woods in such a short time?"

"Yeah. That would be some coincidence." None of this makes sense.

"Did you get the results from Byron Foster's polygraph?"

"Just now," I say and blow out a breath. "Inconclusive."

"Great. That's no help."

"Nope. And he was at work last night. I talked to his supervisor, so he wasn't out in those woods."

"Who else could've been out there, Rita?"

I shrug. "Who knows."

"No way it could've been Mr. York?" Lauren asks.

"Doubt it. He doesn't seem the type to punch someone, and I think Mr. Crosby could've handled him pretty easily. Still, it's a mystery." A mystery amid a dozen others. I glance out the window. Another gray, chilly fall day.

Lauren heads back out to the squad room.

I fumble with my phone, scroll through my email. Nothing new. I can't seem to concentrate sitting here in my office, so I grab my jacket and head out.

# CHAPTER 42
# Esmé

I BARELY SLEPT ALL NIGHT, A BLOODIED JACK AND THE MAN IN THE woods running through my mind. Who could it have been? The man who killed Kara? My phantom? What if they are one and the same?

As tired as I am, I'm still glad I'm at work this morning. Maybe serving coffee and pastries will help me settle. Collin is off today, so it's just me and Margo. We've been slow. The morning, so far, is chilly and raw. But maybe it'll pick up as people get out to run their Saturday errands.

The bell tinkles, and Detective Myers walks in. Margo moves to the counter, while I refill the water in the coffee pot. I hear them behind me.

"Hi, Detective. What can I get you?"

"How about a decaf and an apple turnover?"

"You got it. I'll bring it over to you."

"Thanks." The detective lowers her voice. "Ask Ms. Foster to stop by my table a minute, would you, Margo?"

"Sure thing."

She takes a seat by the window and looks out on the square. Margo fixes her order and places it on a tray.

"I guess I'll take it over," I say.

Detective Myers attempts a smile as I place her cup and plate on the table. "Had a rough night, I hear."

"Yes." I know my weariness must show on my face.

"I read the report. You have a minute?"

"A few."

"Have a seat. How's Mr. Crosby? I read that he got the worst of it."

I drop into the chair across from her. "Yeah. Poor Jack." My heart thumps loudly as I think about what might've happened. Jack and I dead in the woods maybe.

"You have no idea who attacked him?"

"No. I never saw him, and Jack couldn't tell in the dark."

"Could it have been Ray Ridley?"

I blow out a breath. "Maybe."

"Did Ray know Kara?"

"Yeah. We used to all hang out when we were teenagers. Well, Ray really wasn't part of our group, but since he lived next door, he'd sometimes come around when we were out at the pond."

"Did Kara see him nowadays?"

"I don't know. I don't think so. Like I told you, Detective, I really lost touch with everyone. I don't know who Kara was hanging out with." My eyes meet hers. "Do *you* think Ray might've killed Kara?"

"We don't know," she says.

"Oh. I ran into Cynthia, Ray's sister, the other day. I didn't know she had come home." I pause, look out on the gray day. "You know about Cynthia?"

"Yes," Detective Myers says, writes in her notebook. "We've been talking to her. But it was definitely a man who attacked Mr. Crosby?"

"Yes. It wasn't her." I shake my head. I almost wish it was. We could fight Cynthia. I feel myself shaking inside, the picture of my phantom running through my mind. I know that everyone thinks he's a figment of my imagination, and maybe he is, but I've got to know before I drive myself insane.

"Detective?"

She sips her coffee.

"I know this is out of nowhere, and I don't even know if it's real."

She sets her cup on the table. "Tell me. The more I know, the better, no matter how insignificant."

"I don't know if this is relevant."

"Let me decide that."

I clear my throat, avoid Detective Myers's eyes. "Thirteen years ago, my mother was killed in a car accident. My father was driving, and I was in the back seat."

"Okay."

"We crashed into a tree. It was dark. Winter. And the road was icy. And my mom . . ." I take a napkin from the metal holder and wipe my eyes. "She didn't make it. My dad wasn't hurt, but I got a concussion." I clear my throat. "Anyway. Before the ambulance got there, this man pulled up behind us. He tried to open my mother's door, but it was crushed, and he couldn't." Tears mix with my voice. "So he opened my door and he started yelling." I stop to catch my breath.

"What was he yelling?" Detective Myers asks quietly.

"He said, 'I'm going to kill you. I'm going to kill you.' "

She nods. "When was this again?"

"I was sixteen."

"Who was this man?"

"I don't know. It was dark. I couldn't really see his face. I crawled out of the back seat and fell into the snow." My voice trembles. "Then he grabbed me." I touch the back of my neck, where I can still feel his rough fingers. "Then I remember hearing sirens in the distance, and the man disappeared."

"Okay."

"I know this sounds crazy, Detective, but after the accident, I kept seeing this man around town, like he was following me."

"How do you know it was him if you never saw his face?"

My gaze settles on the table. My words sound paranoid even to my own ears. "I don't really. It was just a feeling."

"Did you ask anyone about him?"

"My dad. But he said I imagined it."

"Trauma can do that, Esmé. It happens sometimes that we don't always remember things the way they really happened."

I shake my head. "I think he was lying. My father."

"Why would this man want to kill you?"

"I have no idea. But maybe, I don't know. I had this other guy send me scary letters for a while when I was living in Syracuse. He went to one of my ballet performances."

"Did you report him to the cops?"

"Yes. I gave them the letters, and they went and talked to him."

"Did he leave you alone after that?"

"Yes, thank God."

"How old were you when the accident occurred?" She's writing in her notebook.

"Sixteen."

"Had you been performing at that point?"

"Not professionally unless you count *The Nutcracker* when I was little."

She nods. "Okay."

"Can you look at the old police report of the accident and see if it mentions a man?"

"I will, and I'll let you know."

I take a deep breath. Customers are starting to queue up, and I need to get back to work. "Do you think that man could've killed Kara? Maybe he thought she was me."

She tries to smile, be reassuring. "I'll definitely look into it, but it's highly unlikely a man from thirteen years ago has decided to kill you—or your friend, for that matter. But I wouldn't go into the woods again, okay? Be careful."

"I will. Thank you." I feel strangely better as I walk back to the counter. Like a burden has lifted. Someone listened to me about my deepest fear, and she didn't shrug it off.

# CHAPTER 43
# Rita

WHEN I GET BACK TO THE STATION, THERE'S EXCITEMENT ALL AROUND. I pass a young woman being escorted back to the lobby from the interview rooms. I crane my neck to get a good look at her. Something about her is familiar. I run into Doug in the hallway standing next to his office door, a large envelope in his hand.

"Rita, you got a minute?"

"Sure. What's up. Who was that?" I point over my shoulder.

"Let's meet in the conference room."

Lauren is already sitting there, laptop open. Doug pulls a clutch of photographs out of the envelope and lines them up on the table.

"We just got these back from the lab. Connors took them yesterday with our new camera and zoom lens." Doug is grinning, something you don't see every day.

I sit and pull the pictures to me. There's Ridley, up close and personal, without a doubt. He's standing next to the side of an old brick building. Place looks familiar, but I can't say where it is. He's holding a bag.

Then there's a picture of him and a woman. You can see her from the side. Hair pulled up, a nice short jacket over a skirt and pumps on her feet. Like she just stepped out of the office. Another picture shows her hand Ray something. Then the bag is in her hand. The pictures were taken in a burst, so you almost get a movie-like effect. Money to Ray, bag to the lady. Then we see her walk away, face toward the camera.

My heartbeat kicks up. "I've seen her before." My gaze meets Doug's. "That who you just had in here?"

"That was her."

"She's the same woman. The Mercedes woman who pulled up in front of Ridley's place the other day when Chase and I were there."

Doug nods. "Could've been."

"Who is she? What did she say?"

"Her name's Hannah Dabrowski. She's an addict, although she says she's not. Just a woman who hurt her back water-skiing last summer."

"Uh-huh."

"But she threw Ray under the bus, so I don't care what she thinks her problem is or isn't."

"When are you going to pick him up?" I ask.

"Hopefully, in the morning. I've got to get the paperwork done."

"You want me there?" I'd like to be there. "I'd likc to get a look at the house again."

"Yes. I think that would be prudent," Doug says, tapping a pen against the table. "Can't hurt to have both of us. And he knows you."

"Yeah. Let me know what time."

# CHAPTER 44
# Rita

It's early morning, and everything is ready to go for the Ridley arrest.

Doug and I, accompanied by two cruisers of uniformed officers, head out to Hogsworth Road. On the ride out, I think about what Esmé told me. It's highly unlikely that a man who threatened her thirteen years ago would suddenly turn up and murder her friend, but stranger things have happened.

The sun is peeking out. The birds are twittering when we pull up in the Ridley driveway. A curtain moves in the window that I know is in the living room. Hopefully, this will go down without incident. Serving a warrant and making an arrest can go sideways on the turn of a dime.

We're wearing our vests, standard procedure in this type of operation. My hand skims over my sidearm, double checking that it's there, like people tend to do with a cell phone these days. Doug carries the pertinent paperwork.

Before we can knock on the door, Ray opens up and stands barefoot on the threshold.

"Well, this doesn't look good," he says, gazing out at the cruisers, lights strobing. We show him the warrant. Read him his rights.

"I need to call Cynthia's aide," he says. "Let her know," he smirks, "that I'll be gone a while."

"That's fine." We wait while Ray makes arrangements for his sister. He ends the call, sighs, and turns around for Officer Connors to put the cuffs on him.

Doug blows out a breath. "That went well," he whispers to me without sarcasm because it really did.

I nod. "Ray's had some experience with the law. Knows the routine. Let's see what we've got inside."

The house is dim, smells distinctly of weed. The living room is fairly bare. A pizza box sits on the end table next to the springless, treacherous couch. An old action movie blares on the flat-screen, squealing tires and random explosions. The sister's armchair sits empty, knitting gone as well.

We head into the kitchen, the tech team following, snapping pictures. There are dirty dishes in the sink. But nothing of interest in the cupboards or on the table.

The bathroom, although in need of a scrub brush and a bottle of bleach, yields nothing of interest either. Ray's bedroom is also pretty utilitarian, a rumpled double bed with a tangle of blue sheets that don't look like they've seen the inside of a washer lately and a ratty brown comforter. A dresser with an assortment of toiletries on top yields nothing but clothes stuffed in the drawers.

We enter the corner bedroom. It's pretty empty, so we move to the closet. There's a cardboard box on the top shelf. Doug takes it down and sets it on a card table that sits in a corner. Bingo. Inside, we find pills, some in vials, others in small plastic packets, too many for Ray's own personal use.

We step aside so the team can photograph and bag up the evidence.

Doug and I head back down the hall. So far, I've seen nothing tying Kara to Ray, except the pills probably, but we've got enough to hold him until he gets before a judge and makes bail. Being the weekend helps too. He'll have to wait until tomorrow.

There's one more room to check, probably the sister's. I knock on the door, and we proceed inside. She's standing by the window, looking out, wearing a long black coat.

"Ms. Ridley?"

She turns slowly. Blinks her sunken eyes. "Your brother is outside with police officers. We're going to take him into town. Why don't you come with us and speak to him first?"

That way he can explain about the aide. She nods.

"Where did you get that coat?" I ask. It looks suspiciously like the one Kara was wearing when she left work the night she was killed.

Cynthia's skinny hands run over the lapels as if stroking a pet. "I found it."

"You found it?"

She nods.

"Where?"

We follow her down the hall. She opens a closet near the front door. A distinct mustiness wafts out. It's packed with coats and jackets, like Ray's been hoarding them for twenty years.

"You found it in there?"

"Uh-huh."

"Is it yours?"

"No." Her eyes blink fearfully.

"When did you find it?"

"I don't remember."

I turn to Doug. "I'm going to call Judge Fowler. We need another warrant."

# CHAPTER 45
# Esmé

Despite the craziness of the weekend, on Monday morning I'm excited to go over to Mr. York's house. We're going to fit the ballet costume, and my stomach is doing flips. I managed to choke down a bowl of cereal and sit with my dad in the living room for a few minutes before Irene got there. We don't speak these days, not after what she said about my mother.

I drive down our road, swing around to Mr. York's street, and pull up in front of his house. Detective Myers said to stay out of the woods, and she doesn't need to tell me twice. Until the man who attacked Jack and Kara's killer are caught, I don't want to step foot there.

Mr. York greets me at the door, his little dog entourage wagging and prancing beside him.

"Good morning, Esmé. You look fresh as a daisy."

I smile. I don't know how that could be with the lack of sleep this weekend. Maybe it's just my excitement about the costume.

We head into the kitchen, and Mr. York pours tea into small floral cups. He outlines the agenda—fitting in the dining room, then we go up to the third floor, and he'll take the still shots.

"My friend in LA was thrilled with the sketches," he says. "I told him I'd email the stills this afternoon."

"I'm excited," I say, and drain my tea. I can't wait to be in a ballet costume again. When I get up from the table, my hip clicks loud enough that Mr. York hears it. A twinge of pain radiates down my leg, as if to tell me to calm down; a costume does not a dancer make.

In the dining room, Mr. York hands me the lacy bodice and fluffy skirt.

"I've laid a package of tights in the bathroom. Did you bring your slippers?"

"Yes." I still have a few pairs of regular ballet shoes, and I tossed a pair in my purse this morning.

In the bathroom, I remove my jeans and T-shirt, sit on a little chair in the corner, and pull the tights over my legs. I stretch and point my toes. Then I put on the bodice, feel the slight scratchiness of the lace. Finally, the tutu. It's a little big in the waist, but I can't help myself. I turn a pirouette. I glance at my face in the mirror, bun slick and tight at the crown of my head. I rub my cheeks to stir up some color. I should've put on some makeup. Oh well, too late now.

I walk back into the dining room, holding the skirt in place. Mr. York's eyes run over the costume, assessing. He pats the stool, and I stand up on it. He descends on me with his wrist-mounted pin cushion and neatly fixes the skirt's waist. He stands back, nods. "Beautiful."

"I wish I'd put on some makeup," I say.

"We can take care of that upstairs." The room darkens as the cloud cover that has been building since early this morning thickens. Mr. York puts his finger on his nose. "I ought to go ahead and stitch that up, but"—he sighs—"I don't want to take the time right now. Let's get the pictures taken. I'll do the finishing touches tonight. We're just taking the stills anyway, so the pins should hold it."

Up on the third floor, Mr. York flips on the light in the costume room, and I'm speechless. He turns on another light, and the dressing table is lit up with bulbs that surround the mirror. There's makeup, bottles and tubes, everything you'd need on the table.

"Sit, my dear. You know how to do this."

"Yes." While I search for the right colors among the makeup, Mr. York disappears, and I hear the sounds of *Carmen* over the speakers above my head. The music fills me with emotion as I put on my theatrical face. When I'm finished, I turn to see Mr. York in the doorway, waiting for me.

"Lovely." He claps his hands.

I rise, posture erect. Feet turned out.

"Just one more thing." He stands in front of me, so close I can see the pores near his nose, feel his hot breath blowing against my forehead while he places a silk rose next to my bun. He slips it into place and secures it with bobby pins that he pulls from his jacket pocket.

He steps back. "There, that's it. Turn, please."

The tutu rises with my careful pirouette, and I can't suppress my smile.

"Beautiful, Esmé. Come, let's get started."

Like before, Mr. York snaps away like a professional photographer. I feel exultant, listening to the nuanced, passionate music that is *Carmen* as I pose. When we're finished, I close my eyes and drink it in.

"Now," Mr. York says, his face flushed. "That was perfect. My client is going to have his socks knocked off."

"I'm so glad," I say.

"Next time, though, we're going to do video. That will demonstrate how the costume will function during the dance." His gaze meets mine. "Do you think you can manage that?"

It will hurt. I know that. "I haven't done much dancing in the last two years, Mr. York."

"It will only entail a short bit of dancing, to the 'March of the Toreadors' mostly."

My heart swells. I love that music. But . . . "That's the male dancer's part," I say.

"No matter. I just want to see how the costume performs. That short segment, only about four minutes, will encompass vigorous dancing as well as a more sedate section."

"I don't know the choreography. What do you want me to do?"

"Don't worry about that. You've danced most of your life. I just want you to feel the music and improvise. I'm not looking for anything specific. You think you can do that?"

My brain is telling me no. "Yes. Of course. I can't wait."

# CHAPTER 46
# Rita

With Ray Ridley's arrest, excitement fills the station. We're at full weekday staff, and Doug is filled with purpose. He and I will lead the interrogation. The chief returned about midmorning with the news that Mrs. Cunningham identified the coat as belonging to Kara. Bob wanted, again, to do this himself. Now that this key piece is settled, it's time to talk to Ray, so Doug and I head over to the county jail.

We take our places across from our suspect, who's dressed in orange, his long hair a tangle over his shoulders. Ray's agreed to talk to us before he goes in front of the judge this afternoon.

"So, Ray. How are you?" Doug says.

He smirks. "Great. You?"

"Can't complain."

I take out my notebook, flip to a fresh page.

"We need some answers, Ray," Doug says. "How's the oxy business?"

Ridley shakes his head, but I detect a gleam in his eyes as if he thinks we're idiots. "Don't know what you mean, Detective."

Doug jumps up and paces the small room. "We've got our undercover officer's report and two witnesses who said that they buy illegal drugs from you on a regular basis."

Ray shrugs. "I got hurt last spring working construction. The doctor gave them to me for back pain. But I'm not dealing."

"Geno Lewis was arrested in front of the Elm Tree Tavern trying to sell opioids to some of the patrons. When we brought him in, he said he bought his stash from you."

"Freakin' Geno. He came crying to me a couple weeks ago about how he'd got hurt at work and didn't have any insurance, so I gave him some of my pills."

"That so?"

"Yeah." Mr. Ridley crosses his arms and remains silent. I sketch his face, furrowed forehead, tight chapped lips.

Doug pulls the photos from the envelope. He slides a picture of Ray's stash over to him. "We found these in your house. Certainly looks like more than one guy could need for a back injury." Ray leans over the picture and studies it a minute. Doug slides the rest of the photos over, lines them up to show the exchange between Ray and Ms. Dabrowski.

"Shit," Ray says and slumps back in his chair. "Look. I've just helped out a couple of friends, okay? If Geno was selling, it's not my fault. I was just trying to help out a couple of people. A buddy of mine said he had a friend who was in bad shape, and he told her"—he stabs at the photo of Ms. Dabrowski—"I had some pills, okay? She got hurt last summer and was in a lot of pain. Her doctor wouldn't give her any more, so I was just trying to help her out."

"Just being a good guy, huh?" Doug says.

"Yeah. I am." He lifts his chin, dots of perspiration appearing on his upper lip. "I don't see what the big deal is. I'm not some big-time drug dealer."

I add to my sketch while Doug falls silent, sits, and thumbs through his folder. Ray starts jiggling his leg.

"Were you in the woods by that old shack Friday night?" I ask and watch his expression carefully.

"What? No." Confused, definitely.

"You ever sell any pills to Kara Cunningham?"

He clamps his lips, rubs his hand over his mouth.

I blow out a big breath. "Ray, you see Kara the night she was killed? You follow her back down the path that night? After you'd made the sale? Something ticked you off? You just wanted to talk to her?"

Ray shakes his head. "No. I didn't see Kara."

"You sure?"

"Yeah." He folds his arms across his chest.

"You didn't go into the woods the night she was killed?" Doug asks.

"No. I had no idea that someone hurt Kara." He glances at me. "Ask Detective Myers. When she came to the house that day, I had no fucking clue that someone was dead!"

Doug glances at me, and I shrug. "So, Ray, the night that Kara was killed, you never saw her?"

He shakes his head.

I pull a photo from the folder and set it in front of him. "That your hallway?"

"Yeah."

"That your closet?"

He nods. I point to the lump of wool fabric draped over my arm in the photo. "Your sister told us she found that coat in there on the floor. If Kara wasn't at your house that night, how did her coat get there?"

Ridley swallows. "I want my lawyer. I'm done here."

# CHAPTER 47
# Esmé

LANEY GREETS US WITH A SLEEPY INFANT DRAPED OVER HER SHOULDER. Her house is comfortable and feels lived in. The evidence of kids is everywhere—the preschool drawings on the fridge, the juice boxes on the counter, the toys scattered in the living room.

"Let me put him down, and I'll be right back."

Laney had organized a little impromptu dinner party, and Christy, Jack, and I are sitting in the living room. Christy's son comes down the hall with Laney's four-year-old tagging after him.

"Mom, can I read Robert a book?" Teddy has Christy's blond hair, a smattering of freckles across his nose. He's tall like his mom but, at seven years old, not yet in the gangly stage.

"I'm sure that's fine, honey," Christy says proudly, her eyes eagerly going over her son.

"Okay, come on, Robert. Let's go in the kitchen."

The boys wander off, and Christy sighs. "He's tested gifted." She smiles. "He's been reading since he was three. Can you believe it?"

"You're very lucky," Jack says.

"You think so?" she asks. "It's been hard on him, growing up without his father. Paul's so busy, he doesn't always take Teddy on his weekends." Uncharacteristic tears gather in Christy's eyes, and she quickly blinks them away. "But that just means more time for me and Teddy."

Laney, sans baby, stands in the doorway. "Food's ready, guys. Let's sit in the dining room."

The table is formally set, but not fussy. The kids have already eaten. Laney's husband is away on a business trip, so it's just the remnants of the old gang.

"I can't believe you two got attacked in the woods Friday night, Jack," Laney says, handing around a bottle of red.

Jack blows out a breath. "Yeah. It was scary more than anything. I really wasn't hurt." He self-consciously rubs his jaw, where a bruise hides under the stubble.

"Who could've done such a thing?" Laney asks.

I want to blurt out that maybe it was my phantom man, but I know they'll think I'm crazy. I think I'm crazy.

"Could it have been Ray?" Christy asks.

"Maybe. But why would he attack me?"

"Why would anyone?" I say.

"Good point," Jack says.

Christy sips her wine. "I heard he was arrested for dealing oxy." Ray's arrest has quickly made the rounds of town gossip.

Everyone nods. Laney's face turns pink, and she fidgets with her napkin.

"I wonder if one of his customers might have been out there," Jack says. "He's probably got some unsavory characters going through the woods."

"Well." Laney sips her water. "There's too much going on around here lately, and frankly, I'm a little scared. And now with Cynthia back."

I sip my wine. "Yeah, I never thought about her coming back. It's a little creepy having her home again."

"Well, stay away from her," Christy says. "Maybe she'll leave and go live somewhere else once Ray's in prison. Can she stay there alone?"

Christy looks at me, and I shrug. "I have no idea. But I hope not. It's a little unnerving to think she's there with no one keeping track of her."

Teddy and Robert walk back into the room. "Can we have a snack, Mrs. Addison?" Teddy asks. "Robert said he wanted potato chips. Barbeque. He said there's some in the pantry."

Laney's gaze lands on her little son. "Are you still hungry? You ate a giant bowl of mac and cheese not a half hour ago."

"Please," he says.

Laney stands, drops her napkin on her chair. "Okay. In the kitchen. Be right back."

Christy says, "Well, I'm glad you weren't hurt, Jack. Those woods have gotten dangerous."

"Apparently," Jack says.

"Well, I'm not going back into the woods until Kara's killer's caught." I draw a deep breath, sip my wine. "Did you know that Kara was modeling for Mr. York?"

Laney walks back into the room, throws a glance at Christy.

"Huh," Christy says, batting her eyes. "Kara was always asking to borrow money, which I gave her, by the way. Was he paying her?"

"Yes. I think so," I say. "I've started modeling for him, and he pays me."

Laney shivers. "Don't you think he's kind of creepy, Esmé?"

"No. I mean, he's been our neighbor for years. He and my mother were good friends. I've never felt that from him."

"I guess," Laney says. "I never really knew him, just to say hello."

"He's been really kind to me," I say. "And never did anything to make me feel uncomfortable." But I hate that Laney has brought that up. Just the thought that someone thinks that about Mr. York makes me feel strange.

But images of the red and black ballet costume fill my mind, and I feel a sense of excitement, contentment. It's where I want to be. The pull of that world, my old world, is still so raw. I know it's just modeling a costume, but it's all I've been thinking about since Mr. York showed me the sketch.

The evening flies by, and it feels good to relax and unwind with friends after what happened to Jack and me in the woods. When I get home, there's a dim light on in the living room. Byron is at work, and Irene's car isn't in the driveway. Dad is usually in bed by now. I open the front door and don't hear anything. Funny, if Dad is still up, the TV should be blaring. Maybe he went up to bed and left the light on.

I lock up behind myself and make my way to the living room. A man stands in the middle of the room, a gun pointed in my direction. I swallow. My heart pounds. It's my father.

"Dad? Dad?" The words seem to stick in my throat. "It's me. It's Esmé. What are you doing?"

"Huh? What?"

"Esmé, Dad. Put that down. It's okay." I walk slowly toward him, closer, where he can see me better in the low lamplight.

"Esmé?" His eyes are dazed and unfocused.

"What is it? What's wrong?"

He shakes his head and lowers the gun. "Nothing. I was dreaming. Sitting in my chair." There are tears on his wrinkled cheeks.

I reach out and take the gun from his hand. "What are you doing with this?"

"I thought I heard someone outside." He chokes on his sobs. "I'm so sorry, Esmé."

I lean over and set the gun on an end table and hold my frail father in my arms and wonder if he dreamed it all. Or is someone out there?

I finally got Dad calmed down and up to bed last night. He fell asleep fairly quickly, his snores echoing down the hall. I, on the other hand, was awake most of the night, holding the Glock and peering out windows. Did he really hear something? Or was it his imagination?

When I hear Byron come through the front door, I jump up from the kitchen table, a cup of tea gone cold in my spot.

"What's wrong?" he asks, his eyes tired, his scrubs rumpled.

The Glock sits on the table behind me. "When I got home from Laney's last night, Dad was standing in the middle of the living room pointing the gun at me."

Byron blinks his eyes. "*What?* How did he find it?"

"I have no idea, By. It was in the linen closet where we hid it last time I checked."

"Fuck." He runs his hand over his mouth. "But nothing happened, right? Nobody got hurt?"

"No. He told me he thought he heard something. We'll have to find a better spot to hide it, though."

"*Did* he hear something?"

I drop back down in my chair, pick up my cup. "I don't know. I was up all night checking, but I didn't see or hear anything."

Byron blows out a breath. "I'll put it in my room on my closet shelf. I don't think he can get up there without a chair. Then when I get a chance, I'll buy a safe for it."

"That would be a good idea."

"You're not going back out in the woods, are you, Ez?"

"No. Detective Myers told me not to."

"After what happened to Jack, you need to steer clear."

"I know that, Byron. I'm not about to do something stupid. They still haven't caught Kara's killer, so who knows who's out there?"

"Just be careful, okay? You work today?"

I glance at my phone. "Yeah. I've got to be there in an hour. I guess I should jump in the shower."

Byron nods. "Okay. I'll go check on Dad and get his breakfast."

I finish my cold tea and head upstairs, listening to every creak and groan the house makes.

# CHAPTER 48
# Rita

As soon as we showed Ridley the photo of Kara's coat yesterday, he clammed up. Once he asked for his lawyer, we were done.

Lauren sits in my office, twirling a loose tress of curly hair that's broken free from her braid.

"What did you find out about Cynthia?" I ask.

Lauren clicks keys on her laptop. "I went back through everything—from the statements when her sister was killed to the prison and hospital records. And finally the woman who runs the group home called me back."

"Good work." It is too. That's a lot of ground to cover in such a short time. "What did you find?"

"Not much. Cynthia appears to have been a model inmate slash patient. There's only one discipline record in all those years."

"What was that for?"

"About a month after she killed her sister, she scratched another kid at the facility where she was being held."

"That's it?"

"That's it. No other violent events since. Not in twenty years."

"What about the group home woman? What did she say about Cynthia?"

"No problems other than the running away. She said Cynthia

was quiet. Kept to herself and just wanted to go home. Mrs. Grant, the group home lead, said she would be surprised to hear that Cynthia would do anything violent."

"Huh. Psychiatric evals?"

"Nothing significant there."

I tap my fingers on my desk. "But even if she didn't kill Kara, maybe she knows something, saw something that night."

"Maybe, Rita."

I blow out a breath. "Anything else?"

"Nothing more on Cynthia. Oh, I looked back over the video from the insurance office," she says, clicking more keys.

"Yeah?"

"And I went back through Kara's phone records." Lauren blows out a breath and sits up. "We've accounted for every number coming in and going out over the last two weeks she was alive. All the numbers except one belong to her friends or her mother. Just the one number that's unknown. She called that number numerous times. The last time before she died was Sunday night."

"Burner phone?"

"Yeah. I'm thinking it's Ray's work phone."

We didn't find it when we searched, but he might have gotten rid of it before we got there. Maybe after he killed Kara.

Lauren leans forward. "I think she called him Sunday night looking to score some oxy. He tells her he'll let her know. On Tuesday, he meets her at her office—well, across the street."

"He's the one calling her name off screen." I tent my fingers. "And Ray made sure he was off camera when he met Geno. Could be our Mr. Ridley knows enough to stay where the cameras aren't."

"That's what I'm thinking. He tells her to meet him back at the house, and he'll hook her up."

I take a deep breath. "Sounds logical. It all fits the time line and what we know. But why kill her?"

"Who knows, Rita? That's the big mystery."

"I wonder, though, if Cynthia might be involved. Ray seemed nervous when talking about her and was quick to point out that she knew nothing about Kara's death. Maybe he's covering for her. Maybe being back home triggered her somehow."

"But what about the man who attacked Mr. Crosby? If it was Ray, why would he do that? Nothing makes sense."

"No." I blow out a breath. "Nothing seems to be adding up."

I stand and go to my window. It's raining again. "Did you have a chance to look into Esmé's mother's accident?"

"Oh, yeah. I read the report. It all looked routine. When the ambulance got there, EMS didn't see anyone but Esmé and her parents. Then the report by the responding officer confirms that. Nobody but the three people in the car. Well, Esmé was found in the snow next to the vehicle, after she had apparently exited the back seat. She wasn't ejected or anything. Her injuries were fairly minor, a concussion and a few bruises. They kept her at the hospital overnight. Mrs. Foster was dead at the scene. And Mr. Foster was unhurt and refused medical attention."

"What about the condition of the roadway? Any signs that another car might've been following them? Ran them off the road?"

Lauren shakes her head. "Report said only one vehicle was involved and that ice was to blame. Does Esmé really think someone was out there that night, someone who wanted to kill her?"

"That's what she says, but she did have a head injury."

"Maybe she's just freaked out by her friend's murder. That's why she's remembering the accident. She's paranoid. I know I would be if my friend was killed in my backyard."

"Yeah. That's what I'm thinking, but I told her I'd look into it."

# CHAPTER 49
# Esmé

TODAY'S THE DAY. I'M GOING TO DANCE AGAIN. OF COURSE, IT'LL only be for a short time, one performance, but I'll be in costume, under stage lights, the music of *Carmen* surrounding me.

I jump into my car, and when I turn the key in the ignition, nothing. Just great. I try again, with the same result. I check my phone. I'm supposed to be at Mr. York's in ten minutes. My gaze shifts up to the woods.

The morning is dark with clouds, a few sprinkles dot my windshield, but it is daylight. Byron's asleep, his car keys in his room, and Irene and Dad are settled into their morning routine. Irene's car blocks Dad's in the driveway, and there's no way I'm going to ask her to move. Besides, Byron said that Dad's car hasn't been started in months. I don't know what to do.

I get out of my car, swing my bag over my shoulder, and head for the path. If I hurry, I'll be through the woods and into Mr. York's backyard in no time. Nothing has happened out there in the daytime. I trot across our back lawn, the wet, weedy grass slapping at my ankles. I enter the woods and feel my heart start to race. I pick up the pace, my breath coming in quick gasps as I break into a run. The chilly scent of rain and rot pervades the forest. I hear a flutter of leaves and glance over my shoulder. Just the wind. Our house has disappeared by now, and I'm almost at the pond. I glance back at the way I've come. Maybe I should go back. I shouldn't have come this way. But I'm more than halfway through. Too late to go back now. I press on, hurrying. I circle the water, averting my eyes from its fetid, gray depths. I hear a rustle of dead leaves again and peek over my shoulder. Someone's coming down the path from Ray's. I sprint to the path that leads to Mr. York's house. Once in the shelter of the trees, I stop and catch my breath, look over my shoulder. A thin figure appears. My pulse races. Then I recognize her. Cynthia. She's making her way to the pond, oblivious to me, a bundle in her arms. I turn back toward Mr. York's place and run.

The house is up around the bend, but for now, I'm encased by trees, everywhere, like a living prison. I stride quickly, my heart still pumping wildly, my hip screaming in pain. How am I going to dance if I show up already hurting? I slow to a walk. I'm almost there. I take a deep breath, try to calm my breathing. I glance over my shoulder, back at the path. No one is after me.

I rap on the big wooden door, and Mr. York answers right away.

"Esmé? What happened?"

I realize I must look crazed. I swipe sweat from my forehead. "Oh, nothing. I was running late, and my car wouldn't start, so I came through the woods."

He steps out on the porch as if to check my story. "Your car's at home?"

"Yes. I walked."

"I'm so sorry, my dear. If you'd called me, I would've picked you up. Come in. It's starting to rain."

I rub my cold hands together as we walk into the dim dining room, where a mannequin is dressed in the *Carmen* costume. She stands in the shadows, her blank plastic face ghostly.

"Let me get you a cup of tea so you can settle a moment before we get to work," Mr. York says. "And when we finish, I'll drive you home." He disappears into the kitchen, and I walk over to the mannequin, touch the lace of the bodice.

Mr. York reappears with a steaming cup. "What do you think?" He tips his chin.

"It's beautiful."

"I put the finishing touches on it last night."

"I'm so excited." I sip my tea and feel its warmth penetrate my body.

Up in the costume room, I sit before the lighted mirror. My fear coming through the woods has dissipated, leaving only a healthy blush on my cheeks. Music fills the air as I apply my makeup. Mr. York has set out the tubes he wants me to use. A silk rose for my hair and a fan also sit beside the mirror. Once I've finished, I move to the little dressing area, where the costume hangs. I slide my jeans down over my hips and pull my T-shirt over my head, letting my clothes drop into a pile on the floor. I dress quickly in the costume, feeling like I am transforming into the real me. Who I really am is the woman in the mirror wearing tulle and lace.

Mr. York is waiting at the door when I come out. His cheeks are flushed. His eyes run over the costume. He steps forward and adjusts the tutu. Steps back, his hand clutching his chin.

"So lovely." He reaches over and slides a bobby pin into my bun and secures the rose a bit tighter. "Let's get started. Come."

I follow him onto the stage area, where several screens are set up as backdrops. He points to the spotlight center stage. "Stand here. You'll see your mark on the floor."

I do. A little white X made of tape. Mr. York stands back. "Oh, one more thing," he says and walks quickly back into the costume room.

I take a deep breath, close my eyes, feel the music surround me.

"Here," he says.

My eyes flutter open. Mr. York is holding a pair of pointe shoes.

"Oh, Mr. York. I haven't really danced on pointe in two years."

"It'll make the video more authentic. Surely, it's like riding a bike."

It's not, but my eyes land hungrily on the shoes. Oh, how I want it, but I know that I'm too weak. A few minutes in my bedroom hardly count as real pointe practice.

"Won't you at least give it a try?" he asks.

I feel myself giving in. Dreams are like that. Desire overcomes reason. "But they have to be specially fitted."

"Look closely, Esmé."

The shoes are worn. The pink dulled. I catch my breath. “Are those mine?”

“They are indeed.”

I step back. “How did you get them?”

“I found them in a bag by your trash bin a couple of weeks ago. I was out walking my dogs, late, and I sometimes walk clear through to your road, and I saw the bag sitting there. I knew you didn’t mean to throw them away. I knew you’d regret it, so I took the liberty of saving them for you.”

“Why didn’t you say anything before?”

“I wanted to surprise you, my dear.”

# CHAPTER 50
# Rita

Chase, Lauren, Doug, and I are gathered in the conference room. The whiteboard is full of notes, photos, diagrams, you name it, but we're no closer to finding a viable suspect in Kara's murder than we were a couple of weeks ago.

Chase brought in a carrier of Dunkin' coffees and a box of donuts. Maybe the sugar will get our brain cells firing. I'm always game for junk food, unfortunately. Doug eyes the treats suspiciously, while the rest of us dig in. I want to make a snarky comment about his girlish figure but keep a lid on my mouth. We've got too much serious business to get to.

"Okay. It's been two weeks since Kara was killed." I stand by the whiteboard. "Let's take another look at our suspects. Byron Foster. He had opportunity and possibly motive, but so far, we don't have anything else to tie him to the murder. Ray Ridley. We know Kara was probably in his house the night she was killed, maybe to buy oxy."

Lauren huffs out a breath. "We need to talk to him again, Rita."

"Yes. We do. How can we make that happen?"

Chase wipes donut crumbs from his chin. "He knows we've got him for dealing. He knows that, but a murder charge is a totally different ball game. You think his lawyer will let us talk to him?"

I sip my coffee. "This is what I'm thinking. If he's innocent, he'll want to get a deal on the drug bust. That is, if he can tell us anything useful." I tip my head. "On the other hand, if he was involved in Kara's murder, he's not going to talk to us."

Everyone nods in agreement.

Doug huffs out a breath. "What are we missing, Rita? Those two guys are our only possibilities?"

"Mr. York," I say, and write his name on the board. "He may have been in those woods that night, despite what he said. And now we know that he and Kara were working together, which he felt compelled to lie about at first."

I sit back at the table, eye what's left in the donut box. "I'm as frustrated as you guys are. I keep coming back to motive. There doesn't seem to be any reason that anyone would have to kill Kara." I tap my fingers on the table.

"What about Cynthia?" Lauren asks.

"Possible," I say. "Ray's been awful antsy whenever I asked him about her. But it doesn't seem to fit exactly." I stand and add Cynthia's name to the whiteboard. I put it out on the side like it's drifting on its own, not aligned with the men listed there. That seems fitting. "Maybe."

"I'll see what else I can dig up on the men, Rita," Lauren says, eyes on her computer screen.

"Good deal." I draw a deep breath. "But maybe it's someone we haven't even considered yet. Someone unknown to us at this point. But who?"

I close the donut box to stop myself from grabbing a third donut. "We need to find out if anyone else might've been out in the woods that night. We know that people have been coming from and going to Ray's place through there. Maybe one of Ray's clients ran into Kara, and, for some reason, they got into an argument."

"You think Geno maybe?" Chase asks.

"Why?" Doug says. "We've known Geno for years, and while he's been in lots of trouble, he's never hurt anyone."

"We need to get a complete list of Ray's customers," I say. "If he thinks that will take the heat off him for Kara's murder, he might be cooperative." I stand and pace in front of the whiteboard. "I'll give his lawyer a call and see what we can work out."

# CHAPTER 51
# Esmé

MR. YORK IS IN THE BOOTH, AND THE MUSIC RISES AND SWELLS. I spent ten minutes warming up before putting on my pointe shoes, tying the ribbons, feeling the satin slide between my fingers. I spent another ten minutes working on pointe, feeling awkward but soon regaining something of my form, the years of practice surfacing to help me, the pain and the weakness forgotten as I took the first trembling steps across the stage.

"I'm ready, Mr. York," I say.

"Fabulous. We'll start with some of the slower music. Then we'll film the 'March of the Toreadors' section afterward. Okay?"

"Yes. I'm ready."

"Start on your mark. Just feel the music and improvise, my dear. Do give us a few pirouettes and leaps, would you?"

"I'll do my best."

"Good." The lights go down until only the spotlight illuminates me, setting the sequins ablaze. The music begins gently, and a thrill runs through my body. I step out to my left and let myself go.

After a few minutes, Mr. York yells, "Cut!" The music stops, and I rest, my chest heaving, but I'm exhilarated.

Mr. York comes out of the booth. "That was lovely." He hands me a bottle of water. "Mind that you don't dribble."

I laugh and sip carefully.

"Now, then. Do you think you can handle a bit more?"

Pain sparks from my hip down my leg, but nothing is going to stop me. "Yes. I'm ready."

"All right. We'll start again in a minute. Now, with 'the march,' the music is full of energy and passion." Mr. York's eyes meet mine. "Feel the music, Esmé. Carmen was a temptress. That needs to come through in your movements. Use your fan, smile at the camera. Be sure to capture the energy in your steps, and do give us a grand jeté when you hear the crash of the cymbals."

I nod. I can do this. I want to do this, to feel that energy and power and otherworldliness I always felt on stage.

Mr. York collects the water bottle, and I return to my mark. He's in the booth and lowers the lights until it's only me. The music starts, the sharp, infectious march, and I start to move across the stage, my heart beating in time.

# CHAPTER 52
# Rita

Ray Ridley, dressed in his usual ratty jeans and flannel shirt, sits beside his lawyer. Mr. Harvey is a frequent visitor at the station, representing a fair number of petty criminals we see on a day-to-day basis. His suit is rumpled, and his bushy hair needs a good cut, but he seems to shuffle from the station to the courthouse on a nearly continuous loop, as if he has no time to go to the dry cleaner or stop in at the barber's.

"Thank you for coming in," I say, as Doug and I sit across from him.

Ray nods. "What do you want to know?" His lawyer gives him a sideways glance.

"Well, Ray," Doug leans back in his chair, "we might be able to help each other. You're aware we've got all the evidence we need to get a conviction on the drug charges. And since you were dealing opioids, you're going to do some time. But," Doug raises his eyebrows, "as you know, we've got a murder on our hands that we're pretty anxious to solve."

"I didn't have anything to do with that," Ray says, his cheeks red.

Doug raises his hand. "We just want a few answers."

Ray settles back in his chair. "Okay, shoot."

"The night that Kara was killed," I say, "she was at your house."

Doug slides the photo of Kara's coat in front of him as if to remind him.

Ridley looks at his lawyer, and Mr. Harvey nods. They would've discussed this ahead of time, what Ray would admit to and what he wouldn't.

Ray lets go a breath. "Yeah, okay, she was there."

"For what purpose?" I ask.

"She wanted some pain pills. She was in an accident last spring. I was only trying to help her out."

"How many times, Ray?" Doug asks. "How many times did you sell to her?"

Ridley looks at his lawyer, who nods. "A few. She called me last summer, like July, I think. That's when I gave her the pills the first time." He runs his hand through his shaggy hair.

"Okay." Doug stands and paces in the small room. "We're trying to establish a timeline on the night of the murder."

I turn Doug's laptop in Ray's direction.

"Take a look," Doug says, and I play the video from Kara's office. Ridley and his lawyer watch intently. "Look closely. Someone calls to Kara off camera. Was that you, Ray?"

I stop the tape.

Mr. Harvey says, "My client and I need a minute."

"Fine," Doug says, and they step out. We sit in the quiet little room that's suddenly gotten too warm. You either freeze to death in this old building or you roast. After a couple minutes, they come back in and sit.

"So, Ray? What's the verdict?" Doug asks. "Was that you?"

"Yeah. That was me. Kara had been calling me, begging me for more. I told her I'd let her know."

I look up from my notebook. "When I questioned you the first time, the Wednesday that Kara was found, you told me you'd run to the grocery store sometime about five the night before."

He smirks. "Yeah, I stopped by the store, then I swung around to Kara's office to catch her as she was leaving."

"You told her you had the pills for her, and then what?"

"I told her to meet me at the house."

"Park in the far lot?"

"Yeah."

"Then what?"

"She was there in no time. She almost beat me home, and she had to come through the woods. She was in a big hurry."

"Did she say why?"

"She said she was meeting a guy, and she needed to get going."

"Who? What guy?" Doug asks, leaning over the table. We know it was Jack Crosby.

"She didn't say, but I figured it was Byron. Still think it was him. They were going out, you know? And she was found in his backyard, right?"

Doug settles back in his chair. "Could be, Ray. Did she say she was meeting Byron?"

He shrugs. "No, but she was excited. I think that's why she left her coat. I found it later and threw it in the closet. I figured she'd come back for it eventually. I wasn't going to run after her with it."

"So, Kara bought her pills. Left her coat, and that was the last you saw of her?"

"Yeah."

"You didn't follow her into the woods?"

"No fucking way. I never left my place."

"Okay," I say and lean back in my chair. "Did anyone else come to your house that night? Did you make any more sales?"

"No. Just Kara."

"Do your customers all come through the woods?"

"Most do. I don't want them in my driveway. Sometimes I meet them someplace else." Mr. Harvey taps Ray's arm. "And it's just Geno, Hannah, and Kara. That's it. I'm not some big-time dealer."

"Did you see Geno that night?"

"No."

I take a deep breath, tap my notebook with my pencil. "Ray, can you think of anyone else who might've been in the woods?"

He shakes his head.

"You sure you didn't sell to anyone else that night? Someone who might've attacked Kara?"

"No. If I did, I'd tell you."

"What about your sister? Where was she during all of this?"

He blinks, licks his lips. "In her room. I tell her to wait in her room whenever anyone stops by the house."

"Why's that?"

He shrugs. "I don't want her to get agitated. I don't want her involved . . . in my business."

"What about after Kara left? Did she come out?"

"Yeah. But she stayed inside all night, Detective. She didn't go out." Ray's gaze shifts to the door.

"Could Cynthia have seen anything? Maybe she's just afraid to tell us."

Ray shakes his head. "My sister doesn't know anything about this."

Doug leans back in his chair, sighs. "Okay, Ray. You think of anyone who would have a reason to want Kara dead?"

"No. I still think Byron had something to do with it."

"Do you know anything that connects Mr. Foster to the crime?"

He shrugs again. Then leans forward. "The only people around would be Byron's old man, who's too sick to do much of anything. Byron. And Mr. York," he adds, like he just thought of him.

"What about Mr. York?" I ask.

"He's a freaking perv. Maybe it was him."

"What makes you say that?" Doug asks.

I'm all ears, pencil poised.

"Well"—Ray leans back in his chair, takes a breath—"back when we were teenagers, I caught him one time in that little shack by the pond. He was taking pictures of the girls."

"Did you report him?" I ask. "Tell anybody?"

"No. He said he was taking pictures of birds." Ray chuckles. "I told him if I ever caught him bothering the girls, I'd beat the shit out of him." Ray smiles with pride, the great protector.

"Okay, we'll talk to him again," I say, my mind firing with questions.

Ray considers. "But I don't think he killed Kara. I scared him off pretty good, and he's a pretty wimpy guy. I think your best bet is still Byron."

I stand. Doug shuts his laptop. "Thank you for your help, Ray."

# CHAPTER 53
# Esmé

THE MUSIC STOPS, AND I'M BREATHING HEAVILY, HEART HAMMERING. But I feel emotional, powerful, all my pain forgotten. How I've missed this. I swipe tears from my cheeks as Mr. York comes out of the booth.

His face is flushed too, his eyes shining. "That was amazing, Esmé. Why don't you rest in the costume room? I want to look over the tape, just to make sure we've got what we need."

I stretch out on the velvet sofa, prop my feet on the armrest, my pointe shoes discarded on the floor. My feet throb, and I feel the inevitable blisters starting to form. I'm still breathing heavily and laugh at my own lack of endurance. I used to be able to dance forever without breaking a sweat. I finish another water bottle and close my eyes. The pain in my hip pulses as I relax into the soft cushions. I almost drift off when I hear Mr. York.

"Esmé?"

I pop up and swing my feet to the floor. "Yes?"

"I need to make an adjustment." There's a frown line between his eyebrows. "When looking back over the tape, I noticed it. The tutu needs a bit of attention. There's some loose lace on the bodice as well. Would you mind undressing so I can fix the costume? There's a robe hanging on the back of the door." He glances at his watch. "Would you like something to eat while I work? If you have time, I'd like to film again after. I really need it today."

"Yes. Of course." But I'm feeling pretty spent. Maybe because I haven't eaten all day. "Something light maybe? I couldn't really dance on a full stomach."

"Absolutely. I'll be right up."

While Mr. York goes downstairs, I slide out of the costume and put on the robe. He's back soon with a tray. A bowl of chicken noodle soup sits in the middle, surrounded by saltines, like I've got the flu. But it will work. I hand him the costume, and he's gone.

After about ten minutes, he's back, and the food was just enough to restore my energy. I also dug through my purse for a bottle of ibuprofen and swallowed two pills with what was left in my water bottle.

Back in costume, I resume my mark, clutch the fan, and wait for the music to start. Mr. York comes back out of the booth, his forehead wrinkled.

"I just noticed something else," he says. He draws a bobby pin from his pocket and jabs it into my bun, scraping my scalp. "Sorry, but I saw a stray wisp. We can't have that."

I know he has a reputation for perfection, and I'm seeing it firsthand. Oh well, I'm going to dance, and that's all I care about.

He walks into the booth and lays his key ring on the counter. The lights go down, and the music begins. I feel it fill me with emotion, and I begin to dance.

Mr. York stops me, and we begin again. But I'm wilting, tired, and despite the pain relievers I took earlier, I'm really hurting.

The main lights flip on, and I blink my eyes. Mr. York comes out of the booth and moves one of the screens a few inches to the right.

"How was that?" I ask hopefully.

He blows out a breath, licks his lips. "It was lovely, of course, but not quite right." He glances at his watch. "I've got to make a call. Perhaps you could rest a bit? We're very close. I think one more take might do it."

"Okay. I'll do my best."

"That's a good girl. Your mother would be so proud."

# CHAPTER 54
# Rita

By the time Ray and his lawyer leave, it's getting late. Doug has left for home, but I want to go back out and talk to Mr. York. Ray's information about the man has got me anxious. I won't be able to settle until I've spoken with him again.

Chase is standing in the doorway of my office. "You want me to go with you, Rita?"

"No. I'm fine. I'm going home afterward. Why don't you head home? Traffic's probably already a nightmare. I'll see you in the morning."

I pass Lauren. She's head down over her computer. "Wait, Rita!" She jumps up from her desk and picks up her laptop. "Can we go to your office?"

I sit behind my desk, and Lauren perches on the chair opposite me, her cheeks blazing.

"I've been working on our suspects' backgrounds all day. I didn't come up with anything interesting on Byron or Ray, but what I found on Mr. York . . . well."

"What?"

"I found a woman who worked with him back in the early eighties in New York. She was an aspiring actress and model back in the day. York invited her to his apartment for a modeling session. He had her dress up in different costumes, and he took pictures."

"Okay."

"She says he was really creepy, and she got 'a bad vibe' and decided to cut the session short, but he wouldn't let her leave."

"He physically stopped her?"

"He wouldn't unlock the door until the photos were perfect, he told her. She figured her only way out was to comply. She let him take more pictures, and two hours later, he let her go."

"She didn't press charges?"

"She was afraid it would ruin her chances in the business. And he hadn't actually touched her, so she didn't think she had a case."

"Nice," I say. "Wonder how many others there were?" Women made to feel so powerless and afraid that they didn't protest for fear it would ruin their careers.

"She told me she knew of one other woman who had a similar experience with him. But she was in his apartment all weekend. She said she thought he put something in her drink."

"I knew there was something off about him." I drum my fingers on my desk. "Maybe he is our guy."

"Maybe."

"But as far as we know, he doesn't touch them. Just takes pictures?" I say half to myself.

"I think he's a voyeur, Rita."

I nod. Lots of strange people in the world. "I'm headed out to his place to poke around a bit."

"You want me to go with you?"

"No. You keep doing what you're doing."

Darkness is falling as I pull into Mr. York's driveway. His car's there, and the lights are on downstairs.

"Detective?" he says, answering the door.

"You have a few minutes, Mr. York?"

He glances back inside. The dogs sitting by his feet are uncharacteristically quiet. "I'm fighting a deadline," he says, huffing out a breath.

"This will only take a minute." He makes no move to invite me in, so I guess we'll talk on the porch.

"All right. How can I help you?"

I don't want to tip our hand about what Lauren has discovered.

Not yet. But I want to see his reaction to what Ray told us. "We've been talking to Ray Ridley, and he told us something I wanted to run by you."

He folds his arms. "I wouldn't believe anything that fellow has to say."

"Well, that might be. But he told us that years ago, when Kara and her friends were teenagers, he caught you in that little shack by the pond, taking pictures of the girls."

Mr. York's mouth falls open. "That's not true."

"He didn't find you in the shack with a camera?"

He licks his lips, shakes his head. "I was taking pictures of the pond, nature. I do it all the time."

"That's it?"

"Yes. Now I've got to get back to work."

I stand still a minute, wondering, thinking. This guy, to me, is super creepy, and he's certainly violated women, but is he a murderer?

"Look, Detective, I wouldn't believe anything that man has to say. The whole family is crazy, and he's a drug dealer, you know. I'm sure of it."

I nod. "Okay, thanks, Mr. York. You have a pleasant evening."

# CHAPTER 55
# Esmé

I'M DREAMING. ONE OF THOSE WEIRD DREAMS WITHIN A NIGHTMARE. I know I'm asleep, and I'm trying to wake up, trying to claw through the dark webs of slumber. My phantom man is behind me, striding with heavy footfalls through the woods. I run faster and faster but can't get anywhere. I hear him breathing in my ear, feel his breath on my neck. Then I see Kara standing by the pond, and I try to call to her, but my voice is trapped in my throat. I watch helplessly as Kara wades into the dark water and disappears. Terror fills my stomach, radiates down my limbs. Then I wake up. My eyes pop open, and Mr. York is standing above me. My heart is thumping, and sweat covers my forehead.

"What happened?"

"It's all right, Esmé. You fell asleep, but we need to finish our work."

I lean over, catch my breath. My head as well as my hip are pounding. "What time is it?"

"Late, I'm afraid. Let's hurry along so we can get this finished."

I take a deep breath. "Couldn't we do it tomorrow, Mr. York? I'm really tired."

His brow furrows. "I told my client he'd have it tonight. He's on the West Coast, so it's not so late there. How about a cup of coffee? Perhaps that will revive you?"

"Okay. I'll try."

He turns to leave, then comes back with a handful of tissues and powder. "Do clean up. Your makeup needs attention." He reaches as if to wipe my cheek, but stops, hand midair. Then hands me the tissues and powder. "I'll be right back."

I sit and dab powder on my face, then put on my pointe shoes. The music is off, and the third floor is strangely quiet. I'm so tired I don't know how I'll make it through another dance. And I wonder what time it is. I search through my purse for my phone, but it isn't there. Then I remember that I left it on the dining room table. I decide to look around to see if I can find a clock. If it is really late, I'll tell Mr. York that I'm going home. We'll have to pick back up tomorrow.

The stage area and the booth are dark, too dark to see anything, and I'm disoriented. I feel along the walls, looking for a light switch but can't find one. I decide to go downstairs and tell Mr. York that I'm too tired to continue. I find my way to the exterior door, but it's locked. Why is it locked? I pound on it and call, "Mr. York?" But the house feels deathly quiet. I press my ear against the door, but I hear nothing. My heart is beating so hard it feels like it will burst. My skin goes cold.

Has he locked me in on purpose?

I make my way to the booth door, try the knob. Luckily, it's unlocked. Inside, I flip the light switch and blink. Maybe there's an extra key to the exterior door in here someplace. I search across the counter. Nothing. I turn to the filing cabinets, and they're full of photographs. I can't help but be mesmerized by the sheer volume of costumed models. Women dressed as gypsies and queens, wearing voluminous dresses and fancy feathered hats. And then I find other pictures too. Women half dressed, lying on divans, their breasts exposed. I step back. Were these really taken for movie clients? They aren't salacious. There's an artistic quality about them. Still. I shiver. Something seems off. It's in the eyes of his models. The women don't seem entirely at ease, or is this my imagination? Laney's words flit through my mind. "Don't you think he's kind of creepy, Esmé?" I shudder.

I close the drawer and return to the counter. There are two

drawers beneath the work top. I open the first one. There are bits of odds and ends in here. Maybe there's a key. I search underneath a heavy file folder and find more photographs. I'm about to flip past them and stop. Kara. I clutch my hand across my mouth. Kara completely nude. I drop the pictures and close the drawer. My heart is hammering, and I run.

I try the exterior door again, but, of course, it's locked. Then I hear him coming up the stairs. *Think, Esmé.* I walk out to the middle of the stage, eye the screens that make up the backdrop.

He's standing in the doorway, holding a mug. "Brought you your coffee. Sorry it took me a bit longer than I thought. I had a message from a client in LA, and I had to return his call."

I take the cup from him, but don't drink. "It's okay. Do you think one more take will do it?"

"I think so. The last one was almost right."

I nod, pretend to sip the coffee, and put it aside while Mr. York heads for the booth. I watch him setting up and see him take a ring of keys out of his pocket and lay them on the counter. The music starts, but I stand still on my mark.

His voice booms overhead. "What's the matter, Esmé?"

"I think something's wrong with the screen. It's not in the right place." I'd moved it and broken a footing so that it tilted slightly.

He comes out, his brow furrowed. "How did this happen?" he says and drops to his haunches. I inch toward the booth.

"I'll need my tools," he says, sighs, and heads into the prop room. I duck into the booth and clutch the key ring. My heart is hammering, sweat dripping down the sides of my face. I grab my purse out of the costume room and walk quickly toward the exterior door, slip the key in the lock, and I'm through. I close the door quietly behind me and dash down the stairs, my pointe shoes flopping on my feet. I make a quick stop in the dining room and see my phone on the table, grab it, and head out the front door.

It's dark as midnight, and it might be that late, maybe later. I've lost all track of time. I run through the wet grass and stumble toward the woods. I stop short, glance back over my shoulder. Did he follow me? My pulse is pounding. I don't want to go into the forest. The trees, tall and menacing, wave in the chilly breeze. But what choice do I have? I could walk all the way down the road and then cut over to my street, but it's a couple miles that way. I glance over at Mr. York's road. It's dark and deserted, equally scary. At least I know the woods. I could find my way literally with my eyes closed. I take a deep breath, untie my pointe shoes, grip them in my hands, and sprint down the path.

# CHAPTER 56
# Rita

I BARELY SLEPT LAST NIGHT WITH THE NEW REVELATIONS ABOUT MR. York running through my brain. I know I look like death when I show up at the station. Even that expensive makeup Collin insisted I buy didn't cover the circles under my eyes. But I'm determined to make some progress on Kara's case today.

I make my way to my office, not stopping to talk to anybody. I fire up my computer and open my notebook. Nothing in email. I pick up the phone and call the lab. The unfortunate young man who answers gets an earful. Not his fault, but I'm in a bad place. I apologize after reading him the riot act and hang up.

Chase pokes his head in at the door. "You want to head back out to see Mr. Foster?"

"Yeah. Might as well." I drain the contents of my coffee cup. We decided yesterday to talk to him again. "Give me a minute, and we'll go." I doubt that old Mr. Foster is our guy, but it won't hurt to try to jog his memory again.

Irene Musgrave answers the door, crosses her thick arms over her stomach. "What can I do for you, Detectives?"

"We'd like to talk to Mr. Foster."

She huffs out a breath. "He doesn't know anything about Kara. Really, this is getting old. He's not well." But for all her stalling, she leads us into the living room.

Mr. Foster does look worse each time we've seen him, but we've got a murdered young woman, and I don't have time to coddle anyone who might know something.

"Mr. Foster?"

His rheumy eyes meet mine. "Sorry to bug you again, but we'd like to ask you a few more questions."

He nods. Chase and I sit on the couch, and I take my notebook out of my satchel. Ms. Musgrave stands like a sentinel, like she's Mr. Foster's bodyguard, ready to swoop in if we get too pushy.

"The night you heard the scream, you had fallen asleep in front of the TV?"

"Yes."

"You thought the news was on. Was it the six o'clock news?"

"Might've been," his voice is thin, scratchy. He eyes the beer can on his TV tray.

"Did you get up? Go to the window maybe?"

He shakes his head. "I was too tired."

"So, you just sat in your chair? Didn't move when you heard it?"

"I didn't move. I thought . . ."

"Yes?"

"I wasn't sure. Maybe I was dreaming?" He looks at me as if for confirmation.

Irene walks in front of me. "Detective, Tom has nightmares. Sometimes he thinks he hears screaming."

I blow out a breath. "Is that right, Mr. Foster? Did you think you were dreaming?"

"Maybe." His gaze shifts to the picture window, as if he's looking for something outside.

"But you never got out of your chair that night?"

"Just to go up to bed later."

Irene leans toward me and whispers. "Can I talk to you in the kitchen?"

I get up, shoot Chase a look. He stays put with Mr. Foster.

The kitchen is tidy, if sparse and worn. Irene leans against the counter.

"Tom isn't well."

"I know that."

"His mind is pretty well gone."

"Okay." Not sure I know exactly what she means.

"Thirteen years ago, he was in an accident, and his wife was killed."

"We know about the accident."

"He was driving, and he's never gotten over it. Blames himself. Now that he's sick, that's all he thinks about, that and"—she sniffs—"his daughter."

"Why his daughter?"

Her gaze shifts to the back window that looks out on the woods. "He just worries about her, okay? She didn't take her mother's death well, and he blames himself for her problems too." Irene straightens up, crosses her meaty, freckled arms across her chest. "But Esmé's a grown woman, I tell him. If she has problems, it's her own damn fault."

"Okay, what's this got to do with the night Kara was killed?"

"I'm just saying, Tom might not have heard a scream at all. The more I talked to him about it, the more I'm convinced what he heard wasn't real. It might just be a coincidence that Kara was killed while he was having one of his nightmares."

"We still need to ask him, Ms. Musgrave. He's the closest thing we've got to a witness."

"I don't want him harassed. He doesn't deserve to be tormented in his last days."

"I'm sorry about that." I wonder what part this woman plays in this strange family dynamic. "What's your interest in all this?"

Her mouth falls open like it's the silliest question she's ever heard. "I'm his friend. I've known Tom my whole life. I grew up in the house next door to his." She clamps her lips together like I've thrown down a dare. "My father was abusive when he was *sober.*" She laughs a sharp, short guffaw. "For most people, it's the other way around. Anyway, when he'd get a little too handy with his fists, I'd run next door to Tom's. When we got older, Tom told my father he'd knock his block off if he touched me. So I owe him. We're friends, and I won't let you or anyone else upset him."

"Sorry." But that explains a lot. "Don't mean to bother him. Just need to know what happened that night."

She shakes her head. "Nothing that Tom did. He wouldn't hurt a fly. Besides, he couldn't walk out to the pond if he wanted to. He doesn't have the strength."

"He's that weak?"

"Yeah, Detective, he is." She turns and heads back to the living room.

I make a couple of notes and start to drop my notebook in my satchel. I glance up and see Esmé standing in the doorway. She looks exhausted and washed out, as if she hasn't slept in a week.

"Detective Myers?" Her voice is soft and low.

"Yes?"

"I need to talk to you."

# CHAPTER 57
# Esmé

When I got home last night, the house was dark and quiet. I ran up the stairs and locked myself in my room. It was nearly three in the morning. I've never felt so betrayed before. I thought Mr. York was my friend. He was my mother's friend. Why would he treat me like that? The photographs of Kara flip through my brain. I can't unsee them. What kind of pervert is he? Could he have killed her? Why did he keep me locked up? What were his plans for me?

"Esmé?" Detective Myers sits at the table, pencil poised. She's all business, but I see a softness in her eyes. "What do you need to tell me?"

I clear my throat. What do I say? "Um, well, yesterday I went over to Mr. York's house. I've been modeling for him." She nods. "Kara used to model for him, I found out."

"Yes. We know."

My heart starts to beat in quick little thumps. "Have you questioned him? Did he have anything to do with what happened to her?"

"We don't know, but we don't have anything that indicates he was involved in her death."

"Well, um, he had me model a ballet costume." I swipe a tear from my cheek. "And I was really excited, you know? I miss it so much." My voice catches, and I fish a wad of tissues out of the pocket of my robe. “Anyway, I’ve known him since I was little. My mom and I used to go over there and visit. I trusted him.”

“Catch your breath,” she says. She’s drawing in her notebook.

I nod. “Anyway, he wanted to film me in the costume to show to his client. That’s what he said.” I bow my head. I wonder if there even was a client who was interested in ballet costumes. It all seems too convenient, and I must’ve been a fool not to see it. The pull of my old life was too strong. I hear low voices in the living room. I don’t want my dad to hear and be upset.

“What happened?”

“I don’t know. We went through several takes, but he was never satisfied. Then he brought me some soup and said we’d try again later. But then I fell asleep.” I look up and catch Detective Myers’s gaze. “It was weird. I think he put something in the soup. I think he wanted to keep me there. He went downstairs and locked me in.”

She puts her hand gently on my arm. “It’s okay, Esmé. Take your time.”

I wipe my cheeks and nod. “I tried to find a way out. I went looking for a key and I, um, went through some drawers in the booth, and I found some pictures.”

“What kind of pictures?”

“Kara. I found pictures of Kara, but she was, uh, nude.” I close my eyes. The room goes quiet. “Why? Why would he take pictures like that if she was supposed to be modeling costumes?” My voice rises in anger.

“Where did you find these pictures?”

“In the booth where he controls the lights and tapes.”

Detective Myers is writing, nodding her head. She finally looks up. “How did you get out of there?”

“I broke a piece of scenery before we started taping, and he came out to fix it. When he went for his tools, I took the keys off the counter and got away. I ran through the woods to get home.”

“Did he see you? Follow you?”

“I don’t think so.” Once home, I huddled in my bed, the ballet costume a heap of tulle and lace on my bedroom floor, my dad’s Glock on my nightstand.

“Okay, Esmé. That helps us.”

“I’m afraid, Detective. What if he comes after me?”

"You can press charges."

I take a deep breath. I can't think about this now. "Maybe. I'm not sure what I want to do."

"You don't have to decide this minute."

I glance up and catch her gaze. "I've still got his costume upstairs."

"You want to get it for me? Put it in a bag, and I'll return it to him."

"Yes. Thank you." I don't ever want to see Mr. York again.

"No problem." She clasps my arm. "And don't worry. We'll go talk to him, and warn him to stay away from you or we'll arrest him. And you call me if you need me, anytime." She slides a business card over to me. "You've been very helpful, Esmé."

# CHAPTER 58
# Rita

After lunch, I swing by Mr. York's place. He looks distinctly rattled when he comes to the door.

"Detective," he says with a sigh. "Back again so soon?"

"I have something of yours." I hold up the bag containing the costume. "Can I come in?"

His graying eyebrows draw together. He doesn't answer, just swings the door wide, and I follow him into the living room. We sit facing one another amid the antiques and fussy furniture. I hand him the bag, and he opens it slowly, as if it contains a rabid wolverine.

"Christ," he sighs. "What has she done?"

He pulls the costume out of the bag and runs his hands over it. "It'll take me hours to repair it." He huffs out a breath, and I almost think I see tears in his eyes.

"Don't you want to know how I got it, Mr. York?"

His gaze meets mine, frown lines fill his forehead. "Obviously, Esmé gave it to you. I can't believe the girl would be so careless."

"Mr. York?" He's spreading the costume across his lap, pushing away the pug who seems to want to help him.

"What is it?"

"Esmé told me that you locked her in your attic last night."

He sputters a moment. "That's ridiculous."

"She was scared to death, and she told me she got away and ran through the woods."

He sighs and clutches the frothy fabric in his age-spotted hands. "Esmé and I were working on a video for a client. Unfortunately, it got quite late and she"—he waves his hand in the air—"became overwrought."

"Overwrought?"

"Yes. She became emotional, Detective. I guess in retrospect, I may have pushed her too hard. But this is a tough business. You have to be perfect to stay ahead of the competition. I suppose I didn't realize how fragile she was."

"Uh-huh."

"She's quite emotional, you know. I think being back home has brought up the tragedy of her mother's death. That and the end of her dance career. And, of course, her father's illness. Enough to get one rattled, don't you think?"

"She does have a lot on her plate," I say. "How do you feel about losing her as a model, Mr. York?"

"Well, I don't know that I've lost her. She'll come around." He pauses, looks out the window. "Although I don't know that I'll trust her again in the state she's in."

"She didn't seem like she was in a 'state' when I talked to her."

"Well, be that as it may, I might not be able to use her again. She's damaged the bodice here." His hand shakes slightly as he grips the sequined fabric.

"Mr. York?"

"Yes?" He's annoyed. "I need to get to work, Detective. Are we quite finished?"

"Esmé told me that when she was in the attic, looking for the key to get out, she came across some pictures of Kara." He waits, the costume clutched in his hands like a precious family heirloom. "In the pictures, Kara was undressed, completely."

He blinks his eyes, licks his lips. "And?"

"Well, she was concerned. We're concerned, Mr. York. What was the purpose of the photos if Kara was here to model costumes?"

"Art," he says simply. "They were artistic shots, and Kara was agreeable and well paid for them." He clenches his jaw. There's a slight quiver in his cheeks.

"You didn't coerce her?"

"No."

"She didn't have second thoughts? Regrets? Maybe she wanted them destroyed or out of your possession?"

"Absolutely not. It's not illegal, you know. It's art, and Kara was of age."

I nod and scribble in my notebook. "Maybe Kara was going to talk to the cops about you, Mr. York."

He huffs. "For what? Like I said, the photos were consensual."

"Maybe. But maybe you didn't want Kara blabbing about them. Maybe you ran into her in the woods that night, and you two argued. Things got out of hand. You pushed her."

He shakes his head. "No. That never happened, Detective. And if you insist on harassing me, I'll have to get my lawyer involved."

# CHAPTER 59
# Esmé

After Detective Myers left yesterday, I went back to bed and slept, trading one escape for another—dancing in Mr. York's third floor to hiding in my nightmares. When I got up this morning, my dad was already downstairs in his chair. Byron is off today, and he's trying to get Dad to eat, but he doesn't look good. His face is dry and gray. Worry over him has my stomach in knots.

I make tea in the kitchen, and when I turn around, I see Irene standing in the doorway. I haven't spoken to her since the day she called my mother a slut. I place the milk carton back in the fridge, pick up my cup and start to walk past her, but she reaches out a fleshy hand and grabs my arm, her fingers pinching.

"What goddamn business did you have over at that nut's house?"

"What?"

"I heard you talking to Detective Myers yesterday."

"Did my dad hear?"

"No, thank God. I was in the hallway, headed to the bathroom, when I heard you." And probably stopped to listen, no doubt. She snorts. "You had no reason to be over there, worrying your father to death."

"Did he know that I was at Mr. York's?"

"No, but he knew you were out with someone. Your car was in the driveway, and he hadn't seen you all day. When I left for home at dinnertime, he was a worried mess. I had to make something up. I told him you were with your friends." She grunts. "But I guess like mother, like daughter."

"What does that mean?"

"She used to go over there all the time too. Leave your father here, no supper, wondering where she was."

"I'm not talking to you about this, Irene. It's none of your fucking business where I go."

"You ought to think about your father for a change. He's taken care of you, protected you, and this is how you reward him? What if something bad had happened to you over there? What if you ended up like Kara?"

Is she implying that Mr. York killed Kara? Did he? I shiver. My mind has obviously gone there since last night, despite my attempts to shut it out. It is too frightening, too close to the bone that my mother's friend for so many years could have such a dark side. I don't know whom to trust anymore.

"I'm fine, Irene."

"Just stay out of trouble, Esmé. Your father's suffered enough." She turns on her heel and heads back into the living room.

My phone chirps, and I set my tea on the table. It's Jack, wondering if I want to get together later.

The coffee shop is warm and snug. I concentrate on that as my friends group around me. I'm in the corner with Jack on one side and Laney on the other. Christy sits across from me. Laney takes my hand. There'd been hugs all around when we met. Jack picked me up after he finished at school and drove since my car won't start.

I'd been in my room all day in order to stay away from Irene, but I needed to get out of the house for a while. I'd called Collin yesterday and apologized for missing work. He was sweet and so concerned. I promised to show up for my shift tomorrow, although he told me to take all the time I needed.

I'd told Jack what had happened at Mr. York's house, and he told the others.

"How are you feeling?" Laney asks. We sit hunched over our coffee like the group we used to be, united, there for one another.

"I'm okay, really."

Jack shifts in his chair. "God, Esmé, I'm glad he didn't hurt you."

"It was strange. He kept talking like it was all normal. He kept making me dance over and over again. He said it needed to be perfect." My voice breaks. "I don't think he was going to let me leave."

"Is that all?" Christy asks. "You just danced?"

"Yes. But . . ."

Christy and Laney exchange a glance, like they know something that I don't. I get the feeling that I'm on probation or something, not quite trusted or accepted back into the group.

Christy sips her latte. "Well, I wouldn't go near him again, Esmé."

"I won't. But I trusted him. My mother trusted him." I didn't mention to Jack the nude pictures of Kara. It seemed like a betrayal of her. Maybe she didn't want anyone to know about those. It's enough for now that I told Detective Myers. I glance at my friends, Laney with her eyes on her coffee, Christy taking furtive glances out the window. Maybe Laney and Christy already know. Maybe Kara confided in them. That's what any of us would've done back in high school. There were no secrets among us. If so, why didn't they warn me?

Jack rubs his chin. "I thought that guy was harmless. I keep thinking about when we used to see him in the woods when we were in high school. He seemed nice enough, kind of strange, but not menacing, you know?"

Laney leans in. "Could he have been the one in the shack the other night? The one who attacked you, Jack?"

"I don't think so. That guy was strong."

"Maybe he's stronger than he looks."

I shiver, wrap my hands around my warm coffee mug. I don't know what to think about anything.

# CHAPTER 60
# Esmé

It's dark when Jack drops me off. The light's on in the living room, but Irene's car is gone, so I relax a little. Byron and Dad are sitting and watching TV, an old movie of some kind, like they used to when I was a teenager downtown dancing. They liked to turn the lights off and watch old horror films together. But, tonight, it sounds like a western. Horses and gunshots.

"How are you feeling, Dad?" I ask and sit on the end of the sofa nearest to his chair.

"I'm okay, Esmé. Did you have a good time with your friends?"

I wouldn't exactly call it a good time. "Yes. It was nice to see them."

"Did Jack make sure you got to the door okay?"

"Yes, Dad. He watched out for me."

"By, would you get me another, son?" Dad lifts an empty beer can with a shaking hand. "I think there's one left."

Byron gets up without a word and leaves the room.

"Jack's a nice young man," Dad says. "I always liked him. I felt like he'd protect you."

I take a deep breath. "From what, Dad? Why did I need protecting?"

He shakes his head, sighs. "The world's a dangerous place, Esmé."

"That's it? There was no one specific I needed to look out for?"

Byron returns and places the can on the end table. "You ought to go to bed, Dad. You look like you could use some sleep."

He nods. "Soon's I finish my beer."

Dad's asleep and Byron and I sit in the kitchen. "You ought to go to bed too, Ez," Byron says.

"I will soon."

"You look like death."

"Gee, thanks." I feel like death, my mind swirling with thoughts of Mr. York and Kara.

Byron gets up and walks to the window, looks out on the dark backyard.

"Maybe you should go back to Syracuse," he says.

"Why?"

"Nothing's gone right since you've been back."

"And that's my fault?"

He turns to face me. "That's not what I meant. Look, Kevin's a good guy. At least, that was my impression the one time I met him. Maybe you ought to give him another chance. What's here in Graybridge?"

I want to say my family, or what's left of it. And it's my home. For all the pain, there's something deep that connects us to the place where we grew up. The familiar scenery, the smells, the memories, even the frightening ones. It's a sense of belonging that never really seemed real in Syracuse. And my mother was here. Our shared histories. I couldn't seem to conjure an image of her in Syracuse, except in small dribs and drabs, flitting pictures in my brain. But here, in Graybridge, my mother lives and breathes. I can't really explain it.

"I don't know, By. I just don't think it's fair to him to make him think that we have a chance. And, well, my friends are here."

"Friends that you ditched and didn't keep in touch with for a decade?"

"I know. But I've liked being back with them." Especially Jack, I think to myself. There's something comforting about his friendship.

"What about a career? You aren't going to get anywhere working at the café."

"Yeah, I know that, Byron." I feel annoyance creeping up my spine. "I'll figure it out. Isn't it enough that I'm here with Dad?"

He takes a deep breath. "I guess, but he's worried about you, and that's not good for him. Stress doesn't help his illness. He felt a certain measure of calm when you weren't here."

My breath catches. "He doesn't want me here?"

"It's not that. That's not what I meant. He just thought you were safe and happy there."

"I don't know why he worries so much about me. That's not my fault."

Byron walks back to the table, sits. "Maybe not. But he worries about you the same way he did with Mom."

My memories of my mother are mostly caught up in our shared exploits together. Our camaraderie. Off at the dance studio. Dinners together after. Our visits to Mr. York. It's funny, when I think back, times with Mom and Dad together are hard to find in my memory. Surely, we did things together. We were together that fateful night when she died. The three of us. But besides that, my mind is full of Mom and me. Now, looking back as an adult, it seems strange. Their marriage couldn't have been great. I know it wasn't, but as a kid, I didn't see it or care, as long as they both loved me. It dawns on me as I sit in my childhood kitchen with the yellow curtains at the window that my mother hung, drinking out of mugs that she bought while I was with her at a garage sale. Maybe she wasn't the amazing woman who lives in my memory. Irene's hateful words whisper, and I push them away. She was just jealous, like Mr. York said. Maybe my parents' marriage wasn't perfect, but my father's love for her was deep.

"Well, he doesn't need to worry, Byron. I'm not going back to Mr. York's place, and I'll stay out of the woods. I only went through them because of my car."

"Speaking of. I'll help you in the morning. We'll jump it, and you can drive it down to the service station and get the battery replaced before you have to go to work."

"Thanks. That'll help." Luckily, I just got my first paycheck from the café. The battery should pretty well take care of that. I sigh.

# CHAPTER 61
# Rita

COLLIN TALKED ME INTO GOING TO A FLEA MARKET THIS MORNING. It's not often that we have a day off together, and André is in Connecticut visiting family. The day is warm and sunny, but I still need a sweater. I got up early, had my coffee, tried to chase away the cobwebs in my brain. I dressed in jeans and a long-sleeved T-shirt and left my hair down. I'm determined to forget about work for a while. That's why I agreed to go with Collin. My first plan was to sit at home and go over my notes, maybe give Lauren a call and bounce ideas off her. But sometimes your brain needs a break. I know that, so off to the flea market I go.

Collin drives, and we park in the crowded lot. Flea markets draw the early birds, I've learned. I like to go occasionally and look at other people's junk. Ma always said I was nosy, and she was right. I spent my childhood getting into other people's business, much to my older sisters' chagrin. That's one reason, I guess, why I became a detective—too interested in what goes on in other people's lives.

We wend our way through the crowded stalls, walk by a fussy kid or two, probably wanting to get outside and play in the sunshine. Collin spies a table covered in china. Looks like a pattern my grandmother had in her old house in Maine. My memories of her are scant. She was pretty old by the time I was coming up, but I remember those plates arranged in her china cabinet, and her admonition that we kids stay out of her dining room. I remember those better than that damn ceramic chicken Danny gave me.

Collin lifts a plate and flips it over. "I love this." He sighs. "But if I start another china collection, André's going to kill me."

"Why? If it makes you happy."

"We don't have a lot of room in the apartment." I know what's going through his mind. Collin would love to buy a house out in the country. A big place where he could spread out, indulge his love of antiques, and adopt a couple of dogs, but that dream has conditions, which he's reluctant to face. André has no interest. André's a city guy. I swear, nothing's easy in this life.

"Why don't you rent a storage unit?" I ask, trying to be helpful.

"Already have one, and it's packed." Collin sets the plate back in its spot, and we move on.

After a couple of hours, my stomach's growling. "You want to stop for lunch?"

Collin glances over his shopping basket; despite the left-behind plate, he found a few knickknacks. "I guess I'm ready."

"Is that all you're getting?" He points to the framed sketch in my hands.

"Yeah. That's it." I found a watercolor someone had painted of a lighthouse. I don't recognize it, but it reminds me again of going to my grandmother's place in Maine. A couple times a summer, my parents would pack us up in the station wagon, and we'd go see her for a couple days. It makes me smile to think back on those trips. We were stuffed in the car, some of us with no seat belts; there weren't enough to go around. We'd bicker the whole way, and my dad would threaten to pull the car over every ten minutes or so. He never did. I don't know what he would've done. Left a couple of us on the side of the road?

When I get home, I pull my phone out of my purse and see that I've got two missed calls from Lauren. I call her back as I walk through my apartment. I flip through mail I'd left on the counter, check the fridge for snack possibilities.

"Hi, Rita."

"What's up?"

"I've been doing a lot of digging, and I found another woman who said that she modeled for Mr. York." Lauren lowers her voice. "She said he pressured her into posing nude."

I blow out a breath. "A real predator. I swear, I don't know how these guys get away with it for so long."

"Well, times are changing," Lauren says.

"About time," I mutter. "Okay, so we know the guy is bad news. Let me grab a pen, Lauren. Give me the details." I take a deep breath. "I'll give him another call. Time somebody made him feel uncomfortable."

I make myself a cup of tea and tap in York's number. He answers on the fourth ring.

"Yes?"

"Mr. York, Detective Myers here."

He sighs. "I'm awfully busy. What now?"

I go over all the sordid history Lauren has uncovered on him. The line goes quiet. "Mr. York?"

He clears his throat. "Yes?"

"Well?"

"Misunderstandings. There's a lot of jostling and backbiting in this business, Detective. People will say anything to get ahead. There's no truth in any of it."

"So, you don't have a problem with any of these women going public with what they told us?"

"Have they threatened to?" There's panic in his voice.

"They're thinking about it." Silence. I'm afraid he's going to hang up. "Mr. York?"

"All right. What do you want from me?"

"Not me, Mr. York, but these women do deserve to be heard."

He blows out a breath. "Give me some time to discuss a few things with my lawyer."

"Why should I do that?"

"Has anyone made a formal complaint against me?"

"There are no charges—yet. And it seems to me that if you have had a pattern of abusing women, maybe you wouldn't hesitate to kill Kara to keep her quiet to protect your reputation."

He blows out a ragged breath. “I would never . . . I’m not guilty of murder. I had nothing to do with what happened to Kara.”

“I’m not sure I believe you, Mr. York.”

Silence again. It almost sounds as if he’s crying. “These women are going to speak out publicly, are they?”

“I believe so. Yes.”

“All right, Detective.” He clears his throat. “I didn’t kill Kara, but I know who did.”

# CHAPTER 62
# Esmé

Dad is sitting in his chair in the living room, and Byron is cleaning up the breakfast dishes. Byron's off again today, and I'm glad because Dad looks terrible, and I need to get to work. I sit and watch an old black-and-white sitcom with my father, but I'll need to head up to the shower in a few minutes.

"I'll bring you a treat from the café, Dad," I say. "When I get home tonight."

He smiles at me. "Do they make those eclairs I like?"

"Yes. They have amazing eclairs."

"They're my favorite," he says.

And I wonder why I had no idea. If I'd known, I'd have brought some home days ago. I sigh. "I'll bring home a dozen." I get up and walk around behind his chair, lean over and hug him, his dry cheek against mine. "I missed you, Dad, when I was gone." But it occurs to me that I've missed him my whole life.

He reaches up a shaking hand and pats the side of my head. "I missed you too."

My mind drifts back to when I was little, back before I started dancing downtown, when it all seemed to change. My dad teaching me to ride a two-wheeler in the driveway. Picking me up when I fell and brushing the gravel from my bloody knee, holding me in his strong arms and soothing my tears. He was a good father to Byron and me, and it occurs to me now that when Mom and I started going downtown to the big ballet school, we left him and Byron behind. That was really the end of our family, long before Mom died.

And I recall that Mom wasn't always there while I was in dance class. She didn't hang around the studio with the other mothers. Instead, I was sometimes waiting for her after everyone else had been picked up. She'd come rolling in, full of apologies, with some excuse, errands, traffic, but I was a kid. I didn't think much of it. Then we'd grab dinner together, and she'd ask me all about class, breathless and full of excitement. Looking back as an adult, it all seems a little strange, a little incongruous now. In the meantime, Dad and Byron were on their own, and I didn't give it a lot of thought back then, but now I'm filled with regret, guilt even, for the distance that grew between me and my dad. I sigh. Well, I'll try to make it up to him now. I'm home for good, and I'll never leave him again.

I'm in the shower when I hear Byron screaming. I run into the hall, pulling on my jeans, my hair dripping. "What? What happened?" I call, sprinting down the stairs.

Byron is in the living room, his phone clenched to his ear, his hand clutching Dad's limp wrist.

The hospital waiting room is cold and empty, save for me and my brother. They took Dad back to an exam room as soon as the ambulance pulled into the bay. Byron and I had followed in his car, and my brother told me that he'd found Dad unresponsive in his chair. He was breathing, had a pulse, but was unconscious.

Byron is talking to one of the nurses at the counter, while I pace in front of the plate-glass windows. The trees outside are covered in bright yellow leaves, but the cloud cover makes for a gloomy day. I smooth back my wet, tangled hair and cross my arms over my chest. I'm trying not to cry, but the tears come anyway.

Time crawls in a waiting room. I glance at my phone just for something to fill the minutes. I text Collin and let him know that I won't be in today. He's going to think I'm a total mess. I've missed more days than I've been in lately. But he responds quickly with a nice note, telling me not to worry and that he'll add Dad to his prayer list.

A woman and a little boy show up. The boy is about ten years old, crying, bubbling with tears, holding his arm. They displace Byron at the desk, and he comes back over to me.

"I called Irene."

I wheel on him. "You didn't!"

"That's what Dad would want, Ez. And that's what's important."

I want to tell Byron what she said about Mom, but I don't have the strength. Besides, it would only cause trouble. More pain at a time we don't need it. "I know," I say. "I guess you had to."

Byron draws a deep breath. "I don't think he's coming home. We've got to be prepared for that."

"Why?" Tears tremble on my cheeks. "Why did it get this far? Why didn't he get help?"

Byron drapes his arm around my shoulders. "He feels guilty for the accident. In his mind, he killed Mom. He told me that once, late one night a few years ago, when his drinking was starting to escalate."

"It wasn't his fault. I was there. It was icy and dark and . . ." But I think about their fight. Mom begging Dad to slow down, and the headlights behind us. I shiver. Maybe it was his fault, partly. I wipe my face with my sleeve. I don't know what to think. But I know the last thing he ever wanted was for Mom to die.

I turn, and Byron hugs me tight.

The sliding doors whoosh open, and Irene, in her royal blue jacket and stretch pants, strides through. She grabs Byron's arm, and we break apart.

"Where is he?" Her dark eyes flash behind her glasses.

"They're examining him, Irene. We haven't heard anything yet." Byron goes on to tell her how he found Dad in his chair. I walk away from them and sit on a slick vinyl couch near the window. There is a stack of rumpled, outdated magazines on the end table next to me, but I can't read. I can barely think. I gaze out the window instead, out past the trees to the parking lot and beyond, mindlessly watching traffic at the light.

# CHAPTER 63
# Rita

MY BREATH CAUGHT WHEN MR. YORK CLAIMED TO KNOW THE IDENTity of the killer, but despite my questions, he refused to name him over the phone. He said the murderer threatened to reveal his past if he were to come forward, but now that we've found these women, it no longer matters. *Sheesh.* Apparently, his reputation counted more than a young woman's death.

I drove to the station since Mr. York agreed to meet me there after contacting his lawyer. I worked at my desk, going back over my notes, made a few phone calls, and watched the clock. But the afternoon ticked on, and no Alan York, with or without an attorney.

I call him again, but his phone goes to voice mail. *Shit.* He better not have gone on the run. My heartbeat kicks up. Did he put me off so he could get a head start? I can't sit around here and wait, so I grab my satchel and jump into my van.

Of course, I hit every red light getting through town. People are out running errands and taking in the nice autumn day, while I've got a murderer to catch and don't have time to sit in traffic. I drum my fingers on the steering wheel. Finally, I turn down his street. I pass the little area where Kara parked the night she was killed. I push the accelerator, and my van makes a clicking, coughing noise and slides to a stop, engine dead.

"Shit!" I turn the key in the ignition, nothing. Just then a car flies past me heading away from the York place. It was moving so fast I couldn't get a bead on anything other than it was a dark sedan. I jump out and take off toward York's house on foot.

As I approach the residence, I notice that York's car is in the driveway and the front door is ajar. I pull my weapon from my side and slowly climb the steps.

"Mr. York?" I call, pushing the door open with my foot. It's quiet inside, still. Then one of the fluffy white dogs patters into the foyer. I stop in my tracks. The dog sits, tips his little head, and lifts a paw as if to show me the blood covering his feet.

The place is crawling with crime-scene techs, and the ME, Susan Gaines, is assessing the body of Alan York. He's sitting on his velvet couch, the back of his head splattered on the wall behind him, and a large oil painting is dotted with his blood.

He was still warm when I discovered him, so he hadn't been dead long. And then there was the dark car speeding from the scene. I radioed the station to put out a BOLO on the sedan, but I had no description to give them, other than it was a dark, four-door vehicle.

Susan shouts out orders and comes over to where I'm standing in the dining room among the bolts of cloth.

"No weapon?" I ask. I hadn't found one but wondered if anyone else did.

"Nope."

"So it wasn't a suicide?" Just want to cover that base, even though the car leaving the scene might suggest otherwise.

"No. Someone shot him in the forehead from several feet away, if I was going to venture a guess," Susan says. "And it is a guess, Rita."

"Got it." Susan is always loath to speculate before she's done a thorough postmortem.

"He told me he knew who murdered Kara. He was supposed to come in and give us a statement." I shake my head. "I wasn't sure I believed him."

Susan snorts. "I'd say he knew." But then she holds up her hands as if she'd said too much. "Your department. Let me get things figured out here, and I'll let you know what I find after the postmortem."

"Right. Thanks. Talk to you later." I take one more turn around the living room, finish my notes. Then I head back to the station, hitching a ride with a young officer.

I walk past Doug's office, where I hear him on the phone. He's digging into where Ray was getting his supply. Lauren's waiting for me in my office, her computer on her lap.

"I can't believe it, Rita," she says before I can even get my jacket off. "Someone killed Mr. York to keep him quiet?"

"Looks that way." I drop into my chair, blow out a heavy breath. "But how did they know he was about to talk?"

"They had to be watching him or have the place bugged."

"I guess." I shake my head. It couldn't have been random. That defies all common sense. My gaze meets Lauren's. "This is more complicated than we knew."

She draws a deep breath. "I still can't believe he'd let Kara's murderer go free to keep his past hidden."

I nod. "It takes all kinds, Lauren." She's young. Me, I've seen enough criminals over the years to know how evil and selfish the human heart can be.

# CHAPTER 64
# Esmé

Dad is tucked up in a hospital bed on the fourth floor. He hasn't regained consciousness and looks sunken and gray under the white, woven hospital blanket. Oxygen tubes run from his nose, and he's hooked up to other machines that monitor all his bodily functions. Byron circles the room, unable to sit still. He checks the monitors like he's on duty.

I sit in a chair next to Dad's bed and periodically rub his hand to reassure myself that he's still warm. Irene glowers at me from a chair in the corner. She's been on her phone, reading, texting, and totally ignoring me other than occasional severe looks from under her eyebrows. But she can go to hell for all I care. If it weren't for Byron insisting that Dad would want her here, I'd have thrown her out at the get-go.

The sun is starting to set, and we've been here all day. The room is a dull gray, and Byron leans over and snaps on the bedside light.

"Why don't you go down to the cafeteria, Esmé, and get something to eat. I'll sit with Dad. When you get back, I'll go."

I can't even think of food but know that Byron is right. "I won't be long," I say. "You want me to bring you something?"

"No. I'll go later. I want to talk to a couple people here anyway. See if I can find out if they've got any results from Dad's labs yet."

The doctor had told us little when he'd called us back to the exam room earlier, just that they were going to admit him and monitor him, run some tests. He didn't know when or if Dad would wake up.

I start down the hall, where nurses stride quickly in and out of patient rooms, hunched over their computers, documenting everything they do. No one looks in my direction as I walk past and head for the elevator.

The cafeteria is quiet, only a few other people mindlessly sliding trays along in front of random food stations. The smells are a homogenous blend of fried food and overcooked vegetables, with a tinge of antiseptic underneath it all. I grab a premade salad in a clamshell. It looks completely unappetizing, but I haven't eaten all day. I pick up a banana nut muffin, one of those mass-produced in an industrial bakery someplace, which makes me think of the café and all the carefully crafted pastries there. Oh, well. I probably won't taste it anyway, just something to keep my stomach quiet.

Luckily for me, when I return to Dad's room, Irene is gone.

"She had to go home to take care of her mother," Byron says. "But she'll be back in the morning."

"Great. Well, at least she won't be glaring at me the rest of the night."

"I'm going to go talk to a couple people, grab some food. Then I'll be back."

Byron leaves the room, and silence falls like a heavy blanket. I can almost hear the ticking of the machines hooked up to Dad. The curtains are still open, and the lights of the town flicker in the dark. I feel a sense of deep melancholy, realizing that I soon could become an orphan. Which is silly, since I'm a grown woman; still, almost thirty seems a young age to be parentless. I sigh, thinking about the years ahead, when I get married and Dad won't be there to walk me down the aisle. And if I have children someday, they won't have grandparents, at least not on my side. And I think about the time I've wasted staying away from Dad and my hometown. I threw myself into my dance career and hid from everything else, content, or so I thought, to separate myself from my past. And now, here I am, at my father's bedside when it's too late.

My phone vibrates. A text from Jack. That reminds me that I

haven't let anybody know about my dad, so I respond to Jack's text and then move on to my other friends.

When I finish, I stand and stretch. The muffin I ate earlier feels stuck in my throat, so I decide to go down the hall and buy a soda from the vending machine. The hospital has taken on that quiet after-dinner feel. I see no other visitors as I walk along the corridor. The doctors have completed their rounds and have left. Only the night-shift nurses are here now, the seven-to-seven shift that Byron usually works.

With a bottle of Coke in hand, I start back toward Dad's room. The building is eerily quiet. I pass a bank of windows. They are all dark, giving the hospital an otherworldly feel, as though we are cocooned in a building on another planet maybe. As I near Dad's room, I hear a voice, a hoarse whisper coming from inside. I stop outside the door and listen.

"Hello, Tom. Remember me? It's been years, I know." The voice is low, a man that I don't recognize, yet there's something familiar. My heart starts to hammer, and I look toward the nurses' station. There's no one there at the moment. I listen as the man begins to speak again.

"You killed someone I loved, Tom. How would you feel if I killed someone you love?"

I drop my soda, and the bottle rolls until it bumps up against the wall. My feet are planted, glued to the floor. I hear the man moving, the sound of footsteps. Is he leaving? Coming for me?

I turn and run down the hall and nearly collide with a nurse as she comes out of a patient's room. I reach the small waiting area and glance back over my shoulder. I see him at the end of the hall, a man in a thick winter coat, cap pulled low. My breath comes in gasps. He sees me and starts walking in my direction. I turn and run down the opposite hall, looking for the door to the stairs. I almost run past it, skid to a stop, bang it open, and fly down the concrete staircase. My breath is caught in my throat, and my hip pulses with pain. *He's real. He's real.*

I lean against the door, listening. I'm down on the second floor in a ladies' room across from another nurses' station. When I hear several female voices, I quietly exit the restroom and head to another small waiting room, like the one on the fourth floor. I hear laughter. It's the maternity ward, a place where there are reasons to laugh and be joyful, and there are people around. The man wouldn't dare bother me here. I sit where I can see down the hall and feel reassured by the sight of an elderly man, a grandparent maybe, talking excitedly with a nurse, a clutch of pink balloons in his hand.

I text Byron. He didn't see me in Dad's room, so he's been looking for me. I don't want to tell him what happened over the phone, so I just tell him that I'm coming up. I walk tentatively to the elevator. Its doors slide open, empty, so I get in and push the button for the fourth floor.

Byron is standing outside Dad's door, and I tell him what happened. "I can't believe a man was in here threatening Dad. Are you sure?"

"Yes, Byron. I didn't imagine it." We head into Dad's room. There's a stench in the air, something like body odor and unwashed clothes.

Byron checks Dad's monitors, holds his wrist.

"Well, he seems okay." He walks to the door and tips his head.

I follow him to the nurses' station, where a young nurse with a long blond ponytail is filling out paperwork.

"Stephanie?" Byron says. Her head bobs up. "Was anyone in my father's room, oh, about ten minutes ago?"

"Not that I saw. Why?"

"My sister says that when she came back from the vending machine, she heard a man talking to my father. Then he left."

She shakes her head, throws a look at an older nurse hunched over a computer. "Did you see anyone go into Mr. Foster's room, Linda?"

The woman takes a tired breath. "Nope," she says and returns to her work.

Byron glances down the hall. "Well, can you guys make sure that no one goes in there while my sister and I talk to security, just to be sure?"

"Of course, Byron," Stephanie says. "Is there a problem?"

"I don't know."

Byron uses his hospital badge to buzz us through to the security office. A young guy in a blue uniform is sitting behind a desk surrounded by TV monitors. His name tag says: Kent Dearborn.

Byron introduces himself, shows him his hospital ID, and asks to see footage from the fourth floor. The young man happily complies and runs the tape back. Graybridge General is a small-town hospital, and he probably doesn't have a whole lot to do. Dad's hall comes into view in crisp black and white. Byron and I hang over Kent's shoulders as he lets the tape roll.

We see Stephanie head into a patient's room and even see Linda working at her computer. She doesn't look up as the back of a man walks into the picture. My heart starts to race as we watch the man confidently walk past Linda and down the hall. He hesitates just a moment outside Dad's door, then goes inside.

I let out a long shaky breath, and Byron wraps an arm around my shoulders. "Shit," he murmurs.

"Who are you looking for?" Kent says. "That guy?"

"Yeah. Let the tape roll. I want to see his face when he leaves." We continue watching, and there I am walking toward Dad's room. I stop. I drop my soda on the floor and turn and run back out of the screen. A moment later, the man emerges from the room. I catch my breath. He looks older, Dad's age. But I don't recognize him.

"Who is it, Byron?" I plead.

He shakes his head. "I have no idea. An old friend of Dad's maybe?"

I turn to my brother, tears on my cheeks. "A friend who threatened to kill someone Dad loves?"

"Whoa." Kent jumps up from his desk. "You heard this guy threaten to kill somebody?"

"Yes." I drop down on a chair in the corner.

Byron turns to me. "You sure, Ez? That's what this guy said?"

"Yes, Byron." I take a deep slow breath. "I think he's the man from Mom's accident." I tip up my tear-stained face. "Believe me now?"

# CHAPTER 65
# Rita

It's getting late, and we haven't heard back from the guys on scene at the York residence. Bob's been pacing the station, poking his head into cubicles and offices. Two homicides in a couple of weeks, unheard of in Graybridge.

Finally, I hear raised, excited voices in the squad room, and I head out into the hall. Officer Simmons is standing, Bob and a group of others gathered around. He sees me coming and nods to me.

Simmons holds up an evidence bag containing what looks like something small and metal.

"Listening device," he says proudly. "We found it underneath the freaking coffee table."

Huh. All this over a young woman with no money, no power, with seemingly no reason that anyone would want to kill her. *Jesus.*

Lauren and I head into the conference room. Simmons and a couple of other officers who were at the scene follow shortly after. Simmons tosses the listening device on the table.

"I just got a call, Rita, from the guys still there. They've got three more. Found them in some of the other rooms."

I pick up the bag and examine the device through the plastic. Home surveillance has gotten so mainstream now, you can buy the damn things at Walmart. I get that people want to keep an eye on the babysitter. Some people even want to check on their pets when they're at work, but in this case, the technology was used for criminal purposes, something becoming more and more commonplace. Was someone listening on their phone or computer? Heard Mr. York talking to me? I wonder how the person who planted them got in. Was it someone that York knew?

I draw a deep breath and head to the whiteboard, glance over the list of suspects in Kara's murder, pick up a marker, and cross Mr. York off the list.

"That leaves us Ray and Byron, Rita," Lauren says. "Maybe Cynthia."

I blow out a breath, not an impressive list. "Let's see if Byron has an alibi for tonight. And check that Ray hasn't left the house or cut off his ankle monitor. And I'll talk to Cynthia again." But I feel like we're missing a huge piece of the puzzle. "I don't like any of these guys for it," I whisper. "Among other things, I just can't see Byron or Ray planting listening devices in York's house. And I seriously doubt that Cynthia was able to do that." My gaze shifts away from the cops sitting around the table. They're looking to me for answers, and I've got nothing. Nothing that I'd hang my hat on, that's for sure. And I'm standing here in a faded pair of jeans and an old concert T-shirt, the clothes I put on early this morning to go to the flea market. I look as incompetent as I feel right now.

My phone vibrates in my back pocket, where I've stashed it, like a teenager. I glance at the screen. Hmm. Byron Foster. That's convenient.

"Be right back," I say and walk out into the hall.

"Hello."

"Detective Myers?"

"Yes. What can I do for you, Mr. Foster?"

"I know it's late, but could you come up to Graybridge General?"

"Why? What happened?"

He sighs. "My dad's in the hospital. And Esmé overheard a man in his room. We've got him on security tape threatening my father."

This is strange. Maybe the break we need, and Mr. Foster is the closest thing we've got to a witness to Kara's murder. Maybe there's something there. "I'll be right over. By the way, Byron. How long have you been at the hospital?"

"Me? All day."

"What time did you get there?"

"This morning, early. Why?"

"You leave at any time?"

"No. We've been right here with Dad. He's not good, Detective."

"Okay. I'll be right there."

I get into a department unmarked vehicle, my new ride until I find out from my mechanic if my van can be saved, and make my way to the hospital. In the security office, two uniformed guys stand behind a desk surrounded with screens. Byron Foster stands with them. Black-and-white images of the hallways and entrances and exits flicker. Esmé is huddled in a chair in the corner.

They probably haven't heard about Mr. York yet. The media coverage has only just started. I decide to keep mum about it for now. One thing at a time. I pull my notebook out of my satchel while Kent Dearborn runs the tape in question for me.

I lean in and peer closely at the unidentified man. "Neither of you has any idea who he is?" I ask the Fosters.

"No, Detective. Never seen him before," Byron responds.

"Esmé?"

She shakes her head. There are tears on her cheeks, and she clasps a clump of tissues in her fist.

"So, what did you hear him say?" I ask her.

She draws a trembling breath. "He said, 'You killed someone I loved. How would you feel if I kill someone you love?' " Her gaze darts up at the two security officers.

I nod. "Okay. Let's find a quiet place where we can talk."

We find a small consultation room off the waiting area. Byron and his sister sit opposite me, and I lay my notebook on the table between us.

"You guys sure you have no idea who this guy is?"

"No," Byron answers. "Dad didn't have too many people around in recent years. Just Irene. He was embarrassed, I think, because he was so sick."

"Has your dad said anything about him? Does he know who the man is?"

Byron shakes his head. "Dad's unconscious, Detective. And probably won't wake up."

"I'm sorry." *Shit.* "Okay, then. So, who did your father kill?" I ask probably a little too bluntly. Now my mind is clicking all over the place. Maybe Mr. Foster wasn't as weak and out of it as he seemed a couple of weeks ago. Could he have killed Kara? Could that have happened?

Esmé chokes on a sob, and Byron answers. "He must've been talking about our mother, Detective. That's all I can figure."

I lean back in my chair. "You sure? Someone's that mad about something that happened thirteen years ago?"

My meaning slowly settles on them, and Byron shakes his head. "Not Kara. Dad would never have intentionally killed anyone. The guy had to be talking about our mother."

"But it was an accident. There were no charges filed."

"I know, but he never would've hurt Kara. Besides, he wasn't strong enough to have walked out to the pond. That's where she was attacked, right?"

"Yes. But maybe, in his mind, he felt threatened. Had just enough strength to make it out there and back. Thought Kara was someone else maybe."

"No way, Detective."

But this brings us back to Mr. York. How would Mr. Foster have managed that? He's been in the hospital while that murder took place.

"The man had to be talking about our mother. And my dad, well, he blames himself. That's why he drinks. It was an accident, but he was driving, and Mom died."

That brings up an uncomfortable question. "So, then, who loved your mother enough to threaten your father, especially all these years later?"

Byron shakes his head. "I have no idea."

"Esmé?" She seems to shrink into her chair.

"I don't know." Her voice is quiet, childlike. "But what if he is the man from the accident? The one who said he was going to kill me."

"Did it look like the same man?"

She shrugs. "I couldn't tell."

"Did it sound like him?"

She clears her throat, which sounds clogged with tears. "Maybe. It was a long time ago." She sits up straighter, her eyes brighten. "But it must be him, right? Who would threaten me then and now, basically say the same thing? And Dad was always worried about me. I didn't realize how much, but he was. Always asking if I was all right. Telling me to be careful. Making sure I was with friends." She flops back in her chair. "But everybody said I was crazy."

"No one said that," Byron says.

She turns on him. "You all did. 'There's no phantom, Esmé. It's your imagination, Esmé. You had a concussion.' "

"Okay, guys. Let's assume there was a man at the accident all those years ago and he threatened to kill you. Where's he been all this time?"

Byron shakes his head. "No idea." He studies his hands, then looks up at me. "But Dad pulled a gun on Esmé a few nights ago."

"What?"

"She told me." Byron glances at his sister. "She came in late after being out with her friends, and Dad thought she was someone else. So maybe this guy has been lurking around, and Dad knew it."

Maybe this mystery man was on his way to the Fosters' house a couple weeks ago and ran into Kara and killed her. Who knows? "Did he say who? Did he give you any clue to this man's identity?" I ask Esmé. But she shakes her head.

"No. He said he heard something. But then he said he was dreaming."

"Let me do some more digging." I make some notes, then glance up at the two of them. "In the meantime, be careful. Don't go out alone or be at the house alone. And I'll have an officer sit outside your dad's hospital door."

They nod. Bryon wraps an arm around his sister's shoulders.

I head out into the dark, chilly night.

# CHAPTER 66
# Esmé

WE'RE BACK AT THE HOSPITAL EARLY, AND THERE'S BEEN NO change in Dad's condition overnight. Just as Detective Myers promised, there's a uniform officer sitting in a chair next to Dad's door. He nods a greeting as we walk in. I'm just getting settled in the chair next to Dad's bed when my phone vibrates. I set down my coffee and check my texts. Jack. He says to call him.

Byron is right outside talking to the nurses, who've all been told to monitor Dad's room closely and to look out for an older man. I step into the hall and motion for Byron to go in and take up my place next to Dad. I wander down the hallway, keeping a sharp eye out, but there are quite a few people around this morning, and I feel fairly secure. I call Jack.

"Hi, Esmé. How's your dad?"

"The same. No change."

"I'm sorry."

"Thanks." The line goes silent.

"Um, I thought I'd let you know before you heard it on the news."

My heart starts to hammer. "What?"

"Someone killed Mr. York yesterday."

My breath catches in my throat. "Are you kidding?"

"Nope. They say someone shot him at his house."

I drop down on a vinyl chair in the waiting room. "When did it happen?"

"Sometime yesterday. I'm not sure when."

I don't know how to make sense of this. Even though my feelings for Mr. York have drastically changed in the last two days, I don't want him dead. My mind reaches back to my mom and him, laughing, talking, while I played in a corner of the parlor. He adored my mom and always reassured me that she was a good person, but now I don't know about either of them anymore. I put my hand over my mouth, trying to stop frustrated tears.

"Esmé? Are you all right?"

"Yeah. I'm just in shock. Who would've killed him, Jack?"

"Who would've killed Kara?"

"This is a nightmare." I think about the man in Dad's room last night. Maybe he killed Mr. York, then came up to the hospital. Maybe he's someone who was obsessed with my mom and knew that Mr. York was her friend. Maybe that's why Irene said what she did about my mother. Maybe because of this guy. "Um, I need to call Detective Myers, Jack. Can I call you back later?"

"Yes. Sure. Let me know if you need anything."

Detective Myers confirms what Jack told me, and she says that they are still investigating and don't know if there is any tie to Kara's murder, but she'll keep me posted. I got the feeling that she was busy and didn't really want to talk to me. I get it. Another murder so close to Kara's. The cops have got their hands full.

When I get back to Dad's room, Irene has taken up her post in the chair in the corner. Byron is standing next to her, and they're deep in conversation. Byron looks up at me, his eyes wide.

"Somebody murdered Mr. York," he says.

"I know. I just talked to Jack. He told me."

Byron paces the room. "This is crazy, Ez."

"He had enemies," Irene says.

"Like who?" Byron stops in front of her.

She waves her hand in front of her face. "He was a flake. Had women over to his place all the time. I heard things."

"What did you hear?" I ask.

"Nothing worth repeating."

"You better talk to the cops, Irene," Byron says.

She whooshes out a breath. "I don't know who would've killed him, Byron. I just know he was a nut, that's all." Irene's gaze meets mine.

I think she knows a lot more than she's saying. "Did you tell her about the man?" I ask Byron.

He shakes his head. "Haven't had a chance."

The door opens, and Dad's doctor comes in, carrying a laptop. "Good morning." He glances at me and Byron. "You want to step out into the hall? We'll go over your father's lab results."

# CHAPTER 67
# Rita

THE MORNING IS DARK WITH CLOUDS, AND IT LOOKS LIKE IT'S GOING to rain. I'm running a little late and quickly get ready for work—white-collared blouse, black pants, blazer, hair pulled up in a bun. When I called the station, Lauren told me that Ray Ridley was right where he was supposed to be yesterday. He hadn't left his house, but I still want to take a ride over there and see for myself and talk to his sister. As far as we know, they're the only two people who might've been home in the area when Mr. York was killed.

The house is quiet, and it takes Ray a few minutes to answer the door. He yawns and scratches his stomach. Guess I woke him up.

"You're up early, Detective," he says. "Don't you ever take a day off?"

"Too busy. How's it going, Ray?"

He jiggles his leg to draw my attention to his ankle monitor. "Okay. Not a whole lot to do except watch TV, play video games."

"It beats sitting in a cell at County."

"You got that right. Anyway, what're you here for?"

"Had a few questions."

He arches his bushy eyebrows. "Don't have anything to say without counsel, Detective."

"Yeah. I know. Can I talk to your sister, actually?"

He wrinkles his mouth like he's thinking. "What about?"

"You hear that Mr. York was killed yesterday?"

"We heard. Crazy." He takes a step back. "What happened?"

"Why don't we go inside, and I'll fill you in?"

"Yeah. Okay."

I don't see any sign of Cynthia, but I sit and tell Ray what I can about Mr. York.

"Shit." He glances out the window. "It's getting too dangerous around here. Might have to move."

Cynthia appears in the living room doorway. She's wearing an old jacket that's way too big for her and holding the large orange cat in her arms. Her nose is red-tipped and running slightly. Looks like she just came in from outside.

"I don't want to move, Ray," she says, like I'm not even in the room. "I want to stay here."

He glances up at her, smiles. "Just kidding, Cyn."

"Miss Ridley, could I talk to you a minute?"

She slowly shifts her gaze in my direction. "Why?"

"Just have a few questions."

She sidles past me and sits in the armchair in the corner and sets the cat on the floor, where he curls up at her feet. "Okay."

"Were you home yesterday?"

She nods.

"Did you go outside at all?"

"Yes."

"Where did you go?"

"Just down to the pond."

"That's all?"

"Yes."

"You see anyone out in the woods. Hear any noises?"

"No," she says quickly.

"What time, Cynthia, were you out there?"

She looks at her brother.

Ray scratches his head. "Early," he says. "I think it was morning, wasn't it, Cyn?"

She nods.

Ray jumps up. “She wouldn’t know anything about Mr. York. She knows better than to go near that place.”

“All right. Is that true, Cynthia? You didn’t go near Mr. York’s place yesterday?”

She shakes her head, leans over, and pulls a knitting needle from her basket. “I never go over there,” she says, looking at the floor.

“Okay.” I extricate myself from the couch, stand. “Neither of you saw or heard anything from Mr. York’s direction yesterday?”

“We heard the sirens later,” Ray says, shrugs. “I thought maybe Mr. York had a heart attack or something. Not like I can go anywhere to investigate.” He glances down at his ankle monitor.

“So neither of you saw or heard anything from Mr. York’s direction before the sirens?”

“No, Detective. We have no clue what happened over there.”

# CHAPTER 68
# Esmé

WITH KIND BROWN EYES, DR. DELGADO TELLS US THAT THE NEWS isn't good. Dad's organs are starting to shut down, and there's nothing they can do. Years of heavy drinking have done their work, and Dad's body can't take anymore. He can't tell us how much time Dad has, but it isn't much, and it will just be a waiting game.

Byron wraps an arm around my shoulders, and we head back into Dad's room. I sit heavily in the chair next to his bed and take his withered hand in mine. I wonder if he even knows we're here.

Irene follows Byron out into the hall, and they're gone a while. I feel utterly alone, so after wiping my face with a rough hospital tissue, I text my friends to let them know about Dad. After a few minutes. I hear a gaggle of voices in the hall.

Officer Dearborn stands with Irene and Byron and the Graybridge cop. "We haven't seen any trace of the guy this morning," the security officer says. "But we printed out a picture from the tape and gave it to our people at the doors." He hands one of the pictures to my brother and another to the Graybridge cop.

Irene's face is creased with confusion.

"Thanks," Byron says, and Officer Dearborn heads back down the hall.

The Graybridge cop sits back in his chair and pulls out his phone. "I'll send a copy of the picture over to the station," he says.

As we start to walk back into Dad's room, Irene asks, "What was that about?"

Byron clears his throat. "Last night, Esmé heard a man in Dad's room." He tells her about the incident, and Irene snatches the picture from Byron's hand. She bites her lower lip and nods.

"Do you know him?" I ask, my throat rough with tears.

She snorts. "Why don't you two come down to the waiting room with me." She whispers, "I don't know if Tom can hear us, but I don't want to take a chance." She walks away, and I grab her arm. She whirls on me, her eyes flashing.

"You know who he is, don't you!" I scream.

She almost smiles. "Yes."

# CHAPTER 69
# Rita

I HEAD BACK TO THE STATION. THE CHIEF HAS CALLED EVERYONE INTO the conference room to go over the York case. There are big bags under Bob's eyes, and he holds onto the back of the chair as he speaks, taking huge breaths.

I'm sitting at the table, notebook open, when Connors walks in. She hands me a photo, black-and-white, of the man caught on security cameras at the hospital. I look back over what Esmé told me about her mystery man. This is the most tangled web I've ever investigated, even counting my years with the Boston PD. Is it possible that someone from thirteen years ago is back and did kill Kara because he thought she was Esmé? Maybe Mr. York saw it happen and the man threatened him with exposure of his past if he didn't keep quiet. It would've had to be someone who knew of York's past. Someone who'd been around a while, so maybe. I flip back and forth in my notebook.

"Rita?" I realize the chief is looking at me. "Anything?"

I stand with the photo. "This was captured on hospital security cameras," I say and fill in everyone on what we know about the mystery man, which is all conjecture. "It seems apparent that whoever killed Mr. York also killed Kara. That's the bottom line. We have Byron Foster, who says he was at the hospital when Mr. York was killed. We have Ray Ridley, whose ankle monitor puts him at home during the murder. Then there's his sister, Cynthia. And now we have this mystery man."

"Maybe it was two people, Rita," Lauren says from the back of the room.

"Right. Two people working together. That's a possibility." I turn back to the board, my eyes going over the photo. "But who is this guy?" I blow out a breath. "Anyway, these are our people of interest," I say with little gusto. "But I'm open to any ideas."

People start to filter out of the conference room, Bob in the lead, until only Lauren and I remain standing in front of the whiteboard.

My phone vibrates on the table where I'd left it next to my notebook. I glance at the screen. The lab.

"What's next, Rita?" Lauren asks.

I hold up a wait-a-minute-finger to Lauren. "Hello?"

"Detective Myers? Mark Goodson here."

"Yes. Mark. What do you have for me?" I ask, hopeful.

"We finally got the report back on the victim's fingernail scrapings in the Cunningham case."

"What took so damn long?" My heart is thumping.

"Sorry. We're really backed up, and a couple priorities came in."

"And this wasn't?"

"You know how it goes, Detective."

"Yeah. Right." Politics. Someone with more clout than the little Graybridge PD. "So?"

"We got DNA."

My gaze meets Lauren's, and I can hardly breathe. "What?"

"After eliminating Kara, we ran it, but it didn't match anyone in the system."

I blow out a breath. Put my hand to my forehead. "Okay. Great," I say sarcastically. "Thanks, Mark."

"Wait a minute."

"Yes?"

"I do have one bit of information that might help."

"What's that?"

"The DNA was female."

# CHAPTER 70
# Esmé

MY HEART IS THUMPING SO HARD I THINK OTHER PEOPLE CAN HEAR it. We sit in a corner of the little waiting room, which smells like old coffee and Lemon Pledge. A woman sits in the opposite corner talking on her phone. Irene shoots her an annoyed glance.

"What do you know about this man?" Byron asks.

Irene draws a breath, eyes the woman again. "Your dad didn't want you kids to know."

"Why not!" Byron shouts, and the woman, finally taking a hint, gets up, still talking on her phone, and walks out.

"All right." She stares directly at me, and I feel a cold chill work through my bones.

"He and your mother had an affair."

My breath flies out of me, and I slump forward like a deflated balloon.

"For years," Irene continues slowly, as if relishing each word.

In the back of my mind, I knew. Had always known. My mother's dissatisfaction with her life, her lingering looks across empty rooms, odd smiles as if she'd thought of something or someone who wasn't there. But I didn't want to believe it was possible.

Byron blows out a breath, his gaze on the floor. "So why didn't she leave? Why did they stay married?"

"Your dad claims they didn't want to hurt you kids." Irene glances around the room. "If you ask me, Jennifer played both of them. Liked having two men fighting for her."

"Jesus, Irene. My mother's dead. Give her a break," Byron says.

She clears her throat. Adjusts her glasses. "Sorry. Just my opinion."

"Was he following us that night? The night of the accident?" I ask, my voice raw and throaty.

"Yes." Irene sneers.

I shiver and shake my head. I feel Byron's arm around my shoulders.

"And I guess you want to know why your dad said you were mistaken about the man at the accident, am I right?" Irene says, her voice tinged with triumph. I nod. "Well, he wanted to protect you. He never wanted you kids to know that your mother was catting around."

"Hey," Byron says, his voice low and dangerous. "Be civil, Irene. You want to stay here at Dad's bedside, watch your tone."

She snorts. "Sorry. Anyway. It all came to a head that night. Tom told me afterward that he and Jennifer had been fighting. He told her she needed to get rid of this guy, or he would take you kids and leave. He'd had enough. But the guy was waiting for them outside the restaurant and followed them. The road was icy, and, well, the car skidded into that tree." Irene clears her throat and looks at me. "Your dad was devastated when Jennifer died. It was the last damn thing he wanted. For whatever reason, he loved her."

I shake my head, try to slow my breathing. "But why . . . why did the guy threaten to kill me?" I dissolve into tears. "He . . . he . . . said, 'I'll kill you! I'll kill you!' "

Irene nearly laughs, her stomach ripples, and she clears her throat. "He wasn't talking to you, you idiot, he was talking to your father. Why would he want to kill *you*?"

"But I heard him last night. He told Dad, 'How would you like it if I killed someone you love?' "

Irene takes a deep breath, swishes her hand in the air. "He's all talk. He isn't going to hurt anybody." She chuckles.

"You know this guy." Byron straightens up, looks squarely at Irene.

"Shit. Of course I do." She points at Byron. "And so do you."

"What?" I manage to whisper. "Who?"

Irene crosses her arms, her glasses gleaming. "Ray Ridley Senior."

# CHAPTER 71
# Rita

LAUREN AND I LOOK AT ONE ANOTHER IN ASTONISHMENT. "CYNthia!"

The chief has poked his head back in at the door.

"Rita? When you have a minute, stop by my office." He must see the looks on our faces. He comes in and shuts the door. "What?"

I walk over to the whiteboard and slash through the names on our suspect list. "It wasn't either of these guys. At least not for Kara's murder."

"What happened?"

"Just got a call from the lab. DNA under Kara's fingernails was female."

"A woman?" Bob says, shaking his head.

I let go a deep breath. *Shit.* "How did I not see this?" I say, pacing. "I should've known better. Cynthia could very well have been in those woods. And she's already been incarcerated for killing someone."

Lauren is sitting at the table, clicking the keys of her laptop.

Bob shoots me a look. "Still, when a beautiful young girl is killed, statistics back up the perp being a man."

I whirl on him, angry at myself. "Yeah, but there was no sexual element; the vic had scratches on her arms." I tick off the clues on my hand. "The weapon was a rock, something handy, which makes me think this was a fight, not something planned out, and the fact that Kara's injuries weren't immediately fatal."

"How does that say a woman did it?" Bob sinks down into a chair, settling his bulk with a groan.

"It just points in that direction, but I was so hung up on Byron Foster and Ray Ridley. And everything we dug up on Cynthia seemed to indicate that she hasn't been violent in the twenty years since her sister's death."

"The men were the most obvious perps, Rita."

I start pacing again. "Then when we found out about Kara and York, he seemed like a possibility." I stop walking, place my hand on the back of a chair. "But I didn't even seriously consider Cynthia. Not like I should have."

"We don't know it was her, Rita. Just because she knocked her sister out of a rowboat twenty-some years ago." Bob peeps up at me from under his bushy eyebrows.

I blow out a breath. "I know." I draw a frustrated breath. "But maybe she and Kara got into an argument. They tussle, thus the scratches on Kara's arms. Men don't typically scratch in a fight. I should've seen that the killer was a woman. From her injuries, we know that Kara must've turned her back on her killer at some point, so she wasn't all that concerned. Would a woman do that if she were fighting with a man? I don't think so, unless it was to run, but that doesn't fit either. I think Kara knew her killer, got into an argument; it turned a little physical, and when Kara turned to leave the woods, her killer picked up the first handy thing and, in a rage, struck Kara in the back of the head, but not hard enough to kill her outright. Again, a man probably would've been strong enough to strike Kara down right there at the pond." I collapse into a chair and blow out a breath. "Jesus, Bob."

"Don't be too hard on yourself. No one was really thinking about a woman."

"But then who killed Alan York? That could've been a man. A man who wanted to protect Kara's killer." I bang my fist on the table. "Or maybe it was the woman who killed Kara. Cynthia pretty much has the run of those woods. She was around. Fuck."

Lauren looks up from her computer. "I'm going back through all the women we interviewed, Rita. We probably should start from scratch, now that we know the killer was a woman."

"You're right. Let's be thorough. I don't want to make any more assumptions." I hop back up and go to the whiteboard, pick up a red marker. "Okay. Let's go back and look at every woman who we know knew Kara before we decide the killer was Cynthia. Laney Addison, Christy Bowers, Esmé Foster." I take a breath, put my hand on my hip. "Irene Musgrave. Let's include her. Shit." I turn toward Lauren. "What was the name of that older lady who works at the insurance office?"

Lauren scrolls through her laptop. "Marie Romano."

I write her name on the board. "Anyone else you guys can think of? Bob? You were her neighbor."

"That was a long time ago, Rita. I can't think of anyone else."

"Okay. Well, that's a start. Add Hannah Dabrowski. She could've been in those woods."

Bob pulls himself to his feet. "And if this woman also killed York, she would've had the wherewithal to monitor York's place and had a gun to kill him with."

"Or had someone to help her," I say.

# CHAPTER 72
# Esmé

WE'VE LEFT IRENE WITH DAD, AND BYRON AND I ARE HEADED TO the police station. Detective Myers needs to know that we've identified the man in Dad's room and see if he has any connection to Kara. Strangely, the sun has peeked out, and the autumn leaves nearly shimmer. It's a beautiful day, and I try to let that fill my mind and displace Irene's words. I can't dwell on them now.

We pull into the small visitors' lot and check in at the desk in the lobby. The building is old, brick, and smells slightly of mold and paper inside. A young officer comes to get us and escorts us to Detective Myers's office.

She's fast at work on her computer and hastily finishes typing and closes the top when she sees us. The office is small, and there's only one chair for visitors, so the young officer brings in a folding chair from the other room, and we get settled across from Detective Myers.

"How's your dad?" she asks.

"Not good," Byron says. "He doesn't have much time."

"I'm sorry to hear that." She sets her notebook on the desk, opens it, and picks up a pencil. "What did you want to talk to me about?"

"We know who the man was at the hospital last night," I say. "And he was the same man who threatened me, or actually my dad, after the accident when my mom was killed."

Detective Myers drops her pencil, and her eyes meet mine. "Okay, so who is he?"

Byron says, "Ray Ridley Senior."

Her eyes widen. "Really? Who identified him?"

"Irene Musgrave, my father's . . . friend. The security officer at the hospital showed her a picture from the tape."

"She sure?"

"Yes," Byron says.

"Didn't know he was still around." Detective Myers is rapping her pencil against her notebook, biting her lips.

"None of us did. We hadn't seen him in years," Byron says. "You think he could've killed Kara?"

"We'll talk to him." She stands abruptly. "In the meantime, stay away from him."

The meeting is clearly at an end. Detective Myers seems eager to get us on our way, which is fine. I want to get back to Dad.

"Oh," she says. "You wouldn't happen to know where Mr. Ridley is staying, would you?"

"Not a clue," Byron says, and we head for the door.

# CHAPTER 73
# Rita

RAY RIDLEY SENIOR—WELL, THERE'S A BLAST FROM THE PAST. I remember him. Ramblin' Ray, the country music DJ. I didn't listen to country music much, but he was something of a local minor celebrity. His picture would pop up occasionally on a billboard. Handsome, long dark mullet haircut, cowboy hat, and his trademark mirrored sunglasses. But the radio station had been bought out years ago by a national company, as so many stations were, and Ray faded from local view. I hadn't heard anything about him in years, and frankly, when I spoke with Ray Junior, I hadn't even thought of his dad. The connection seemed incongruous, like Ray Senior had no family or people he was attached to.

So, Ray Senior is back in town. And it just so happens his daughter is a murder suspect who probably would've needed help in eliminating a potential witness. Cynthia doesn't seem capable of bugging Mr. York's place, but Ray Senior, with his knowledge of radio, might know how to do it. And maybe visiting Mr. Foster, an old adversary, was just a side trip for the ex-DJ.

I've had Lauren looking into Ray Senior all afternoon, while I reread Cynthia's old arrest files and notes we got from her incarceration. According to the reports, Cynthia said she didn't mean to kill her sister. Maybe she didn't mean to kill Kara either.

Dark has fallen, and I get up to check on the weather outside before I head home. The streetlight in front of the station illuminates the small lot. Everything's quiet, no rain. My radio's on low, and I hum along to CSN's "Dark Star," one of my favorite songs. It fits my mood right now.

Lauren raps on my door frame. "I think I've got all there is to find on Mr. Ridley, Rita."

"Great. Have a seat." I sit behind my desk, fold my hands across my stomach.

"Okay." Lauren's eyes are on her screen. "The Ridleys divorced the same year their daughter died, and Ray moved out. Rented an apartment downtown. Mrs. Foster died eight years later. Ray was still working at the radio station another two years after that, until it was bought out. After that, I traced him to Manchester, New Hampshire, where he got a job at a radio station. But, a year later, he was arrested." She looks up and meets my gaze. "Felony drug charge."

"Like father, like son," I say.

"Looks like he was in a treatment program but reoffended and went to prison."

"How long was he incarcerated?"

"Looks like until last year. He got out about eleven months ago."

"Where was he after that?"

"I couldn't find an address for him until he pops up last March in Boston. According to what I've been able to dig up, he stays most of the time at a homeless shelter downtown."

"How the mighty have fallen." I think back to those '90s billboards. I write down the address and phone number for the shelter.

"What are you thinking, Rita?" Lauren asks.

"I don't know. But I know enough not to make any more assumptions. I want to see if Mr. Ridley will talk to us. See what he has to say. If Cynthia killed Kara, would daddy cover for her? Would he have killed Mr. York?"

# CHAPTER 74
# Esmé

It's late, and I'm exhausted. The revelations of the day and Dad's deteriorating condition have sucked all the energy from my body and soul. I watch him from my chair, his chest slowly rising and falling. All in one day, I feel like I've lost both my parents. My mother isn't the woman I'd hoped she was. Just like my artificial world of dance, my mother wasn't real either.

Irene left after delivering her secrets like a messenger from hell, but said she'd be back in the morning. Neither Byron nor I had the strength or interest to try to prevent her return. Byron walks into the room after talking to Dad's nurses.

"Let's go home, Ez. They'll keep a good eye on him. Stephanie said she'd call me the minute anything changes."

I shake my head, wipe tears from my cheeks.

"Come on," Byron says. "He'd want you to get some rest."

I stand, reluctantly, my legs shaky, and we head out.

The house is dark and lonely, and I avoid the living room where Dad's chair sits, the remote on the end table next to it, never to see its owner again. No one last old movie or noisy game show. They will go on without him.

Byron and I sit at the kitchen table and drink tea. Someone rings the doorbell, and Byron gets up. If it's Irene, I think I'll scream, but she'd just barge right in, so it's someone else.

Jack follows Byron into the kitchen. He's holding a takeout bag. "Hi. I thought you guys might be hungry." He sets the bag on the table. "I remembered that you used to like Chinese."

I wipe my eyes with my fingers. "Thanks. That was really sweet."

Byron lays the containers on the table and gets out plates. "Join us, Jack?" he asks.

"Sure, if you feel up to me hanging around." He stands, fidgety.

"Please," I say. "We could use the company."

When we're settled with our food, I clear my throat, look at Jack. "So, how's school?"

He swallows, sips a glass of water. "Good. Fine. Homecoming's next weekend, and I've got to chaperone that."

He seems to get that we don't want to talk about our dad and launches into all that's happening at Graybridge High School. "Had to break up a fight on Friday," he says. "Two girls. I thought, no sweat, so I got between them, and before I knew it, I was flat on my back, and they were still going at it."

Byron laughs, and Jack smiles. "Yeah. Talk about embarrassing. The school resource officer showed up a minute later and helped me up."

"What happened to the girls?" Byron asks.

"Out of school suspension. Could be worse since I technically was assaulted." Jack manages to lighten our mood, just a little, as the clock over the stove ticks toward midnight.

I get up to go the bathroom and see a car go past the front window. The car slows and comes to a stop in front of the house. It's too dark to see anything but the headlights. I move to the window, past my dad's chair. The car is definitely sitting in front of the house. I shiver. Is it Ray Senior? I hurry into the front hall and snap on the porch light. But its glow doesn't extend far enough to make out any details. The car moves off in a hurry and continues down the road toward the main street.

# CHAPTER 75
# Rita

On Monday morning, Chase parks the squad car in a lot down from the shelter. Boston smells like it always does, exhaust, fried food, and a touch of seawater. We walk along the street, past the snarled traffic and honking horns. A sharp urine odor wafts from an alley as we pass. Down the block a man stands, resting his back on the front of the shelter building.

He's bundled in a thick tatty coat of indeterminate color, but instead of the cap he had on at the hospital, he's wearing a stained, gray cowboy hat. He looks over when I call his name.

"Detectives?" he asks, voice rough. He drops a cigarette and crushes it into the sidewalk with the heel of his battered boot.

Chase and I show him our identification. "Can we go someplace and talk, Mr. Ridley?"

"There's a diner on the next block."

I know how this goes. He's angling for a free meal, which I don't mind. Least we can do for a guy down on his luck. And he'd readily agreed to talk to us when I'd spoken to him this morning. I was lucky to catch him at the shelter before he started his day on the streets.

It's warm, almost too warm, inside the restaurant. It's been here a million years but isn't as shabby as it could be. Smells like donuts and coffee. Chase slides into a red vinyl booth, and I sit next to him. It takes Ray a minute. He's seen someone he knows sitting on a stool, hunched over a mug at the lunch counter. They trade some light banter, and Ray slaps the man on the back before sitting down across from us. Doesn't act like a guy who recently killed somebody, but you never know.

I finally get a good look at him, long gray hair dangling over his shoulders, rutted cheeks, and that hollow look of a years-long addict—or former addict, as he told me on the phone. A definite stench emanates either from him or the old coat, maybe both.

He orders a full fried breakfast, and a tired, elderly waitress places cups of coffee in front of the three of us. Ray lifts his to his nearly toothless mouth and smacks his lips. "They make good coffee here."

"So, tell us, Ray, what you've been up to," I say, pulling my notebook from my satchel. I'm almost excited to draw this guy. His face definitely tells a story.

He leans back, pulls in a deep breath. "What do you want to know?"

"Were you at the hospital in Graybridge on Saturday evening?" No sense beating around the bush.

He nods, eyes suddenly vacant. "Yes. I was there." His speech is strangely formal; he enunciates his words carefully, with a slight lisp, owing to the missing teeth probably. But I remember his occupation or former occupation. Elocution was part of his stock-in-trade.

He coughs. Sips his coffee. Chase is pouring a buttload of sugar into his own from the glass and metal container on the table.

"I went to visit an old friend." He removes his hat and sets it on the seat next to him. His gray hair is thin on top and greasy, stuck to his pink scalp.

"Who would this friend be?"

He sighs. "Tom Foster. But I guess you figured that out already."

I nod, sketch his withered face. "You threaten him, Ray?"

He shakes his head. His gaze shifts out the plate-glass window. "No."

The waitress slides a big oval dish with fried eggs, bacon, sausage, and toast in front of Ray. "Thank you, darlin'," he says in his DJ voice.

"Mr. Ridley, how long have you been back in Massachusetts?" I look over my notes. "We discovered that you lived in New Hampshire for some time."

"That I did." He stabs a corner of a piece of toast into glistening egg yolk. He chews a minute, swallows and smirks, sips his coffee. "Would you like to hear the whole story? The sorry life of Ramblin' Ray, your country music DJ?"

Chase looks up from his phone, where he's been taking notes. I have a feeling this may take a while but may be worth it. We'll see.

"We're all ears, Ray."

"Okay. Where to start?" His gaze drifts to the stained ceiling for a moment.

"How about the night Jennifer Foster died?" Might as well get all the background.

He blows out a breath. Taps the table with long, yellowed fingernails and shakes his head. "Beautiful Jennifer. Yes. That's the place to start. Everything went to hell after that." He takes a deep breath. "She was the love of my life, as the phrase goes. She and I had been together eight years when she died. Amazing, but tumultuous years, but that was Jen. Every man in town wanted her, so I put up with it. I wanted her to leave Tom, of course." He cuts into the sausage and spears up a bite. "I used to work out past Graybridge, a little building in the country where the radio station was at the time. She'd sneak away and join me there sometimes. There were only a few people who worked there besides me. Jen would sneak in a bottle of wine or peach schnapps, something, and I'd play music, all the country hits." Ray smiles, the memories transporting him to a bygone time.

"What about the night she died?" I ask, trying to get him back on track and move things along.

"Right." He nods. "They were out to eat, and I'd followed them to the restaurant. Things were getting dicey. Tom wasn't going to put up with it any longer, and Jennifer was going to have to choose one of us. Well, when they got into their car, I followed them down the road. I felt like we three should talk. There were three of us in that relationship. Anyway, it was cold as a bastard that night, freezing rain, and Tom was driving too fast. When he hit that curve on

Miller Road, his tires wouldn't hold the pavement, and he skidded into a big tree."

Ray's eyes water, and he wipes them with his napkin. I wonder how one woman could have such an effect on a man all these years later. Who knows?

"I was devastated, Detective." Ray's gaze finds mine. "I got out, and I could see that Jen's side of the car took the brunt of the impact." He takes a big breath. "I tried to reach her, but she was dead. All I could see was her beautiful blond hair, blood everywhere. Well, I lost it. I opened the back door, trying to get to Tom."

"Esmé thinks you threatened to kill her."

Ray falls back against his seat. "Little Esmé? Really? She was in the car, and, thank God, she wasn't hurt. I picked her up out of the snow where she'd crawled out of the wreck. I screamed at *Tom.* I'd kill *him.*"

I drop my fist on the table with a thump. "Esmé's been freaked out for thirteen years thinking some man wants to kill her."

"Aww, God." He clasps his hand over his mouth. "I wouldn't have hurt her. I wouldn't have hurt anybody except Tom." He lets out a slow breath. "Jennifer loved Esmé. She was so proud of her."

"So, Ray, when you went up to see Tom Foster at the hospital, you didn't threaten to kill someone he loved? That's what Esmé heard."

"She heard that?" Ray hangs his head. "I didn't mean it. I shouldn't have said it. Don't get me wrong; there's no love lost between me and Tom, but I should've stayed away. I just happened to be in Graybridge when I heard he was on his deathbed at the hospital."

"What were you doing in Graybridge?"

He sips his coffee, looks away. "I took the bus out there to check on my daughter."

Bingo. "Cynthia?"

"Yes. She's living back at the house with her brother. But I'm her legal guardian. I got that squared away after I got out of prison."

"Were you there Saturday?"

"Yes. That was the day."

"What time? What time did you talk to Cynthia?"

He looks up at the ceiling again. "I don't know exactly. Morning sometime."

"Where?"

"At the pond. She likes to meet there."

"Then what?"

"I left. Walked back through the woods and up the road to the bus stop."

But did he stop off at Mr. York's place? "That's all you did after you spoke to Cynthia?"

He draws his eyebrows together. "Yes."

I look down at my notes. "But you weren't spotted at the hospital until hours later. What were you doing all that time in between?"

"Nothing much. Went to Graybridge Square. Walked around. Had a bite to eat. Then waited for the bus that went out to the hospital."

"Huh. That's it then?"

He shrugs. "Yes. Why?"

"You'd protect Cynthia, if need be?"

"Of course. She's my little girl." He clears his throat. "I haven't always been a good dad, Detective. But I've always loved my children."

"You know that Ray Junior's been arrested for dealing?"

"Yes. Damn shithead. I knew he'd never amount to anything. That's why I'm so concerned about Cynthia."

"Tell us about Cynthia."

Ray bows his head. "She never should've been sent to juvie," he says quietly. "She never intended to hurt her sister."

"What happened that day?"

"I wasn't home. I was never home. My wife was supposed to be watching the kids. But Maura wasn't the best mother in the world. She'd gone out and left the kids alone. She thought Cynthia could watch the younger ones." Ray looks at me. "But Cynthia was never right. She got hurt, Detective, when she was just a toddler. Brain damage. She had a hard time thinking straight and didn't always act rationally. I would never have left her alone with the kids. Last summer, when I heard that Cynthia had run away from her group home, I started coming up to Graybridge to check on her." He sighs. "When Junior heads off to prison, I'm going to have to find a place for Cynthia to live where she's got supervision."

"Why aren't you living at the house?"

Ray smirks. "Belongs to my ex-wife."

"Okay." I've got enough information now to clear up the whole man-threatening-Tom-Foster mess. My pulse kicks up, thinking about the Cynthia connection. Could she have gotten into a fight with Kara? Mr. York sees it happen, and then Daddy swoops in to get rid of Mr. York? "So, Ray, you'll stay away from Tom and the rest of the Fosters?"

"Yes. Absolutely. I regret going up to the hospital that day, Detective. The last thing I want to do is upset Jen's daughter."

"Okay. Good deal." I lay my pencil on my notebook, watch Ray as he scrapes his plate clean. "You know a man named Alan York?" I ask.

"Yeah. The costume guy. Lives on the other side of our woods." Ray lowers his voice. "I heard someone killed him."

I assess Ray a minute. Watch his body language, but I don't get any vibes one way or the other. "Yes. Saturday." I let the implication sink in.

"Wow. Shit. I didn't hear anything when I was with Cynthia," Ray says.

"You sure?"

He shakes his head. "When we were in the woods Saturday morning, everything was quiet."

"On your way out, you see or hear anything from Mr. York's direction?"

"Not a thing, Detective."

The waitress drops the check on the table, and Ray slides it over to me.

"If you don't mind. My Social Security check only goes so far." He plunks his hat back on his head.

"No problem." We stand, and Chase takes the check up to the register. Ray and I wait for him outside. The wind tosses Ray's long gray hair over his shoulders. He pulls a cigarette out of his coat pocket, turns his back on the wind, and lights up.

"You got a phone, Ray, so I can get in touch with you?" I ask. Also, I want to know if he'd have a way to monitor Mr. York's conversations.

He inhales deeply and lets go a slow stream of smoke that the wind carries off as quickly as it leaves his wrinkled lips. He digs in his frayed coat pocket. "Yeah."

I hand him my business card. "Here, in case you need to reach me. Call me now so I have your number, okay?"

He grips his cigarette in the corner of his mouth and punches my number into his phone. My phone vibrates. "Good. Got it."

Ray's wizened gaze meets mine. "Well, it was nice talking to you, Detective." He sighs just as Chase walks out of the diner. Ray extends his grubby hand to my partner.

"See you around, Ray," Chase says.

Ray's gaze shifts down the sidewalk to the busy streets. He reaches in his shirt pocket and slips on an old pair of mirrored sunglasses. He punches himself in the chest and coughs, settles his cowboy hat more firmly on his head, turns, and walks away.

# CHAPTER 76
# Esmé

We've been at the hospital all day, waiting and watching. Dad's chest still rises and falls, the monitors still record his every bodily function. Irene's words have sunk deep into my soul. How could I not have known about Ray Senior? Mom was good at keeping secrets, apparently, and I was lost in my own world of dance. Even as a child, and then a middle schooler and up through the first two years of high school, when the affair would've been going on the whole time, I was lost in my own childish world. Happy with my friends and enchanted with the world of dance. Every little girl's dream. The music and the costumes, the makeup. And the attention. Everyone made a big fuss over me, my mom leading the charge. I drop my head in my hands.

"Brought you coffee," Byron says, standing in front of me.

"Thanks." I take the warm paper cup from him. He and I've had little to say to each other about Irene's revelations. I don't think we know where to start. The fact that I was right about the man at the crash scene is a bitter victory.

At least, Irene went home last night. Her pleasure at destroying our mother's memory, despite Dad's request that she not tell anyone, especially us, had left her with a little shame, I guess. And she's still not here yet.

Dad's doctor walks into the room. Right away, I know what he has to tell us is not good. I can see it in his eyes, the grim set of his mouth.

"Byron," he says nearly in a whisper, "would you and your sister step out into the hall?"

We oblige, and Dr. Delgado watches the door shut behind us. "Well," he clears his throat, "we've got your dad's latest labs."

Byron peeps over at the open laptop in his hands. The doctor turns the screen so my brother can see, one professional to another. I see Byron's face fall. The doctor looks at me. "I'm sorry, Esmé. He's failing fast."

I bite my lips. Tears tremble in my eyes, and I blink them away. "What does that mean exactly?"

He understands the hidden question that I'm really asking.

Dr. Delgado takes a deep breath. "We don't think he'll last through the night."

A sob bursts through my lips, and Byron's arm circles my shoulders, and he pulls me to his chest.

"I'm so sorry," the doctor says. "Please let us know if you need anything." And he's gone, his soft shoes barely making a sound as he walks down the hallway.

Irene's back, and Byron tells her what the doctor said. She nods, and her glasses fog up. She leans over Dad's bed and whispers something to him and rubs his mottled arm. Then she collapses back in the chair across the room.

Byron stands, looks out the window into the dark, then walks back to check Dad's monitors every few minutes. I need some air and walk down to the waiting room at the end of the hall. I sit and wipe my eyes, glance at my phone. I've got a text from Laney, so I call her.

"Hi, Esmé. I just wanted to check on you."

"We're up at the hospital. Dad's not doing well." My voice catches.

"I'm so sorry."

"We just spoke to the doctor this afternoon." I take a deep breath. "He probably won't make it through the night."

Silence. "I'm so sorry. Do you want company? I know how lonely it gets in the evenings at a hospital."

"I don't want to bother you. I know you're busy."

"We just put the kids down for the night. It's no bother, really. Dylan is just sitting watching TV. I can come up."

I take a deep breath. "If it's no trouble."

"Not at all. I can at least bring you some decent coffee."

I manage a smile. I have good friends. "Thanks, Laney."

Laney and Christy tap on Dad's door, and Byron lets them in. Laney sets a cardboard carton on the counter by the little sink and hands Byron and me each a Dunkin' coffee.

They speak quietly to Byron and then retreat to the waiting room. Thankfully, Irene is down in the cafeteria. The room is eerily quiet, and it makes me think back to a poem, one of the few I remember from senior-year English class. Something about waiting for death by Emily Dickinson. What I remember is the normalcy with which she described it, a natural thing. But nothing feels natural right now. My head swirls with images, mostly my mother's laughter, which I can't seem to quell. Why think of that? Hear that now? Not mocking laughter. Just joyful. Like we were when I was little. Before she seemed to change. That I can see now. She changed about the time that Wendy died. Maybe she realized that life was short, unpredictable, that she should live the life she wanted but had been too afraid to embrace. Maybe she was reaching for her own personal happiness, no matter who got hurt in the process.

I sip my coffee, gaze at my dad, as if I could figure out his life as well as hers. How did he put up with it for so long? Could you love another person so much that you'd overlook everything they did?

Irene shuffles back into the room, holding a bottle of Pepsi. She looks old, older than she did just yesterday. What's she thinking, now that Dad will no longer be the center of her life? I do look forward to her disappearing from my life. Let her go back to her mother and find someone else to cling to. But maybe there's no one who can fill that role for her. Maybe she'll just shrivel up in a recliner and watch game shows until it's her time. Who knows?

I lean over and clutch my dad's dry hand. I feel the bones just beneath the skin. And think about the family we should have been.

I glance at my phone. Eleven-eighteen. Byron gasps, and I look up, his eyes on the monitors. He squeezes my arm and circles the bed and grabs Dad's other hand. Dad's eyelids flutter, his breath rattles, and he's gone.

Irene stumbles over to the bed and wails. Byron and I hug and cry on each other's shoulder. After a few minutes, we walk out into the hall and meet Dad's nurse on her way to us. She nods and bites her lips.

I break away and head for the waiting room. Laney and Christy stand and pull me into their arms. After a few minutes, we move apart, and I see Jack standing in the hall. I go to him, and he wraps me in his arms, where I sob against his chest, his hand stroking my hair.

# CHAPTER 77
# Rita

When I get to the station in the morning, Chase and Lauren are waiting for me in the conference room.

"Tom Foster died last night," Lauren says.

"Okay." I blow out a breath. "That was expected. The family doing all right?"

"Byron called and said they were okay."

I walk over to the whiteboard, glance over the list of women. "We need to talk to them." Although everything points to Cynthia as our number one, I don't want to presume and miss something.

Lauren raises her eyebrows. "Where do we start? Chase gave me his notes from your interview with Mr. Ridley."

"Good. So, what do you think?"

Lauren closes her laptop. "Ray Senior could've killed Mr. York. He had opportunity. He admitted to being in the woods Saturday. His background in radio would've given him the knowledge to use listening devices, I imagine, and he does have a phone he could use to monitor them."

Chase says, "And he would know how to get an illegal firearm, Rita. He did a pretty good stint in prison."

I nod. I feel like a teacher with two A-plus students. "All good ideas. And if Cynthia killed Kara, Ray even admitted he would do anything for his daughter." I tap the table with my pencil. "Anything from traffic cams on the dark sedan I saw leaving York's road?"

"We couldn't find it, Rita. There aren't many cameras out that way."

"That's the only thing that bugs me about Ridley. If he killed York, it stands to reason he would've walked through the woods. He doesn't have a car. But maybe the car I saw was just someone who'd made a wrong turn." I sigh. "Let's look at the other women before we concentrate on Cynthia, just to be sure."

I walk over to the whiteboard. "Marie Romano. She was at the insurance office after Kara left." I look at Chase. "Go back over the video we got from them and figure out what time she left. Then dig into her background."

He nods, his fingers flying over his phone.

"Lauren, see what you can dig up on Hannah Dabrowski and Irene Musgrave. I'll take a ride out to see Laney Addison and Christy Bowers." I put my hand on my hip. "I guess Esmé can wait until tomorrow, since her dad just died. And it doesn't look like it could be her. When she arrived on scene, she said she'd just come in from Syracuse. Should be able to locate somebody there who saw her. Hopefully." It doesn't feel right anyway. "I still think Cynthia is our best bet. But let's eliminate these other women first."

# CHAPTER 78
# Esmé

SOMEHOW, I SLEPT ALL NIGHT STRAIGHT THROUGH. NO DREAMS. NO nightmares. But now I have to face the day knowing that Byron and I are all alone. The house is dim and shabby and filled with stuff that Dad had accumulated over the years. I didn't seem to notice before. Newspapers dated to last year, folded over to the crossword puzzle, waiting, dust-covered, and undone. An old radio, its guts hanging out on the kitchen counter. One of the many things Dad thought he could fix and ended up abandoning.

Byron and I head up to what was our parents' room. The bed is a rumple of old sheets and a worn quilt, as if Dad thrashed in his sleep. The nightstand still holds the picture of our mom, her smile brilliant in the summer sun. Days now long gone. Without a word, Byron lays it facedown.

Byron shakes out a large black garbage bag and opens Dad's closet. He stands back and draws a deep breath, as if he can't go any further.

"Maybe we should donate his clothes," I say.

Byron shakes his head. "They're too old, too worn out. He wouldn't let me buy him anything new. He said there was no point."

That makes me sad. Dad's life just seemed to fold up like an umbrella with him inside. He went nowhere, saw no one except Irene. I feel a tinge of anger. For him, for our mother. How did they let their lives become so hopeless, so useless? Mom with her destructive decisions, and Dad giving up on life.

Then I stop to think about my own life. What have I done with it lately?

After cleaning most of the day, I'm exhausted, both physically and emotionally. Just as I head downstairs with the last bag of trash, the doorbell rings. Christy.

"Hi, I was in the neighborhood and thought I'd check on you."

"We're fine." I set the garbage bag on the floor and let Christy in. "You want a cup of coffee?"

"If it wouldn't be any trouble. It's freezing out."

We sit at the kitchen table, and I'm suddenly self-conscious. This is the first time she's been at my house since I've been back, and I can't help but feel how shabby it is, especially compared to her place. This was something I wasn't concerned about when we were kids, but now it feels strange, like I've failed adulthood. And the house isn't even mine.

Christy squeezes my hand. "What can I do to help?"

"Just being here is wonderful. I'm so glad I have you guys, not that I deserve you," I say. My gaze drops to my black coffee. "Jack brought over dinner for me and Byron the other night. He was so sweet."

"That's our Jack."

I nod. "I feel like I let you all down, leaving." My eyes meet hers. "I know I let Kara down."

"Don't be silly. You were a good friend. You had to do what was best for you at the time. Besides, we've all have had our troubles here, believe me."

"Not Laney," I say suddenly. "She seems to have done everything right."

Christy's gaze shifts to the window. "Well, Laney's had her problems."

"Like what?" I sip my coffee.

"Well," Christy takes a deep breath, "she went through a pretty rough patch a couple years ago."

I instinctively lean forward, like in the old days, when there were no secrets among our little group. "What happened?"

"You remember her big brother, Sam?"

"Yeah. We all thought he was so hot."

Christy nods. "Laney really looked up to him. They were close. Well, Sam got married, had a couple of kids, everything is going good. Then the family finds out he's doing drugs. Got caught up with a bunch of other young execs, partying, trips to the Caribbean, living the high life, in more ways than one. Anyway, Sam was out of his mind half the time. His wife left him. He lost his job. Then, one day, the family hadn't been able to get in touch with him for a couple days. Laney had a key to his apartment, so she went over there." Christy's gaze shifts to the window, then back to me. "She found him dead on the kitchen floor. Overdose."

"That's awful," I say.

"Yeah. She was a mess. I was worried about her for a while, but she went to therapy. She's doing better."

"I wish I had known." I don't know what I'd have been able to do, but it looks like I let another friend down. I take a deep breath. "Poor Laney."

"Yeah. And now with Kara. Laney was the one who figured out that Kara was taking pain pills. She said that, after Sam, she could spot an addict a mile away."

"Kara was taking pain pills?"

"Yes. We told you that, didn't we?" Christy's eyes open wide.

This is news to me. "No." I feel left out again.

Christy waves her hand in the air. "Sorry."

"When did Laney figure it out?"

"Just a week or so before Kara died." Christy stands and pours herself another coffee. "And they argued about it. Kara didn't want to hear it. She said that she was fine and only needed the pills occasionally for 'lingering back pain.'" Christy leans against the counter and sips her coffee, jiggles her leg like a nervous bird.

"Was Kara buying her pills from Ray?"

"We suspected. There was some talk around town, so we weren't surprised when Detective Myers arrested him. And Laney's not doing as well as you think right now. The last time Laney spoke to Kara, they had a wicked fight about the pills."

I remember what that was like when we were teenagers. We occasionally squabbled, and it was an awful feeling, a primal kind of emptiness to be separated from the group, even if it was just some crazy teenage issue. We all made up quickly enough. But now, how much more difficult are these adult problems? I feel bad enough about leaving Kara, leaving my friends behind, but poor Laney. How must she feel, knowing that the last conversation she had with Kara was an argument?

"Well, anyway. Things sometimes happen." Christy draws a deep breath, then sets her mug in the sink. "I need to get going. Let me know if you need anything."

After Christy left, I tidied the kitchen, was thinking about dinner options, when Jack called and asked if I wanted to get out of the house for a while. That was a definite yes.

# CHAPTER 79
# Rita

I WENT BACK OUT TO TALK TO LANEY ADDISON AND CHRISTY BOWERS. They had nothing to add to their previous statements and said nothing to arouse my suspicions, so I decided to swing by the Ridley place and talk to Cynthia before heading back to the station.

The old farmhouse looks forlorn, the rain making it seem even grayer than it is. A curtain flutters in a window in what is probably a bedroom. I sit a minute and think. I probably should just head home and give Ray Senior a call tomorrow, arrange for him to bring Cynthia into the station and make it more official. That's what I should do.

I knock on the door, and it takes Ray a few minutes to answer.

"Back again, Detective," he says with a grunt. He's muffled in two sweatshirts, one on top of the other, like he's freezing. It is cold, drafty, as I follow him into the living room. My gaze shoots to the armchair by the window, but it's empty, the knitting basket overflowing with bright pink yarn. Cynthia must've finished up the yellow skein.

"I'd like to speak with your sister," I say as Ray collapses on the couch. He picks up a game controller but reluctantly sets it aside.

He huffs out a breath. "Why? She doesn't know anything about . . . anything."

"Still. I'd like to speak to her."

Ray tips his head back and shouts, "Cyn!"

Right away, she pokes her head around the living room door as though she'd been hiding, listening.

"Miss Ridley, can we talk a minute in the kitchen?"

"Right here's fine," Ray says.

I swallow. "Okay."

Cynthia sits in her armchair. The big bomber jacket she's wearing over a dress deflates around her like a parachute. The orange cat appears at her feet, almost as if he'd been hidden in her voluminous outfit.

"Thank you for talking with me, Cynthia," I say from where I'm standing in the middle of the living room.

She nods, her eyes anywhere but on me.

"Have you seen your dad lately?"

"Yes."

"When did you see him last?"

She scratches her head; a hank of white-gray hair slips over her forehead. "Saturday."

"Why didn't you tell me about meeting him when I asked you before?"

She shrugs.

"What time? Morning? Dinnertime?" Ray Senior had already told me it was morning, but I want to see if Cynthia will corroborate this.

"Morning."

"Where did you see him?"

"In the woods, by the pond."

"Why didn't he come into the house?"

She shrugs. "We like to meet there."

"Okay. What did you two talk about?"

"Just things." She shoots a glance at Ray. "My brother is going to go away soon."

"Is that all you talked about? Where you were going to live then?"

Her face creases. "I want to stay here. Home."

"It's okay. I'm sure your dad will take care of everything. Did he say anything to you about Mr. York?"

"No."

"When he left, where did he go?"

"I don't know."

"He didn't talk about anything else, just about your brother leaving?"

I hear Ray shifting on the couch as if he's getting ready to spring like a lion at any moment.

"That's all."

"Did you know Kara Cunningham?"

Cynthia nods, folds over her knees, and drops her hand to the floor to stroke the orange cat.

"When was the last time you saw her?"

She shrugs.

Ray says, "That's enough, Detective. Of course, she knows Kara. We all knew Kara, all right?"

I turn to him. "We just need to know if Cynthia saw anything that night."

Ray jumps to his feet and motions for me to join him in the foyer. "Well, she didn't, okay?" His gaze meets mine. "Cynthia's in the woods a lot. It doesn't mean anything. She had no reason to hurt Kara, and she would've told me if . . . I've already asked her about that night. She has no idea what happened to Kara."

"All right, Ray. I talked to your dad yesterday."

"Really? Why?" This catches him by surprise.

"Just getting some background on everybody."

"What does he have to do with anything?"

"Well, he was in the woods talking to Cynthia the day that Mr. York was killed. We wanted to know if he saw anything, knew anything."

"He doesn't know jackshit, Detective." There's a flash of anger in Ray's eyes.

"You talk to him often?"

"Not too much. We don't see eye to eye on a lot." Ray blows out a breath. "He wasn't exactly father of the year when we were growing up. But I guess he'll have to step up when I'm gone. But Cynthia was always his favorite, so hopefully he'll take care of her."

"Would he protect her?"

"I guess. From what?"

"I don't know. Anything she might've done."

Anger is replaced by something akin to panic in Ray's eyes. "She hasn't done anything, Detective, so if you don't mind . . ."

"Sure thing, Ray. I'll get out of your hair. For now."

# CHAPTER 80
# Rita

BACK AT THE STATION, I REREAD A TEXT THAT DANNY SENT ME EARLIER. He wants to meet after work at Hartshorn's Brewpub. He has a meeting downtown and will be passing Graybridge on his way home. Don't know what he wants, maybe nothing special.

I pull into the lot, and it isn't too crowded on a Wednesday night.

I see Danny's already here and sitting in a corner booth, a short glass in front of him. I stop by the bar and order a glass of wine, wait for it to be poured, and carry it with me to the table.

"Hey, how's it going?" I say, pulling off my leather jacket and hanging it on the post next to the booth.

"I'm good, Rita. You? How's your big case?"

I blow out a breath as I slide across from him. "Not going well, actually. I'm hoping things might move along now. We just got some information from the lab that I hope will be the key that we need."

"Sounds good. You want to order food, or are you in a hurry?"

"No. Food's good. You not seeing Vivienne tonight?"

"She's busy."

"So I'm second choice?" I smirk, trying to be funny, but Danny doesn't smile, his eyes on his drink.

"You're never second choice."

Huh. "Why so glum, bro?"

"It's nothing. Just worried about Charlotte, I guess."

Now I'm worried. "What's wrong with Charlotte?"

Danny heaves a big breath. "Nothing really. It's just she wants to head up to Maine. She wants to start a doctorate program up there."

"Well, it's not like she'd be moving to Alaska."

"Yeah. I know."

"So?"

Danny sips his drink. "Just missing everybody for some reason. Time of year, I guess. The holidays coming up and all."

In recent years, we haven't had the whole gang together for Thanksgiving. It just seemed like too much work to get organized. Besides, our sisters all have several kids and grandchildren, and they all had their own plans.

I sip my wine."You want me to call Maureen?" Although I'd rather eat mud.

Danny's gaze meets mine. "We could all gather at Ma and Dad's place like the old days."

"Maybe Maureen would be agreeable." Although agreeable and Maureen seldom belong in the same sentence. But Danny looks so down, and I know that the whiskey is only making it worse, but what can I do about that? "I'll call her. See who would be up for a McMahon family Thanksgiving." I take another big sip of my drink just as the waitress comes over to take our order.

The food was just what I needed. Didn't realize how hungry I'd gotten. I haven't been eating regularly since this Cunningham case started. Danny has perked up, and we've relaxed into our usual snarky banter.

I hear laughter from a table not far from us and see Esmé Foster and Jack Crosby. He seems to be doing his best to entertain her. She's actually smiling and looks better than she did the last time I saw her. I keep an eye on them while making conversation with my brother. You never know what insights you might gain observing people associated with a case when they don't know you're watching.

"I need another glass of wine," I say. But the waitress is really busy and hasn't stopped by since she delivered our food a while ago. "Think I'll go up to the bar and get it myself."

Danny looks up at me, raises his empty glass.

"How many have you had?" I ask, palm raised before he can object. "I don't want you ending up in the ditch or hear that one of our officers pulled you over for driving under the influence."

"All right. Get me a ginger ale."

"Good choice."

I walk past Esmé and Jack, but they're deep in conversation and don't see me. I stand at the bar, waiting for my drinks, when I notice a man, big and fit, sitting on a stool with a clear view of their table. He's got a little notebook out and is writing in it. He sips his ice water, stares across the room. If I'm not mistaken, this guy is a reporter maybe. He's clearly got his eye on Esmé and Jack. Hmm. Jack reaches over the table and holds Esmé's hand. They certainly look cozy. My drinks come, and I sip my wine. Linger a bit. As I walk past the reporter guy, I peep over his shoulder but can't make out anything on his notepad.

I sit back down with my brother but can't help but take furtive glances at the man at the bar. Danny and I finish our meal, and I notice that Esmé and Jack and the bar man are all still there as we leave.

# CHAPTER 81
# Rita

THE NEXT MORNING, RAY SENIOR WAITS IN AN INTERVIEW ROOM FOR Chase and me. When I open the door, that familiar Ray smell of unwashed clothes and body odor wafts out. Ray is sitting, cowboy hat on his head, drinking a cup of coffee someone must've brought him from the break room.

We exchange pleasantries, and I start the recorder. Ray seems jovial, as though he's the DJ of old giving an interview.

"So, Ray, thanks for coming in," I say. Chase takes out his phone to take notes while I open my notebook.

"Not a problem. How can I help?"

"Did you know Kara Cunningham?"

He sits up straight, takes a deep breath. "I heard that she'd been killed in the woods. I didn't remember her specifically, but Junior reminded me that she was one of Esmé's friends."

"You talked to your son about the incident?"

"Yes. He filled me in. Just a shame." Ray wags his finger at me. "I warned Junior about having all those dirtbags around. You know, there to buy . . . It could have been his sister who was killed." Ray leans back in his chair, his gaze on his coffee.

"Uh-huh. You have any reason to believe it was one of his customers?"

Ray shakes his head. "I didn't know anything about it until recently. I told Junior he was a goddamned idiot, and now look." Ray catches my gaze. "You hope your kids learn from your mistakes, Detective, but I guess he didn't."

"Anyway," I clear my throat, "we're wondering if Cynthia was in the woods that night. Maybe she saw something."

Ray takes a deep breath. "She was only looking for her cat, Detective. Cynthia had nothing to do with that girl's murder. Nothing."

I drop my pencil next to my notebook. "She told you that? She was in the woods when Kara was killed?"

Ray coughs and rubs his hand over his mouth. He shakes his head. "She doesn't know anything, Detective."

"We need to get her in here to give us a statement, Ray. We've been treading carefully with her since she's disabled."

"That's right." There's a glint of anger in his eyes. "Cynthia is legally of diminished capacity. I have a legal right to be with her during any questioning."

That's an interesting phrase to use, an old legal term. Like he's given this a lot of thought. "But we still need to speak to her again. If she was out there that night, she's probably the best witness we've got."

He looks down at his hands. They are clasped on the table as if the weight of the world is on his shoulders. "All right," he says at last and heaves a sigh.

We would really like a DNA sample from Cynthia. That would either implicate her or eliminate her, but fat chance Ray will agree to that. We'll see.

# CHAPTER 82
# Esmé

I SPENT THE DAY CLEANING THE HOUSE, TRYING NOT TO THINK ABOUT Dad's funeral tomorrow. I sigh as I open a cupboard, looking for something to make for dinner. But before I can get started, Christy calls and asks me to come over. She sounds upset, so I agree.

Her house is uncharacteristically dark. It's nearly six o'clock, and yet she hasn't turned on any lights that I can see from the driveway.

I ring the bell, and she answers quickly. Her eyes are teary, strange. "Come on in," she says and closes the door behind me. I follow her down the dim hallway and into the massive kitchen. A low light over the stove glints on the shiny cooktop surface.

A glass of red wine sits on the counter, and Christy pours another for me.

"What did you want to talk about?" I ask as we sit at the table.

"I know your dad's funeral is tomorrow, but . . ."

"What?"

"I don't think I'll be able to make it." I know she doesn't like funerals, but this is odd.

"Okay."

"I wouldn't cut out on you like this, but I'm leaving in the morning for Florida. My mom's had a stroke."

"I'm so sorry. Of course, you need to go. I wouldn't expect you to stay, really." I sip my wine.

Christy stands. "Well, you'll have Laney and, of course, *Jack*. And my mom is okay. It was a mild one."

"Still. I understand. I'll be fine."

She nods, refills her glass, and tops mine off.

Christy sits back across from me, and I get a tingling on the back of my neck. Something's wrong, more than her mom. We sit sipping for a moment. Christy glances off across the room; her lips pull into a grin. "Let me show you some pictures. I feel like we've never truly caught up since you've been back."

She hops up and goes into another room, returning quickly with a photo album. She turns up the kitchen light as she walks by. "I thought you might like to see what you've missed out on over the years."

"Okay."

She flips open the album, and there's a picture of her in her wedding gown, looking like a chic Hollywood princess, her husband, Paul, whom I've never met, standing next to her. He's much older, good-looking, but definitely of another generation.

"There I am." She points. "The perfect trophy wife." Christy looks up at me. "My dress cost ten thousand dollars."

"Wow. Uh, it's beautiful."

"Yes. I landed in a butter tub. My grandmother used to say that. A stupid expression." She taps the photo with a blood-red, manicured fingernail. "You can't even tell I was nearly five months pregnant here, right?" She laughs and flips the page over. In the next picture, she's holding a tiny, wrinkled newborn. Her hand caresses the page. "And here I am again, just a few months later with Teddy."

"He was a beautiful baby," I say.

She's teary. "My perfect little man. He was worth all of it."

"I'm sorry, Christy, about your marriage."

She snorts out a laugh. "So am I. He started cheating on me the week after we took Teddy home."

"That's awful." I finish my wine. I don't know what to say to her. I need to go home, but Christy looks so distraught.

She jumps up. "Let's have another glass. I'll open a new bottle. Something rich and expensive."

I don't really feel like more alcohol, but I don't know quite how to say no.

She's back and expertly uncorks the bottle. "I'd do anything for my son. That's the attitude I've taken over the years. I was going to survive Paul. Divorce him and take him for everything I could get. Which I did, by the way. Not that I needed his money. I've been very successful on my own."

"That's good, Christy. Something to be proud of."

"Right." Her gaze catches mine. "But pride's a lonely bedfellow." She pours more wine.

"Surely, there've been other men in your life since Paul?"

She shakes her head. "A date here and there. Nothing worth talking about." Her eyes fall back to the album, where she's turned the page to a montage of photos of Teddy playing baseball, in his scout's uniform, one where he's holding a striped kitten. "I miss Kara," she blurts out. "I told her everything. All my troubles." Christy smacks the album shut. "And I was so good to her. Listening to her. And could she *bitch* about everything and anything, but I listened because that's what friends do, don't they?"

Christy stands and walks to the counter, picks up the wine bottle, sets it back down. "I even gave her money whenever she needed it."

"That was generous. I'm sure she appreciated it."

Anger flashes across Christy's face, chasing away her beauty. "No, she didn't, Esmé. She didn't appreciate a fucking thing!"

The room feels warm. My heart ticks in my chest in funny little jerks. "Well, Kara could be thoughtless sometimes, but you know she was good-hearted."

Christy grips the edges of the counter, her knuckles white. "I told her how difficult my life had been with Paul. I told her the only man I'd ever really loved was Teddy's father."

"I don't understand."

"Paul wasn't Teddy's father," she says with a laugh. She takes a sip of her wine, her deep red lips part. "Jack is."

"*What?*" The breath flies out of my chest.

Christy circles the room, glass in hand. "Oh, yes, Esmé. Jack, our perfect Mr. Crosby, is Teddy's father."

"Does he know?"

She shakes her head. "Not yet. No one knows." She sits back down across from me. "Well, Kara knew. She's the only person I'd confided in. You see, Esmé, when you left us all, went off to your illustrious ballet career, I stayed here, went to college. Interned at Paul's company senior year. And he was after me from the minute I stepped through his plush office doorway. I was fucking twenty-one years old, and he was almost my dad's age. Anyway, I avoided him as best I could because it was only Jack I wanted. So, at the end of the semester, I drove over to Albany. Invited myself up to Jack's, and he was happy to see me. We partied with his college friends all weekend and ended up in bed every night I was there. It was perfect. I was thrilled. I thought we were going to be a couple. But then, on Sunday afternoon, while I was still in a sex and alcohol happy haze, he told me that we'd made a mistake. That we'd always be friends, but that he shouldn't have taken advantage of me that way." Christy rises from the table again and refills her glass.

She leans against the counter. "I was devastated. He's the love of my life, Esmé," she nearly shouts. "But what was I going to do? We hadn't used any protection, and I was scared and hurt, so when I got home, I started sleeping with Paul. A month later, I knew I was pregnant. And Paul was more than happy to put a ring on my youthful finger."

"How do you know that Teddy isn't Paul's then?"

Her mouth droops. "Really, Esmé. I'm not stupid. I had a DNA test run. Paul never knew, but when Teddy was six months old, I grabbed Paul's toothbrush and also swabbed Teddy's cheek. The lab I used came back with the report. No way that Paul had fathered Teddy." She smiles.

I swallow. Beads of perspiration have gathered on the back of my neck. I feel drunk. My head is swimming, but I haven't had that much wine. "I'm so sorry, Christy." Suddenly, she's looking at me like she's confused by my presence in her home.

"Anyway," she snaps, "Kara knew. I poured my heart out to her. And then, last month, Jack came home." Christy fills her glass and smacks the empty bottle on the table. She shakes her head. "I said to her, 'Kara, you can have any guy you want, you know that,' " Christy lowers her voice. "Not that she could keep them. But that's beside the point. 'You can have anyone you want, just not Jack.' "

Christy's face reddens, and I shrink back in my chair. "I was going to tell Jack about Teddy, but before I could do that, Kara's going after him." Christy's crying, tears dripping down her face. "Was it too much to ask for her to steer clear of one guy?"

"Well, Kara's gone now, Christy," I say quietly.

Christy's mouth contorts. "I didn't mean it, Esmé. I was just so angry. I felt so betrayed. And you know what she said, the ungrateful bitch?"

I shake my head and slowly get up from my chair, my legs shaky. "Christy, I know you're upset. We've all been through a lot the last couple of weeks. I need to go. Byron needs me at home." I start to inch toward the hallway. But she stands and follows me.

"She said, 'Too bad, Christy. You don't own Jack. You can't stop me from seeing him.' "

Christy backs me up against the wall. Mascara stains her cheeks. Saliva drips from the corners of her red-lipsticked mouth. "And I said, 'Oh really? After all these years of me being your best friend? Listening to all your problems? Giving you tons of money? You're going to act like a mean little middle-school bitch? I have a son to think of.' " Christy's face goes slack. Her eyes meet mine. "Then she pushed me." Christy's hot breath hits my cheek.

"Oh my God." I can't catch a breath. I try to make my way to the front door, but she grabs my arm, her fingers pinching my flesh.

"It was dark in the woods that night, Esmé. Cold too, and she'd forgotten her coat at Ray's."

"How did you—"

"I drove over to the insurance office to talk to her. She told me earlier that she was meeting Jack. Just the two of them. And I wanted to talk her out of it! Make her see what a betrayal to me it was. But as I drove up, I saw her across the street, talking to Ray, and I decided to follow her." Christy nods. "She turned down Mr. York's road. I waited a few minutes. Then I parked next to her and walked to the pond and waited. After a while, I saw her coming down the trail from Ray's. She was surprised to see me there. That's where we got into the argument, and she pushed me." Christy's wide eyes meet mine. "She started it."

"Anyway," Christy continues, "Cynthia's home. What luck, huh? When I heard that, I breathed a sigh of relief."

"You think Detective Myers will decide that Cynthia killed Kara?"

"If she doesn't blame it on one of the guys. Why not? Maybe with a little hint from me." Christy's voice explodes. "I can't go to prison! I have a son and a job. People depend on me."

"You won't get away with it, Christy," I manage, trying to catch my breath.

She cocks an eyebrow. "Oh, really? They believed Cynthia killed Wendy."

I collapse back against the wall. A memory surfaces in my mind from long ago. The day that Wendy died. Christy and Laney had come over. We played hide-and-seek, and after Byron had found Laney and me, we all searched for Christy, who eventually emerged from the woods. My jaw drops. It was a week after school had let out for the summer, and Christy was angry. Angry that Wendy, who was in her class, had won a prize, a small trophy. The pieces click into place. It hadn't occurred to me before, but I'd seen that trophy just a few days ago sitting on a shelf in Christy's home office. The realization hits me like a clap of thunder, and I can't breathe.

Christy smiles. "I know. I shouldn't have done it, but I was only nine, and that fucking trophy should've damn well been mine."

"But Ray saw Cynthia knock Wendy out of the boat." My heart is hammering, sweat pouring down the sides of my face.

"Yeah. I saw her do that too, when I was hiding. Then Ray ran off to tell on her, and Cynthia paddled to shore and followed him up the path. I came out to see what was going on, and I saw that fucking trophy in the rowboat. And then I saw Wendy trying to swim to shore. She was a little woozy. She'd been hit in the head with an oar, for Christ's sake." Christy shrugs one shoulder. "She probably wasn't going to make it anyway, so I picked up the oar and shoved her back into the pond."

"Oh my God, Christy."

"I was only a kid! And Cynthia was the one who knocked her out of the boat, so she got what she deserved. Does adding Kara to her list really make a fucking difference?"

But the realization hits me, and my heart feels like it's going to explode. Christy wouldn't be telling me all this unless . . .

Christy steps back, raises her arm, and points at me. "And now you come back." She laughs. "You! Esmé, you always had a way of upstaging us all, didn't you? Nice pun, huh?" She shakes her head. I try to move around her, but she blocks my path. "But your little world was shattered, wasn't it? It sucks to be you now. Career over. No longer the little star, but then, like a knight in shining armor, Jack comes to the rescue."

I start to step around her, but she grabs my arms again so tight it hurts. "Let go, Christy. I don't want Jack. He's all yours." I see there's no reasoning with her. She's gone off the rails, and my mind flips back to our younger years and the times I'd seen Christy lose control. We always laughed about her temper, never thinking it was more than a willful disposition. Her anger was quick to flare, but her apologies seemed sincere and quick as well. But now she's basically confessed to murdering our friend *and* Wendy Ridley.

"I won't lose him to you. I've got too much riding on this."

I manage to pull away from her. "Have you been following me? Harassing me?"

She shakes her head. "Me? No. My PI. I pay him well, and he's got a flexible conscience, especially if the price is right. I just had to see how serious this thing between you and Jack was. That's all. I had to be sure."

So that's the man who's been following me, peering in the window of the café, following me down the road from Jack's apartment, sitting at the bar at Hartshorn's. And who knows how many other times.

Christy laughs, then pulls her mouth into a grim line. "Then my PI actually punched Jack in the face out in the woods in the shack.

I was pissed, but he explained that if he hadn't, the whole operation would've been compromised, so . . ."

"There's nothing going on between me and Jack," I say quietly, trying to reason with her.

She hoots. "I'm not stupid, Ez! Christ, can't anything go right for me? Anyway," her voice drops. She sniffs. "I didn't mean to do it. I didn't mean to hurt her. It was an accident." She blinks her eyes, and I see young Christy there somehow, for just an instant.

"I know you didn't," I soothe, needing to calm her down. Anything to get out of here.

She shrugs. "But now I've got you on my hands."

"No. I'm going home. It'll be all right, somehow." She stares at me. "Uh, go to the cops, Christy. They'll understand what happened when you explain it. Kara attacked you, right? And we don't even have to mention Wendy. Like you said, you were just a kid, and Cynthia is really responsible. She knocked her out of the boat."

"Nice try, Esmé. But that won't work, so I've got no choice."

She's going to kill me. The thought hits me like a punch in the stomach. This can't be happening. I start to dart past her, hoping to reach the front door before she does. But a tall man steps out from the dining room and blocks the way. I whirl around and run back into the kitchen and head for the back door.

I stumble out into the cold night air, Christy and the man behind me. I sprint across the manicured lawn. There are trees behind the property, and I head to them. I'm quickly engulfed in woods, the cold, piney scent filling my gasping lungs. But I can't slow down. I hear them behind me. The neighborhood is old, the lots expansive, and I can't make out any lights anywhere through the trees. Branches slap my cheeks, and I trip over roots and rocks, staggering, falling headfirst into a clump of wet, fetid leaves. But I scramble quickly to my feet, ignoring the pain in my right side. I hear them behind me, crashing through the undergrowth, and pray that I can outrun them, get somewhere safe, but my hip is throbbing, my ankle sore from where I twisted it when I fell. I break out into a clearing. I'm on a golf course. It's wide open here, nowhere to hide, and no one at this hour to help. I lean against a tree, gasping for breath, trying to decide which way to go. Which way is safest?

I hear Christy swear under her breath. They're close. I take off like a shot, heart pumping, across the green. Then I'm hit from behind. A huge thump takes me to the ground, my face shoved into the sharp grass. The man is on top of me, and I can't move. Tears wet my cheeks, and I try to struggle. I call out to my friend, who is standing over me.

"Please, Christy."

# CHAPTER 83
# Rita

Although it's getting late, I'm stopping by the Ridley place on my way home. Ray had called and said his dad was there, Cynthia too. They all wanted to talk to me. I asked if they'd come down to the station, make it official, but Ray said no. It would be easier for Cynthia to talk to me at home, where she was comfortable.

I pull into the driveway, and the little house sits in the dark, lights on in the living room. Inside, Ray Senior sits on the couch, huddled in his coat. Ray Junior paces in front of the window.

"What do you want to talk to me about?" I ask, reluctantly taking a seat in Cynthia's tattered armchair.

"Well," Ray Senior draws a deep breath, "Cynthia wanted to speak to you, Detective. I told her we needed to go down to the station, but she said no, she wanted to talk to you here."

"Fine." I pull my notebook out of my satchel, my nerves tingling as I wonder if this will be it—a confession.

Ray Senior draws a deep breath. "Junior and I have been asking her questions, and she admitted she knew more than she told you. She's just scared to death that you'll send her away. She doesn't want to leave this place. God knows why, but she has a strong attachment to it."

"What does she know?"

"Well, she was in the woods the night that Kara was attacked," Ray Junior says. "She was out looking for her cat after Kara left. I had no idea she'd left the house, Detective. I swear."

Right. "And?"

"She said she knows what happened to Kara. She wouldn't give us any details. She said she'd wait for you."

"So where is she?"

Ray Junior says, "She's in her room. I'll get her."

"Okay." I quickly reread the notes I'd already taken when I'd spoken to Cynthia before. Again, wish they'd agreed to come down to the station where we could get Cynthia on video, but at this point, I'll take what I can get.

A minute or so ticks by. Ray returns without his sister. "She's gone."

# CHAPTER 84
# Esmé

It's dark, and the smell of motor oil and dirt assails my nose. I'm shaking, sweating in the trunk of a car. The man had zip-tied my arms behind me, pulled a hood over my head, and, despite my thrashing, carried me like a rag doll in his strong arms, back into the house. He spoke quietly to Christy; although I couldn't make out his words, his voice was familiar. I racked my brain to place him. Then it hit me. Christy's party. I'd met him for a fleeting moment. She had introduced me as the ballerina. Looking back now, was she trying to put a face to my name for him? I can't remember what he said exactly, but I remember the slight Russian accent, and I shiver.

I hear a garage door open and close, and now we're driving. I wiggle my legs to where I think the taillights might be and try to break them with my feet, but it's not working. I can't seem to get any purchase, and I'm just flailing in the dark. My heart is skittering like a caged animal. I've got to think of something.

After about ten minutes, the car stops, engine cut. My heart is hammering in my ears. What am I going to do? Where are we?

The trunk pops open, and cold air wafts over me. The man swings me to my feet and pulls the hood from my head. I'm disoriented in the dark for a moment. Then my mind clears. I know exactly where I am. The parking area up from Mr. York's house.

Christy is there in the shadows, her dark coat buttoned up to her neck, hood covering her hair. "Don't scream, Esmé. There's no one to hear you. Mr. York's gone. Ray's stuck in his house with his ankle monitor. Byron's at work. We're all alone out here." She starts down the path, the man pushing me to follow her, his hand on my shoulder.

"Please, Christy. We're friends."

She stops, turns. Blinks her eyes in the moonlight. "We *were.*"

I stumble along, finding it difficult to walk in the dark with my hands bound. *Think, Esmé. Think!*

The pond glitters in the moonlight, its dark depths rippling in the breeze. I try to swallow my panic as the man squeezes my arms behind me, keeping me immobile. Christy darts into the woods, then backs out dragging a small rowboat from the trees.

It can't be. Has it been there all this time? It's covered with dirt and pieces of vegetation, like a relic of the past. I swallow, despite the cold, sweat drips down the sides of my face. She knows I can't swim. Christy shoves the boat through the weeds and into the cold water, and it bobs at the shore.

"Just a little boat ride, Esmé."

The man pushes me forward and forces me into the boat. He gets in beside me, and I wonder how it will support the two of us. A picture of Wendy and Cynthia flits through my mind. Two young girls, all those years ago. Why is Christy doing this? Is she setting this up to make it look like Cynthia . . .

I try to get out before we can get into deep water, but Christy pushes the boat away from the shore as the man holds me in his arms. We drift farther into the pond, and I'm desperate to get away. Then the man picks up an oar.

# CHAPTER 85
# Rita

"WHERE IS SHE?" I JUMP UP FROM THE ARMCHAIR, HOPING I haven't wasted my time. Ray Senior is on his feet too.

"That's strange. She was determined to talk to you, Detective."

The only place I can think of that Cynthia would go would be the woods. "She looking for her cat again, maybe?"

"That's probably where she is," Ray Junior says. "Or maybe she got scared about talking to you and ran off. I'll look for her."

I glance at his ankle monitor. "No. You two stay here. I'll go."

I drop my notebook in the chair and head out the front door and around the house. The air is brisk, cold and breezy. I enter the woods, and all is quiet, spooky. At least, the moon is casting enough light that I can see where I'm going. The air is humid, thick, and fetid. I run down the path, turn around a bend, and get smacked in the face by a branch. *Shit.*

Then I hear a noise. Panting. Someone running. Maybe Cynthia realized she was supposed to be home talking to me. I run too and nearly collide with her. Cynthia's eyes are wild, her gray-blond hair tangled over her shoulders. She grabs me by my shoulders.

"What is it, Cynthia? What's wrong?" She can't seem to speak. She grabs my arm and pulls me toward the pond. I run after her, my breath coming in hard gasps.

# CHAPTER 86
# Esmé

THE MAN DIPS THE PADDLE IN THE WATER, AND WE SILENTLY MOVE into the center of the pond. Christy is standing on the shore, watching, her face a ghostly oval peering from her hood. My teeth are chattering, and tears spill down my cheeks. But I try to clear my mind to think. There's got to be a way out of this.

The man will have to cut the zip ties. They'll never believe that Cynthia put them on. He'll cut the ties, then . . . I'll fight him. I'll find a way to tread water and get away. I'm stronger than he thinks I am. Years of ballet training have left me strong and nimble.

He drops the paddle in the bottom of the boat and pulls a knife from his pocket. He roughly grabs my arms, which are screaming in pain, cinched behind my back. I feel a flood of relief as the ties fall away. But before I can stretch my arms out, the man grabs them and pulls me to my feet. I instinctively spread my feet wide until they're anchored on the sides of the boat. I feel the strength in my legs, the power in my balance, and I throw my weight to the side, rocking the little boat. The man's caught off guard and flails to catch his balance, but he grabs me, and we both go over the side.

The frigid, dark water takes my breath away, and I'm kicking, sputtering, trying to keep my head above water. But then, like a stone, I'm sinking down into the murky depths, where Wendy died so long ago. I try to hold my breath to fight my way to the surface, but the man has grabbed me and is pulling me down. I'm trying to fight my panic. I know it will only work against me, but my mind is swirling, my lungs screaming. I choke out a breath, try to keep from inhaling. But I'm losing control, and my body is working against me, starting to go limp, almost wanting to let go. My lungs pull for air, but there's only water, and panic fades to surrender.

# CHAPTER 87
# Rita

Cynthia and I break out of the woods just in time to see Esmé Foster and a man go over the side of a small boat in the middle of the pond. A woman stands on the other shore, but I don't have time to deal with her. I shuck off my jacket, tear at my laces, drop my boots on the shore, and charge into the water. The chill takes my breath away as I swim toward the man flailing in the center of the pond. But where is Esmé?

When I reach him, the man backs away from me, struggling in his heavy coat. I scream for him to stay away as I dive down looking for Esmé. I hope all my lifeguard training from forty-plus years ago stands me in good stead. I seriously need backup here, but I'm in this alone. The water is murky, but luckily the pond is small, so I hope I can feel my way to her. My lungs are burning, and I'm fighting panic. I've got to hurry. Drowning doesn't take long. I'm at the bottom, feeling along rocks and mud, but I'll have to surface soon.

I keep kicking to keep myself on the bottom, my hands working quickly, but my fingers are growing stiff with cold. If I don't find her soon, I'll have to go up for air. Then I feel a leg. Limp, but I've got her. I walk my hands up to her shoulders and grab Esmé under her arms. I push off the bottom as hard as I can. I break the water's surface and gasp for breath, but Esmé's nonresponsive. I paddle to the shore and lay her on her back. I hear people around me, but

I'm laser-focused. She's got a pulse, but it's thready, and she isn't breathing, so I start rescue breaths. Nothing. I start to panic. Am I doing this right? When was the last time I was trained on this? *Think, Rita.* Then Esmé starts to cough, and I turn her on her side. She throws up. She's alive.

Cynthia is by my side and hands me my jacket. I place it over Esmé, and I glance up. Ray Senior has his phone clasped to his ear, talking to a 911 operator, I hope. Ray Junior is dragging a screaming woman out of the woods. He has her clutched in his arms, where she sputters and kicks, but he's a big man, and she's going nowhere. Christy Bowers. I'll be damned.

The man in the pond has disappeared. Ray Senior breaks off his phone conversation. "The police are on the way. Ambulance too."

"Where's the man?" I ask. Cynthia is standing next to her father now, her face white and otherworldly. She points at the path that leads to the parking area. I want to run after him, but it's better that I stay on scene and coordinate from here. I grab Ray Senior's phone from him. Mine's soaked, sidearm too. I talk to the 911 dispatch operator to fill them in. Tell them about the man. Just as I finish, I hear the sirens in the distance. I check on Esmé. She's trembling, but she's alive. I sit next to her and offer words of comfort.

# CHAPTER 88
# Rita

I'VE BEEN UP MOST OF THE NIGHT. COLD SEEMS TO HAVE PENETRATED down to my bones. That'll teach me to dive into a pond in the middle of October. But Esmé Foster is alive, and that's all that matters. Of course, I need a new phone, and my gun needs a good cleaning. Not to mention that my favorite white blouse is now a dirty brown.

The station is a hive of activity. The chief, despite his fatigue, has been here all night too, and his weariness has been replaced with a lightness I haven't seen in him since we got the call about a body in the Fosters' backyard.

Christy Bowers is finally over at the county jail. The whole time she was here, she sat like a wronged princess in the interrogation room, indignantly spilling her guts before her high-priced lawyer got there and told her to shut her mouth. I sat opposite her, a blanket someone brought me wrapped around my shoulders like a cape.

Ms. Bowers claimed that she never harmed anyone. She and Kara argued, and Kara attacked *her*. Then she only planned to scare Esmé. She wasn't supposed to end up in the pond. And when I asked about Mr. York, she blubbered that her instructions to her PI were to monitor him only. He planted the bugs after Kara died. She never told him to shoot Mr. York. When I asked why they were monitoring him, she said that he'd seen her the night she argued with Kara. She'd been getting in her car at the parking spot, and he drove by, stopped, and asked her if she was all right. She was a wreck. Kara had attacked her, after all. She told him that if he ever told anyone he'd seen her there, she'd expose him for the pervert he was. Apparently, when Kara started modeling for him, Ms. Bowers had her PI compile a file on his past. Suspicious of him, Ms. Bowers tried to warn her friend, but Kara wouldn't listen and started working for the man anyway.

Finally, we had what we needed for the night, and she was escorted out in handcuffs. I went into the locker room and stood under the shower, letting the hot water try to lift some of the chill from my bones. Then I went into my office and shut the door. One of the young officers tapped timidly on my door and brought me a cup of hideous but hot coffee. I relaxed in my chair, still a little shaky.

Christy Bowers. How did I not see it? The strange bonds among high school friends, bonds that work more like harnesses that keep the group in line, hiding jealousies and ill will beneath the pretty veneer of friendship. Most of us outgrow those adolescent ties. But some people don't. It's not the first time I've seen those juvenile impulses manifest themselves in adults who should know better. All this over a man.

At some point, I fell asleep in my chair and jolted awake as the sun was coming up. Bob got a call that the FBI had picked up Ms. Bowers's PI at the airport. Kirill Petrov was born in Russia and moved to the States with his mom when he was a kid. He has dual citizenship—American and Russian—and had his passport and a buttload of cash on him when they nabbed him at Logan. He had prebooked a flight to Moscow for this morning. Luckily, the good guys got to him first.

Lunchtime came and went a while ago. Someone brought in sandwiches and chips from the deli on the corner, but I was too tired to eat. I sit at my desk, in relative quiet, and I'm bone weary but satisfied that justice will now prevail in the Cunningham case.

I lean back in my chair and listen to the radio, where an old, dreamy Al Stewart song plays. I feel myself start to drift. Then someone raps on my doorframe, and my eyes flutter open. There on the threshold stands Special Agent Joe Thorne.

I drop my feet to the floor and run my hand through my tangled hair.

"Hey, Rita." He walks in, closes the door behind him.

"What are you doing here?"

"Tried to call. Couldn't get you, so I ended up talking to Detective Broderick when I called the station. Sounds like you had quite a night."

I glance at my water-logged phone sitting on the desk. "Yeah. It was . . ." I glance up and meet his dark eyes. "Scary, if I'm being honest."

Joe folds his tall frame into the chair across from me. "But you got the collar. Potential victim saved. Sounds like everything worked out right."

I nod. "I guess you heard about the PI from your guys?"

"Yeah. That's how I knew you'd been involved. Agent Metz, my old partner, was working his case. They've been watching Petrov for a while. He's been involved in other crimes in the area, and they were waiting to catch him in the act. Looks like we have the Graybridge PD to thank."

I blow out a breath. I know I must look like hell. My hair's full of pond water. I didn't have any shampoo in my locker. I'm wearing an old pair of jeans and a sweatshirt I keep here at the station for emergencies. And Joe sits there, all handsome and dark-eyed.

"Well, I'm just glad the hard work is over. I've got other cases pending that I need to get to." I glance at my laptop, which sits closed on the corner of my desk. As I reach for it, Joe takes my hand in his, and I feel a ripple run over my skin.

"Not today, Rita. Surely the chief will give you a couple of days off."

"I guess it can wait."

"I had an idea."

"What?"

"How about dinner and a glass of wine?"

I glance out my window. Darkness is starting to creep in. "Well, I guess it's about that time."

"Then you need to go home and get a good night's sleep."

I nod. "Yeah. That I do." I blow out a breath.

"I had another idea."

"You're full of them today. What?"

"How about I pick you up tomorrow, say noon?"

"Why?"

"They just opened a new indoor skating rink ten minutes from here."

"Skating? You want to go *skating*?"

"Yeah. I haven't gone since my kids were little, and I've decided to turn over a new leaf."

"What, like break a hip?"

He laughs. "We're not that old, Rita."

"I haven't been on ice skates in years." Not since Danny and I, and Jimmy, before he died, used to go on Saturdays in the winter.

"Me neither. But that new leaf I mentioned. A New Year's resolution."

"It's October."

"I don't want to wait. Why waste time?" He drops my hand and leans back in his chair. "I've decided I work too much, and it's time to get back to some play. What do you say?"

"Skating?"

"What? You can't skate?" He lifts his chin like Danny used to when throwing down a dare, and my hackles rise.

"I can skate, Joe. Swim too."

"I heard." He shakes his head. Smiles. "Let's have some fun, Rita."

I glance out the window, where darkness has dropped like a blanket. October is fading fast, and Thanksgiving will be here before you know it. Time just seems to run faster and faster.

My gaze meets Joe's. "Okay."

# CHAPTER 89
# Esmé

Byron wanted to postpone Dad's funeral, but I was determined to go through with it. They kept me at the hospital overnight, and by morning, I was fine, thanks to Detective Myers. That afternoon, I went through the short ceremony like a robot. The chill from the murky waters of the pond was hard to throw off, and I dressed in layers and topped my outfit with a heavy winter coat I bought, tearing off the tags in the car on the way to the funeral home.

In the weeks since, I've felt a strong sense of purpose, like the real me had been hidden, first in my ballet world and then in the cocoon of what I thought was friendship. But now, for maybe the first time, I feel like the real me has emerged, into a cold and difficult world, maybe, but one that I'm determined to handle. Laney and Jack have been trying to comfort me. We are all dazed and numb at the realization that Christy was Kara's killer and attempted to bring about my death as well. And they were stunned when I told them about Wendy. We looked at each other, questions hanging unasked in the air. What didn't we see? How could we not have known? But none of us is in a place right now to discuss it.

And I told Detective Myers what I'd learned. Cynthia deserved that and more. If she hadn't gone for help that night, I probably wouldn't have survived.

Jack was incredulous when he learned that Teddy was his son. The boy was temporarily placed with Christy's sister and her husband. They too were stunned to learn what Christy had done. Luckily, Christy's sister was agreeable to doing another DNA test, and it confirmed that Teddy was indeed Jack's son. Paul, Christy's ex-husband, was more than happy to relinquish his parental rights, and all parties are working out the custody details.

Byron and I called a realtor, determined to sell the house and move on. But I'm staying in Graybridge. That I'm sure of, but things will be different now. No more secrets. And it turns out that Dad had a decent life-insurance policy, one that not only paid his funeral expenses, but had a little left over that, along with the sale of the house, will allow Byron and me to be all right for a little while. Enough that I'll be able, along with my café pay, to afford a little apartment of my own.

After another long day of sifting through Mom and Dad's belongings, Byron and I sit at our little kitchen table and drink peppermint tea. Maybe this has drawn us back together, back where we were before Mom and I headed off downtown to the big ballet school, leaving Dad and Byron behind. Maybe this is real life now, and maybe it's not so bad.

# CHAPTER 90
# Esmé

*Three months later*

THE TINKLE OF PIANO MUSIC FILLS THE STUDIO. THE SMELL OF RESIN and a tinge of sweat lingers in the air. Eight twelve-year-old girls stand at the barre, an elegant line of pink-clad, bun-topped dancers standing at attention.

I walk down the line, dressed in leotard, tights, and ballet skirt. I stop to raise an arm, demonstrate a position. And my students nod and work to emulate me, eager to dance, their hearts beating with excitement.

I'm eager too. I had considered teaching after my company had let me go two years ago, but I didn't know where to start. Then Kevin pulled me into his world so quickly that I let that dream drop.

In December, after coming out of the haze that surrounded Dad's death and Kara's murder, I started looking around, energized and with a plan. I found a school thirty minutes from Graybridge that was looking for a teacher. And here I am, back in a ballet studio, and I couldn't be happier.

Laney and I see each other occasionally, and Jack too. But going back to the way we were in high school is the last thing I want to do, so I've broadened my horizons. I'm taking classes at the local community college. Meeting new people. I might pursue a degree, or I might not. I don't know yet. I just know I'm happy here, back in my dance world. But it's different now. My art is just that—art. Not an escape from reality. Reality lives beyond the studio, out in the world, where there are people to meet and new things to learn. And I'm excited to get there.